W9-AHH-822

GALLAGHER'S TRAVELS

JOHNS HOPKINS: POETRY AND FICTION

John T. Irwin, General Editor

GALLAGHER'S TRAVELS

Jean McGarry

THE JOHNS HOPKINS UNIVERSITY PRESS
Baltimore and London

This book has been brought to publication with the generous assistance of the G. Harry Pouder Fund.

Printed in the United States of America on acid-free paper
06 05 04 03 02 01 00 99 98 97 5 4 3 2 1

The Johns Hopkins University Press
2715 North Charles Street
Baltimore, Maryland 21218-4319
The Johns Hopkins Press Ltd., London

Library of Congress Cataloging-in-Publication Data will be found at the end of this book.
A catalog record for this book is available from the British Library.

ISBN 0-8018-5634-5

FOR TOM, MARY, DEB, AND REGGIE

PART ONE

CHAPTER 1

To get the job, first she had to write the obituary. It was early evening, and the streets of Wampanoag were vacant. Urban Renewal had plowed through downtown in 1973 and by 1974 had cleared a thriving Times Square of its three department stores and Newberry's, jewelry store, several bars and movie theater. Left behind were a widened street, the five-story *Wampanoag Times* building and the cement block next to it, Rocco's, " 'Gansett on tap. Music Nitely."

Gallagher pushed through the door of the *Times* building, and up a flight of steps. A tall, white-haired man (MANAGING EDITOR) received her in his glass cubicle. On the desk was a mound of newspaper and wire-service tape, anchored by several sticky-looking jars. After a history of the paper, and highlights of the *Times* obituary style, he handed her the rough draft—ten pages long!—and led her back into the newsroom. It was empty. No—two gawky young men were sitting at adjacent desks in the rear: "Nightside," the older man said. "Don't bother with them." But the two reporters were already ankling forward. The introductions were terse. The M.E. told Nightside not to help the girl with her obit. Eying the ten pages, one laughed, but the M.E. shooed them both away, and they slunk back to their desks.

The applicant sat at the assigned desk, stripped clean but for an ashtray and a baseball. She spread out the pages of obituary. The M.E. rolled over a portable typewriter: Did she touch-type? He told her how to "slug" in her name and OBIT, how to signal to Composing the number of pages and the end of the story. The idea, he said again, was to fix the obit so it could run in the paper tomorrow. The tall, skinny one, Vinny, would tell her when her time was up.

She wanted to ask him how long it normally took to write such an item, but the M.E., Mr. O'Callahan, was already gone. The applicant (slugged GALL) commenced by skinning off her sweater to expose her arms. Without even turning to look, she could feel the eyes of Nightside fixed on her. They had stopped talking, and weren't typing either. Mr. O'Callahan had said in passing that the last female recruited was in '59.

One of the nightsides was now typing fast, while his mate circled the room, stuffed a plastic cylinder into a rubber tube, jumpshot a balled-up paper, missed the wastebasket, and then flipped up the volume on the police radio. Gallagher opened her purse and fished out a pair of eyeglasses. Minutes ticked by and the obituary was awfully long—why *was* it so long?

Taking up the first sheet, she read:

> Mrs. Ethel ("Cheapskate") Flynn Magnet, 60 years of age, of Old Custard Road, Wampanoag, Rhode I., was found dead in her bed of a fatal heart attack, by her daughter-in-law, Frances R. ("Reenie") Magnet of 21 Woolnut Street, Woburn, who happened to be visiting her mother-in-law when the sad event occurred. (Mrs. Magnet, Jr. is separated from her husband, Lonnie F. Magnet, Jr., who remarried and now lives out of state, and who was away on business when his mother collapsed.)
>
> Ethel Magnet (Flynn that was) grew up in Wampanoag, where she was born and raised, made a poor record with the nuns at St. Margaret's Grammar School on School Street, Wampanoag, until she was 15, when she was sent out to work. The father was a Teamster—a drinker, according to neighbors—and didn't always show up for work. The mother, Ethel ("Fatty") Hanrahan Flynn, former seamstress for the Coats & Co., Rumford, kept a slovenly home for her ten children, and for years they lived on what she earned taking in washing and ironing, and shopping at Goodwill. The deceased was second-oldest, born with crossed eyes.

Gallagher wondered if Nightside, silent again, had heard her laughing. She skipped to the last page of an obituary that Wampanoagers would kill to read in the *Times* (especially if they *knew* the Magnets), but which would have to be picked clean or they might be killed *by* it. She knew that much about newswriting, having grown up, like Cheapskate, in Rhode I, and having attended those same sister schools, where she had made a good record, scoring herself right out of Rhode and into a top college, only—and she could savor the irony—to bounce right back and be begging for a job on a tenth-rate rag like the *Times,* and why? Because in the movies didn't the bright news-hen go straight to the top by starting at the bottom? And Catherine ("Beanpole") Gallagher was going there, too. For now, she lived with her aged parents on Old Kilgore Street, Providence, Rhode I. Everyone thought she was going to be a hotshot doctor or lawyer, but think again.

Catherine picked up a pencil. She scanned Mrs. Magnet's story. She'd wasted ten minutes, and there wasn't a jungly line of it that didn't need hacking. On the last page, the obituarist—Mr. O'Callahan, she suspected—had hand-written:

> Ethel Flynn Magnet was laid to rest with her husband, Patrick F., in the Mt. Pleasant Cemetery, after a Requiem High Mass at St. Xavier's R.C., under a drenching rain, and with only a handful of mourners. The rest had already congregated at the Magnet Home, Old Custard Road, and were eating chicken salad and Danish, and taking a nip. Mrs. Magnet will be missed by the parishioners of St. X's R.C. and by her family and few friends. Those sending a wreath or cut flowers were: the Dugan family . . .

It continued (MTK), but Catherine felt she had read enough, and rolled a sheet of newsprint into the bulky machine. The other Nightside, perched on her desk, put out a cigarette in the ashtray, and was pawing the ball. She looked at that dopey face and told him to bug off. "You know what she said to me?" he bellowed to Vinny. "Hey, Lupo, you know what she said?"

Catherine typed MAGNET OBIT/GALL. She datelined the story and scrolled up to put "1 of 1" under the slug. Once she had raked out the slander, sentiments, and filigree Mr. O'Callahan had had so much fun knotting in, there was scarcely enough to fill a page. It took ten minutes to make the obit clean and bone-dry as such an item had to be. Readers who knew Cheapskate were already in on the dirt—and felt that this was their *right*—but they also feared a scandal, and as the obits were the paper's best-read section, they were the most heavily censored. Mr. O'Callahan had told Catherine how much they pulled in, too. For every stiff the *Times* got a paid ad, and for the tiny story printed the funeral home got one lousy plug.

Catherine rolled out the sheet. Lupo was hanging over her shoulder, telling her where to put the dash-30-dash, but she left the page alone—she wasn't supposed to know everything, and Mr. O'Callahan might wonder if she did.

Then Nightside invited her out for drinks—the first beer of the night! they bragged—but Catherine saw the M.E. still lurking about. She declined, then got up to slip the story under the M.E.'s door. He pretended not to see. Walking downstairs, she was surprised at how stiff her neck and back felt: was she that tense? Once outside, her spine relaxed. Times Square was sunk in darkness, with only a greenish light from the *Times* windows striping the sidewalk. And in that light she could see the bulky shadows of Nightside, gawking.

For a printable obit, Catherine got the job, and started work Monday on Dayside. For her first job on a real newspaper (DAILY SINCE 1864) she bought some new clothes: black blouse, gray slacks, black ribbon, and wore them that first day, although "it was your ass," the city editor told her a month later when everyone was on a last-name basis, "we noticed, Gallagher."

The city editor sat in the far corner. McGuire his name was, and Gallagher had already heard it a dozen times ("McGuire'll see you after deadline," one reporter had said, "in the confessional") before O'Callahan led her to his desk, boasting—shouting over the din of typewriters—that Jack McGuire was their star, and almost too bright a beam for a hometown paper. His muckraking series for the *Long Island Clipper* had cracked a long-running kickback scheme and brought down a mayor and his city council, winning McGuire a Pulitzer.

Gallagher had been in the newsroom less than an hour, but even a fool could tell that all the force, the light, the heat came from McGuire's corner. But when she arrived at the City desk, thronged by reporters blurting out their stories, the editor barely looked up.

After a tour of the composing room and presses, O'Callahan introduced the newcomer to the rest of Editorial, all too busy to talk, so they proceeded to the wire room, where Gallagher saw the four machines spewing out miles of tape: national and international news, features, columns, recipes, weather and comics, plus that day's worth of boilerplate. Next to the wire room was the curved desk where the copyeditors penciled and ripped the day's top stories, shooting them down the vacuum tube to Composing. The desk was too busy to pay attention to the new cub, but later on, when the paper was put to bed, they too would get their chance to notice her ass.

On the other side of wire was Sports. In a whole year working at the *Times,* the sports editor would never greet nor show any sign of recognizing the new reporter. He didn't think young broads belonged in the newsroom. Once he had called in from St. Petersburg, Florida, and only the "night chick," an intern, there to take rewrite. He ended up, according to Mr. O'Callahan, spelling his whole column on spring training. The girl was blackballed for muffing one of the few things—besides death and scandal—that counted in Wampanoag; namely, what in January, February, and March the Sox were *prepared* to do; what in April, May, June, July, August, and September they did; and what, after the season was over, they *had* done. Wampanoagers were nearly as keen on college basketball, pro hockey, and football—especially after the Pats moved to Boston. Schoolboy sports were big. The intern, before she was banished to Nightside and then canned, was the only reporter in *Times* history who couldn't, in a pinch, sit at Sports, write the round-up piece on the high school sport of the season, or edit the wire, check scores and point-spreads, get the early call into the bookies.

When Gallagher heard this story, she was scared. But that first day, no one asked her to sit on Sports. She was given a desk in the middle of the newsroom, along with a mound of blank newsprint, some pencils, and glue. At first she just sat there, circled by men busily—frantically, as the morning passed—pounding out the day's news. Eventually, the assistant city editor (A.C.E.), a woman, six feet tall, handed her a press release about a new line of stoves at Apex, and the summer reading list at area high schools. Gallagher fell to work, but was interrupted by the A.C.E. yelling, "Obit!" The men typed faster. A reporter who'd been reading the sports page and chewing a donut leapt up, ran to the police radio, pressing his ear against the speaker. "Fire on Key Street!" he yelled to the A.C.E., still trying to pass the obit.

Catherine Gallagher's head was up. "Cathy!" the A.C.E. roared, "Cathy Gallagher! Take one from McNaughton's." Gallagher felt the crackling room calm as the staff eyed the new writer. Gallogly, at the next desk, helped with the headphones, inserted a wad of paper and carbons into her typewriter, and told her to type from dictation. With his arms around her head, he typed in a slug, made up on the spot: (CG) because there was already a Garrihy (GAR), a Gannigan (GAN), McGaughy (GAU) and himself, Gallogly (GAL). 'Phones on, she was set for rewrite. The undertaker spoke up: "Got the headpiece on?" he said. "Paper in the typewriter? We'll take it slow," and then: "Mrs. Giuseppina (Guicciardini) Del Giudice, 84, of 8509 Quonochonchaug Avenue, Pascoag—." Gallagher made a stab at the names, but the undertaker asked her to spell them all back, and some of them were right! "Good!" he said. "Next time I'll ask for you."

Catherine pulled off the headset. Before she had a chance to roll in a fresh sheet, the A.C.E. grabbed the obit out of her hand. There wasn't time for a polish, she said, we do it right the first time.

Gallagher was rifling through more press releases—someone had dumped a couple of weddings on top—when through the din she heard her name. She turned. Across the floor, the city editor was standing on his chair. "Are you deaf?" he bellowed, as she approached his desk. She was smiling at the jest. "Siddown, Gallagher," McGuire said.

And *this,* she thought, eying the extra chair pulled up alongside the desk, was the "confessional." She sat. Jack McGuire was short and muscular with a big block of a head and greasy mop of grayish blond curls. Denim sleeves were rolled up to the elbows and dusted with cigarette ash. His thick fingers were stained molasses color, as were his lips and moustache. Plying a gnawed ruler and pencil, he blocked the day's pages, his layout pad resting on an edge of desk ringed by tipping mounds of paper, anchored by mugs, paper cups, and ashtrays. Most of the cups still had liquid in them, and one had sprouted a growth like cotton candy. While the editor talked to Gallagher, he sized heads and cuts, read material that was dropped on his desk, barked orders across the still-thundering city floor, had the librarian fill the cup with fresh brew—he even took a call from a reader about a recipe. "Call back after deadline," he said. "Was it coffeecake or ice cream? Sure I like to cook!"

When the last story for his pages was headlined, measured, and shot down to Composing, he looked up at Gallagher for the first time. "So you want to be a reporter?" he said. He seemed to be thinking about something. "You won't see me busting *my* ass anymore on a story. What did you say your name was? And how old are you—25, 35? Older? My ass, you are." He grinned. "We'll talk about that later. You want to know why? I'll tell you why. I'm tired. It's as simple as that." He looked as if he expected an argument. "Make a lousy newsman," he muttered, then grinned again. "Say, you know the difference between a newsman and a journalist?" He was showing both rows of yellowed teeth. "You dirty dog! You're blushing and I haven't even told you yet!"

Leaving the confessional, Gallagher was sure she was going to love the news biz, but next day, when O'Callahan assigned her to the Women's desk—hadn't he already mentioned it to her? He was sure he had because that's where the opening was—she was liking it less. It was a dirty trick, but the cub felt too cowed to complain. Instead, by noontime of the second day, she'd thrown herself into this new beat: weddings, fashion, food, and advice. The immediate reward was an assignment to "50 YEARS WED!" a *Times* specialty, and one that kept circulation high among elderly citizens. This staple ("Fifty Years Dead!" the city editor would roar, when he had a new one) was run daily. The *Times* went to the trouble and expense of sending out a reporter and fotog, but usually printed just the pic and cutline on page 3.

The staff despised the "Deadbeat," as they called it. And, reflecting their contempt, what they wrote was so trite and treacly that even the golden-anniversary couples themselves sometimes complained. So why not assign one to the new kid? What could they lose? Gallagher spent an hour—45 minutes more than the story needed or ever got—although it was always booked for 90 minutes, and the team sopped up the remainder at Rocco's, the cement block next door, drinking beers and shots.

Gallagher was thrilled by her material: Mr. and Mrs. Lapham had done some notable things in their half century—they came from the little Yankee enclave across the river, where the cloth industrialists lived, and continued to live there even after all the mills went broke. The Laphams collected Audubon prints, were staunch conservationists, walked five miles every day, and knew by heart the landmarks and personalities of historic Wampanoag. There was more, Gallagher told McGuire, when she filed the story (Mrs. Adele was a guest at FDR's first inauguration; Mr. George had flown for the RAF in World War I), but she knew the paper would run only half a page. "Less," McGuire said, but he used the whole eight inches, after some chaffing about acing the Deadbeat cold.

But even after this coup, Gallagher got no more of that week's Dead. Her time was spent editing Women's: scouring letters to Abby and Ann for references to sex, which His Excellency, the Bishop of Wampanoag—an avid Women's-page fan—didn't want to find in his favorite daily. Was it only sex that was objectionable? Catherine asked the city editor at the end of the first week, before showing him a letter ("Stuck with Stuffy") about a husband who, when he went to a bar or restaurant, always stuffed eight or more olives up his nose. "So?" McGuire said. "What does she say?" Gallagher read Abby's reply: consult your minister, stay home nights.

"What's the problem here?" snapped the editor. He had himself been out the night before and his eyes were puffy. Sorry to have bothered him, Gallagher took her letter back to Women's. She was halfway there when she heard, "Hey! Women's desk!" Gallagher turned to see the editor, his head cocked back, twisting a crumpled cigarette butt up his nostril, another butt ready in his other hand.

Miss Agatha Toohey, Gallagher's immediate superior and a forty-year fixture on Women's, hated McGuire, and he knew it. The city editor could use his new writer's post—across the desk from Toohey—to telegraph his grossest jokes and pranks, so the old biddy couldn't help but hear. So when Catherine arrived at her desk, the phone rang and it was McGuire; he had come up with another solution to the olive problem, and just at the moment when Miss Toohey, reading that very column, was composing one of her headline howlers. Gallagher, unable to stifle her laughter, hung up on him. Shortly after, McGuire appeared at their double desk to finish his story in person.

There was trouble the next day when the Abby letter ran. Complaints had been routed to the publisher, Mr. O'Callahan said. Some callers reached McGuire—always a mistake, he said, because the city editor was death on circulation. No matter who it was or how grave the complaint, McGuire always had some crack prepared for his readers. The switchboard knew this, but somehow the calls still came through.

It was amusing, yes, but for all the fun and the occasional Deadbeat, by week 2 Gallagher was disgruntled. Trying to help, McGuire suggested she teach the "turkeys" on the floor how to read the bridal info sheets and write up weddings. That way Gallagher would be free, as he put it, to learn the trade: how to collect the facts, how to be quick and pushy, to write on deadline and craft the punchy sentences in the dit-dot style the *Times* was famous for. Gallagher had much to learn. She was wordy, she was slow. When he'd sent her over to the cops the first week, she couldn't write up a lousy three-graf item that wasn't actionable. And the cops complained because of all the nosy questions.

So, by the end of week 2, she was back to Women's, and spent the entire day on the food page. Copy flooded in from the canned, boxed, and frozen food companies, the growers, ranchers, and fish farmers, and had to be cleansed of brand names. The local stories, on the other hand—the ones from the Wampanoag chapters of the D.A.R., the L.W.V., the Y, the Girl's City Club, the Order of the Eastern Star, the Rosary and Altar, the Mothers' Clubs and Veri-Dames—all had to be checked and rechecked for accurate names and addresses, but the rest shaved down to a phrase or sentence. This went for the clubs of fat people, single parents, Girl Scouts and Girl Guides, the stitchers, knitters, bridge players, businesswomen, gardeners, watercolorists, and readers, who sent their minutes to Miss Toohey. When Gallagher was finished with the news, she edited the daily columns—WHY GROW OLD, TELL DOROTHY, ABOUT YOU, recipes, household hints, and sewing patterns that filled out the page.

That whole week the young news-hen seethed and fumed. Didn't they realize that she wanted to be a news*man!* She envied those twelve men—half fresh from college, the rest nearing retirement—out on the floor, free to bark into their phones, pummel their typewriters, read and rip the daily paper, and race out the door after the explosions, holdups, accidents, and homicides that were splashed above the fold on page 1.

And Gallagher had no patience—the way the older hens did—

for waiting her turn, swabbing the bridal decks for 10, 15 years, before a desk opened up and no man available to fill it. Patience was a useful byproduct of a Wampanoag childhood: patience was ground into the infant mind, as it lay in its crib hour upon hour, with nothing to do but crackle its rubber pants, or wriggle up the mattress to stick a leg through the bars; when it mastered its legs, it found itself boxed into a pen, strapped in a harness, or tied to a backyard tree. The nuns banked on this patience, cultivated in large families by overworked mothers, to enable their pupils to stand long hours in sun or drenching rain for the endless fire drills and "air raids," or just to hear the principal issue her daily complaints, commands, and requests for prayers. By the time the Wampanoag girl-child was in high school, it had the patience of a dead tree trunk, ready for 40 or 50 years stapling earrings to cardboard backs, or tapping an adding machine, or simply producing and curbing the next generation. Gallagher had started out patient, but the secular college she had attended, and the associations with "society" leeches and slugs, had softened her. She wouldn't wait even *one* year, toiling on the slag heap of Women's, just for the chance to cover zoning board with four grafs and a cut. She wanted that zoning board *now!* And tomorrow she wanted the State House!

Why was she in such a hurry? Her new editors might well ask that question. It would have made more sense if reporting had been the ambition of a lifetime. For Gallagher, it was more recent; in fact, it was so recent that, before taking her first job on the Pascoag *Newsletter,* she had scarcely ever read a newspaper. In college there was too much else to do, and the news that mattered traveled by mouth. Back in high school, she had avoided even those columns written by other students for the Saturday-night teen page, telling of proms, games, and debates. Some high-ranking senior, with an eye toward a news career, was always picked to write this column, which read like a page from a typing manual. The rest of the paper—*Providence Bull* or *Wamp Times*—crafted in short, punchy sentences, seemed mostly about Democratic ward politics, a subject Catherine couldn't get interested in, and didn't even try.

The lateness of this urge did not blunt its force—if anything, it made Gallagher even more avid. She felt she made up for her lack of experience by being—like most Wampanoagers—a natural.

And although the *Bull,* the state's paper of record, which relied entirely on out-of-state talent, was too proud to tap this rich resource, the *Times* policy was to hire "local." Catherine was the first reporter in memory who hadn't gone to Wampanoag State for J-school. This was a handicap, but the editors hired her anyway: they needed someone right away, and Gallagher—bored stiff at the *Newsletter*—had applied. The former Women's writer, Sally Dolan, had earned a promotion—first time in history—to the A.C.E. desk, a post vacated by Jimmy Murray, an old-timer (regular at the Swansea Dog Track and communicant at St. Mary's R.C., an Elk, five kids: one in the mayor's office, one in jail, one in the convent, one in a sheltered workshop, one married to the bishop's nephew), who died in his sleep.

So they were looking to hire, and Gallagher turned up. She was born in Providence, but had gone to a Wampanoag high school. She even won the Hibernians' prize for her essay, "Johnnycake, Potatoes, and Pastafazool: A Rhode Island Sampler." Best of all, she was young, cute, and just the type, they thought, who wouldn't bridle and bitch about sitting on Women's. Even Miss Toohey seemed to like her.

Mr. O'Callahan warmed to Gallagher as soon as he heard *where* she went to college, and what she had written for a senior thesis. "Tell me again," he had said, during that first interview. He loved to hear this title: "Crazy Eights: The Mid-Career of Federico Fellini."

"'The mid-career,'" he'd chuckled. "I've never even heard of the guy." He asked, then and after—in that phony way—if she might not be a hair *too* polished for a small-town paper. Catherine felt sure that whatever slickness she'd picked up in college had been left there. And even if it hadn't, it amounted to nothing. Only a rube or a snob like Mr. O'Callahan would make so much of it. Even her boyfriend, Danny Juscik, could see right through it, and Juscik hadn't heard of Fellini, or of anyone.

Danny Juscik, from Market Street, had done his four years at Wamp State, and one day had wandered over to the East Side, Il Gatto Nero Café-Bar, where Catherine happened to be hanging out. There was trouble over an egg sandwich. The Nero had eggs, but wouldn't make egg salad. It was not on their menu, the waiter must have told Juscik ten times. Glancing at Catherine's table, Juscik happened to notice the stack of film quarterlies. "What's that you're reading?" he asked. Then the waiter thought to offer a croque-monsieur, "ham and cheese to you," and Juscik took it.

Catherine had flipped her magazine over so this nut couldn't see the title, *Cinema/Signified?* "Nothing," she said.

"Oh." He got up a moment later to stand near her table. He studied the *Cinema/Signified?* cover and flipped the pages, stopping at the movie stills.

Juscik went back to his own table. A minute later: "Do you ever go to movies in English?" he asked. Then he swiped the *Cinema/Signified?* and showed it to his waiter. "You know this?" The waiter said no, but he had heard of it.

The croque-monsieur arrived next and Juscik opened the two halves of French bread and looked inside. "You got some mayo here?"

Dan Juscik was over six feet tall, fair, lithe, and slender. He was good-looking and he knew it, but his grooming of those looks stopped at the point where he could still patronize the ethnic clubs in Wampanoag without risk of chaff from potbellied men with all-consonant names who guzzled their 'Gansett and still used Wildroot.

Juscik's blond curls were cut short; his clothes were cheap but well fitted to a body kept trim by visits to his tennis club. Beyond these suburban clubs, the outside world had never beckoned to Danny Juscik; he had found ways to be content with Wampanoag city, and skeptical of the beyond. The Nero on its East-Side street, with its Nathanael Greene and Evangeline Angell students, was the outside world in spades, but to his mind Cathy (as he called her) Gallagher was not, and he told her so that afternoon.

But even six months of dates—the steady ribbing, needling, and sarcasm by Juscik; the separations, drinking, fighting, and good times—hadn't rubbed off all the polish from the Kings College graduate. At least, Mr. O'Callahan, whose wife made him watch public TV and attend the occasional concert by the state "Fillamonik," could still spot it, and it was there on the resumé, too.

Mr. O'Callahan didn't ask what this "refinement," as he called it, had to do with journalism: he only wondered (out loud) what would draw a girl of such caliber back to Wampanoag, but Catherine assured the M.E. that she was thrilled to land such a job; it was the highlight of her career—"apogee," she had said, and

Mr. O'Callahan had savored the word; he loved this kind of talk. "Thus far," he added. And so Catherine Gallagher had gone home that first night after writing the obit, confident that the affable Mr. O'Callahan was really wowed, and not the cagey gladhander who would—after demoting her to Women's—never fail to mention, at least once a day, the "crazy 8-and-a-half" as a hint of how far the mighty had fallen.

But she had conned O'Callahan, too, into thinking she had a keen interest in the bland portrait the paper drew every day of the city, the second-largest in the state, disdained and all but ignored by those lucky enough—like Catherine—to live in Providence. Juscik had taught her this subtle game of superiority: you could play it with nearly nothing to feel superior about.

When Catherine was away at college, far away—at least in spirit—from Wampanoag, she'd planned to have an interesting life. And, although her resumé listed many studies and accomplishments, she'd spent most of her time dreaming about that life, and very little on the academic offerings at Kings. She could ape the arguments, popular at the time, to defend such dreamy idleness—like the one that you were in college not to learn *something,* but just to *learn.* Most of the students then at Kings bragged about how little they did and how much of that little for nothing, although it turned out most were secretly stockpiling courses for careers in medicine, business, and law, eager for the day when they'd be too busy and too rich to bother with such pious nonsense.

Looking back from the newsroom—and the dunce's corner she was in—Catherine could see how much time (her whole life) she'd wasted, and the price to pay for acquiring nothing more than polish. It was her fourth week at work when she laid a copy of *The Autobiography of Alice B. Toklas* on her desk, to ward off the unenlightened, or to attract them, by the only means she knew. She had settled at her wooden desk and rolled in the first wedding of the day. There were twelve such stories to write and then lay out for Saturday's page. She took not a single obit that day, although the phone rang off the hook with undertakers eager to dictate. There was a drowning, a walkout, a three-alarm, a mayor's commission report on housing, and a full police blotter, but Gallagher kept her head bent over her brides. It was her own fault.

She had done it to herself: she could be studying doorknobs and keyholes at I Tatti, or memorizing the ten thousand inferior bones of the thumb, or building tax shelters for rich people—and what was she doing? "Miss Helen Arlene Jankowitz of Seekonk, graduate of East Senior High School, was wedded to Paul Carmine Delgado in a Mass of Christian Burial"—no, make that a nuptial Mass—

> at the Church of the Holy Angels. The bride, daughter of . . . , attended by . . . , wore a gown of champagne peau de soie with appliqués of Alençon lace. The neckline was fashioned with seed pearls and a detachable, cathedral-length veil.

Gallagher stopped to move the veil up to the head.

> She carried a bouquet of phalanoepsis orchids, pompons, and baby's breath. The bridesmaids' gowns . . .
>
> After a wedding trip to Puerto Rico, the couple will make their home in Wampanoag. The bride is employed at the Sanitary Bake Company; the bridegroom is a machinist at Griswold Tool & Die.

As the wedding checksheets were, one by one, converted to copy, Catherine found herself absorbed. It was hard to describe the gowns because the brides had just *bought* them; they didn't know what was on them, or how to spell it. There was a pic, but just a headshot, so while Catherine had no trouble with the veil and headpiece—which she could see—the bodice, skirt, train, and decorations had to be confected. By her third wedding, she felt her write-ups were smoother and more savvy. They sounded like ad copy or a fashion show voiceover. Miss Toohey was reading over her shoulder and patted it: "You've got the knack," she said, and Gallagher, who thought she'd hate this job most, felt cheered, and embroidered a bit more, using a stilted, etiquette-book style, the phonier the better, especially on the brides with a grade-school education and a gown from the mill outlet. She could help them—if not to look right, then to read well. By midmorning, Gallagher knew the laces, the silks and synthetics, the cuts then in fashion, even the rare orchid types, and was freely improvising.

Next came the task of fitting all twelve pix and stories into the newshole. There was one rule, Miss Toohey said: the brides' faces should be turned one toward the other. You could put three or four heads together, so long as the faces on the right looked toward the middle. If they were facing straight ahead, fine, stick them anywhere, but no one should be left staring off into the "gutter." Catherine was using a ruler to X in the copy when a hairy hand fell on the layout pad. Miss Toohey was at lunch, as was most of the staff. Catherine hadn't noticed how quiet the room had gotten. The hand lay flat on the layout sheets, then walked on its fingers to where *The Autobiography* lay—electrifying the air around it, just as it should. "Don't waste time on that shit," she heard, and looked up to see the hanky that McGuire had pinned on his thick, matted hair, and his hands now folded in a prayerful pose around the book. The few reporters left in the room tittered—Chuck Bohan, McGuire's favorite, was shredding a still-wet page 1 and tossing it at the editor's veil. McGuire waited for the room to quiet down, then said, "I might have something for you. Are you free today?"

"Yes," she said, pushing aside the pix and layout pad.

He smiled. "Never say that to a man, Gallagher. You're not 'free,' you're available, just like everyone else." He picked up the book again: "I'll have a look at this, if you don't mind. You didn't say—are you free?"

Gallagher was speechless.

"Good. What I want you to do—first, finish up the brides, then come over to my office. I'm going to lunch. You've got time to finish."

McGuire and Bohan always left the newsroom together, after the paper was down, for a lunch at the Streamline Diner. As they walked by, Gallagher saw that McGuire was still carrying *The Autobiography*. "I'm going to borrow this," he said. "You don't need it, do you?"

Gallagher was so dazed by the sudden attention, she forgot the rule about heads, and had to redo the page because two paired brides were wall-eyed and a solitaire was looking into the gutter. Simple enough to change. Miss Toohey praised her for her skill in arranging twenty-five heads on two pages with only a small flub or two, and offered her a hard Italian biscuit, which she would do each time Gallagher finished a Women's-page task.

Gallagher spent her lunch hour roaming the broken-down streets of Wampanoag. In spite of McGuire's offer—and the biscuit—she felt gloomy. As bad as the job in Pascoag had been, there were no bridal heads or wedding dresses. And that afternoon (as a *reward!*) Miss Toohey promised to give her all the Saturday columns (TELL DOROTHY, COOKING BETTER ON LESS FOR ONE, Heloise, Beth, and Dr. Scholes) to edit and head. Later, Miss Toohey would show her how to lay out Thursday's feature, a story the canned-peaches cartel had sent, along with five glossies of dessert dishes with the slick, orangey fruit peeking out from every nook and cranny.

The bonus was a feature assignment from Miss Toohey: a piece on the opening of a new department store in Centerfield; or, if that didn't grab her, a think piece on the chair-elect of the Wampanoag Women's Club, former treasurer of the county Arts and Garden Club. Gallagher liked the "arts and garden" idea, but wasn't eager to interview a peppy matron pouring tea and marshalling her well-heeled volunteers to beautify downtown Wampanoag—as the press release had put it. Besides, Miss Toohey abhorred feature stories. She still had a file of unprinted stories written by Miss Dolan. Gallagher had seen the editor, feature in hand, brooding over the layout sheet, irked and even bitter at the prospect of sacrificing good space—so much better utilized by the checkerboard of recipes, hints, and patterns. This wasn't *news!* It was more like housework!

In the course of this cheerless rumination, Gallagher covered half a mile of Wampanoag sidewalk and stood by the Chalkstone River with its silvery falls and eighteenth-century millhouse. Here they had set up the first Arkwright mill to spin thread and yarn, which in the surrounding mills was woven into ginghams, muslins, calicoes, and worsteds. Set on the river bank, the mill was a graceful edifice of rusticated stone with white-wood trim, a standout among the hundreds of ugly brick barns built as soon as Wampanoagers got the knack for manufacturing cloth. Now the mills were vacant, windows smashed, weaving machines moved, junked, or salvaged for parts. These days Wampanoag turned out a few oddments connected to its rich textile past: zippers, bits of elastic and braid, but no real cloth, and the city still felt the loss. Unemployment hovered at 20 percent. The only bureaucracies with cash to spend were Welfare and Urban Renewal, whose job it was to raze the last of the city's bankrupt industrial core and replace it with discount marts, parking lots, and extra lanes. You didn't even have to read the "Swamp" *Times,* as it was called, to get the idea: you could simply use your eyes. Plus the *Times,* like most papers, ignored the big issues; it had (and wanted) no memory to contrast such a rich past with the present.

The Chalkstone River was still pretty—deep and rapid—although pollution from the newer industries had killed off the fish and useful vegetation. Some days the river stank of rotten eggs, but today it had no smell. Gallagher sat on the grass—the strip left by the roadbuilders, so eager to cut exits out of Wampanoag. It was peaceful. When Gallagher looked again at her watch, she saw she had five minutes to run the half mile to her desk. The streets were empty and still, and nothing stood in her way. She hit the glass doors of the second floor four minutes past the hour, but no one seemed to notice.

On her desk was a stack of Thursday's columns and the peach story, if needed. Gallagher set to work. She was reading a letter about restyling an old wig when the phone rang: "What in hell," the voice said, "are you doing, Gallagher?" She hung up after he did, turned the columns face down, and made her excuses to Miss Toohey, who looked like she might cry. (The exact relationship of Women's to City desk had never been spelled out. With Mr. O'Callahan in that job, Miss Toohey had met the very few demands City made of her writer, but now, although she feared McGuire and his filthy mouth, she begrudged every minute of her new girl's time and attention.) It was up to Miss Gallagher, however, to set the city editor straight; Miss Toohey was not going to get involved.

After her girl had left, Miss Toohey snatched the stack of columns and 'plate. This was an interesting job, but if Miss Gallagher didn't have time for it, she could read proof for the rest of the afternoon. There was a fresh Italian biscuit sitting on a napkin. Miss Toohey grabbed it and tossed it in the wastebasket, then called her friend, the A.C.E., and told her what was up.

McGuire, balancing on the back legs of his chair, his feet hooked to the desk, was reading "the other *Times*" and marking it with a pencil. Gallagher settled herself, blue dress, white flowers—a seedbag, a pup tent, Juscik called it—in the confessional. McGuire hadn't shaved and the grizzle on his cheeks was the same grayish blond as the grizzle on his head, uncombed, unwashed. His eyes were bright blue behind the polished lenses. Eventually, McGuire (who had other things to do, and was doing them) assigned Gallagher to a story on a local nursery school that was closing down. The school was there when he was a kid, although you needed more bread than his old man had to attend. It was a prep-kindergarten, he told Gallagher, and a venerable Yankee institution. Even in the old days, he said, when the rich weren't as anxious, they enrolled their children at birth in the Asa Bosworth Perry School. At Perry, you were prepared for Elijah Brown or Loring, and then, smoothly and safely—with your set—on to Lincoln, St. George's, or Moses Brown, then to Greene or Angell, Dartmouth, Princeton, or Harvard.

Perry was the last of its kind, he said. Genteel Wampanoag was dying out, its offspring too scarce now to support a society nursery school. So Mr. and Mrs. Charles Bosworth Perry IV, who had inherited the school from Mr. Perry's father, "Boz," and from his father, the late "Bozzy," were forced, against their will and inclination, to close the doors of the Victorian clapboard on Cherry Street. McGuire handed Gallagher the press release; it was actually a letter from Alice Hickok Perry, who taught the classes, and who hoped the *Times* might include a notice and words to the effect that this graduation, Class of 1974, would be the last.

"Now, Gallagher!" McGuire roared, although Gallagher was sitting right beside him. "I want a good story. None of your Ain't-That-Nice, How-Sad-It-Is. I want you to find the *story* in this. Know what I mean? This school was a breeding ground for upper-class scum, the factory owners who sat on their asses while Wampanoag industry went down the tubes."

"Yeah!" said Gallagher. (She was already writing it in her head. When she was on the *Newsletter,* all she needed was the idea, and the story grew on the page. That convinced her that she had found her place in life.)

"A story *I'd* like to read, Gallagher," he said, rocking back on two chair legs again. "And take this!" he added, shooting *The Autobiography* across his desk, where it hit the spike with its thick ruff of newsprint. "Don't be pickling your brains in tripe."

Gallagher took the book—it had done its work—and made her way across the city room. Some reporters had noticed that

McGuire was paying a special kind of attention to the new chick on Women's. They were keeping an eye on it.

It was tricky, hard, but Gallagher managed to slip out for two hours that next day and beat it over to Cherry Street to meet the Perrys. (The fact that it *was* the Perrys made it easier.) There was nothing quite like being out on a story: no one was watching, your object was as yet vague; if you took a little extra time, stopped to gawk at the boxy houses on Cherry with their quaint bits of trim—widows' walks, belvederes, and fan windows, rose-covered trellises and gazebos—it was legal, you were "free" and, contrary to what McGuire liked to think, completely unavailable. This was what Gallagher liked best about the news biz: being out of the office and in the world with a mission, a target, and a skinny reporter's pad.

When she tapped the Perrys' iron knocker, a starchy maid appeared to lead the way through a foyer with columns and marble busts, a dark parlor with layers of Oriental rugs, into the garden room, all white wicker chairs and chintz, where Mrs. Perry was poised to serve tea. The Perrys—Mr. and Mrs.—rose to greet Miss Catherine Gallagher and to inquire after their friends at the *Times,* especially Miss Toohey, whom they had known for years, and who had always been so courteous and helpful.

The Perrys were both slight, white-haired, and eager to put the reporter—such a lovely girl, and so young!—at her ease. The tea and coffee arrived, each pot on its heavily bossed silver tray, each with its cognate pitcher and bowl. Already arranged on the table were demitasse cups for coffee, blue-on-white china for tea; a plate of petit fours and one of watercress sandwiches. Suddenly nervous and even giddy, Gallagher blurted out that this was her first story. The Perrys became even more charming; Mr. Perry pressed a bell on the wall, and when the maid appeared, he requested a bottle of Madeira and they drank a toast to the first story ever, from crystal so fragile, Miss Gallagher took one sip and set the glass down (she didn't like Madeira anyway, too sweet).

Besides, she needed her hands. Already she had a sentence about the house and needed to jot down other details. The Perrys sipped their tea; when Gallagher stopped writing, they began to talk. They were sincere, they were kind. Having devoted their lives to education, they were eager to show the city and its readers the impressions they had made on its first citizens, and indeed they had letters from prominent alumni full of memories and compliments. Gallagher saw photos from the school's heyday, when the twelve pupils—girls in white dresses, boys in sailor-suits—gathered with their mothers on the lawn of 12 Cherry Street for the opening tea. The children learned their letters and numbers, they sang and marched, they made a trip to the doll museum, the athenaeum, and the arboretum. There was an annual tea dance, a May breakfast, the Christmas bazaar, dancing lessons, elocution, pony rides, and gardening. Mrs. Perry had another photo of the 1948 graduation, and there they all were: the Perrys, the two maids and the secretary, the children in white duck and white organza.

The Perrys seemed so pleased that the girl reporter could appreciate their school, and would she take another cup of tea? She seemed more like a friend than a society editor. Then she mentioned her plan to interview some of these eminent '48 graduates (now in their fifties), and the Perrys looked puzzled. None of the graduates, she discovered, lived anywhere near Wampanoag, or even in New England, for that matter. They had drifted south with the cloth machinery to new factories in Atlanta, Richmond, Charlotte, and Jacksonville. Mrs. Perry suggested it might be unnecessary to meddle with persons so directly involved in the economic and social life of the nation. Mr. Perry hinted that persons so substantial might not be as willing as the Perrys—still, as it were, "local"—to talk to a smalltown paper.

He was polite, she smiled, but Gallagher felt less snubbed than annoyed. Why *couldn't* she talk to a few graduates? Were the Perrys worried that the school was just as local and insignificant as the *Times?* Or maybe these high-rollers hadn't liked the Perry School as much as the Perrys liked to think? Gallagher asked for a list of more recent graduates and was again rebuffed; the Perrys had to respect the privacy of graduates and their families. When the reporter said that she couldn't write a story as one-sided as this, on the basis of a single interview, Mrs. Perry urged her to go back and have a word with Miss Toohey. Miss Toohey knew the Perrys well, she knew the school and the school's history.

Gallagher considered. Yes, if Miss Toohey was editing the piece, she'd stop here, thank the Perrys for their hospitality. She might apologize for pumping them in an upstart, pushy kind of way. But the story was for McGuire, and she hadn't gotten it out of them yet.

One of the Perrys must have rung the bell, because two maids appeared and removed trays, pots, cups, and glasses, and the Perrys themselves stood and flanked the doorway, hoping to dismiss the gossip columnist by the chill of their phony smiles. But the girl stood fast. She wanted to know: 1. How old the Perrys were? 2. The financial condition of the school upon closing? 3. The real reason for the closing, and several other matters that were none of her—or the paper's—concern, and the Perrys were sorry they had countenanced this snoop, when they could so easily have phoned in the notice, or sent out the school's secretary. Gallagher, who, at an earlier moment, would have slunk out, mortified and shamed, now insisted: it was her feature, her *Times,* her McGuire waiting for the story, whatever it was. For the Perrys, the game was over: they were old, rich, and guilty about something. The school, its demise, the bank balance, and the cover-up, were now exclusively the property of the readers of the *Wampanoag Times.*

The reporter asked her questions and got the kind of rude check that would serve her purposes quite as nicely as the facts, had they been willing to spill them. Mr. Perry himself let her (pushed her?) out the door and shut it harder than was necessary. It didn't matter: Gallagher's mind was fired as she raced back to Times Square.

Only the Perrys got there first, with *his* call to the publisher, who apologized, then routed the call, with a stiff preamble, to the M.E., now waiting to speak to the cub—in fact, looming in the doorway as the girl bounded into the newsroom. He signaled her, and she—fingers itching to get this story, so rich in possible ironies, on paper—stalked into his office. Mr. O'Callahan sat for a moment, playing with the straightedge he used to lay out page 1. First, he said, she wasn't in any real trouble. She was too green to appreciate the delicate protocol that buffered the paper and its representatives from the first families of Wampanoag, some of whom *used* to pay the rent and measly salaries and, even if they didn't any longer, were intimately connected to the one who still did.

At first, Gallagher didn't know what he was talking about. She wasn't born in Wampanoag, he was saying, and hadn't really been there long enough to discern that the Perrys had a purely philanthropic stake in the city, and could well have spent their millions elsewhere. It wasn't her fault, because, the M.E. went on, his eyes bright, his face pale, his bland expression unchanged, *he* knew she hadn't come up with this absurd idea on her own. He knew whose asinine idea it was, he said, his voice rising, to send her to harass the Perrys.

He went on, but Gallagher had stopped to think. Did Mr. O'Callahan hate McGuire? That didn't square with what he'd said her first day. If McGuire was such a troublemaker, why had they hired him? And why had the prize-winning newsman taken the job? She had filed the McGuire story (MTK) and now there was something fresh to add to it.

But Mr. O'Callahan was still talking, ranting, using the most pathetic euphemisms to describe just how the paper groveled to the few Yankee families left behind in the bankrupt, bulldozed town their forefathers had made out of a fast river, a stolen invention, and native greed. She studied the scene outside the M.E.'s window: an empty square whose traffic light flashed red, green, yellow, and red again before a single car rolled up to obey it. She was watching the street to keep from crying—it was dumb, it was pure Women's desk, but the strange tensions of the afternoon had produced their effect. Mr. O'Callahan sent her to the ladies' room. At least, she thought, spreading a dripping paper towel over her cheeks, he had shut up. As she'd exited the M.E.'s cube, bypassing Women's, and skimming the news pen, she'd felt many pairs of eyes boring into her. Coming out, she felt only those corner eyes, light blue lasers. (So, if they were such lickspittles, why did they recruit McGuire? And why did he *take* the job?) Before she reached her desk and the downcast eyes of Miss Toohey, the phone was ringing. Instead of answering, she tracked past the desks of still attentive but covert eyes until she was in the confessional, the inner window sliding open.

McGuire knew the scoop. Even if he hadn't gotten the call from the publisher, *and* the benefit of O'Callahan's hangdog look, he could've guessed, he said, the upshot. He looked at his reporter, round-shouldered, deflated, eyes still burning with shame, and laughed in her face.

- 25 -

And somehow, in the interval between Wednesday and Friday, when the story was edited, McGuire had outflanked (and out-yelled) both O'Callahan and the publisher: the Women's writer was assigned to him! and her obligations were only to her readers! The days of editing the paper from Cherry Street were, as McGuire told Gallagher, over! That was why the publisher had agreed to hire a real newsman like himself, who, in addition, knew Wampanoag and its plutocrats like the back of his hand.

Gallagher wrote her story (McGuire sent it back: baseless claims, too arch; lifeless, now libelous!) and sent her back to the files and to make a few phone calls. The story was blocked for Saturday's Women's page. Before he shot it down to Composing, McGuire showed Gallagher the soft roll of wrinkled sheets glued end to end. There, over the lead and under the slug (SKUL/CG), he had block-printed the head:

]Posh Perry Boots Gilded Tots[45 pt. bod.it. BF
]Finishing School Gets Finished[18 pt.bod.

Then, while she was still standing there, he penciled in: "By Catherine Gallagher, Times Staff Writer." She need only inform Miss Toohey, he said, of column inches, size of the head, and Miss Toohey could budget the story for her Saturday hole.

Miss Toohey seemed eager to showcase the girl's work—which she hadn't read, but had heard enough of the scandal to be sure that *this* time the scum in the corner would get what he deserved—and used the entire newshole on page 18 for the feature. She was nice as pie, but Gallagher thought she heard in the old lady's voice a crackle of malice, an eagerness to see the bolt strike this willful girl, so brassy, so different from the other helpers who had wished, like Miss Toohey herself had at one time, to become a society editor.

Gallagher had Saturday off, so she drove downtown to pick up the *Times,* and there it was on page 18—every coy, sly, biting word of it, with all its mocking bits of dialogue—and the newsroom phones, she imagined, would be ringing off the hook, one pat to 50 pans and 100 subscriptions canceled.

Gallagher took the paper home. She had made the mistake of telling her father about the story and the ruckus it had caused, and he was still upset that a child of his would criticize a family so respectable, so top-drawer. He was beside himself and her mother had to keep changing the subject, but he kept coming back to it. "Goddamn it to hell! Why do you have to *do* things like this?"

Catherine's mother reminded him that the Gallaghers didn't live in Wampanoag, so what did they care? But that made him even madder. "I *know* people who live there, and they read it!" he shouted, but Catherine wasn't afraid of her father's bluster. She carried the red-hot—as McGuire had called it—story upstairs and unfolded it on the bed. (Before she had gone out that day to the Perrys, Ben Dugan, the foto ace, had been sent to Cherry Street to snap Mrs. Perry sitting behind a desk in the schoolroom-parlor, with little tables and chairs set in front of the fireplace.) Gallagher hadn't seen the pic till now. In it, Mrs. Perry played the loving teacher everyone thought she was, while in the story . . .

Gallagher held her breath; her hands and feet were cold and damp as she read the first few grafs of the McGuired article. So many editorial cuts and adds had sharpened the tone, made the remarks more absurd, hilarious. McGuire had said, "Gallagher, the piece is homicidal, it's *suicidal.* They'll be after you with baseball bats." But *he* was happy, and on that day, she was happy.

Now, she wasn't so sure. She could see it, through her father's eyes, for what it was: a smart-ass smear. Why take a bland bit of society news like this and cook it up so hot? And who was she cooking it for?

"Your tongue," her mother would say, when a stray remark had driven Catherine's father through the roof, "will be the death of you."

Gallagher looked at the article again. It was bad—no, it was funny! It was, as McGuire would say, fabulous, and it would slay them.

CHAPTER 2

But a lot of readers used to being bored by the *Times,* who didn't even read the Women's page, liked the article: it was different, funny, and it was these readers—although only two—not the insulted bluebloods that O'Callahan had expected, who called the *Times* that Monday. No subscriptions were canceled and, oddest of all, Mr. Perry sent a note to the publisher, thanking him for the write-up and picture—no mention, of course, of the staff writer. After all the build-up, Gallagher was disappointed, but McGuire said, "Don't try to second-guess your readers. Just write the best you can." And then: "Some day you'll hit the jackpot. And they'll string you up by the thumbs!"

And so, her first article complete and bylined, Gallagher went about her business on Women's, doing four days of brides, Abbys, food, and fashion to one day's work on a feature, sometimes at McGuire's behest, mostly at Miss Toohey's. Not all of Toohey's ideas were lame; most were, but as McGuire had said when Gallagher beefed about a story on a Wampanoag matron—husband an undertaker, one of the biggest—named to head this year's heart fund, "Gallagher, you scurvy bullshitter, you could squeeze a story out of a trip to a phone booth!" It was gross, but still a compliment, and Gallagher felt, returning to her desk and a press package from the canned-fish combine—text and glossies of a July 4th picnic with the meat of canned crab, clams, tuna, and mackerel mixed with pink mayo and heaped into red, white, and blue bowls—a surge of pride.

That Fourth of July night, she had a date with Juscik. He was taking her to the Tent to see Johnny Mathis. Catherine had wanted to say no—she almost laughed in his face—but Juscik refused to see how anyone not a "snob or phony asshole" could spurn such a quality act (the guy had top billing at Caesar's!). So Catherine affected not to have recognized the name, eager to be taken and shown. "Nice save," Juscik sneered, but the date was on. Juscik liked to keep these things simple: call his girl and make the date, zip over in the Firebird, spend the odd half-hour soft-soaping the parents, then escort the date to something he was dying to see or hear, followed by a few drinks at one of his hangouts—preferably one, like the airport lounge, with no low-class, ethnic overtones—then park for a few minutes, neck, and it was over and done with for another weekend. Juscik liked routine: he already had his tennis night, his TV night, season's tickets to the Bosox, Wasox, Patriots, and Wamp State basketball, a night left over for the Polish Club, the date night, and a spare to sit around, do his laundry, and call his mother.

Since they'd first met, he'd taken Cathy to the headliners of the season: Bobby Orr at the Arena, a trip to Boston to see Steve Martin, the Blue Angels at Quonset Point, the opening of *Jaws,* three times to the Rustic Drive-in where *The Godfather* (longest-running hit since *The Ten Commandments*) had returned and was held over, and a few toots to the mall to eat at Rooney's Steakhouse and Make-Your-Own-Sundae.

The ease they enjoyed together had taken some work on Catherine's part, but less now that she understood that Juscik was not, and never would be, interested in—and he counted them on his fingers—(1) movies with subtitles; (2) classical, jazz, or country; (3) any restaurant he hadn't already been to; (4) walking and gawking, including any art museums or exhibit, except for the annual boat, bike, and auto shows.

Catherine went along. She wasn't, she didn't think, slumming; she was taking a break from a life she could go back to at any time, simply by visiting the East Side. Reporting on her love life to Else Canby, her last link with Kings, she said: "He thinks I'm Stella and I am, but I've got a lot of Blanche in me that he can't see." Else thought it sounded steamy, but what she didn't know was that Catherine had never seen the inside of Juscik's apartment, much less his bed. Juscik was cautious, he was leery, he'd been "stung" the last time, so he was playing it safe.

However, once the Stanley Kowalski trope had slipped into

the correspondence, nothing could shake Else's conviction that Catherine was, as usual, getting it all—whereas, by her own account, Else, a grad student at Berkeley, was getting most of what was there. She had slept with her professors, and once with the dean; she had a couple of affairs with upperclassmen, and was dating a filmmaker from San Francisco State. But Else always wanted whatever someone else had. Envy, she admitted, was her vital principle.

It was during Catherine's senior year that Else appeared on the scene, moving into the suite across the hall. First thing she did was rope off her door with the silk braid that had kept gawkers, she explained, from invading her debut ball at the Plaza. In her present situation, Catherine noticed, Else seemed to need the rope less. Besides Catherine, she had few visitors, and didn't seem to want any. Her chief interests were money and sex, and for these she didn't go looking in the girls' dorm. Else did her hunting in the large lecture classes—economics, political science—where she preyed on the sleek boys, whose jackets were cut in Bond Street, and who had mastered the talk of proxy votes and controlling options.

Money was of interest to everyone at Kings, but as the curbs and scruples of the anti-capital '60s were still in style, it was cooler to poormouth than to leave so naked a sign of class as that debut rope right where people could see. But Else was unembarrassed. She didn't cut her conscience to suit the times; she waited for the old days to come back, and they would. Even in her letters, once the subject of money was "mooted"—there being so little of it at Berkeley—she reveled in the crude details of sex play with the "hunkies": odd and inappropriate places, the names, the theatricality, aloofness, pain, vigor, speed, and repetition. The letters were instructive, even if Else's expertise—like her command of such subjects as mineral-and-mud spas, ponies, and diamond mines—was beyond Catherine's experience. What irked and "smoked" Else—and what bewildered her elderly parents, who had spent a fortune on English saddle, lycée, Kings, Europe, debut, etc.—was that the girl, at age 24, heiress to the mucilage millions, had never once been married. Now she was killing time as a postgrad in psychology. And although Else was smart and even, in some ways, learned, she was bored stiff by psychos. Still, she managed to suck up the contents of her courses—methodology, nomenclature, etiologies—like a vacuum cleaner, reserving her best energies for the plentiful supply of "hanging ham" and "golden hunkies." Catherine wondered if, for all her flippancy, Else was going to end up a lousy doctor, and not the blue-chip odalisque she so longed to be.

Reading these weekly letters—Else loved to scribble and ordered reams of fine paper in blue, eggshell, and oyster gray, which she blackened with a small, dense script, often illegible—Catherine marveled at the capacity (Fitzgerald had said it would either make you a genius or a nutcase) to have friends so unalike as Else Canby of Amagansett and Juscik of Wampanoag. What (besides Catherine) did they have in common? Else was sorry to be only a grad student, and Juscik needed the extra five grand per annum to keep his bookie relaxed, yet in their day-to-day lives they were equal to the task of managing their own happiness, and Else, at least, knew what that happiness should consist of.

Catherine folded up the six-page latest from Berkeley, and tried to cram it into the white-lined envelope, splitting the seams open. She put the exploded envelope in a drawer of jewelry, ticket stubs, and medicine, pushing it all the way to the back. As a rule, Mrs. Gallagher didn't snoop, but why tempt her beyond her limits? Catherine had heard the Firebird come to a screeching halt out front, and now Juscik was jawboning her father, although all she could hear was Mr. Gallagher's booming voice, the roar that only a Juscik could induce, with his ironic politeness and the way he lounged in the doorway, stretching his long limbs, and flashing the feline smile. Even Mrs. Gallagher, harder to impress, would slip into the room to gawk.

Catherine took her time. First, she tried on a black dress piped in white, then a red linen sheath. She chose the red, screwing on black, dangly—her father would hate these—earrings, and tying her hair back in a low ponytail. People dressed up to go to the Tent, and she hadn't done quite enough for *them,* but just right for a concert in Kingstown. And Juscik might go for it, even though he himself preferred to blend in, wearing the self-belted pants and short-sleeved shirt considered dressy by every Wampanoag male. He'd never admit it, but he liked the novelty of dating a snob, whose hair wasn't bleached and who wore no makeup or nail polish. Catherine found her patent leather slingbacks and slipped them on bare feet. Reflected in the bureau mirror, the dress was short and snug (it was Else's—Bergdorf Goodman; she was ready to turf it, along with a skirt, shirtwaist, and two purses, but Catherine snatched it), and such a deep dye that it cast its own crimson haze, bronzing Catherine's neck and the inside of her pale arms. Still, the look needed something, so Catherine borrowed a lipstick from her mother's dresser. The red sheath, red lips, and pale face, framed only by the dangling earrings: this was chic, and people—even if they couldn't place it—would know it.

Catherine stepped out of her room and descended the stairway in a state of satisfaction. She stopped, a tall red stripe, just in the doorway of the cool kitchen. The gazes fell on her, some critical, then her father returned to the story he was telling, about the kindergarten closing down, and where he'd read the article, and how it griped his ass to see what a low blow, and by whom.

"Nobody needs that!" he barked. "And people don't want to read about it either!"

Juscik was listening, but his eyes had wandered to Catherine's burning face, then back to the father.

"Why does she have to do things like that to us?" he was saying. "Who the hell asked her!" He broke off, his voice vibrating with rage.

"Go easy, Eddy," said the mother.

"I will *not* go easy!" he shouted.

When he got up to fetch the article, although Juscik said he'd already seen it, Mrs. Gallagher tried to shoo the couple out the door: "Go while you can," she said, but the father was back, shaking the paper in Catherine's face. "Take it! I don't want this scandal sheet in my house!"

"Have fun," Mrs. Gallagher was saying, as the couple squeezed past her. Mr. Gallagher, who still clutched the paper, was trying to get his daughter, or someone, to take it. Catherine turned her back on him. But Juscik, after seating his date in the car, returned to the porch and took the newspaper, tucking it under his arm. "Don't worry, Mr. Gallagher. I'll take care of her."

Mrs. Gallagher kept waving until the car was gone. Mr. Gallagher was anxious to yell at his wife, and he did, until his anger ("Over what?" she said to him later; "Why do you let every little thing bug you?") was spent, and he could breathe again, sit down, catch his breath, only to have his wife bring up the subject of the skimpy "shift" his daughter was wearing to the Tent, and he was off again.

Catherine didn't hear about this second theme until the next day, over coffee with her mother, while her father was out "collecting" at Jesus Savior. "He took it out on me," her mother said wearily, "and why?" Catherine offered to keep her articles out of his sight from now on. Her father read his evening *Bull,* cover to cover—he missed nothing—but he would never have to see the *Times,* if Catherine didn't bring it into the house.

"I brought it into the house," Catherine admitted, "but I never gave it to him."

"Well, how did he get it?" her mother asked, then went on to something else she'd been waiting to say: "*I* enjoy your articles. They don't bother me. I don't know those people. What do I care?"

Catherine promised again to keep the *Times* out of the house, but what neither of them knew was the father had taken out a subscription. He had seen the kindergarten story long before Catherine had. It just hadn't come up until the Juscik boy came over and "pushed his buttons." And he intended to read *every* article the girl wrote—how could he not? These people could come over to his house in the middle of the night and burn it down! He wasn't doing it for amusement: he hated dirt like this, he exploded, he yelled at Catherine and her mother. Maybe some day, later on, he'd laugh, he could savor a nasty slam, a painful dig; he was pretty good at giving them himself, but Goddammit, he did it in private! He didn't go out and write it up in the paper! What kind of a goddamn fool . . .

"Did you have a nice time?" her mother asked. "You don't have to talk—you look so tired," she added, before Catherine could even answer. She must have seen that the answer wasn't coming as easily as it should. And she didn't want to work Catherine up, this early on Sunday, and be worked up in return. She could tell just by looking at the girl's drained face that it had been the usual ordeal. Catherine's life—which always started out so well—never lived up to her or anybody's expectations. "Why? Why do things like this happen to you?" her mother was forever asking. But who had the patience to listen to the long—and always different—explanation that came with the answer? For Catherine, everything was hard. So, they'd both learned from experience to suffer these things in silence. It spared them both "the agony," and Catherine found her mother's mute company soothing. It gave her time to think. And the date the night before was a fruit already ripe for thought.

It had started out in the usual way. "I like him!" Juscik said, as they were sailing down the street at high speed. "Who?" "Your father." When she didn't respond to his point, Juscik said, "Don't you?" Catherine said she thought her father was okay, but what was so great about him?

And with this remark, Juscik clammed right up. Recalling the little he had ever said about his own father, Catherine wondered if he was being sincere about hers. Once she had gotten Mr. Juscik on the phone. "Y'allo!" he bawled into the receiver. "No one at this number," he said quickly, hanging up.

"Y'allo!" when she redialed.

Eventually, Mrs. Juscik picked up. She had a heavy accent, too, but a better command of English, and for that reason, more than any other—and the mother had many good qualities—Juscik adored her; he favored his younger sister, a bank teller, cute and sharp, but his dour Polack of a father and lumpy older sister—pregnant every other year—caused him such grief, such shame, that he never spoke of them. By contrast, Catherine had to admit, her own father—even raving—might seem like Fred Astaire or Cary Grant.

"Talk to me," Juscik said, as he cut the wheels of the speeding 'bird onto the ramp of the interstate.

So Catherine expanded, since he seemed interested, on the kindergarten story and the ruckus it had caused, but how it had died down in one day.

"Go on," he said, cutting into the speed lane. "I'll tell you when I've heard enough."

But Catherine had nothing more to say on that subject, so they drove in silence, 80 in a 45-mph zone, tailgating a Porsche. Juscik took the time to give Catherine a long look, like he always did, to see if there was something he missed, a tone, a secret sneer, then shifted his gaze back to the road and crept up yard by yard until the Porsche, and the car right in front of it, scrambled into the right lane. Juscik sped up to tailgate a Lincoln. "Okay," he said, "tell me something else then. Talk! I like to hear you talk."

"What about?" she said.

"About the people at work," now nudging the Lincoln into the gutter, and with nothing ahead of them for miles, he slowed down and blocked the cars behind him.

Catherine warmed to the subject of "people at work," already cooked in previous conversations, leaving out McGuire, whom she wasn't ready to dish in the way Juscik so liked to hear. She remembered the time Juscik had stopped short in the middle of Broad Street and dropped his head down on the steering wheel. She had been telling the story of a girl at Kings and how, with ferns and potted palms, a white satin bedspread and tall candles, she had turned her dorm room into a funeral parlor. Cars were beeping behind them, but Juscik made them wait until he showed Catherine, by a sidelong look, how little of this canard he swallowed, but that he'd savored it anyway.

At State, he hadn't met so many "way-out" types. When Catherine asked what types he had met, he said, "You know, types from around here. People, Cathy, nothing special." The subject of types *he* knew, including his family, depressed him or made him mad, so Catherine didn't press. She *had* noticed that these depressing types were the same "people at work" he loved to hear about when *she* was talking. It depended on the angle, apparently, the distance, and Juscik didn't feel like he had any.

She had already covered Sports, police, the A.C.E., Women's, the librarian, the editor in the key, M.E., Composing, but she kept at it until Juscik cut the blue 'bird, screaming on two wheels, into the parking lot of the Kent Tent, a green- and orange-striped wood structure—a tent in the old days—now surrounded by miles of parking lot.

"You take yourself too seriously," Juscik announced, braking sharp, bouncing, then shoving the gearshift into N.

Although Catherine knew he made cracks like this just to get back, just to show there was nothing she could tell *him* that he couldn't see right through to the conceit that drove it, she found his remark worth considering. How could attention paid to the details of other people's lives be taking *yourself* too seriously? It was exactly the opposite, she felt like saying, and would have, if he didn't hate analysis—analysis bored him; he'd always rather hear a story.

He was so different from the "last one," who preferred analysis any day to dreary details of people's lives. To the last one, letting "clowns, symptoms, human stubs" distract you from the real business of life (Schenkerian analysis, say, color theory, or Benjamin's arcades) meant you had no self to start with. So which was it: too much self or not enough? she wondered, climbing out of the hot car, still shuddering from the abrupt stop.

They strode with others toward the Tent, where a crowd was milling around a poster of Johnny Mathis in white tie and tails. Catherine could sooner imagine Else marrying Juscik and shacking up in a Wampanoag three-decker than conceive of that last one shouldering up to the Kent Tent for a night of pop.

Juscik hustled her into the theater, they found their seats, and the house lights dimmed. A lucky thing the show was starting and Juscik's busy eye glued to the round stage and the tiny dark man in white, because Catherine was filling up with thoughts about the last one, and now as good a time as any to air some and ease the pressure.

She'd told few people about Dana Falkenberg; the story was too weird. And there was also the tendency that McGuire had praised for squeezing stories out of nothing. This *was* an asset on the job where assignments were so routine. But where personal life was concerned, such a mind was too productive. When it came to herself, Catherine could never extract or "boil." Even the everyday could, with a little work, thicken and tangle, and Dana was not the everyday.

Even after all that had gone wrong, Catherine was still cowed by Dana. He wasn't like anyone else, and nothing so bewildering had happened before, or since. So Dana was still, as he would put it himself, pure quiddity. And there he lay—or stood—in her mind, a fearsome oddball, making a batch of bitter coffee in a dimestore pot, while the sun licked the greasy scurf on the walls and shelves of his dump of a kitchen. The linoleum was splashed with paint from the previous occupant, but it was Dana who had clogged every inch of counter space with his sauces and oils; the wooden table was crowded with soy sauces alone. Dana liked to cook foreign and cheap, some dishes he covered with green or black sludge, others had a garlicky, deep-fried crust. He washed down the homemade dinners with wine in clear glass jugs, the kind the winos liked. He loved to cook and eat, but never seemed to bulk up; he weighed less than Catherine, and when he stretched out on her at night, as he liked to, and rested his head on her neck, his body was so light it felt like a wooden folding chair.

She had met Dana at a protest in Kingstown. A boy had raced through the corridors of the dorm screaming how the pigs had arrested street people just for gathering in the common, as they always did, to build fires in the trash cans, to sleep and to panhandle. It was early spring and the nights in K-town were still cold. The Kings students beat it down to the common to add their numbers to the besieged street people, to storm the line of helmeted cops and be stormed in return, when the cops felt the rioters had pushed too far. The student mass was forced one block north, where it regrouped and inched back to the edge of the common. The cops held their own line with ease: they had the helmets, shields, canisters of tear gas, guns, and billy clubs; the college demonstrators only had their winter coats, if they thought to wear them, while the street people—the object of the clash—had vanished into the residential neighborhoods that bordered to the west, or onto the Kings campus on the east.

Catherine Gallagher—or Caff, as she was then called—didn't know why she, a person with almost no politics, was in the fray. She felt the summons—as others had—when the young voice, hysterical with rage, had shrieked down the corridor at the sleepers behind their wooden doors. The bulletin, as often happened early in a clash, was exaggerated, even distorted: panic and injuries (deaths?) from an unprovoked attack by the K-town ("shoot to kill") riot patrol on a helpless community trying to rest in the park. And what was there to do after this, but jump out of bed, or die a coward?

But there was no mayhem to witness that night; not one tear-gas canister had been winged at the wave of protesters occupying, then yielding, their one-block zone. Cold and half-asleep, Caff was scared one minute and bored the next. She was jammed in the midst of the angry, chanting mob, forced each time to surge or be trampled. It was dumb—sneaking ahead, taunting and insolent, only to be shoved back, screaming in terror. Caff could barely hear her own small voice in the furor. Were they all that maddened, or was it just the shock of the late-night awakening, the thrill of boots pounding the sidewalks, the tense faces purpled under the floodlights, and the alien sight of the riot cops, armored in plastic?

Suddenly, slow to retreat, Catherine found herself alone in front of the crowd, facing a line of cops, 20 feet away, arranging themselves in V-formation—now getting ready, now charging with billy clubs braced across their hard, plastic chests. She stood for a moment, dazzled by the sight, then was grabbed by the arm and hauled backward by a stranger, trying his best to save her from the stampede.

Did they fire? she asked him later, when they had pierced the mob of protesters and were again sheltered in the soft center, but her rescuer couldn't hear, so frenzied was the crowd, buzzing and milling. Shortly after—and for no particular reason, since the cops had reformed their line—the exhausted crowd began to disperse. There were rumors that downtown was trashed, store windows broken, looting, arrests, and the National Guard on their way.

Not true: no Guard, no windows broken, although a few were waxed. The streets of downtown had emptied while the cops held off the protesters in the park. A few students were arrested—one with a spraycan, another for spitting right on a badge, a third had sat down in the middle of Battle Street and refused to budge. When the pylons and sawhorses were removed, and Battle reopened for traffic, the cops dragged the sole protester—chanting—into a squad car. All this and more was reported in the next day's *Kingstown Bugle,* with the emphasis on the bratty Kings students and the courageous cool of Police Captain Downey and his SWATs. The Kings College *Russet* carried the story under the headline: "Brutal Pigs Foiled in Park."

While these stories were being typeset for morning delivery, so that both papers lay outside the doorways in the Kingstown dawn—some of the copies already "liberated" for burning in the braziers of the K-town common (the street people had reconnoitered minutes after the last police car rolled off Battle, and were snugly bedded on their benches)—the rescuer walked the shattered Kings student, snagged in a police charge, into a coffeeshop north of the park. Catherine remembered it well. At the doorway, the stranger, with cameras and extra lenses slung around his neck, had stopped to snap her picture.

And here it was already, intermission. The first half of the concert was over. She was clapping. Johnny, resplendent in a series of sequined costumes, mostly all black or all white, but once in purple head-to-toe, took several curtain calls, each involving a long run the length of an aisle to the top row of the wooden tent and down again, and this after singing twenty songs—it seemed like twenty; Catherine recognized some of them from the days before the Beatles, when the radio played no other music but this. People were charging out of the tent—before the singer had even finished his last run—to line up at the refreshment stand.

Juscik stuffed his program in a pocket and turned to Catherine, who had been staring so hard at the stage her eyes felt dry. He kissed her, with a touch light yet intense, and again. It was certainly not the first time, but something was there now, a sharpness, and for the moment, as they walked hand-in-hand up the aisle and into the luminous night, she released what she had been so closely thinking. Juscik pushed a plastic glass of red wine into her hand, and she had time for a few sips before the lights flickered to signal the second half.

When they were settled on their green canvas chairs, the stage went black, then dazzling white, as Johnny raced—this time from their own aisle—down to that glittering circle and climbed up on a lone barstool. He was in black tie, small and neat. As he sang one love song after another, he swiveled on the stool to face a different segment of fans. Juscik was still holding her hand and at one point kissed it. She was a staff reporter, famous, half these people—or at least a few of them—had read a bylined article last Saturday about a classy kindergarten gone broke, shut down, end of an era. Every word of it was hers, except for the few twists McGuire had added. After so much wandering and flightiness, bad boyfriends and sudden reversals, she had found her place. And it wasn't on the Women's desk, either, but that would have to do for now.

Johnny had stripped off his jacket and was now dancing with four guys in black tie. Four gals trotted onstage in red satin. Little by little, the small, round stage filled with dancers in evening dress, and Johnny ran offstage and then returned in a white jumpsuit and matching headband. As he sang, he waded into the audience, kissing old ladies and shaking hands with husbands. He leapt up the steep aisle, and the audience was fanned by spotlights, then streaked and showered by beams radiating from the revolving silver ball. By then the audience was ready to sing along to "Smile, though your heart is aching. Smile, even though it's breaking . . ." Back onstage, Mathis quieted the audience and began a medley of "Apple Blossom Time," "Tangerine," and "My Funny Valentine," each song with a love-wracked sob or sigh built in.

Catherine felt the gooseflesh rise on her arms and at the back of the neck. Did the world these songs reflect ever really exist? What happened to those wistful romances once the war was over and life began again with housework and squalling babies? Popular songs no longer bothered to elicit such tender feelings. Did that mean the feelings were outdated, or had they vanished? This was sad, but embarrassing, too. What did it amount to but cultural backsliding? What had happened to the brainy girl who spent afternoons in comparative listenings, arranged by Dana, of Furtwängler, Karajan, Munch, Toscanini, and Ormandy, while they read scores (she could barely read, but he'd play reductions on piano) of the three Bs—Beethoven, Brahms, and Bruckner—in a room crammed with nothing but music: piano, scores, and stereo parts, the thousands of 78s, LPs, and reel-to-reel tapes?

Dana would sit on a box or the edge of a table—there were no chairs—under the ring of naked lightbulbs, and listen for hours, drinking cups of his grainy coffee. There were countless interpretive differences in performances of the same piece—sometimes conducted by the same person—and Dana prided himself on detecting not just the most dramatic inflections of phrasing, dynamics, rubato, but the really *tiny* nuances, sometimes in the articulation of a single note. Then he would explain what the inflections amounted to, how and why they were done, what their connotations were and where they fit in the history of performance practice. He would stop and start the tape recorder—fast forward, pause, rewind—to make sure she heard them. They read letters by the three Bs, biographies of major, early-century conductors, and learned analyses of the key symphonies. It was hard and sometimes tedious, but Catherine, no music specialist—she hadn't had a single piano lesson—applied herself. Even when it sounded like gibberish, even if she could understand only a fraction of what this man said, she might manage someday, with his help, to see into—if not entirely enter—the hermetic sphere of art. Dana was in that bubble already.

Dana was the first person she'd ever known who fully inhabited the world of art. There wasn't a moment in his long, varied day when he wasn't making it or absorbing it, reading, thinking, or talking about it. There were few breaks or distractions—or this was how it appeared. In fact, he did have his compulsions and his hobbies, but they weren't as ordinary (or as normal) as, say, Juscik's, where everything was right on the surface, and it was all surface.

The hermetic sphere proved impenetrable, and Dana himself, too strong, too peculiar a dose for an average girl, a dishrag like herself. It was because of Dana that she was "beaten" back to Wampanoag. That's how Else had put it that last week in Kingstown. Else had flown back from Italy to find her friend sealed up in a dorm room, with no food or water, nothing to do, nothing to say, nothing. Of course, Else didn't know for a fact that Catherine was planning to beat it back to Wampanoag; but it was easy enough to guess from the room and sight of the suds-less dishrag—grimy from use—that Dana had wrung her out, or worse.

Else wanted to know what exactly the scag had done, but she didn't press for details. She took the sodden rag back to her uncle's flat at the Ritz, where she ordered delicacies and stimulants from room service. When the first tray arrived with tea sandwiches, fruit, and a pot of fragrant coffee, Catherine managed to rise and sit opposite Else at a table the waiter covered with heavy linen, and laid with silver and a bunch of violets in a vase. She could just make it out through slitted, puffy eyes. The table stood near a window overlooking the public gardens. It was nearly summer and the gardens—so sad—were in flower, round and oval pools of wavy color against the streaming green.

Personally, Else scorned psychology, she was leery of analysis, but believed in the curative powers of hot water, good food, and subtle luxuries, so that entire day and part of the next she steadied her friend with bath oils, saunas, makeovers, elegant repasts, asking not a single rude question, but receiving, in due course, a weepy, jagged account. She listened, and countered with juicy narratives of a few fiery affairs, and one, even briefer, nuclear fling, which had transmogrified the feverish nights of the week in Rome.

By the time Else was ready to board her train south to Greenwich, Catherine was solid, and went with her friend to the station. But Else was not fooled. It was then that she predicted—in that ruthless way she had of foreclosing on the future of friends, or of any classmates she happened to know—that Dean Saltonstall (or whatever his name was) had pulverized what little metal Kings and Else had hammered into Catherine's spine; she was pigmeat now, hopeless, fit only to retreat to that fleabag city, wherever it was. It was a shame, but coming from that hole, she just couldn't play games, and if Else had only been there—instead of where she was—she would have seen it and intervened. Even in her slurried state, Catherine was surprised to hear just how bad things were. And this prognosis from a girl who sampled men like so many marinated mushrooms, spitting out the soggy ones, avoiding the spoiled or putrid—unless she happened to crave that distinct thrill.

Now less porous, Catherine reassessed the generous coddling and nasty sendoff that Else had offered that spring. Maybe Dana had been a little too interesting, even for Else.

Now it was over. People were clapping, but was it really over? Johnny Mathis raced down the aisle once more, and was composing himself while the orchestra struck up a slow, syncopated beat. Then, first humming the tune in its uneasy key, the singer took a breath, began: "There may be trouble ahead—." Catherine had heard this before. "There may be dah-da and dee-da and love and romance." What was it called? The song—and finally he hit the title line—was a gallant, prewar ballad, and Mathis opened his throat to accent the sad whoop in the main phrase. Then he slowed it down until the song was unbearable, creepy in its gloom, his low notes pulsing and swollen with pain. "There may be music and danc-ing, and love and . . . roma-an-n-n-ce." Her skin rough with chills, and finally: "Let's face the music . . . and dance."

A painful thought was hooking its way through her brain. She had willfully hurt the Perrys; she had taken their act of gallantry, their lifelong sacrifice, and crudely sent it up for the titillation of the *Times'* most jaded readers.

Mathis seemed to be singing the song again, or was he just repeating a verse? Catherine felt she was rolling on the waves in the Titanic, yellow champagne, the glossy dance floor, then the crack. The song was finally over and the house lights poured down on an audience tasting and snuffling its own salt tears.

The stage went dark and people streamed up the aisles and into the soft, black night, a briny slick to the summery air. The ocean was never far away in Wampanoag, one reason Wampanoagers were so satisfied with their lives. Juscik led Catherine to the Firebird. He was silent, and had been silent, but there was a strange negative charge snapping around him: where had that mood come from and how long had it been building? Catherine had experienced something like it before, and trouble ahead was what it meant.

Mrs. Gallagher had, in the meantime, gotten up to make a fresh pot of coffee and broke into her daughter's daydream to offer a cup; now she felt like talking. She had snuck the article out of the stack of reading matter on Mr. Gallagher's table when he was in the bathroom, and she had read it, too. It was funny—was it meant to be funny? she asked her daughter.

"Did *you* find it funny?" Catherine asked, once she figured out what the hell her mother was talking about. But now she didn't want to dwell on it: it was a bad mistake, and one that could never be rectified. Better to have written nothing. Better to let people live their lives and cherish their illusions in peace: this was her new stance. And, in fact, the *Wampanoag Times* had always taken that stance. The *Times* never bothered to inquire into anybody's business: be it the city, the county, the zoning board, the redevelopment agency, or just its citizens. Timesmen took notes, they quoted profusely—they often checked the finished story with sources, just to be on the safe side. Or at least, that had been the policy before McGuire arrived with his Pulitzer prize and buttinski ways. He wanted his reporters to dig, to pump and ferret, while the M.E. and the publisher clearly discouraged all such extra effort, fearing what it might turn up. The *Times* was the only game in town, and it owed its comfortable existence to the pokey way it covered the city, without ever ruffling a feather. The schools, too, Catherine was thinking, and rich patrons like the Perrys, deserved better than to be roasted on the Women's page, and for what? Just so readers—like her mother, for instance, with no respect for anything—could see them for the pompous asses that they were, and laugh.

But even her mother, Catherine noticed, this Fearless Fosdick, doubted that a story about such nobs as the Perrys was really safe to laugh at. And as she looked at her mother's attentive face, set to laugh or to stifle, the worm began to turn. Recalling some of the asinine, the snooty things those egomaniacs, the Perrys, had said—no one put a gun to their heads; and how faithfully, how scrupulously these "howlers" were reproduced on the pages of the *Times*—without commentary, because none was needed; Catherine laughed right in her mother's face. "Their Sunday was *ruined!*" she jeered.

"Whose Sunday?" her mother asked.

"Those Perrys."

Her mother hesitated, then said, "You mean, their Sunday was ruined because of you?" Her face was beginning to twitch with mirth suppressed too long.

"Yeah, because of me."

"Because of you, their Sunday is ruined?" the mother croaked, milking it now.

"Ruined."

And they both laughed, so loud they didn't hear the father coming up the porch steps, across the porch, and into the kitchen, but when they saw him—and the look on his face—the party was over.

CHAPTER 3

Catherine sat at the Women's desk for the next three weeks with nothing good to write. She typed brides, headlined the regular columns, laid out pages and edited food copy, ate the biscuit Miss Toohey gave her every day now that she was doing everything right and in half the time it took the Women's editor and her former desk-mate working together. There was hardly a mention of the kindergarten story. That was Saturday—Saturday was history: new papers had to be written, printed, and thrown away; the only paper that mattered (the pressure of deadline steadily building) was today's. The editors were blasé about a story, however sharp-edged, that ran on Women's, and the reporters scorned anything that wasn't hard news or sports. The stars, Kennedy and Bohan—City Hall and State House—razzed Gallagher, when they spoke to her at all, about the KO punch delivered by the champ, Kid Gallagher. Other reporters, jumping on the bandwagon, toasted "The Kid!" and "Killer!" with cups of coffee until McGuire, hung over and crabby, cruising the city room with his filthy mug surcharged with java, told them to stuff it and get cracking. He circled Gallagher, who had bought a new pair of black slacks and black sweater to cut a figure in the roomful of polyester, tan, and navy blue, but he had no use for her talents that day, that week, or the following weeks.

"It's like being a whore" (Catherine wrote to Else), day after day cold-shouldered by the only person who counted, forced to rely on Toohey for story ideas, not even getting the chance at a single lousy 50 Years Wed! because none had been phoned in. When Gallagher had asked old Eddie Flynn about the dearth of fiftieth anniversaries, he just shook his head: "They're dying like flies out there."

"What I mean is" (Catherine explained in her letter), "you're in bed with him one minute, and a stranger the next."

The more McGuire ignored her, the nicer Women's and the M.E. were to the new cub. One Tuesday Mr. O'Callahan asked if he might have the pleasure of taking her out "for a bite," and Miss Toohey, who overheard, doing—as usual—nothing but passing things that happened to land in her box to her assistant, then watching as the girl typed, blue-penciled, and headlined, scribbling a list of cues for Composing, said yes, Miss Gallagher was always free for lunch at 12. As soon as Mr. O'Callahan had shambled off to the men's room, Miss Toohey congratulated her assistant. Not everyone in the newsroom had received such an invitation, and some had been here over forty years. She fumbled for the box of biscuits in her personal drawer and offered one to Gallagher, who said no, it was too early. And Miss Toohey, so easygoing since McGuire's retreat, chirped: "Well, to each his own." Then, a minute later: "Don't you think he might have asked *me?*" She was whispering although the newsroom, like a factory floor, boomed and clanked toward deadline. "I wonder why he didn't?"

At the Streamline Diner, where he was greeted as a long-lost friend, Mr. O'Callahan ordered a meatloaf on white and a coffee cabinet for himself, a grilled cheese for his girl. When their order came, he ate and drank with concentration. Gallagher nibbled a sandwich dripping with grease from the grilltop, which the skinny cook, in tee shirt and knit cap, a rag stuffed in his back pocket, was now cleaning with sweeps of his flipper, only the oily tide kept flooding back. The diner was so mucky that the menu was barely legible through the scummed plastic; the aluminum ceiling was waxed over, and the stools at the counter were growing a black fur, especially rich around the bases. Even the red banquettes, in one of which sat the Timesmen eating their lunch, were gummed with the residue of 50 years grilling and deep frying in an airless cubby—a small fan pointlessly paddled on the shelf. Even the cook and counterman, and the one other customer, chain-smoking Luckies, seemed slick. The picture windows were opaque with a dust gel.

Filth aside, the Streamline Diner, famous for its excellent coffee, dark and rich, smelled delicious. Embedded in the funk clogging every surface was the pungent odor of the hundreds of pots brewed every day. To step, on a cold winter's day, into the Streamline (O'Callahan had told her on the way over) was God's gift to the working man. Walking the Streamline side of the street, nine-to-fivers were tempted to stick their heads in the door and order a "reg'la," as the counterman said, "with legs." The diner brewed with two antique coffeepots, double glass globes fitted together to make a retort. Cook made no more than one pot at a time, and customers didn't mind the wait, even if they were in a hurry, if there was a chance for a cup from "the fresh."

Before Mr. O'Callahan could finish his sandwich, the bread was soggy from ketchup poured on the hot meat. He drank his cabinet without a straw so that after each pull, he had to wipe the moustache off his upper lip—Gallagher told herself to stop gaping, stop spying—he began to talk about his hometown, and his hometown team, the old Wampanoag Quahogs, and a little about the *Wampanoag Times*, where he had worked since graduating from W.T.C., which is what, he explained to Gallagher, W.C. used to be, and before that, W.N.S., and that meant normal school, another name for teacher's college. And did he want to be a teacher? Gallagher asked politely. Yes and no, Mr. O'Callahan said. What he really wanted to do was pitch for the W.T.C. Redballs, and did Miss Gallagher remember the 'Balls? Gallagher said she might: what were they? Mr. O'Callahan rolled his eyes up and, at the same time, called the waiter over. "Two quaw-fees," he said, having, through all the talk, noticed that the rusty-looking lower globe had filled with fresh brew. "Tell this youngster," speaking to the waiter, "who the Wampanoag Redballs were."

"The Wamp Reds!" the waiter croaked. "Hey, Ernie," he yelled to the counterman, "O.C. here wants to know who were the Reds."

Cook, without having to turn from the grill, where he was still sluicing grease, said, "Tell him, we don't give out that imfamation."

Before the chaffing could get started, Gallagher managed to recall that the Reds had been a college baseball team so good it served as the unofficial farm team for the minors, and the minors themselves as good as the majors. Or nearly, Mr. O'Callahan explained in a voice so loud that the staff and all its patrons could enjoy the story heard so many times, yet to their ears never stale. Gallagher listened, too, but kept her eyes on the counterman, who had lined the inside of his arm with a dozen frankfurters, and was painting each dog with mustard, then squeezed a line of ketchup or spooned out relish. The counterman then forked onions on one, and slid the line of dogs into two cardboard boxes and started pouring the fresh into paper cups. No sooner had he dosed each cup with a tablespoon of sugar and a squirt of cream, pressing on the lids with one hand, when a telephone lineman, with the grappling hooks still on his boots, swung open the door and scooped up the box, waiting to be handed the bag of stacked coffees. This process was repeated several times: once for a lady from the historical society, then a real-estate agent, followed by the mayor's assistant, who strode up to the table when he saw the mayor's crony from the *Times*. The "mare" and O.C. went way back, and at least halfway back with them went the mare's assistant, whose hair was snow white. And all these people had the same order, although some took their dogs with fries or onion rings, some with "sinkers" or packaged cupcakes. The diner still ordered individual fruit pies from the baker, and Mr. O'Callahan munched a lemon pie with his coffee.

Once she'd gotten an eyeful of the Streamline, Catherine began to wonder what the purpose of this luncheon was. He took the last bite of the hand-held pie, a slurp of coffee, flicked crumbs off his suit, then pushed his cup away. "Catherine," he said, "or do they call you Cathy?" Before she could say "Gallagher," the waiter appeared with the last cup of the fresh and poured half in O'Callahan's empty cup, and topped off Gallagher's.

"You haven't touched your quaw-fee," Mr. O'Callahan said in a shocked tone. "And what about the samwitch?"

Catherine picked up the sandwich and put it down again. The coffee was the most delicious she had tasted since Kingstown, where in even the lowliest joint the coffee came from an espresso machine, the beans roasted in every conceivable way. Mr. O'Callahan drained his half cup and pushed it away again, folding his hands. "So," he said, "how do you think you're doing so far?"

Before she could answer—and already a tight smile was fixed on her face and a curt answer ready, as it was when any teacher, boss, boyfriend, or relative ever dared suggest that her performance could in any way be questioned—Mr. O'Callahan said that yes, he could see she was doing fine, enjoying herself and helping the Women's editor with her page; people seemed to like her—

no one had said anything bad—she was never late a day for work, and had proved willing to stay after five when needed, without even putting in for the overtime. Yes, people had noticed, he said, and although it was none of his business—maybe even illegal for him to interfere—there could be union problems if she didn't put in for it, even if it was just the lousy, odd 15 minutes.

Catherine didn't think it worth the trouble to tell Mr. O'Callahan that she *had* mentioned her overtime to Miss Toohey, who told her not to bother; nothing less than three hours a day counted. Miss Toohey couldn't get used to the union—anyone could see that. She had started on the *Times* in the '30s when the Seeleys of North Wampanoag, who'd made their original fortune in slave-shipping, called the shots, hired and fired at will. The Seeleys were proud to pay less than a living wage, well below the minimum 25 cents an hour, yet counted on everyone to help out in a pinch. Reporters in those days, Miss Toohey had bragged, shaking her head in amazement, had done everything short of peddling the papers themselves, and once, when the newsboys were down with the mumps, she'd delivered the papers door to door, and then in heavy lots to the downtown newsstands. "People really worked for a living then," Miss Toohey said wistfully, because for all the Guild had done to improve things, she hated the interference and low-class associations.

Mr. O'Callahan, who as management was a sworn enemy of unions, secretly loved the Guild, since he too had worked many a Saturday for "no," in Classified, or in the photo lab, when the Seeleys, skinflints all, were in power. Those were not glory days, Mr. O'Callahan said, unless you're of the mind to favor a plutocrat and his politicians-for-hire running roughshod on the small fry. "We were all in it together in those days," he went on, whether you sewed on buttons for Coats & Co., or penned editorials and endorsements at the behest of the T. R. Seeleys, Senior and Junior. Miss Toohey had described the pre-union days and now Mr. O'Callahan was giving his version. He still loathed the Seeleys, mostly dead now, and the *Times* long since sold to a chain, which had in turn been absorbed by a game-show syndicate, with the very latest Seeley, a grandnephew, returned as publisher.

But there were some good things in the old newsroom, he allowed; you didn't need a college degree to get a press pass, and hardly anyone had more than a night course or two under his belt. No matter: the best writers, he went on, then and now—Eddie (mayor), Jackie (county), and Vinny (school board)—had no college to speak of, never read a book, and what they filed was tight and bright, written in the five-cent words that even the greenhorn in West Wampanoag, ten children and a sixth-grade education, could grasp.

That was the way to go, O'Callahan said, and Gallagher took this to mean that a recent Saturday story might have contained a few million-dollar words that the greenhorn did *not* grasp. Yes, Mr. O'Callahan said, when she voiced the thought, but something else too. Catherine waited. O'Callahan signaled the waiter and pointed at the two cups. Catherine let hers be re-filled, but never before had she drunk so much coffee in one sitting, and, in addition to having to "go" in a diner with no facilities, she was feeling peculiar: her scalp was tightening like a vise on the thin walls of her skull.

Those Seeleys still drawing breath, O'Callahan went on, who happened to be friends of the Perrys, did not relish a satire at the expense of one of their own. But, he added, tough patooties! He and certain others on the staff—wire and city, even the sports editor—could appreciate a jab at the plutocrats, who were, incidentally, he said, pointing his coffee spoon at her head, running short on dough, now that the IRS didn't coddle them like before. But the average Joe—and that Joe was the *Times'* bread and butter and the reason the paper was so packed with neighborhoods and names—did not go for it. Such a subtle story went over his head and alienated him from his hometown paper, which, given how fast readers were converting from print to their color TV screens, needed him now more than ever. "Just thought I'd mention it," the M.E. concluded, wiping his mouth with the napkin he'd already balled up. "Ready? You want them to wrap that?" he said, pointing to the sandwich, which had oozed rings of grease onto the cold plate.

O'Callahan picked up a reg'la with legs and squired his reporter through the shabby streets of downtown, past Seeley's department store, Woolworth's, and a Kay's Jewelers—all big advertisers—which never seemed to be doing any business.

– 50 –

Not long after the Streamline lunch, Gallagher found herself back again on the crooked, ghostly streets, nibbling cookies from a paper bag to clear her palate. She was on assignment, a secret just like the kindergarten story, and although the brass knew she was out, they were given no clue as to her object, "a feature," McGuire told her to tell them. "And if they have any questions, refer them to me."

Gallagher was on an itinerary that would take her to every café, soda fountain, restaurant, automat, greasy spoon, diner, candy store, luncheonette, dime store, tearoom, and lunchcart that served a cup of hot coffee with its BLTs, hot dogs, pancakes, crullers, Boston cream pie, baked beans, chowder, eggs and bacon, blue-plate special. The object was to evaluate the coffee served in each establishment within a one-mile radius of Times Square. People had their notions on where to get a good cup—everyone knew about the Streamline—but what about all those other mediocre and lousy cups? What would happen, was McGuire's bright idea, if you took a high-toned Kingstown grad, nursed on the espressos, café-au-laits, mochas, and cappuccinos the poor bastards of Wampanoag had never even heard of, and sicked *those* tastebuds on the thin, weak, purplish seepage, either scalding or barely warm, that locals were forced to swallow and to classify in their minds as "coffee?"

Gallagher laughed as McGuire delivered hints and instructions, drinking ("sewage-treatment plant run-off, liquefied fetal platelets . . .") from his own dingy mug. "Stop it!" the queasy reporter cried, overdoing it a little, thrilled to have the editor's attention.

"Skip the Streamline," he added. "Do it as a sidebar. We don't want to throw the curve off. When you've done your research, I'll take you to the 'Line and we'll do some tasting together. I might write that 'bar myself." The paper was dull as dishwater, he went on, relations to advertisers were just a little too cozy. This piece would shake things up. He warned the cub—new striped blouse with the black skirt—that she'd better drink her fill, because the article would put every Swamp eatery off-limits to a fink like herself. "A fink?" she said, grinning at him.

"Don't be a smartass," he said. "Be fair. Drink the coffee. Try to be pleasant. Don't go thinking you're the restaurant critic for *Cue*."

Gallagher said she wouldn't.

"And don't be so agreeable!" he snapped. "What's wrong with you anyway?"

Gallagher started to rise from the confessional, but McGuire yanked her down by the sleeve. "Did I tell you to go? You're not dismissed yet. Stay a while, cool your heels." He leaned back on his chair, his knees propped against the desk heaped with the morning's worth of stories, wire and cuts, layouts, pencils, glue pots, stamp pads, a roll of toilet paper, Bromo Seltzer, a beer can, cigarette packs, and dead ash.

Gallagher settled herself on the straight chair, tugging her short and narrow skirt as far as it would be tugged. McGuire watched, then with his own hand brushed a speck of ash that had settled on the black skirt.

"I touched you!" he said, when Gallagher raised her head to stare. "I touched you! Go ahead. Slug me. Call O'Callahan. Call the fire department. Do something, Gallagher! Think!"

Gallagher reached over to his desk and flicked more ashes onto the black skirt, then waited. It was a bizarre thing to do, and it floored him. They sat tense and silent, eying each other, until Bohan, with the latest version of a story for tomorrow's page 1, rescued his editor. Gallagher then retreated to Women's to satisfy the myriad piddling demands of Miss Toohey, to eat lunch with her, then spring the plan for the next day's trek across the Swamp.

Gallagher loved to be on the deserted streets, sliding along anonymous and free, just like the other bums, pensioners, retirees, City Hall flaks, all out for an extended coffee; housewives and biddies, like bored children, dragging their rickety shopping carts behind them. It was beautiful out here on the street (in fact, humid and overcast) and Gallagher felt she would never return to the office. She peered into every face, alert to questions or suspicions, but there was no truant officer for girls in their 20s, out on the lam in broad daylight, wearing their glad rags and carrying a pocketbook: no one cared. She stopped to glance at a photographer's window—mostly pictures of babies and bowlegged toddlers in blue or pink sitting up on a box with little hands curled around a white rail, or clutching a pedestal; another picture of four children's heads cropped in ovals on pearly blue paper; an engaged couple whose photo was matted in the shape of a heart—the bride-to-be so young, her hands, resting on a satin-padded bar, looked infantine, with boneless fingers and nails bitten to rawness. The Swamp "foxes," as they were called by their fans, married young, sometimes in high school, if they could; some were already pregnant, most would be "carrying" by the next year. The baby fat that rounded hands and cheeks swelled their immature bodies until, four years and four kids later, they looked bloated, flabby if not obese, and old; the tender, girlish faces never fully matured—not even for one year—before they were faded and overblown.

They never, Gallagher was thinking, got to roam the streets of the Swamp solo, with a press pass in their pocket. Then she felt ashamed to think it. What fault was it of theirs? They were doing what they were told, and even if they were told nothing, they seemed driven, magnetized by inner necessity. First there was the example of the mothers, old—and huge!—at 30, stuck at home in the squalor of their cramped tenements, breeding a batch of brats, and the cooking, washing, bathing, feeding, napping, accidents, weeping, doctor bills, oil bills, sticky floors, musty bedrooms, children to whack, slap and whale, tug and push, but nasty and yelling all the more for it. Growing up like this—Gallagher was losing steam, having sampled not a single cup in the ten minutes spent idling on the streets—where did these girls get the idea (no, it was stronger than an idea) to get pregnant in their senior year and marry a boy from a family as poor and chaotic as their own, with fewer years of school, in and out of trouble with the law, with nothing but an old junker and the dim promise of a job at a gas station, or factory, or—if he happened to have the pull—filling potholes on the sinking Wampanoag streets, or just sitting around—to hell with the potholes—killing time, which was what city workers specialized in, since there was never enough money for asphalt and tar, and the trucks were seldom available. The art of running Roads and Public Works was keeping a full quota of men on the payroll and, to that end, making sure all the "big wheels" were greased. It was a high old life working for the city—good work if you could get it (Catherine could quote her father on the scandal of "bums feeding from the city trough"). But, unfortunately, idling was all they did, winter after fall, spring after winter—except for the occasional spot work for some wheel living in North Swamp (not where the Perrys lived; no one catered to the old families anymore), a new suburb where pols and the syndicate lived side-by-side, and whose streets were always in mint condition, if not rerolled every year, plowed first in every snowstorm. That was how things worked in Wampanoag, and no one seemed to mind the graft or complain about the inequities, but it didn't make for better husbands, or wean them from drinking beer by the case, walloping their wives and children and throwing money on the horses, the dogs, or any game with a published score. So this engagement picture—two heads in a heart, Catherine was thinking (and now must be shoving off, before her feet were stuck in the soft blacktop that the city substituted for concrete, so the sidewalks melted, buckled, and sunk every summer) marked the high point in the life of a fox, a moment when she was treated by family and fiancé as an asset, and why she looked so glossy and puffed out, so perfectly relaxed—or was stupefied a better word?

Somehow, Catherine—who had moved on, marching up to the corner and Curley's Hamburgs, the first target on the caffeine trail—envied them. Why? Who, lucky enough to escape that short, cramped, and painful life, could be envious? Gallagher pushed open the glass doors of Curley's and a bell tinkled overhead. No one was eating in the narrow luncheonette, no one behind the counter. She sat on a round stool. The menu was typed on cardboard and filed between the sugar and ketchup jars. Under "beverages," the usual soda, milk, coffee, Sanka, Postum, and cocoa (in season). Through the swing door from the back came a redhead with freckled face and yellow—were they really yellow?—eyes. Gallagher waited until the waitress wheeled around with a thick white mug, then brought a metal pitcher of milk and demanded the 32 cents, to recheck, and they *were* yellow. Although shadowed and rimmed in blue, the eyes were yellow as a cat's. Gallagher poured a stream of milk (maybe it was cream) into her coffee and emptied two packets of sugar. The waitress brought her a plastic spoon, and Gallagher slid her reporter's pad out of her pocketbook and onto her lap. She sipped, scalding her tongue. Slapping the mug down on the counter, she stared at the waitress's back, her eyes tearing from the pain, intensified when the searing stream ran down her throat. I'm too dumb for this assignment, she thought, with palate, lips, and tongue burned insensate for the day's first trial. She cooled the blistered parts with ice water—they still stung, but never would she forfeit an assignment because of mere pain. And perhaps the local java would have more of a chance with a palate dulled by burns, and doesn't that kind of tissue repair itself instantly?

The waitress had vanished and Gallagher wondered how far along in fox life she was—too thin to be married, but no one as young and attractive as she, even with yellow eyes, could be unmarried. Why were women—the thought occurred to Gallagher as her swollen tongue touched her hard palate, always the most painful spot—so drawn to pain? Or was it only Swampers? They at least seemed to get something out of their suffering; it was a way of life—dark, miserable, full of odd twists and intensity. Gallagher emptied her cup and burned her food pipe all the way down to the stomach, and maybe into the stomach, watching while the waitress refilled the thick cup with still hotter liquid, smiling now at Gallagher, one tough cookie, despite the black weeds and lank hair.

Gallagher made another note in her pad—to capture something of the atmosphere—and was gone. On the soft-tarred streets, it felt even hotter now. A crone in a faded housedress and straw hat was laboring up Market Street, red sneakers and no socks. Gallagher followed her, first into the A&P, where she bought an onion and a pack of cigarettes, then to the Seaside Laundromat, where she pulled her matted wash from a jumbo machine and poked it into an even larger dryer. After lighting up, she loosened the tangle of clothes, her head stuck in the dryer and butt hanging out of her mouth. When she was satisfied with the layering of the raggedy sheets and towels, she slammed the dryer door and wiped her eyes, tearing from the smoke. Sitting down, she opened a *Messenger of the Blind* that had been left on the folding table, and smoked her cigarette down to the filter without once taking it out of her mouth.

Gallagher moved on. For a fox, old age was the reward of a hard life: it was still miserable—Gallagher couldn't guess how many blocks, or even miles, the crone had to walk her laundry and haul her groceries, because these old ones never drove—but the husbands were long gone (lung cancer, heart attack, strokes from smoking, booze, and a pent-up rage so great that not even a lifetime spent punching wives and children, cursing, swearing, and smashing dishes could exhaust it). They always died young (happy to go), long before their widows, who were left at last in peace. The children were married and living in hells of their own, and Ma was left with a tiny house or apartment in the old neighborhood, with her own things, the best chair, her choice of TV and radio programs, spare time to pray and study the kindly face of Jesus, the best of the bedspreads and sheets (ancient wedding presents put away "for good" and refound when the house was given a good cleaning after the last child was married and the husband planted). Now the aged fox was set free, living on "Social" and a little pension, with Medicare and, most times, her health still good—too busy with brats and scullery and fending off the husband's rage for her own rage to grow and then to kill.

The rest was well earned, Gallagher concluded, moving on to Stuckey's Hot Shoppe, and so was the short unhappy life for the bastard. It was the '60s Lib movement, which she had joined and allowed to scrub her mind clear of its instincts and prejudices, that had preserved her from a fox's life, and (even though some of the old ideas had reseeded themselves) convinced her that men, the lousy bloodsuckers, should pay through the nose. It wasn't such a radical stance after all, since, in a covert form, every Wampanoag fox believed it in her heart.

Slowly, over the next few days and the free hours in them—and in spite of the many Swampers of every age she saw and brooded over—the coffee story grew, and McGuire edited it in chunks, with art and a layout that would fill the Saturday hole in a way that wouldn't insult his intelligence or hurt his eyes. He did all the graphics himself, leafing through books for dingbats, logos, bullets, and symbols. He came up with a simple system using filled-in coffee cups, half-cups, and empties to rate the product sampled in each of the humble and unsuspecting joints his writer had visited. So far there were twenty ratings made on brew from drum-like percolators, glass globes on hot plates, small pots bubbling on grills, dripmakers with individual pods of ground coffee exposed to the air and forever stale; laced with cream from metal pitchers, porcelain jugs, sealed paper cups; some squeezed from kegs with sour-looking yellow pastes clinging to the silver pumps and puddling on the counter; and sugar in beads, lumps, squares, and bricks.

It wasn't an easy story to write, despite Gallagher's inborn confidence and zeal for the subject. McGuire had estimated 30 inches for this item, a story gripping not in itself, but in the blow it would deal—and when the M.E. got wind of it, he'd hit the roof—to friends (read: advertisers) of the *Wampanoag Times,* who owned, ran, or cooked in the downtown eateries, and whose lives—and livelihoods—had never before been so rocked by scandal.

Once the story had been blocked, when McGuire had blue-penciled the scroll of copy, excising five pages of "blubber," when Gallagher had crafted and recrafted the lead and the top graf until, out of frustration and shame at the jabs about gold-plated and useless educations, turgid, brittle, and overly subtle styles, the absence of rip and spark, the constipated, prissy, craven truckling to the self-interest of a claque of small-time crooks and operators, she wrote a two-graf opening so arch, shrill, and razor-sharp that he roared with laughter. Then, the roar quieting to a cackle, he said that her days in the rag trade were now strictly numbered.

Gallagher, on pins and needles all morning, felt relief at not having to write the lead another hundred times, but it was followed by something sharper. The feeling had grown with the story, but it had been there from the first day, when she saw who it was behind the new fierceness of the old *Times,* heard the lashing tongue, and saw the muscular forearms and meaty hands, the strong fingers, so precise and deft.

Now the editor was talking—he had been talking a blue streak, but he must have seen her eyes roll up in her head because he snapped his fingers in front of her nose: "Gallagher!" he barked. "It's not over yet. You got one, two good grafs. There are another 29 to go and they have to be better! It's not over, girlie, don't die on me."

But he had noticed, too, because his voice dropped down when he said, "And don't be flashing at me, unless you can deal with the consequences." His voice was harsh, and—as there was no response to this kind of remark—Gallagher was ready to bolt. But she didn't, she stayed and gazed at McGuire's animated face, now flexed with anger—or maybe it wasn't anger—until her eyes dropped, and she went wobbling back to Miss Toohey, who had of course been spying, but how much could be seen from that far away, and through the back of Gallagher's head? (As it turned out, you didn't need eyes to see what everyone in the newsroom already knew, and could see coming, before Gallagher even sat down to write that first obit, when Nightside had spotted her in

O'Callahan's office, sexy, the right age, and later McGuire had told everyone in earshot how much he'd like a piece of that: it was what he always said, no matter what walked in—fox, crone, or biddy, so long as it had legs, an ass, and enough hair to cover its scalp. But those who knew him well—Bohan and Kennedy, and others, too—could see the difference with Gallagher.)

To say that they knew, however, wasn't to say they weren't alert that next day when McGuire—who rarely lunched, and if he did, it was with Bohan, and it wasn't lunch so much as beer and pickled eggs—and Gallagher, who always went out alone and wandered the streets (people had seen her and reported back that it wasn't shopping, or meeting a girlfriend, or going to the bank), left the office at noon *together*—McGuire signaling the A.C.E. to keep an eye on the hospital story that hadn't made deadline. Earlier, Gallagher had said to Miss Toohey that it was the city editor himself who'd asked, and she couldn't very well say no, but also offered to lay out Thursday's food page and had already finished Saturday's brides, so it was hard for Miss Toohey to object, but what she didn't say she folded into a hateful look, then clammed up for the hour before lunch, conspicuously eating a single biscuit, breaking it into tiny bites on her napkin, then flicking off the crumbs as if the cookie was dusted in arsenic. Miss Toohey seemed to hate McGuire more with each day that he exchanged even a single word with her reporter. She knew about the coffee story and thought it was asinine, beyond—as she said several times to Catherine—being a needless insult to good advertisers, and to people who liked the coffee around here, and no one cares *that* much about it. But she had no choice but to run the story in the Saturday hole, knowing it would come from McGuire's desk edited, headlined, laid out with a sidebar, cuts, cutlines, art, with only a few slivers of space for Miss Toohey to fill with a motto or household hint.

Miss Toohey was used to rude treatment at the hands of this son of Wampanoag—and from such a prominent family! Bill McGuire was professor emeritus at W.T.C. and on the board of directors for the Y; he had been commander of his VFW post and always led the United Way and Heart Fund drives. In the eyes of many, Big Bill was second only to the mayor and maybe the bishop, and who would believe that a chip off this sturdy old block would brazenly blacken the reputation of the city's paper of record, and in the ugly way he did it. Miss Toohey knew the McGuires socially and they were lovely people. They adored their only son, although even they—she could tell this without their having to say a word—hoped he would do his muckraking at the *Long Island Clipper,* the *New York Engraver,* or even the *Boston Letter,* rather than churn up the quiet waters of the Chalkstone, where nothing flushing from Times Square had ever troubled them before.

When Agatha Toohey had run into Mary McGuire at the Ape-Mart, the kindergarten story was still fresh in everyone's mind, and they deplored the way it had nearly killed the poor Perrys, but Agatha couldn't bring herself to admit that the savage who'd written the piece, wiping her feet on the good Perrys and their fine school, was her own assistant. Why should she? She had nothing at all to do with the story—Mary McGuire would know that much—it had been hatched and cooked somewhere else, and Mrs. McGuire had no illusions about who was behind it. She had actually laughed at her son's open season on the bluebloods, and her husband laughed, too—they weren't that surprised—but she could also see the flap through the eyes of poor Agatha, a pillar of the church (The Little Flower) and model of old-maid rectitude. Mary and Agatha played bridge at the same club; they had had the same nuns and still lived two blocks apart in the houses they were born in, but they had never been intimates, or even friends: Agatha was too much the prude; in fact, Big Bill, named "Mr. Wampanoag" in 1957 when Jackie was in fifth grade, couldn't be in the same room with her for more than a minute.

Thus keen on the "item," the newsroom eyed the couple—Gallagher a few inches taller—making off for the Streamline (they knew because McGuire left the number with Bohan in case of a breaking story). Then they could only wait for the couple to return at 1, to see if the japes and innuendoes in circulation at 12:02 matched what could be read on the guilty faces. The newsroom, nerved up by the sudden jag of talk and laughter, settled down, quieted, and now there were only clicks from the wire machines and hums from the presses downstairs to break the intense concentration. When the hour elapsed, a charge again began to coil, rousing the staff from the post-deadline drowse, the news faces tensed up, every eye fixed on the glass doors, which were not opened by the lunching couple for yet another 45 minutes, at which time, and after so agonized a wait, there was scarcely any interest left: what else could it be, was the thought, but lunch, the lunch McGuire took with every one of his writers every few months to nag, needle, bust, and to egg them on?

But it hadn't been a mere pep talk, as Catherine wrote that night to her friend Else, describing the lunch more freely than she would had Else been within striking distance of Wampanoag. Gallagher—as she now thought of herself, even though the idea of a news-driven bloodhound was still new to her, and totally alien to Else—was here using her last name, Else figured, to cluck and preen over the latest lover in that jerkwater town no one had heard of.

Caff Gallagher, even Else could see—and Else wasn't keen to see something so alluring in a friend—was in love. Every phrase on the cheap letter paper reeked (this was the word that came to mind) of it. Even the handwriting, usually smooth and nunnish, had a suspicious tremor, yet the lines slanted to left and down, a sign of relaxed inhibitions. Else read the letter in the waxing salon, her whole body throbbing from the agony of having the stubble yanked—she had cried—in agonizing strips from her slender legs; the colorist—whom Else visited every other week for a gilding—had to bring her a glass of wine, and hold it for Else to sip as she lay, white and trembling, on the massage slab. She was in no mood for the hyperbole that was half lies anyway, so she skimmed the rest of the letter and tossed it away, only to retrieve it to study certain phrases, so tenderly exact, then tried again to read the tedious case history she was presenting in the morning, but instead, feeling so warm and relaxed, fell asleep. When she woke again, with Elena kneading her back, the letter and the writer (practically a stranger) behind it didn't matter in the least.

The key phrases, on their thin paper, were back in the wastebasket: "ate his sandwich, then mine," "palms calloused from some kind of hard physical labor—woodworking?" "I think they live together," "lanced by the sharp blues" "non-stop. My throat was sore . . ."

Gallagher wondered how McGuire had managed to drive the lunch conversation when she'd done all the talking; he'd merely sat there, nailing her with those sharp blues. She forced herself to write a month's worth of heads for Abby, barely skimming the contents of the letters. It was better that way, for then she could write the bland, gutless headlines required, if they were going to run Abby at all, especially in the last few years, when the letters had ripened into bold histories of perversions, sordid agonies, gross lures for the seven deadly sins. Wampanoagers, who would normally deplore such sleaze, read these columns avidly. After all, if their own *Times* saw fit to print them, and made them look so humdrum, who were they to quibble?

For surely he had driven it, Gallagher thought as she tidied her desk, even if she herself had done all the talking—and he all the eating and drinking—"blabbing my whole life story," she said aloud. "What?" the old lady said. Gallagher looked up, surprised, for she had forgotten anyone was there. "I finished these. Is there more?"

Toohey looked at her. "That's *not* what you said."

It wasn't like her to insist. "I was just thinking out loud," Gallagher admitted.

"Oh?" said Toohey, whose eyes showed she wasn't fooled. She, too, had contemplated the political aspects of the lunch date and its effects on Women's. For thirty years, nothing—and I mean nothing, she liked to tell the bridge players—had changed at the *Times,* and the Seeleys liked it that way, but now, every week, there was a rumpus, a staff rotation, different people flying off to do inane things. They were even, God forbid, thinking of redesigning the masthead, killing the day's motto and the little American flag—things people loved!—the joke about the weather that ran under the weather, and the copperplate rendering of the paper's name. "Think of it!"

"To do what?" Mrs. Perry had asked.

"Just think of it!" Toohey repeated. "Oh yes," she added, taking a sip of lemonade and, in her snit, spilling some down her chin, "they want to change the *name,* too. They want to take the 'Wampanoag' out, and call it 'The Valley Times'! That's what they want to call it!" she shrilled above the sniffs and titters of the Wampanoag bridge players, who so obviously heard and understood.

"I just had lunch with Mr. McGuire. We went to the Streamline," Gallagher offered, hoping this might do it.

"You told me that," said the Toohey, reaching inside her desk for the biscuits, although she wasn't at all hungry. "Did you enjoy yourself?"

Gallagher considered: what did such a question mean? If she said yes, would Toohey assume that she'd been given another assignment? Toohey had an odd look on her face and, studying it, Gallagher saw that Toohey (when had she become "Toohey?") had smelled a rat. Exposed to the look and its blunt message, Gallagher reddened, and there it was, Toohey had it.

The phone rang. "Women's desk!" Toohey sang out, then, "It's for you," she muttered, handing the old-fashioned hook phone to Gallagher. Gallagher knew who it was and she could hear the thrill in her own voice, just as Toohey was also hearing it. McGuire was telling a joke: it was about the old bag and it was, as the bag herself assumed, smutty. (Gallagher wrote to Else that even as the joke was in her ear, cracking her up as only McGuire could, the bag's eyes were on her, and registered the joke and its butt, but how? Did she have ESP or what?) "Things," Gallagher wrote to her friend—who didn't for a minute buy it—"can only get worse." And yet, she thought but didn't write, in some ways, they could only get better.

A week later, the coffee story, spread over two pages in Friday's thick, not Saturday's thin, paper, with pix, charts and a 'bar on the Streamline, came out, and the phones rang the minute the paper hit the street. Most of the "restaurateurs," as McGuire called them, had already gotten wind. Someone had leaked and they were braced, but the printed reality with its 20,000 copies (rushed to every county, hamlet, and outpost) was something more. Everything Gallagher thought would happen, as McGuire had once predicted, happened. Ads were pulled, subscriptions were canceled, complaints were forwarded to the publisher—even one of the surviving elder Seeleys called, Miss Toohey informed her reporter. She heard about it through the Perrys.

But then B.T.U. (Ted) Seeley III, the butt of the family, who graduated from Greene only to end up coaching high school fencing, had another idea. He thought the article a pip, just what Wampanoag needed. He wrote a letter to the editor, offering his views on outlying roadhouses and diners and the bilge they served as an excuse for coffee, but O'Callahan—who had to run the letter—penciled out all references to product: enough was enough. He edited all incoming letters—each with its different list of pats and pans, but after a week, with the letters and calls still pouring in, the publisher switched course: "Print them as is," he ordered, and the controversy brewed on the letters page, some readers offering definitions of what coffee was, its origins, trade routes, and history; others simply listing their choices, or recipes for how they made it at home.

In time, the lunchroom owners cooled off and Gallagher no longer needed an escort (Bohan or Kennedy) to walk her to the bus stop because of threats flaring from the pushier hashers and short-orders; the rest had stopped sending letters of protest. They, too, could see that business had never been better: customers never before seen were doing tastings of their own with a rating chart like McGuire's, and often ordering a meal to go with their beverage. Even if business hadn't picked up, the unpaid ad and all the unsolicited letters of praise and censure—it made no difference which—were unbeatable, and two weeks later, ad lineage for food services was up 50 percent, and the ad department was using quotes from the story in their page dummies. Every literate citizen in Wampanoag had seen the story, and the publisher suggested that Women's try another piece, say, on hamburgs, or milkshakes, but nothing doing, said McGuire, right to the publisher's face. He was the only one griped by the outcome, and he offered nothing to Gallagher for a month, nixing the few ideas she so gamely tried to pitch.

Miss Toohey and Mr. O'Callahan urged the Women's reporter to go ahead, to write the piece on hamburgs or hot dogs, and O'Callahan himself would edit it for Women's. But when he got wind of the plan, McGuire blew his stack and the idea—for the sake of peace and also because Toohey and O'Callahan were afraid of McGuire—was dropped, as was Gallagher, who had nothing to do but brides, columns, food, makeup, and Abby. And she was famous! The only reader still upset about the coffee story—because he had seen it the very day it came out; he had his own paper delivered, but Billy the cigarman had saved him another copy which he read at Joey's Tap—was Mr. Gallagher, who blew up several times in one week, and then went mute, spending most of his nights at Joey's, slinking home late and going straight to bed to avoid the sight of the girl's or her damned mother's face.

Inside of a month, as her father would say, and that month was the driest ever for assignments, Gallagher and McGuire were leading a double life. There was the one that people could see, where the city editor snubbed the famous hen on Women's, and was instead gunning for police, against the grain of that beat's reporter and an unbroken tradition of amity with the police chief—whoever it happened to be—and making trouble for the school board and its reporter, and sometimes even for the mayor's office. Things were cooking in the newsroom, except for the one corner, and Sports—where, if it were baseball season or any of the months before and after, things were always hot. And there was the other, a life that no one could see, because it was happening elsewhere, although some people had their hunches. It had started at the Streamline, where the first off-duty date was made.

CHAPTER 4

Gallagher consulted no one. On the appointed Thursday, she left work at the usual time, following the city editor by an hour. He always waited for a copy of the first run, along with the rest of the newsroom, skimmed the front page, sometimes having to race down to Composing with the typo (or worse), ordering Ernie, the foreman, to stop the presses and reset page 1: an electrifying moment in the *Times* building—even the people in Ads and Accounting would hear about it. More often, if page 1 passed inspection, McGuire would grab his jacket and out the door at 3:00, goodbye to no one. At four, Gallagher washed her face in the ladies' room, using the grainy hand soap, then applied a little color here and there to a skin already inflamed by the detergent and cheap paper towel. She combed her hair, and then stood quietly in one of the stalls waiting to see if she was going to throw up.

Once the skin had cooled from its unaccustomed sanding, Gallagher could see how pale—except for the rouged patches—she was. She had gotten only a few hours sleep, so the lids hung low over sunken eyes, but the rest of her body was feverishly alert. Was she excited, or just nervous because they were sneaking? She had asked McGuire again and he explained, as he had that day at the Streamline, that he was going to end things soon with Ariel ("Not *Aerial,* dummy!"), who, though young and beautiful, was a disappointment to him in ways that made Gallagher uneasy. A man disappointed in one woman could easily feel that way again. (Sometimes, as Else had pointed out, it was the man *himself* who'd created the problems he would come to despise.) Even in couples she knew, Gallagher had seen one party master the other in a series of swift steps. First came the flood of worship—this was the best part—followed by subtle erosions of character and will. Last came the slug state, when the victim—boneless, dependent, parasitic—was put to the test, as in: You aren't the woman I thought you were. Or: Where is the goddess I used to love? Ariel, according to McGuire, had reached this stage. Lazy, shiftless, wouldn't get a job or contribute one penny to their upkeep. Spent her time sulking or primping, cold to McGuire's two kids from the first marriage, when it was, as McGuire put it, a joy, a privilege for a woman to shape the lives of young people, no matter whose they were. But Ariel was, by then, too neurotic and infantile to hear. She spent her time soaking in the tub, brushing the corn-silk hair, riding her horse, expecting McGuire to shoulder the whole burden, plus boost her confidence and pull her out of her depressions.

It hadn't started out this way. Early on, McGuire had raved to Gallagher about Ariel and how great she was in bed. Gallagher was familiar with this phrase, and had the advantage of Else's many glosses. Some of it—dynamo, gymnast—she could guess at, but there probably was more. As time went by, though, and McGuire became more expansive, Ariel's lovemaking began to fall off, so that—by the time of the Streamline lunch—she stunk in bed: inhibited, boring, corpse. A little shocked, Gallagher asked how a woman could be so great and fail so fast.

"You can skip the sarcasm," McGuire said.

"I wasn't being sarcastic."

After a look designed to shrink her down to size ("You think you're so goddamned hard!"), Gallagher let the subject drop. It must mean one of two things: McGuire had lied and Ariel—or "Aerial," as Gallagher still preferred—had never been all that great, or she'd once been great but the months of aggravation, and all that time spent soaking in the tub and cantering across the farmyard had sapped her. Or maybe she did it just to spite him.

What does frigid *really* mean? she asked Else in a letter. Else wrote back saying not to worry about it, every woman was frigid: sex was the man's problem and frigid was, too. Gallagher was tickled by the decisiveness.

However frigid the girl was, and however much McGuire longed to "throw her out on her ass," Aerial was still part of the household: thus, if Gallagher and McGuire wanted to date, it would have to be on the sly. "And don't tell me," McGuire had said when the date was made, "you don't get a thrill putting the horns on 'Aerial.' "

Gallagher unlocked the white compact, and drove off to the Chateau d'Etoile, a cement-block palace off Route 50, site of a recent Mafia hit, according to her father, who always knew things long before the papers did. She parked the bug-like car in a huge empty lot. There was one other car: WAMPANOAG TIMES its front doors said—so how secret, she wondered, could the date be? A secret, she figured, only to Aerial: everyone else was in on it because only management kept company cars, and Mr. O'Callahan didn't use his, and the publisher had a limousine and driver. But you'd have to be blind not to notice that the city editor lived for the pleasure of rubbing people's noses in whatever smelled funny. It might be a professional handicap, although McGuire claimed he was no longer part of the profession. He had declared his independence the day he left the *Long Island Clipper*—"a real paper"—as that journal's prize-winning ace and all-round hard-drinking troublemaker. He had authored a series of deep-digging probes (on a big sewer project) that had toppled two municipal governments, and thrown a pair of mayors and five councilmen in the slammer.

But something else had happened; maybe it was the fame and high expectations, but suddenly, McGuire explained, he was a fuck-up, inconsistent, unreliable. He was eased out, forced—Miss Toohey had said—to take the charity of an editing job on the hometown (lousiest, dreariest, said McGuire, in New England, and maybe the world) newspaper. McGuire, as he himself had claimed, was finished with the rag trade; he was saving up to buy more land and raise thoroughbreds with Aerial's expert help—and work as hard as he could blacksmithing, the real love of his life. He already had a forge, a barnful of equipment, and ironwork commissions from Plymouth, Sturbridge, and Mystic. McGuire did love iron; he spoke of it as he used to speak of Aerial. He loved its ores, its slag, its brittleness; the sheen of iron, its gorgeous red in fire, its malleability, magnetism, and resistance. It was a tough metal, pure, never completely one thing, and very nearly alive.

Gallagher loved to hear the editor warm to the subject of iron;

and, once warmed, he loathed all the more the gutless, craven business of journalism, and would often leave the office in disgust, even before the day's paper was up and proofed.

On rubbery legs, Gallagher tracked through two of the Chateau's musty bars, both empty, dark, and smelling of vacuum cleaner, before—in a third, and even gloomier lounge—she found the editor sunk in a leather chair with his foot resting on a glass table. When she approached, McGuire waved but remained seated, or rather flopped, in his rounded chair. He signaled the barman, whom Gallagher hadn't noticed in the murk. This third bar, chilled by some powerful machine rumbling in the background, was also empty. Someone had just mopped the floors, so that essence of ammonia hung in air pockets not yet blasted by the cold stream.

The Chateau was famous for its chandeliers. The original newspaper ad showed a single, streamlined chandelier, and every lighting fixture in the hotel was based on this model. There were at least twenty chandeliers in each lounge—the individual tears, balls, and pendants were welded together into a hoop, and fitted into a larger hoop, but where were the light bulbs? Each hoop glowed like neon, but out of the center hole something incandescent and white-hot poured out, so if you passed beneath you were hideously skeletonized, a corpse in the morgue. That's the problem, McGuire was saying; there was also the scandal of not being able to turn them all on because of certain fire codes, unearthed for the first time in memory. Given the ugly word-of-mouth, and stories like the one Mr. Gallagher had heard, the hotel was never more than half-filled, yet forever slashing its rates.

The bars and lobby were ugly in other ways, too, Gallagher noticed, but it was mainly the lights that drove people away. The ad had eventually been changed to show an ultramodern lobby with crimson rug and metal chairs, shot just below the level of the lights, but the Chateaux—there were five of them scattered throughout the state—still failed to catch on. Even before McGuire hinted at it, Gallagher could smell the rat: garishness had never been a problem in the hostels and restaurants of Wampanoag, but no one in the state, until now, was fool enough to give out big building contracts to the low bidder, then fail to budget a substantial chunk for payoffs and protection. The hotel chain was a California venture, McGuire said, and they knew nothing about how things worked here. Gallagher nodded. She had heard stories like this before, and knew that even a maverick like McGuire wouldn't touch this one.

The bartender had brought Gallagher a glass of burgundy that was the sourest wine she'd ever tasted. "Don't go high-hat on me," McGuire said. "You're not out on a wine-tasting." Gallagher smiled, but it was vinegar, undrinkable, dead in the bottle, and McGuire was just talking tough. The barman reluctantly took the wine back—he tried to argue about it—then brought a glass of Cold Duck, the only other wine they had, left over from a wedding: it was sweet and flat, but Gallagher drank three glasses to McGuire's four bourbons and branch. She was gazing through the dusty picture window at the miles of empty parking lot. There was nothing out there to see, but still preferable to the sight of McGuire's softening face. He was saying things like how attracted he was to her and how, as soon as possible, he wanted to take her to bed, and maybe she didn't get it yet, but they were meant for each other. Gallagher, staring out the window (finally, a car cruised into the lot, a bellhop or someone in uniform), wondered how, at a time like this, he would still be calling her Gallagher. "Gallagher!" he said suddenly in a harsh voice, and she burst out laughing.

Still he was more right than wrong. Something was going to happen. She was drawn to him. It was one of the first things he'd noticed, he said: she couldn't have kept it from him if she'd tried. They finished their drinks, laughing one minute, mute and electrified the next. He would roll his chair and crowd her in until they were leg to leg, and she could feel his breath on her neck. Then they sat out in the *Times* car and pressed into each other, kissed and touched. The windows were closed, and by 7:00—when McGuire had to leave—they were all steamed up.

After the Chateau, there was another secret date in a steakhouse, where they ate nothing, but drank buckets of wine, water, coffee. For the third date, McGuire wanted to go all the way to Boston. No one knew them in Boston; in Boston they could *really* talk. How long, she asked in the steakhouse, did he want to stay in Boston? How much time did he have? In an edgy tone, snarly, McGuire explained once more that he didn't have any more time to give her than he was giving her already, and he hoped she wasn't going to start moaning and griping about it this early on. She didn't mean to moan, Gallagher—who knew this game and played it well—said; she just wanted to know whether she should drive to Boston or take the bus. "Shit!" he yelled, grinning. "You are one hell of a tough broad."

While they waited for the next week and the Friday when they were going to Boston (he by car, she by bus) for dinner and whatever else they could squeeze into the two- or three-odd hours he had to spare before racing home to the sullen Aerial (more a bitch, said McGuire, every day, but still to be feared, even respected), McGuire assigned Gallagher to a meaty story: city women on welfare. "Skip the stats," he had said. "You never seem to be able to get them anyway. I'll have Bohan do a checksheet. That way you can ask the naive questions in good faith, snoop around, get an eyeful. Find out how these people *really* live."

He wanted her to spend time with two or three women on the dole: go grocery shopping with them, stand in line at "the welfare," have lunch at home, play with the kids, sniff out any boyfriends. When Gallagher told him how much she loved this idea, that she could hardly wait to begin, he interrupted: "I'm not sure you're up to it, but I can't spare anyone else."

But Gallagher could see right through the editor's derisive ways. Not only was she *ready;* she was the only newsman in Wampanoag who could write this story. The trick would be getting Miss Toohey to (as McGuire put it) unlock the leg chains.

Although the women's editor still loathed McGuire and his big ideas, she had grown fond of her assistant and now leaned heavily on her. She might—grudgingly—let Cathy take the time for these hurtful and totally superfluous stories, if it weren't so pleasant to keep her close at hand. It was nice having someone there to nag, passing copy back and forth, eating biscuits, and even gossiping about any funny business developing on the floor—like, say, the upcoming marriage of Art Oakley, metro reporter, to the only daughter of F. X. (Ox) Mullins, sports editor.

Sally Mullins was about to have her engagement picture published in the *Times,* and the Misses Toohey and Gallagher had had to scramble to supply a few lean sentences, antecedents, and accomplishments for both bride and bridegroom. And there still wasn't enough copy.

That very afternoon, Gallagher was on the horn with Sal, an athlete, lettered in four sports, but not smart enough, even with all that varsity promise, to get into Wamp State. Having lately graduated from the local j.c., Sal was now devoting her time to the selection and receipt of nuptial china, silver, and linens. She had been a tomboy—this any clod could figure out—long enough; now, a young lady, she was getting married and the *Times* would please skip the all-star basketball, the MVP in ice and field hockey, CYO softball and soccer—all material that Ox had showcased in Schoolboy Sports.

Gallagher was trying to dig out other items of note: clubs, hobbies, amateur theatricals, reading, sewing, anything, but Sal had done zip other than graduate Fizz-Ed from the j.c., bottom third of her class, and then sit around with her mother and six younger brothers, waiting to get married. Sal asked if Miss Gallagher might be free to come and eyeball the hope chest, jam-packed with matched sheets, spreads, "monogram" towels, napkins, and also the dozen sets of things that couldn't be wedged in there. Gallagher wasn't all that eager, but agreed, hoping a half-hour spent at the Mullinses' would spring something suitable for padding the stark paragraph about the bride-elect. If they couldn't come up with a decent couple of grafs, they'd be "in the soup," Miss Toohey had said, "with Ox."

Part of the clique that drank beer nightly at Rocco's, and occasionally at the Polish club, the bridegroom rooted for the Sox and the Hens, the Friars, Reds, and Patriots, and had nothing but contempt for the old bat and that pushy twist who roosted at Women's. However, he was cowed by the father of the bride, who, kingpin of a clutch of Catholic and Hibernian clubs, the "pope" of Muldoon Stadium, and a part-time boxing ref, considered all the college boys on the floor—with the possible exception of Bohan—greenhorns, dimwits, or fairies. He had tried to smarten up his only daughter with regard to the gutless "Slovak" she'd picked, even after his wife pointed out that the Slovak might be Sal's—a nice girl, homebody, but plain—only chance. The idea of it still turned his stomach. He wouldn't give Arty Oakley ("How did that Slovak," he had asked his assistant, DiMuccio, typical meatball, "get a name like Oakley?") the time of day. So poor Arty, a lonesome guy, craving a family right here at the *Times*, went begging for it, or for any crumb the bluff sports editor might toss him.

Miss Toohey's assistant had a few good laughs watching Ox and the bridegroom, but neither she nor the society editor felt up to the task of quizzing the sports editor for extra details on his daughter's engagement, yet they knew there'd be bad trouble if that bridal notice didn't look just like all the others—no shorter, no longer. So Gallagher, with the welfare assignment burning in her skull, drove out to West Wampanoag Heights to meet Sal, to see the chest and get the story.

The bride-elect was out waiting for her on the porch steps. The girl leapt up when she spotted the *Times* car, and raced over to open the door. "Oh, Jesus!" she cried. "I can't believe they'd send a reporter just to see my things!"

Gallagher studied the tall, gangly girl—20, but had pimples—with the small head and button eyes, and decided not to correct Sal's impression of what the *Times* was up to. The two girls went inside, where Mrs. Mullins was setting out teacups around a white-frosted cake. Sal rushed Gallagher into the hope-chest room—the parlor—where the heavy wood locker, big as a casket, sat crushing the pile of the beige shag. It was carved mahogany, Spanish Modern, Sal pointed out, stripping away the protective bedsheet. She hoisted the lid to show dozens of pastel bed linens, digging out layers of tablecloths and napkins, dishtowels, potholders, doilies (some aunt still tatted), and, at the bottom, a small rug braided by yet another aunt. The sheets were still wrapped in plastic, the towels had paper cuffs, and the napkins were pinned together in sets. When Sal had restacked the layers, she opened the bottom drawer to reveal a heap of filmy nightgowns and wrappers, silk panties and lace-edged slips. "People *gave* me these!" Sal screamed, blushing to the hairline. She seemed reluctant to touch the filmy mass, but encouraged Gallagher to dig in and fish something out—a sheer nightie in pink nylon, with its matching "penwa," piped in satin ribbon and appliquéd, as Gallagher might have written, "with scallops of Venetian and Alençon lace."

Once the nightie had been loosed from its secret drawer, Sal snatched it and held it up to her broad shoulders, a strained expression on her face. "I just can't picture it," she said. "Are you married?"

Gallagher said she wasn't, but added that she knew what Sal meant—especially (she thought, but didn't say) if Sal was a virgin. Gallagher herself was not, as they say, inexperienced, and had never in her life been as innocent as Sal. Yet she felt closer to that raw state than to whatever it was that made people tease and bully a virgin, as if the reward of married sex was the chance to spook the next generation. With every shower, and every gift of something "personal," usually from otherwise prudish matrons—Gallagher knew the type—there also came a lewd joke or prank, a bit of chaffing or leaden innuendo. And that was why poor Sal didn't have the heart even to lift the flimsy slips and sacks from their perfumed hideyhole.

At first, the bride-to-be seemed stung when the reporter didn't tender any of the now-stale jokes and remarks, but Sal soon inferred from this a naivete greater than her own, and attempted to twit, in her own way, the visiting Timesman. "They'll be howling at *your* door!" she teased. "Every dog has its day!" Then, after forcing shut the narrow drawer, the raw wood screeching against metal runners, she dropped the lid. "So much for that," she said, bounding up from the floor and down onto the flowered couch. Gallagher sat next to her. "What more do you want to know?" Sal asked, leaping up to throw the sheet over the glossy box.

Gallagher asked some routine questions about the wedding plans, Mrs. Mullins came in with tea and cake, and Sal jumped up again. She pulled out the wedding books and flipped through the pages: caterer; flowers: orchids, white roses, baby's breath; bridesmaids' gowns: teal blue and rose, with matching pillbox hat; the band: Hal Touchette and the Frenchies; one-hour open bar and sit-down dinner: roast beef or chicken, fruit cocktail, champagne punch, and best of all—here were sketches and ads—the gown: ivory peau de soie, sculpted sweetheart neckline, and a cap of chapel-length, re-embroidered Valenciennes and side panels, rosettes, fitted bodice and leg-o'-mutton sleeves, dropped waist, scalloped hemline, cathedral-length train . . .

Gallagher, trying to listen (the m.c., the rings, the garter, the five-tiered cake with "Happy Birthday, Dad" incorporated on a lower tier, because it would be Ox's 55th; the many fittings, parties, bridesmaids' gifts, favors at the wedding tables, etc.), found herself drifting off the subject. Sal didn't object: she said what she had to say, repeated it, then sat and watched while the cute reporter, having pulled a tissue from her pocketbook in the heat of the bridal litany, was balling it up, smoothing it out, making a fan of tiny pleats.

Sal took a tissue from the box and blew her nose. What was the girl making? But Sal didn't want to pester Miss Gallagher with an annoying question. She was so glad to have the company—and for so long!—that she settled back on the couch, folding up her long legs, content to enjoy the reporter's thoughtful mood. (Maybe she was planning her own wedding?)

After a while, still savoring this intense air gathered around the thoughtful girl but bored anyway, Sal picked up a *TV Guide* and started to flip through it. By then, the reporter was finished. She thanked Sal for the pleasant afternoon, wished her well, and Sal offered to send a wedding invitation, if Gallagher thought she might come. "Oh," said the reporter. "Maybe, if I'm free." "You work on Saturday?" Sal said. "Sometimes." "Wait a minute!" said Sal, bouncing hard on the couch cushion. "It's not a Saturday! What a stupe I am. It's a Sunday! *Now* can you come?"

Gallagher said she would if she could, then exited the bridal house and sped off in the blue car. It was after four, so no need to return to work. She pulled into the *Times* parking lot, waved to Charlie Bobs, the attendant, and walked through the deserted streets past the Cup & Saucer, past Eddie's Hot Top and the Jasper Café, turning away from the plate-glass windows and any customers lurking inside, and continued on to the bus stop. She was between buses, so she sat on a bench marked with the city motto: "Wampanoag: Clothmakers to the World."

After clapping on sunglasses, for privacy, she was ready to return, in that automatic way—as if she lacked the will to stop—to that now-distant moment when she had gained the experience that put her ahead of a muscular maiden like Sal Mullins—and yet behind, too, because the thought of having to go through it again filled her with dread: and it was on the horizon, wasn't it? She was grateful for the shades, as her eyes were already bugged out. And now the damned bus, always late, was here on time. Gallagher stepped to the rear and settled in the second-to-last row—no one ever sat this far back, except school kids, and they were already home.

The puzzling thing, and what always made the experience hard to relate, even to someone like Else, resistant to shock, was the fact of never having liked Dana Falkenberg, not in *that* way, and yet being his girlfriend and—she balked at the sappy word, even if the facts, sentimental and gross as they were, demanded it—lover. Everything about him, except for his brain, was sickening. (She had to laugh: even his brain could be sickening.) He never bathed, so he stunk; his clothes, of no interest to him except as warmth and protection, were rags, dated and cheap. He had a few slimy nylon shirts, and one pair of tight, skimpy trousers, a sky-blue windbreaker and old sneakers, which he wore with black socks. Before going to bed, he stripped, dropping his garments (no underwear) on the floor for quick retrieval in the morning. Catherine had never seen him make a trip to the laundromat, but he must have gone, for his clothes weren't filthy, just "high," as Else said, the one time she met him. The bedsheets were even higher, slick and thin as cobwebs.

But there was a logic behind the squalor. Dana's dwelling was first and foremost a lab: the bathroom—no windows—functioned as a darkroom, with chemicals in the sink and tub; tripods, lenses, boxes of film and photo-paper were lined up in the kitchen, and sometimes along the hallway. Even though the rooms were always dark—the sunlight blocked by sheets, and sometimes blankets—Dana had pinned hundreds of photographs to the walls and doors.

But the cold, smelly hole of an apartment was *not* the reason why—Catherine, fully into the scene now, was shaking her head "no"—the "experience" had been so revolting. The lab, and the spartan life unfolding within its damp walls, actually drew her to him. This repulsive scag was exactly the kind of person she longed to understand, and then to become. When and how did he decide to chuck all the routines and comforts of normality, how had he honed his life to this fine edge? And Dana's life was no arty pose: three passionate endeavors—picture-making, music, and aesthetic analysis—consumed his days and nights and occupied his thoughts, and even his feelings, as far as she could tell.

It was the solitude, the reek, the slow turn of the artist's tedious day that Catherine loved. No place was farther from Wampanoag than Falkenberg. Whatever Wampanoag stood for, Falkenberg stood against: where Wampanoagers turned by rote, under surveillance of watchful neighbors, driven by guilt and fear of scandal, Falkenberg turned—by what? (Gallagher noticed she had steamed up the window with her breath.) He turned *himself!* He had no neighbors or family (just a mother in California), no past to worry about. He took orders from no one, lugged no baggage; communing only with the perfect works of dead geniuses. He was the apex of the modern, the overman, and Wampanoag—what was Wampanoag? Gallagher wiped the perspiring window to see several dark bodies trundling down Westminster Street, some humped around the wooden newsstand. Wampanoag was the machine.

The contrast struck Catherine—even in her present mood—as funny, because Wampanoag was hardly ever a machine that worked. Twitches and blips of revolt and perversity were ever threatening to shut it down. Yet, strangely, it was the sum total of the millions of idiosyncrasies that made the place seem automated. The *Times* newsroom was a perfect example: it seemed regulated as a factory floor with a staff drawn from the Catholic laboring classes, but within this mass there were factions and partisans, fiercely loyal only to neighborhood and nationality. That's what people meant, Catherine was thinking, when they dreamed of a melting pot, although, in reality, nothing melted in Wampanoag—things rubbed and ground, maybe at times they had a melted *look,* but not a single ethnic soul ever willingly yielded to another.

Here was her stop. She rose and pulled the bell-rope to alert the driver, but he knew her stop and had already stamped on the screeching brakes and sent the passenger toppling down the aisle. This often happened because bus drivers in Wampanoag were the most individualistic conformists of them all, always with some trick or humiliation planned for each of their quirky passengers.

Gallagher knew she would have to take some time to unfurl the entire length of this memory, long coiled by time and pain. If she tried to halt it, it would come back stronger. There was nothing to do but yield, and no safe place to let it flap. Her mother and father were both at home, eager—anxious even—for her presence. The telephone would be ringing, odd jobs, chores, dinner, and the news would thwart the smooth unwinding until, at bedtime—well, it wouldn't wait till then. But there was nowhere to go, and dangerous to walk around, too easy to trip or get hit by a car.

Guided, but by nothing conscious, she walked past her turnoff, down the avenue, and up the steps to Jesus Savior R.C. Church, her old church, a dark and quiet place this time of day. Sitting in the side aisle, a colonnade blocked her from the altar and the view of any priest or sacristan who might happen to be loitering there. The crones in black, scattered here and there whistling their beads, were too blind or nutty to notice. She settled herself on a wooden bench slick with a dozen coats of varnish.

She gazed straight ahead, aware of the pleasing series of groined vaults and rounded arches leading, bay by bay, to a side altar, just a darkened hollow now, half blocked by a thicket of vigil lamps. The colored panes of the clerestory broke the cloudy afternoon light into a burning puzzle: flame blue and red, tannic yellow and agate green, streaming down and faintly shading the statue of the Little Flower in brown habit, roses in her arms and tumbling on her pedestal. A nest of shadows complicated marble reliefs of the Sixth and Seventh stations, mounted on the opposite wall. An even fainter light picked out ivory threads in the green marble tiles. Soon the sacristan would come to switch on the lamps, but for now the church well was sunk in a dusky gloom.

She half-knelt, half-sat, resting her chin on her folded hands, a pose that might have looked devout, but that was just a cover for the brazen reconstruction of old crimes, mentally repeated here in the house of God and right under His Nose—not to mention the firm resolve to recommit them as soon as possible, and with a divorced man who had a live-in girlfriend named Aerial. But too late now for scruples; the deed was done and redone, and the rethinking more penance than fresh sin.

After a few minutes more of peace, she closed her eyes to the church and viewed the days as they unreeled. How quiet his apartment could be. Except when selected records were playing, Dana lived and worked in a soundless void. She'd wake into that dark void, its atmosphere of coolness and moldy smells: the aroma of brewed coffee sometimes snaking through the jungle of nighttime airs; the unwashed clothes and sweaty bodies, thick dust, photochemicals, the gluey smell of books and paper. If Dana hadn't yet started the coffee, it was like waking up in a clothes hamper.

After eating a heavy breakfast which he made himself, Dana would disappear into the front room to work on a review (he was the rare artist who could write, and was much in demand as a critic of exhibits and books), then to plan the day's shoot. The heart of the day was for outdoor picture-taking, although most of the prints on the walls were taken indoors. These were all shots of nudes—girlfriends, Catherine assumed, even before he told her: who else would be willing to pose, confidently exposing their flesh to the lens, only to end up looking like rotten legumes or horse blankets? Dana was proud that his pictures did not flatter, yet each image pleased the eye with the mystery of formal beauty. Catherine had studied the famous shots of peppers and flowery calyxes, of paint peeling on walls, of old bones and tumbleweeds lying in the desert or stark and fine against the livid wall of a great sky. These were art, unquestionably: even she could see it. It was harder to perceive—and this might be just a personal thing, she'd confessed to Dana—in a naked lump of a woman with a huge ass ballooning like a parachute, and with legs scratched, bruised, or covered with stubble.

They had argued about the difference between his work and the Diane Arbus photos, Catherine claiming that Arbus's mugs at least knew why their pictures were being taken, and even seemed to like the idea. This was the alluring element in her portraits: the subjects volunteering as grotesques, and then, at the last minute—the critical one—having second thoughts. She didn't suppose, on the other hand, that Dana's old girlfriends ("What do you mean by old?" he asked) offered themselves as studies in spare tires, piano legs, fat asses. Why, for a change, didn't he photograph some pouchy man?

She had offered these and some even more benighted views, thinking, maybe I can go home now and never come back. But, as it turned out, Dana was unfazed by her naive opinions; there was nothing to learn from such a banal critique. Her uncomplicated gaze, warped by the conventions of ad photography, had sapped the aesthetic faculty, made her blind to form—the only thing that really counted.

Dana was good-natured about it. He was never offended. Discussions of photographic art and its criteria recurred, and the arguments were always different. In his mind, art was extramoral, divorced from life—especially personal life—in which he had almost no interest. To him, others were no more than mass and surface, and he himself the sensitive, trained eye.

Yes, but there was evidence, she argued, that contradicted this purist view. For one thing, there was some personal reference in each of his captions: "Jeannette, Christmas 1971," "Miradel, on her 30th birthday, January 5, 1970," "Angela, 5 months pregnant, 1972," "Madeleine, after her father's funeral, 1974," "Jeannette, spending a day in bed." How could he deny the biographical element?

In his favor, on the other hand, was the fact that he rarely photographed a face or, if he did, he'd solarize the head, so all you saw was torso, or torso with solar disk, spread legs, fat backs and grainy-looking breasts; or, the ones she could never get used to, but studied nonetheless: the "muffs," as he called them, or the "pussies." Catherine had seen raw photos like this in men's magazines, but there the object was, at least in theory, to please; whereas, in Dana's pictures, the effect was as repulsive as plates in a medical book. The pussies were all black-and-whites, and some models posed so awkwardly that they looked like victims of a bad accident. "Someday," Dana had threatened, "I'll photograph you." Even then, at that early point when she was in awe of Dana and his life, she doubted that this would occur.

Catherine sat back in the pew; now, nothing in the church, no arch or beam of light, could distract her. From the start, Dana's notion had been to shack up (as Juscik might put it) with the classy girl from Kings, and have sex with her whenever he wanted—at night, mainly, when his other work was done, but not always. She was a novelty—attractive to him in ways his models, older and more experienced, were not. But he had also found life with her irksome. She shared with him no social world, no experience, no books, no all-consuming drive to spend five, six hours on the Charles River Basin taking a million shots of a few blades of grass, now bent by a heavy dew or by snow, beaded by frost, dry as straw, or freshly green in spring. She had come with him for a few of these all-day tramps, with the back-breaking intervals of shooting, but his absorption made her feel restless and—even if she had brought a book along—lonesome.

He had other women friends, and had warned Catherine that there were some in the vicinity who might drop by. Catherine could stay or go. One ex—and Catherine had met only the one—seemed quite happy, when she arrived, to find Catherine there with Dana, and together they fixed dinner and drank a half gallon of wine, listened to music, and looked at Dana's new prints from the Charles Basin. Deirdre, who looked about 30, 35, had as little to say as Catherine about the photos. She did say she liked the nudes better than the grass, but her field was literature, and she was shrewd enough, Catherine noticed, not to overreach. But Dana, piqued by that restraint, had urged Deirdre to jump in and "read" the images along "narrative" lines, if she chose, then seemed to enjoy the complimentary things she said.

It was clear, as they sat on boxes in the living room and listened to a new recording (weird and scary) of *Lulu,* that Deirdre didn't plan to leave that night, and as there was only one bed—no couch, not even room for one—Catherine decided to retreat, against their protests (especially Deirdre's, a very friendly woman), to the dorm.

Although she told them that it was perfectly all right with her—she had work to do and she was tired—she resented it. The next week, she refused to take any phone calls from Dana, now eager for her to come back.

"Tell him I'm out," she shouted to the hallmate who knocked on Catherine's door, phone in hand.

The break had, at least for a while, been pleasant. She mostly stayed in the dorm, read for classes, talked to her hallmates, who'd assumed she'd moved out for good, and drank espresso with them at night, listening to their own kind of music, Marvin Gaye and Billie Holliday, Eric Clapton and John Fahey.

One night, after the three friends, Else, Marguerite, and Catherine, had smoked a few joints and lay on the floor of Else's huge suite (reserved for visiting faculty, but Else somehow managed to claim it) listening to Bessie Smith, "Tricks Ain't Walking," Catherine chimed in with a thin voice. "Poor baby," Else crooned, when it was over, and Marguerite already up to play the flip side. "Are you kidding?" Catherine surprised them by screeching. "I'm glad it happened!"

Else laughed. "You're just relieved to be rid of the head trips. Excuse me, what do you call that crap he plays—music-to-kill-yourself-by?"

"Don't be so ignorant," Marguerite sniffed. She was a music major, studying composition with Roger Sessions. "And you, too," she said to Catherine. "No wonder that guy got bored."

Else barked in outrage, but Catherine felt she did bore Dana, but he bored her, too!

By then, the church was dusky: light flared from the votive

candles in their red glass; the lamp over the altar illuminated frescoes of the life of Christ painted on the apse. The low lights took the divine element—God the Father in His celestial triangle, with the holy bird—out of the story. The sacristan, heels ringing on the marble tiles, had come and gone. Catherine was alone. It was useless to tease out from her retentive mind the tawdry scenes of her and Dana worming around on that slick-sheeted bed. Conjured in the dimness of the church, such scenes could be made to stink of sulfur and glow with infernal light, but now they seemed only dull and foolish. And yet Catherine would not renounce. Although she'd drawn the line at a night à trois, and balked at the gross nudes, she felt drawn to Dana's world, with its lures and dark mystery.

Next day she completed the item on the Mullins-Oakley BETROTHAL—sometimes they'd use ENGAGEMENT, AFFIANCED or SOON-TO-WED, but BETROTHAL was the most solemn, reserved for bluebloods, the very rich, and children of politicians or of the sports editor. The page proof was brought in, and there was Sal in a white angora sweater, her lips glued together to form a smile thin as a new moon, but pretty—the angle flattering, the lighting soft. The cut was clear and sharp; Sal had been shot by the *Times'* own Ben Dugan, and Miss Toohey herself had studied the twelve contact sheets, and ordered several dozen prints before she—in conference with Ben and Sports, the A.C.E. and McGuire, who got into the act at the last moment—selected the fetching three-quarters headshot.

When the bridal notice had been cleared by Ox, who had no complaint (no compliments, either—that was his way), Women's could take a breather, and it did. Then, Gallagher put together a food page with pix supplied by the Bean Growers of America. "South of the Border," read the 48-point head that Miss Toohey devised to go with a giddy account of a Mexican supper party. The women's editor had already scratched out all consortium and brand names, checking to see if any had been snuck into the twelve adjoining recipes (yes, in every case). Then, when they had celebrated with coffee from the morgue and two biscuits each, Gallagher asked for time to visit the first of her welfare mothers, and Miss Toohey, with nothing to do but tidy her desk and take a long lunch with the A.C.E., said yes, why not, and not to bother coming back, just for the sake of appearances. Her quick acquiescence was noted.

But the reporter forgot Toohey and her caginess, as soon as she'd backed the *Times* car out of the garage and into Federal Street. A three-part series, McGuire had said. The *Times* had never before run a serial, and it published little, besides the occasional editorial blast, on the subject of welfare. The paper had always been fiscally conservative and staunchly Republican, even though—when the time came and the first dozen Democrats unseated Republicans—the paper was quick to endorse the winners. The Yankees were out, ward heelers in. It had all started in the '30s, when a more liberal franchise and radical redistricting gave the swarms of factory workers all the ballot-box clout they would ever need. After that, the old-line GOP papers in Providence and Wampanoag endorsed Democrats, or they were out of business: it was that simple.

In spite of the paper's dissenting voice, welfare politics had long since gripped the city. In the lean years of the early '70s, with the oil embargo and recession that followed, when Gallagher herself was swept out of Kingstown and into journalism, Wampanoag was stripped of its last cloth and jewelry factories. The mills went south, or to Asia, but the workers stayed. The unemployed, proud breadwinners and union men, wouldn't think of moving out of state, or even beyond the city line, and had, as they saw it, three options: drink themselves to death (if they had the cash), sponge off relatives (if they didn't), or just go crazy. And only if forced—children sickly, wives crying for money (unless they had already followed the husband to the barroom, Ladies' Entrance)—did they show their faces at the welfare office, downtown where everyone could see, to prove their eligibility and worthlessness.

The state was also broke by then, and only too glad to dump its dependents—the sad but necessary byproduct of a streamlined economy—off the rolls and onto a federal agency, so "qualifying" was, as everyone knew, a cinch.

Still, no matter how easy, and how handy—especially in those hard times—to get the green check, and sometimes the gold check, too, and the stamps (if you could bring yourself to use them)—going on welfare meant leaving the ranks of the decent and joining the deadbeat horde, the freeloaders, the chiselers who wouldn't lift a finger, but sit on their asses and feed from the public trough.

That view, as McGuire explained, was what the *Times* shared with its readers—even though the *Times* management had had a ringside seat when the deals were struck that had driven skilled workers from their jobs. The Old-Money Yankees, who had once owned all the factories and supplied the city with what art and culture it had, had themselves stripped it bare, and why? Because nonunion labor was cheap down South, winters mild, and the pants suits, cheap bracelets, and sneakers could be made down there for less, in automated plants whose construction would be financed through tax loss and amortization in Wampanoag and capital investment in the Sunbelt. These industries, true, hadn't shown a profit since the '50s, but the cloth and bracelet barons had sold out in time, and their children, set up for life in the hometown their fathers had built and wrecked, could now lash out in family-owned newspapers against free-lunch politics and welfare corruption. Praise was meted out to the new breed of worker who could adapt to smokeless industries (wherever and whatever they were: Wampanoag had no such industries to speak of, if you left out the newspaper and the unemployment office), and who had the stuff their fathers and grandfathers had had, and willing to *work* for a living!

McGuire had wanted his reporter to grasp how the *Times* (and its trustees) felt on the subject, because she wasn't just going to ignore these feelings; she was going to trample them! Gallagher's mouth was watering at the prospect.

Thrilled—and scared witless—Gallagher nearly missed the turn-off into Lake Meadow Terrace. (Why did they always give projects such pretty names?) Lake Meadow was a grassless strip near the city limits, clumped with a dozen low-rise buildings. Flat roofs and sheets of colored metal on cement-block gave the place the look of a beat-up grade school. Gallagher parked in a lot that served as a basketball court. The blacktop was cracked and wavy, strewn with weeds and broken glass. A child in overalls was sweeping the court with a broom whose bristles were worn to a nub. Gallagher locked the car and tracked across a dirt lot to the closest building, "C" hand-printed over the doorless jamb. She walked from there to A, with a knobless metal door, all scratched and hacked; then to the right, past C and on to the far buildings, E, F, and, finally, G, where she watched a sheet sail out the window and snag itself on a chain-link fence. A plastic curtain—the only one—flapped from a first-floor window, its ragged edges dangling into the leaves of a plant so dead you couldn't tell what it was.

From the dark hallway, she made her way to the stairs where something soft and sticky was underfoot. The door to 2G was wedged open with a brick, but Gallagher knocked anyway. When no one answered, she pushed ahead into a kitchen of dazzling brightness. A ring of overhead lightbulbs, 200 watts apiece, burned in a metal dish, a shadeless floor lamp was switched on, fluorescent light flooded the sink, and a Santa nightlight was plugged into the wall. Daylight was blocked out by Venetian blinds; even the little window over the sink had its ratty curtain rolled across the rod. The kitchen was vacated, but the remains of many meals lay strewn on the table: a loaf of sandwich bread spilled out its slices, there were open jars of mustard and relish with knives stuck in them, empty packets of lunchmeat, a half-eaten apple, stick of margarine melting on its paper, jug of Kool-Aid. Tipped-over boxes of cereal, plates with stubs of hot-dog rolls and dried-up cheese macaroni, open jar of instant coffee, along with ashtrays, plates—paper and plastic—a jump-rope and a rolled-up diaper.

The tenement was still except for a voice, cheery and nonstop, coming from a dark room just off the kitchen. "Mrs. Leech? Donna?" Gallagher called, then picked up a sneaker from a kitchen chair and sat down. She took out her narrow pad and pen, but couldn't bring herself to take notes. It wasn't just poverty that turned a kitchen into a pigpen. Besides the litter of food and dishes, brooms and paper bags burst out of the closet, many spills on the floor, fingerprints blackened patches of refrigerator, cupboards, drawers. The story needed a setting, yes, and a credible one, but not this! The squalor would only confirm what the homeowners and timeservers of Wampanoag already prided themselves on knowing.

And here was someone. A woman, according to the phone interview, about Gallagher's age—but five children in six years, a string of bullying boyfriends, the foster homes, the ungraded schoolroom, the borderline IQ, bad lungs, drinking and starchy diet, inertia and the extra hundred pounds (all of which Gallagher would see or hear about that day) made Miss (?) Leech seem old, used up, dead tired, although under the nest of matted hair the fat face was almost pretty.

An army of children padded in after their mother, each blinking in the glare. They settled, as if they were used to being interviewed, around the table, and then aimed a series of rapid questions at the stranger: where was the car, did she come in a car, what kind of a car, "Whatcha name?" how old, how old was the car, did she have a boyfriend, where did she live, "Whatcha name?"—no, they already asked that one, stupe! The smallest girl, 5 or 6, had pulled her chair next to Gallagher's, sat, and smiled up at her face, then took her hand. "You're pretty. What's that you got on your eyes?"

In the barrage of questions, Gallagher heard the mother's voice: did she want a cup of instant? No? A glass of soda? a donut? Was she married? Kids?

Unable to keep up, Gallagher let the children settle some of the questions themselves. She looked around the table at the five sweet, mostly smart, faces, as bony as their mother's was fat. Their sharp eyes, so avid, were the match of any eager-beaver Timesman. They wanted something, but what? Gallagher sent the oldest ones downstairs to check out the *Times* car, and gave the younger girl her reporter's pad—she kept an extra—and the special fat pencil that said WAMPANOAG TIMES. She set the girl to draw a picture of the baby in the high chair. But the girl closed up the pad and handed it back. She pushed her chair closer to Gallagher, circling the reporter's wrist with her fingers and stroking her arm. "She botherin' you?" asked Donna Leech. But Gallagher couldn't find her voice. Besides, the girl had climbed up on her lap and laced an arm around her neck.

Just then, the two boys and a girl came pounding up the stairs, blew into the room, rattling off questions about the *Times* car: how many were there, did you need a special license, who got to drive? But Donna Leech, smacking her fat hands together in a deafening clap, scared them ("Goddamn pesty asses!") out of the room and slammed the door behind them. Suddenly the TV blasted out a commercial jingle, driving Donna from her chair to bang on the closed door: if they didn't turn the fuckin' thing down, she was coming in to beat them black and blue! Wild laughter on the other side of the door, but the set was turned down, and Donna came lumbering back to the table. She was up again to fetch a bottle of apple wine (the reporter had said no thank you) from the fridge, and poured them both a "sniff" in big tumblers. Then she swept food and dishes to one side so there was a clearing between her glass, Gallagher's, and the sweating green bottle. "Are you sure you're not hungry? I gotta feed these kids in a minute, so think about it."

But Miss Leech never fed her kids that day. The kids watched an hour's worth of TV, they filled the tub with water, they bought ice cream from the ice-cream man, got up a game of dirt ball with the kids downstairs that lasted until Jimmy Leech fell down and cut his eye. They watched more TV, and played foot hockey until the downstairs people started banging on the radiator. Then a girl socked a boy and the boy twisted her arm. The baby was screaming.

Donna had taken as much as she could. She whipped out of the kitchen, smacking one, then another—even the one already wailing from the twisted arm. Where was the belt? She was looking for the belt. Not able to find the belt, she locked the children—two in one room, three in the other—in the back bedrooms. Gallagher was right behind her. You could barely see for the gloom. Only one room had a window and no lamps to speak of. The window gave onto another wall, whose grayish light barely brushed the streaked glass. Straining to see, Gallagher could make out the rumpled beds and an open closet with no hooks or pole, just a pile of stuff on the floor. "I *hate* those kids!" barked their mother. She pushed the reporter through the living room with the TV still glowing and chattering. From the kitchen, a hive of warmth compared to the clammy cells beyond, Gallagher could still hear the children's shrieks and sobs.

She drove home to the *Times* lot—it was after eight o'clock—with burning eyes and a headache, but the two pads filled with quotes, heartbreaking, stomach-turning, sometimes both. There was enough for a fifty-part series, and she had interviewed one family. Gallagher had seen and heard things she would never forget: now, how to arrange them so that Wampanoag wouldn't forget them either. It would involve a lot of weeding, she thought, downshifting the car to ease over the bumps and into the garage, because some of what was in the notebooks might cause a tax riot—the way the welfare, for instance, furnished the Leeches with rent and utilities vouchers only to have them cashed (as the social worker Gallagher interviewed had hinted) for apple wine, smokes and candy, trips to the race track, color TV and stereo, handouts to parolees, and a year's supply of reducing fudge, which the children ate when they could find it. Mrs. Leech was a year behind in her rent. Lake Meadow Associates, fattened on federal subsidies for low-cost housing, was loath to turn its deadbeats out and lose not only the monthly vouchers but the extra allotments for welfare clients in arrears. So, in short, the taxpayers often shelled out twice for the Leeches' rent, and the landlord never lost a penny. When Donna Leech's month's supply of food stamps ran out, she'd report the booklets lost and the stamps would be replaced, so the taxpayers footed that padded bill, too.

Her interview with Gallagher was not Mrs. Leech's first crack at the press. She was a believer in its power, and had used it before to shame or scare state employees into compliance. The Swamp *Times* seldom, if ever, ran a story based on a lead from Donna Leech, but the idea that one day they might was enough to threaten the right parties down at the welfare. Like everyone else, Donna had a right, she said, to live: it wasn't her fault she was poor. If she had someone to look after the kids, she'd go out and find a job, but when Gallagher suggested babysitters, Leech laughed.

"What's the good of getting a stinkin' job, minimum wage? All they do is cut your payments off. Or else take it out on you some other way. I got a friend tried that. Boy was she sorry. They tried to take her children offa her. The babysitter drank up all the liquor and left them kids to rot. My girlfriend, she comes home one day, one of 'em's laid up in the hospital, run over. She's not going out to work no more, that girl. Would you?"

This was a complex game, Gallagher was thinking, as Charlie Bobs took the keys and reparked the car. The various angles might not intrigue her readers, sadden them, or even make them laugh. There were too many working families in other slums, families who lived the same cramped, needy life but without the handouts and with none of the extras that a cheater like Donna could afford.

"You think the poor are dopes?" McGuire had said. "Well, you couldn't be more wrong. They're snakes, gougers, thieves, and cheats. They're no different from anyone else—welfare is their *job!* Go out and see. You might be sorry you took this story, Gallagher. It's harder than you think."

And she *was* thinking, standing at the bus stop, that unless the other interviewees were model poor people, McGuire was right again. To produce the story he wanted (or she *thought* he wanted), she'd have to pick and cut, smooth out and dress up what she'd heard, to cast the right pathetic light on these grim scenes. And was that news, or was it—as McGuire had hinted—propaganda?

She dropped 50 cents dime by dime into the slot, nodded to the driver and stumbled, as the bus lurched, to the back. There she found her mind sponged of the Leeches—cleansed of the thousand cuts and stretches needed to pitch the story to the *Times*' flinty readers—by the mere mental voicing of the words "Jack McGuire," for tomorrow was Friday, and, in some dazzling way McGuire had split into two: the "Jack" drinking bourbon in the dim lounge of the Chateau d'Etoile, and the "McGuire" who would insist that she lay it on with a trowel, skate on the sheerest moral ice, so as to satisfy not only his sense of justice, which was merely professional, but his personal mission to stick it to the fogies, to the O'Callahans and Seeleys, to all those working stiffs who lived and breathed just to read the *Times* in peace, with a story crafted to work like a purge—so strong, so offensive to their beliefs and feelings, that only one outcome was possible: to run that bleeding heart and her pinko editor right out of town!

Gallagher hadn't yet grasped the size or exact shape of McGuire's plans to self-destruct, although she could sense her own role in some scheme, one that squared with her longings to wow this fierce and jaded man—to be his star, his tool, his "button," just as he'd been someone else's when he'd exposed those crooked pols back in the days of real newsmen. Times had changed, yes, and those glory days were over, but Gallagher meant to be the resounding coda, and more.

Still bouncing on the bus, she stopped worrying the welfare story, but sank instead into fevered scenes flaring just by mouthing the words "McGuire, Jack McGuire"; separating the words and putting them together: McGuire and Jack McGuire and just McGuire.

Gallagher had been home ten minutes, flopped on the bed reading a letter from Else, when her mother tapped on the door, bearing two messages: her father was home; would she please go down and say hello to him; he hadn't seen her in two days, and she didn't deliberately want to hurt his feelings, did she? And second, she said, as Gallagher folded the multipage letter and stuffed it back in the envelope, *she* hadn't seen much of the girl either, and could she please sacrifice a little of her time for her boring parents? They knew how boring they were—Gallagher could hear her father's voice in this—but could she make the effort anyway? Mrs. Gallagher gasped when she reached the end of her spiel, partly from the labor of charging the borrowed words with all their fretful import.

"Oh, come on," Gallagher moaned. "You haven't seen me for two days. Big deal. I'm home at night, aren't I?"

"Oh," the mother said, grabbing a comb from the dresser to smooth the reporter's fluffed-out back hair, "I almost forgot. Dan Juscik called you yesterday, and he called again today. You've got to call him back, Cathy, or you're going to hurt his feelings. He doesn't want to talk to *me,* you know." She ran the comb through her own hair, then put it down. "But you're never home long enough to call him."

Gallagher wanted to tell her mother that, at 23 years old, she didn't need to stay home anymore. "Her time"—as the *Times* headlined its formula stories on new retirees—was "now her own." She did, like some bum or deadbeat, live at home with them, but this awkward interval was bound to end, she was thinking, as she plodded downstairs to greet her father and sit while he grilled her about upcoming stories. As soon as the welfare story—no matter what shape it took—hit the stands, and her father the roof, she'd *have* to move out, and about time, too. The much-needed R&R was complete, and her parents could no more keep her from the clutches of diehard bachelors like Juscik, or misogynists like—.

But just then, her foot on the bottom step, the phone rang. Juscik: calling to confirm the Saturday night date (*Godfather II* and a steak), and where had she been the last two days? He'd called a bunch of times and had already given her old lady an earful, and she him.

"So?" Gallagher replied, only half-listening, because her

mother was saying something to the father about going easy, and how tense the girl was.

"What's wrong with *you?*" Juscik demanded and, getting no answer, said goodbye, hung up, then called right back to add that he'd pick her up at 7:15, if she still wanted to go.

"Don't be so touchy," she said

"Don't call *me* touchy!" he snapped back. "I'm not begging. If you don't want to go out with me, just say so. You're not doing me any favor."

While Gallagher was reflecting—and after the half-minute of silence—the line went dead.

Gallagher stood near the phone, but it didn't ring again, so she called Juscik, but now his line was busy.

She wandered into the den, where her father had been rustling his newspaper, irked at having to wait while his daughter finished her "yakking." But Gallagher couldn't focus on him either. She *did* like Juscik, and she liked going out with him, but she didn't feel like seeing him now.

"What's eatin' you?" her father was saying.

"Supper's ready!" sang the mother from the kitchen, and soon that ordeal too was over, and Gallagher was alone with the thoughts she had been cradling all day waiting for the moment when she could lock herself in. ("What are you doing in there?" her father yelled, en route to the bathroom. "Reading," she said, then her mother asked: "Still reading?" and she said yes, then "Don't hurt your eyes. Do you have a light on?" And she said yes. "Well, shall we say good night now?" So Gallagher was forced to open the door, first grabbing a book, then switching on the light, for she had been, all along, lying in the dark, blocking with her thumb the glittery halo from the streetlamp.)

"Good night, Cathy."

"Night, Ma, night, Dad." No answer. "Night, Dad!"

"Oh, *good* night," he said, peeved as usual, slamming his door shut.

Gallagher made a mental note to pull the real estate ads on Sunday, before her father had a chance to bundle up the papers with a string, and to look for an apartment, before the welfare series killed him *and* her.

CHAPTER 5

In less than a month—after three day-long interviews with clients and visits to the welfare, to food stamps, and after calls to social workers, to the mayor's office and HEW—Gallagher was ready to write. Each part would tackle a different family, although the last would survey all of them, pinpointing the lacks and miseries they suffered in common.

In her free afternoons—while Miss Toohey kept watch from her side of the desks—Gallagher organized her notes and made an outline. She was going to kick off with the quotable Leeches, wend through the McGreedys, a grim mother and handicapped son, and end up with the Fullertons, decent types, homeowners, five children, husband an invalid, who squeaked by on welfare and workman's comp. Mrs. Fullerton had given Gallagher a copy of their monthly budget. McGuire grabbed it. They'd get Ben to shoot *this* as is, penciled in block letters on tablet sheets. It was fucking pathetic.

As he made out the foto order, McGuire pointed to a budget item that had caught his eye: "Clothes—$10/mo."

"What can she buy for *that,* Gallagher?"

Gallagher shrugged.

"That's important! Find out! What kind of mill-outlet sleaze will she buy for a lousy ten bucks, and who gets it? When's the last time the missus bought herself a pair of slacks or a girdle? Call her! Have you talked to foto yet? I'll do it. I want to talk to Ben myself. Go on. Go back to your desk," McGuire ordered, waving a hand at her. "Your keeper's scoping you."

As Gallagher sweated out the long afternoons, with McGuire tearing back and forth, or just calling up on the hook phone (and once she'd begun dispatching pages, he'd be roaring so loud, even O'Callahan in his glass cubicle could hear), curiosity in the newsroom, already piqued, began to swell unbearably. Gallagher was launched as a newsman; she was invited for beers at Rocco's; she was kidded and mocked. They called at home sometimes, but even in a beery grilling Gallagher—per McGuire's order—wouldn't spill. The editor assigned more brides to Police, to Zoning, to State House and Suburban, and the write-ups were done without a gripe, and without the questions about where a decoration was supposed to go, and what part of speech it was.

"You like this, don't you?" McGuire said one Thursday, referring to her new-found status, or maybe just to the notoriety of the series itself. "You could write your own ticket, girlie—if you could see beyond your nose."

The editor dragged the confessional chair closer to his own. "This," he said, pointing to the stack of edited copy slugged DOLE, "is a sensational piece, but that's all. You're still the last person I'd send out on a breaking story. And you know why?"

Gallagher knew why, but she asked him.

"You're not tough. You're *smart,* but your head's in the clouds. That low-life Bohan is worth a dozen of you in getting out a paper every day."

Tamburino, former Nightside, now School and Business, stopped Gallagher on her way back to Women's. "Did he getcha?" he asked, nudging her over to the morgue for a coffee. "That's his job," Tamburino added, when they got there. "Just don't let him see. He thinks he's such a fuckin' killer, but it's just words. There's no muscle behind it." He paused to fill his mug, half cream, half coffee. "O'Callahan has the muscle, but he's just a dipshit."

Gallagher fixed a coffee for Miss Toohey, cream and sugar, and one for herself. "I know," she said.

"Well, don't let him see. The guy loves the sight of blood."

Gallagher laughed.

"You could hoist him," the Dayside concluded, "on his own spittoon, or whatever it is."

Gallagher laughed. She watched as Tamburino (whose nickname was "Speedy") slouched toward his desk, wondering if he—and how many others?—knew what was going on. She glanced over at McGuire's desk. Sports was in the confessional, and the chair had been shoved way back.

Being busy with Ox, however, didn't mean that McGuire had missed the exchange in the morgue.

In the course of hacking out the three-parter from the masses and tangles of fact, details, anecdotes, and impressions, there'd been a pair of volatile dates in one week with Juscik and McGuire. Gallagher had not canceled the Saturday night plans with Juscik, even though the tryst in Boston would fall the Thursday before, leaving only Friday, when the Gallaghers went out as a family for Italian, as the buffer. With so little in between, something of McGuire's night could leak into Juscik's. Juscik might not know what it was, but he'd know something. Even the Gallaghers, who'd staged their own Friday night fights, could sense, on that intervening night, that something was up.

"Caesar salad," Gallagher told the waitress. Her voice was hoarse, too breathy, and once it puffed into the smoky, garlicky air of Mainelli's, her father pounced, rebuking her for ordering a "goddamned rabbitty salad" in an Italian restaurant. "What's *wrong* with her?" he asked the waitress.

When Mrs. Gallagher pointed out that Cathy always ordered a salad of some kind, the father pounced again: "That's *not* the point!" He rolled his eyes for the benefit of Dora, their regular waitress, and Dora smiled, asking the parents whether *they* were having the usual, and yes they were, so off she went, writing nothing on her pad.

"That's *my* usual!" Gallagher croaked, but her father, disgusted at what he'd detected, ignored her *and* the mother, turning his back on them to speak to the McDermotts from Regent Avenue, sitting in the booth behind. But when Mrs. Gallagher said something—just a pleasantry to cool things down—he swung back, leaving the McDermotts to their steaming plates of shells. "I heard you come in last night," he charged. "What time was it?

"It was 2 A.M.!" he answered himself, too impatient to wait. "Tell me what kind of joint is open at 2 A.M.? No, don't tell me. I don't want to know."

The waitress brought cups of chowder, Mr. Gallagher's two beers—it was happy hour—and four wines. When she'd placed the soup spoons on napkins and turned away, Gallagher began to burble an account—factual, elaborate, but mostly irrelevant—

about the night before. Her father broke in: "I don't care about this!" he said. "Do you think I care about this?" Gallagher was still talking. "Did you hear me?" the father said, raising his voice to cut through. "Did she hear what I said?" the father asked his wife.

"I heard," Gallagher said. "I felt like telling you anyway."

"*I'm* interested," her mother piped up, and here was the waitress to clear the chowder cups.

"What are you so worked up about?" Catherine asked her father.

"I'm *not* worked up!" he yelled.

"Don't upset your father," said Mrs. Gallagher.

Catherine looked at her father—he was upset, but she'd seen worse.

"What the hell's wrong with you?" he exploded. "That's what I want to know!"

But he had nearly exhausted both his interest and his energy, and here was the main course. He liked to concentrate on his food, so the subject was dropped. Passing the bread around, though, he spotted his daughter's moony face, flushed, gleaming, and shot the mother (because she'd noticed, too) a look to kill.

As everyone knew, he liked to have his family *home* at night, and locked in, windows closed, shades pulled. A date could interfere with these plans, throw things off. A local boy was one thing: even a Polack like Juscik could be trusted to respect a father's need, after midnight, to shut himself in for the night. But this latest one he didn't know from Adam, and the girl had come home in a taxicab!

Catherine knew how he felt, but she didn't care. *She* felt full, buoyant: every cell aerated. She began to fill up with air when she boarded the bus on Arlington Street. It was partly the look McGuire was transmitting through his windshield and into the bus window (and kept it up, even as the bus lurched out of the station). And it was partly starvation. Catherine hadn't eaten much since Tuesday; Wednesday, lashing herself to finish Part One before the weekend, she had only drunk coffee. By Thursday, McGuire had edited all but the last few grafs, and was playing with a layout, X-ing in cuts, a sidebar here, boxing the long snake-like copy, then taking it out of the box. He had a head in mind, but told Gallagher to wait and see. At two o'clock he put away his T square, his sharpened pencils, spat—like always—in his coffee cup, grabbed his jacket and left the newsroom, slapping Gallagher's desk on the way out. Under his hand was the welfare fact sheet that Bohan had worked up, for her to incorporate where necessary. But Gallagher's eyes were tracking the retreating figure, ramrod back and flung-back head, as City swung through the turnstile and out the glass doors.

Killing those last two hours was tough. Gallagher fiddled with a sentence, drank more coffee, sharpened a pencil, refilled her glue bottle, then broke down and typed two brides. At the vacuum tube, she was cornered by Bohan and Tamburino, who wanted to crack wise about Arty, that faggot, forced to put on a pink shirt and burgundy tux for his wedding, and was he bullshit! It wasn't just the pricey rental, it was the insult to a guy who wore nothing louder than navy. Gallagher sensed that Tamburino and Bohan, both newly wed, were flexing up for a cruder attack on the bride, so she beat it back to the morgue, and downstairs to Composing. She had no business down there, but felt drawn to the hectic printworks, heaving and crunching. She walked past banks of idle linotype machines and into the thunderous press room, where the last of the late edition, bright with wet ink, was curling over the rollers, ready to be cut, folded, and fall off the belt. She picked up a warm copy and glanced at the headlines. Ernie Abell, master pressman, stalked over, but it was too noisy to chat. She read the page—wire and local—the motto, the joke, the weather, the score box. It was an average news day: the lead story was a three-alarm fire; a Third World coup d'état was tucked under the fold; still lower, a federal agency created to study the comatose New England economy, with unemployment at 22 percent; in a corner box, the school superintendent deploring a dwindling college enrollment, and, boxed with stars, the football teaser, jumped to sports. Sports had its own section, crammed with action blowups—the best pix in the paper—and columns of feverish prose. Good sportswriting, McGuire liked to say, was the highest art—there was one, maybe two talented writers in the country. The rest—indicating by a gesture that even in this, their staff didn't make the cut—were shit-shovelers.

Gallagher told Ernie page 1 looked sharp ("Thanks, hon"), and she walked up the back steps into the comparative peace—even with typewriters clacking and police radio bleating—of the newsroom. It was almost time to go.

Hiding the welfare story in a heap of unfinished brides, and anchoring it with the glue jar, she still felt uneasy, so she grabbed the wad of glued sheets and stuffed it in her shoulder bag. Miss Toohey had already left and, except for an editor on the key—who couldn't see from where he was—and O'Callahan, busy rereading the paper, the newsroom was empty. Gallagher scanned the morgue and Nightside, but no one there to see her "removing *Times'* property from the premises," the first and only significant "Don't" in *Watchwords,* "A Timesman's Codex."

Still, it was prudent, she thought, waving to O'C. in his glass box and gliding out the door, to keep the welfare story under wraps for another day. Once McGuire had the whole thing in hand, she could relax. City was potent, practically autonomous: he consulted the M.E. only when he felt like starting trouble. And if the edited story was stopped in Composing—the likeliest blockade—McGuire could handle that, too. In a showdown—and there had been several—between Old Wampanoag, represented by foreman Phil Jewett, a forty-year veteran compositor, and City, the smart money rode on City. City could afford to wait, to filibuster; the older man, whose job it was to get out the edition on time, with a nervous-Nellie publisher breathing down his neck, was easily worn down. Composing had a grudging respect for the young city editor (they'd take him any day over the fretful, waffling O'Callahan—a king-size time-sponge), but personally they despised McGuire's bullying, boat-rocking guts and, behind his back, called him (or so the newsbag librarian had reported) "the Shitfly."

By six P.M., Gallagher had arrived in Back Bay. She walked along the Public Garden, south on Boylston to Copley Square—the bright blue sky was softening, and behind the public library, a belt of rose pink swelled from the horizon. The Lenox Bar, pitch dark, was where McGuire waited, and there he was—she spotted him, once her eyes tunneled out. He was ordering her a glass ("What kind of wine do you drink?") of burgundy ("Here," he handed her the glass, "try it. Is it drinkable?"). He carried both glasses to a dusky booth in the back, lit by a single lantern with bottle-brown glass. McGuire stepped aside to let Gallagher pass, then squeezed in after her. His arms were around her and his half-opened mouth pressed onto hers. He reeked of tobacco and whiskey—how long had he been here?

For ten minutes they kissed in the dark. When Gallagher opened her eyes, she could see his eyelids shut tight behind the glasses; he looked strange without the cynical glare. After another long kiss, he rested his head—such bristly hair he had, and a thick body, dense as a tree trunk—on her shoulder; then he moved off, sucked on his whiskey, and started to talk, stopping only to bring their glasses to the bar for refills.

They spent the next hour or so squeezed into one side of their booth: a spate of urgent kissing, followed by a string of jokes and jittery talk. Gallagher had never seen anything like it. The old McGuire, prickly and combative, was gone. In his place was this simple soul, delirious, besotted, and content. Was it a good sign? When was the other one coming back?

Arms around each other's waists, they stumbled into the dining room, all dark wood and pewter, the same amber lanterns blooming dimly on the ceiling. McGuire ordered a bucket of steamers, salad, and a T-bone. He urged Gallagher—he still called her Gallagher; it was the only familiar note—to get lobster, but Gallagher felt too rocky. Even that morning, she had managed to cram only a few spoonfuls of cereal down her throat. There was, she tried to explain, a bolus—but he was on her, kissing the spot on the silky neck where, she said, the bolus—. Eventually, she ordered chowder and ate the pilot crackers. McGuire was drinking stein after stein of beer as he emptied his bucket. Taking a breather, he asked if he could pour one of his clams down her throat. Thrilled by the queerness of it, she watched him tear the slimy meat from the clamshell and dangle it ("Don't chew, just swallow!") over her open mouth. She swallowed, but it stuck there, and she coughed it out into a napkin.

Boston cream and lemon meringue pie, Indian pudding, coconut cake, fig squares, vanilla, chocolate and strawberry ice cream—the waitress announced, when the bucket, platters, bowls, and heaps of shells were cleared. McGuire ordered two lemon pies, coffee, and brandies. When the waitress left, he took Gallagher's hands, kissing them palm and back, fingers and thumbs, wrists and every knuckle. "I love you," he groaned. "Have you any idea how much I love you, Gallagher?"

Gallagher studied the pie when it arrived. She pierced its wavy cloud of meringue, then set down her fork. Drinking coffee and most of the brandy, she watched McGuire eat his pie and finish hers. They spent the last hours tracking the quiet streets of Back Bay, squaring the Public Garden, hiking up Beacon Hill to the State House, crisscrossing the common, then arrowing down on Marlborough to Kenmore Square. They ran, they strolled, they paused to kiss in darkened doorways and under the spreading trees. McGuire suggested a nightcap at the Ritz bar—Gallagher had blisters on both heels. McGuire drank another brandy, regaling with stories the waiter and a barman who, stiff and formal though they tried to be, couldn't help but laugh. He told Gallagher how long he'd loved her. When—as the hour of the last bus neared—he drove her to the Greyhound station, he gripped her with both arms and a leg, although the driver had already closed the bus door and was starting the engine. "You don't have to tell me now," he rasped. "But will you marry me, Gallagher? I love you so much."

It was that last bit, Gallagher was sure, that had pumped the air into her hollow and hungry body. All the way home on the bus she filled, and through that whole sleepless night, until her skin felt hot and tight. Shivers shot down her spine and legs. Lying rigid on the single bed, electrified, she wondered if she was losing her mind. Finally, the jolting sensations ceased, and she saw in the dawn light that she must be in love with McGuire, if "love"—not a popular notion in Kingstown, scorned even in Wampanoag—was the word to describe these seizures.

The next day, Gallagher tottered to work, ragged and shaky, with smoked eyes and limp hair, and started the day by filling her coffee cup. McGuire's chair was vacant, and for the rest of the day it stayed vacant. Only the sight of that desk and chair, never before so quiet, made the frenzy of the night before seem real. That, and the way Gallagher's sensitive body was still ballooning with air.

At Mainelli's the next night, the air at last found a pinhole and slowly, eating a roll, then another, and every green and pink thing on her plate, then dessert ("You never order dessert," her mother commented, but they always did, and each was served a wedge of banana cream pie), the air escaped and the voids screamed and howled for food. But the banana cream pie—its ripe smell and the puckers of its creamy cover—made Gallagher's stomach roll. She pushed the yellow-white blob away—just the *word* "blob"—but too late, the air was reversing course and pushing the food that had replaced it. Without a word, she ran, eyes flushed by pain, to the ladies' room. Someone was in there, so she had to wait hovering in the doorway of the bar—shudders and sweats—until, at last, a bulky woman, all in black, waddled out and Gallagher rushed in, bolted the door—. Once inside, safe, the pulsing guts relaxed and the crisis passed.

Gallagher mopped the sweat dripping into her eyes, then soaked a paper towel and draped it over her flaming face. She was rubbery and still twitching, but the dinner was safe. It was now a question of staying in the john long enough to get those wedges of pie—just "pie," no qualifiers—removed. When she made her way back, past tables redolent of tomato sauces, fried veal, and grilled beefsteak, an occasional waft of beer or whiskey, Gallagher felt steady, but seeing her yellow-white wedge still there, resting in place, she pivoted, and tracked down Dora.

When the girl returned, the Gallaghers were smoking cigarettes, and that was a relief. She breathed in the blue smoke and fielded their questions, dodging the nosy ones with a firmness the parents had seldom heard. They respected it, at least for that quarter hour between the meal and the ride home. They could each see that something out of the ordinary had happened to their grown-up daughter, but they couldn't figure out what. They knew little more than they did the day poor Cathy rolled home from college on the bus, half dead, and barricaded herself in her room, then spent the next week acting like a zombie. She snapped out of it, eventually, and went and got herself a job. But was it going to happen again, and—since it was nothing they recognized—what was it?

Next morning, Juscik called twice (Catherine was asleep) to confirm the date, but refused to confirm it—even though he liked the mother—with the mother. "I'll wait till she's up," he said wearily. "My number is—." Mrs. Gallagher interrupted him to say that they knew his number, repeating the digits to prove it. Juscik hung up.

At noon, Catherine drank two mugs of the coffee her mother had saved from breakfast, and fought through the dense tangle of dreams that had replaced the fine air, gone now. She carried the second mug to her room, where she heard her father's car roll into the driveway. He was planning yard work, her mother had said, and could use some help. Catherine said she'd go out as soon as possible, but her mother, as irritable today as *he* had been the night before, snapped, "You'll eat your breakfast is what you'll do. What do you want, to die of hunger? If you want to die, go someplace else and do it."

Catherine, nightgown sticking to her moist back, turned to look. "Why are *you* mad? What am I doing to upset everybody?"

Mrs. Gallagher, still in her housecoat, sat down at the table. She studied the pale face with the shape of wrinkled pillow bitten into the cheek. "I don't know. I'm not really mad, and I'm not cracked—like you-know-who. Why don't you try to eat? Then we can all get off your back."

But they *were* mad, and Catherine knew why, even if they didn't. Once again, their daughter was breaking down, softening, and just when their hopes—fueled by the degree from Kings, when no one in the family had ever *thought* of college—were highest. By now she should, on their timetable, be running Ford or sitting on the Supreme Court, or at the least making a hefty salary, with the kind of husband, houses, and cars that came with it.

Their letdown had been keen when, instead of going, say, straight on to Wall Street, Catherine had come home on the bus. And, sure, it was nice to have a kid, a college grad, home again and available for a Friday supper. It was nice for them, and the girl *did* have a job. But the shape she came home in—skinny, pale, mental-looking—*that* they'd never forget!

And it wasn't only, as Mrs. Gallagher told her husband, that Cathy looked like a refugee; it was the knowledge that this moody, high-strung girl, killing herself to write those upsetting articles, was not, and never would be, an Eleanor Roosevelt, a Margaret Chase Smith, or even a Margaret Truman.

This much—shutting her bedroom door, refreshed after twelve hours of sleep and last night's spectacular infusion of calories—Catherine understood. She was sorry, but their baffled dreams were their own. Her own dreams, dense and knotted, involving much more than a beat on the *Wampanoag Times*, or even the *New*

York Times, were just starting to take shape. She didn't have to pin herself down, not just yet.

Catherine could hear her father bellowing in the kitchen—he was feeling good. She watched him throw open the garage door and haul out his rakes and shovels. He stopped to smoke a cigarette with old Mr. Smaldone, out walking his invalid dog. The phone rang, and "Cathy," her mother yelled, "pick it up! It's *him*."

"Hello?" There was silence on the other end; she could hear breathing. "Juscik?"

"I'll pick you up at between 6 and 6:15. We'll eat first."

"Can't you say hello first?"

"I'm telling you the time," Juscik replied. "What time am I picking you up?"

Catherine had already forgotten.

"Between 6 and 6:15. It's a long movie."

"Is it?"

"What do you mean: *is* it? You told me it was long."

"Oh."

"See you later, all right? I gotta go."

But neither hung up. "Are you in a hurry?" Juscik asked.

After a moment's hesitation: "No, I just got up."

"So what are your plans?"

"I don't know. I have to help my father cut the grass."

"I'm looking forward to this, aren't you?"

"Yes."

"Did you read the book?"

"No, did you?"

"I *told* you I read the book."

"Well, I didn't."

"It's in paperback."

"Yeah, I've seen it."

"You're not in the mood for this, are you?"

Catherine considered. "Why don't you come over and have breakfast? Or we could go out for breakfast."

"Can't. I'll see you later. Tell me what time I'm coming."

"Six."

"Between 6 and 6:15!" Juscik hung up.

The phone rang again. "Hey!" a voice—smooth and rich—poured into her ear. "Are you thinking about me?" He was whispering, so Aerial must be lurking.

"Yes, I slept late."

"I was *with* you."

Gallagher laughed.

"Gotta go. See you Monday, Gallagher. Say, Gallagher?"

"What?"

"I wish you were here." Catherine could hear commotion in the background.

Mrs. Gallagher was hovering in the doorway. "Who was that?" she asked, sitting on the bed, her eyes shiny, eager.

Godfather II, making its second run, was a very long movie. So bloody and gross, Gallagher regretted eating first. Still, they sat through it and saw the beginning again. The Godfather empire, so lovingly amassed by Don Vito Corleone, is eroding, and what's left, crawling with traitors. Michael is a hateful and mysterious godfather; his control so weak that even Fredo, the runty brother, defies him and nearly kills him in his bedroom, "where my wife sleeps, and my children come to play with their toys!" In every scene Michael tries to be a strong don. More and more memories of Don Vito in his old-timey origins seep into the story as Michael loses ground. The empire grows anyway. Michael kills everyone he knows, and ends up alone. With Vito there was always a crowd: wives making sausage or meatballs in the kitchen, cronies piled up in the library; sons, protection, capos, drivers, flunkies, and buttons.

Juscik and Catherine were doing what they always did after a movie: arranging the scenes and filling in gaps to get a clear view of the narrative. Juscik was logical—even literal-minded—and demanded a clarity which no movie of any pretensions delivered on first view, so they always spent hours smoothing it out. He had driven them to Spot's, and they had had a couple of drinks while working on *G-II*. That night, the time was spent unraveling the Frank Pentangeli angle: who set Frank up? Was it Michael himself, or was it the Rosattos sent by Roth to kill Frank, to bungle it, and make it *look* like Michael's order? Was it to simplify things for the Rosatto gorillas, now running the old godfather neighborhood ("doing violence in their grandmother's neighborhood—whores, dope, junk!")? And was poor Frankie—Frankie "Five Angels," a leftover from the old Corleone family of Brooklyn—just in the way?

It was Roth. The order came from Hyman Roth, they concluded. The Rosattos were peons. It was Roth in his homicidal jealousy of Michael who had given the order—not just for the heads of the five families, but for Roth's adopted son, the Jewish godfather in Vegas. It was Roth. Catherine and Juscik were thrilled, they planned to see their movie again with this new light to shed on its twisty narrative. It was fabulous! Remember that second-to-last scene, Juscik said, the flashback where the brothers are back home for Vito's birthday, and Carlo is stuck with the women, Michael trying to get out of it by enlisting, and Sonny, like always, Sonny in a rage, with Tom playing peacemaker: the family most together, and already falling apart? Then Sal Tessio sneaking in to say that Vito was at the door, just walking in: "Surprise!"

They were bushed—it was after one o'clock—exhausted and hungry, so Juscik drove them to the Miss Wampanoag Diner. "I love a diner," Juscik said, as he opened a menu so smeared with honey or syrup that it was stuck to the table. "I'll have pie," Juscik told the waitress. "And she'll have—what will you have?"

They were almost talked out. When the waitress brought the desserts, they ate in silence. "So," Juscik said, after a while, "what's new? What new thing are you working on?"

Gallagher started to outline DOLE, first installment.

"That's not a story!" Juscik retorted. "That's a blueprint for how the chiselers beat the system. Don't tell me they pay you to give out that information."

Catherine didn't answer. She felt irritated that Juscik—like so many *Times* readers—would pass judgment before he'd even absorbed the facts. She decided to give him the highlights of Donna Leech's history.

"Leech!" he roared. But when he had heard more, he shook his head. "How can you fall for crap like that?"

"Do you think people *want* to be poor?" Catherine asked, raising her voice a little. "You think it's fun for them?"

"It's nice not to have to work for a living," he said, relaxing into the booth.

"What I never have been able to understand," said Catherine, wrapping the thread around her teabag and squeezing it, "is how someone your age, who *went* to college, could think the way you do."

"What way's that?" he asked.

"Didn't you ever read anything about poverty?" she said. "What *did* you read in college? My father hasn't read anything," she added. "He thinks the way you do."

Juscik pushed away the unfinished pie. He lifted the top crust and a syrup of bloody cherries oozed onto the plate. Catherine watched. Was this it? She knew this much: every tranquil evening they spent together meant that the movies and games they watched, the concerts they heard, had kept them busy, distracted, with no time to compare notes on politics, or anything else. Right from the start Juscik had said, in so many words, that if it ever came to a battle of wits, he'd bolt. He was no fool. He knew that in a decision, as Ox would call it, between Kings and Swamp, the Swamp must default, even if it had an edge. He had warned her, in what then seemed like a joke, that if he ever found himself in the ring with her, it would be the first and last round.

"You're acting just like Sonny," Gallagher said, "you know that?"

"Who?"

"Santino Corleone," Gallagher said, "the hothead: 'Consider this, Sonny,'" Gallagher grunted, aping Tom Hagen in conclave with Sonny after Don Vito had taken five slugs in the back. "'Just consider it!'"

"You know who you sound like?" Juscik returned.

"Who?"

"Michael."

"Michael!"

"You left the family, but now you want to control it."

Gallagher laughed.

"And you want respect."

"You mean, like Fredo?" asked Gallagher.

"I'm Fredo! I'm the clown. You're the murderer."

Catherine was silent.

"It was bound to happen." he said.

"What was bound to happen?"

"Let's go," he said, sliding out of the booth. "I'm sick of this dump."

Juscik stopped in his flight to the cashier, turned on his heel. He paused, unfolded his wallet and fished out a crisp twenty—

Juscik always had a wad of clean bills. "You can take the girl out of Kings," he said, "but you can never take the Kings out of the girl. Sound familiar?"

Juscik paid for their snack, and opened the door for Catherine. She considered the easy out that he was offering, but decided, out of a stubbornness that Juscik would understand, not to take it. "I think that's a lousy, rotten thing to say. And it's not even true!"

"You don't belong in Wampanoag, Gallagher. No one here is on your level."

They drove in silence, past the rubber company, up the hill, past the church, and left on Gallagher's street. Then, motor off and lights out, they sat.

"So this is it?" Catherine asked.

"I know you're seeing someone," Juscik muttered. "It's true, isn't it?"

"I've never asked *you* that question," she said, tentatively.

"That's right!" he snapped. "Because you don't give a damn!"

"*Are* you?" she asked him.

"I'm asking you first."

Catherine was looking out the side window. "What do you mean by 'seeing'?"

"I mean," he said, "that your mother told me you were out somewhere late on Thursday."

"She shouldn't have told you."

"I *asked* her."

Catherine saw that all the lights downstairs were turned off. "Why did you ask? Does it matter that much?"

Juscik, too mad to answer, bolted out of the car, around the front end, and was opening her door, polite to the end. Catherine was tired and rattled—mad. Why did the question of McGuire and Juscik have to be settled just that minute? And why had he pushed it? And what was wrong with telling the truth? Couldn't he take it? What was wrong with him?

It was only after he'd peeled out—the dark ribbon of exhaust shredding—that Catherine felt sorry. Juscik was an original: he was too smart to be so dumb and defenseless. Why, if he couldn't leave Wampanoag, wouldn't he let *her* take a little of the Wampanoag out of *him?* Why did he have to be all-Wampanoag? Who was making him?

Just then the porch light came on. Mrs. Gallagher waited in the doorway. "Poor Danny," she said. (How did *she* know?) This driblet of sympathy—after the day's, and even the week's, pressures—was too much. Mother and daughter stood a moment under the yellow porch light. They exchanged no more than a glance, but tears, following the zap of understanding, rolled freely down their cheeks.

One by one the pieces of the welfare story came out—on Monday, Wednesday, and Friday. Newsstand sales were brisk, as were incoming calls to the city desk, running 10 to 1 against, hundreds of subscriptions canceled—and in such foul language that McGuire insisted on fielding the calls. For several days, after the day shifts let out and had stoked up on a few tall ones and some stiff talk—and thank God, McGuire lingered till 4:30 or 5—the phones would start ringing, and they could hear City's nasal voice cursing the "smug, ignorant sons-of-bitches," all feeding from the same right-wing garbage can. "Just shut up! No one cares what you apes think!" Then he'd *order* them to cancel their goddamned subscriptions—they didn't have the wits to read a newspaper. But after a week's calls, some so belligerent that O'Callahan could hear McGuire from inside the glass cage—and upon a visit from the publisher, who'd taken a few calls himself—a memo was sent, and thereafter, the M.E. himself took all incoming calls on the series.

It was during those infernal days that McGuire, who had seen both *Godfathers,* collared his reporter, and like Don Vito spurring on weepy nightclub singer Johnny Fontane: "You can *act* like a man!" he bellowed. But that's exactly what Gallagher couldn't do. She was too scared to act like a man. People were calling to say how they wanted to smarten her ass up, teach her a good lesson, punch out her headlights, and might at any hour be gunning for her outside the *Times*' doors.

As predicted, even supine readers were heard from ("Don't sweat it," McGuire kept saying, but even he took the precaution of assigning Gallagher an escort). To think that the *Times* would lavish that kind of space and kid-glove treatment on the cheats, the whores, the gougers, the big fat slobs breeding like rabbits! "When my husband opens his paper at night," one lady screamed into Gallagher's ear, "he doesn't want to see *this!*"

The reporter asked what it was that had so worked up the husband, but the woman had already slammed down the receiver. Her parting words: "Girlie, I hope they kick you out on the street! With all your pals!"

Another caller said he'd heard a few things about that barfly, Christine Gallagher, and was anybody interested? Then, as the raging stream flowed on, McGuire grabbed the phone out of his reporter's hand. As rough-tongued as any reader, even *he* got sick of the yelling. Worst was the first day, when the part on Donna Leech, least deserving subject, hit the streets. The other two recipients had, at least, the tough luck, the accidents and tragedies to force them onto the dole. Leech was, as McGuire put it, a born parasite. "She's your weakest link," he'd warned, "but I'm glad you worked her in. Makes the series credible. You picked a real scumbag-loser and the dummies'll just have to lump it."

The dummies read it—the series broke a 25-year record in newsstand sales—but they wouldn't lump it. The shocker was the calls from welfare clients and their advocates, just as mad, just as outraged. Adam Gregorian, kingpin agitator, whose demagogic gift had stoked up whole wards of the poor and desperate, but worked just as well on timeservers and low-level pols, called up every day, saying things, to Gallagher *and* to McGuire, that spooked them both. Next thing, he turned up outside the *Times*' door. Gallagher spotted him on the sidewalk, and whipped up the stairs.

McGuire happened to leave early that day, and O'Callahan, who usually lingered—puttering, sponging up time—was gone, too. No one was there but weekend Nightside: editor Lou Cone, a wheezy old relic, and his staff, Al Clip. Jaded and easygoing, Clip spent most nights on the town, juicing and sniffing out skirts. Then, slow as molasses, he wrote his way into the next shift, and was still there at deadline, tapping out his five-graf stories. This second-string Nightside had nothing but contempt for the eager-beavers on day, killing the job, too lame to see a cushy deal for what it was. *Times* veterans for twenty and forty years, respectively, Cone and Clip had seen it all, and nothing whatever fazed them.

Al offered to drive the chick home in the company car, but Gallagher turned him down; she had to face the music—now was the time. What could the bastard do? Luckily, though, when she reached the glass door, darkened now as trafficky dusk turned to eerie, street-lit night, Gregorian had vanished.

Next day, she ran smack into him. He tracked her up to the newsroom. After a fiery spat with McGuire, the agitator admitted that he hadn't read the articles, so he couldn't see, as McGuire kept insisting, that they were *favorable,* sympathetic! All he knew, Gregorian shot back, was that years of work muscling City Hall to spring for the lousy supplement, the "handout," allotted the helpless poor was now in jeopardy because of an operator like this Gallagher—he knew the type—trying to hoist a career pandering to the low instincts of bloodsuckers who lapped up the sewage printed in the Swamp *Times*.

This was Gregorian's side of it. For a tense half-hour, he ranted: didn't give a shit, in fine, about those unread articles, no matter how gutless, how bleeding-heart they turned out to be. Under the steady blows, however, of McGuire's nail-studded tongue, the agitator let up. (O'Callahan was present, but silent: he despised a "rabble-rouser" and was tickled—as he later said—that Gallagher's work had stung this hound.)

Gregorian agreed to take a look at the pieces, although he still insisted on meeting the ratbag (quaking behind the ladies' room door). "Fine," McGuire told him. "Read the articles, and give the girl a call. Don't come back," he warned. "This newsroom is off-limits to you, buddy."

No place in Wampanoag, or on earth, howled the agitator, was off-limits to *him!* "I could ruin you!" he was heard saying to O'Callahan as he shouted his way to the door, "and your two-bit rag."

"Whyn't you try!" McGuire returned. "Gregorian!" the editor yelled as the agitator shouldered through the swing doors. "Read the goddamned articles, you gutless pimp!" But Gregorian was, by then, out of earshot.

Next day, the agitator called back. The series had caused him grief, yes, but the articles, he could see now, were good, more or less accurate, sympathetic. There were many things he'd change, and he wished to God the girl had called him! There were people he knew, *dirt* poor, who'd have made stunning copy. And, by the way, they should have left the Leech out of it. Any jerk would know not to lead off with that. He was still mad, he could wring that news squirt's scrawny little neck. But no, he wasn't going to sue, and yes, he'd lay off the girl, he had bigger fish to fry, don't worry.

Gallagher agreed to meet some of his people: leadership, including the famous welfare priest and plumber councilman, and rank-and-file—the students, welfare mothers, disabled vets, and misfits Gregorian was able to round up for sit-ins, marches, and boycotts. Thereafter, whenever the kingpin, or his staffers, had a story to report—and they usually didn't, but needed the publicity anyway—they always called the *Times* and asked for their man Gallagher.

The reporter squared things with welfare and advocates long before things were square with the *Times*' readership, and with management. The series had left many a nerve raw. Talk was that McGuire, working freelance for *Pravda,* was co-opting the society page. Unsigned editorials (inspired by the publisher and penned by O'Callahan) ran in the *Times* lambasting the present handout system, along with the cheats, the government flacks and sympathizers. The editorialist mined the series for scandal to highlight widespread abuses, and the odd pathetic bits to show, in "fairness," the rare case of just deserts. The publisher had his way, and in so doing reassured readers that the *Times* endorsed working for a living, money in the bank, home ownership, sobriety, and the sanctity of marriage—the very values that the page 1 motto hammered home daily. Readers were then free to boast, as they had after the coffee article appeared, about their paper's hard-hitting excellence. There was a flurry of congratulatory letters when the *Times* won a prize for human-interest reporting.

The worm, by then, had long since turned, although with it came the resignation of the 'Fly, the clout behind the series, and everything else good—according to a few readers—that had ever come forth from the Swamp. McGuire was quitting; he had done what he set out to do: the *Times* now covered local government "like a rash." The Women's page, emerging from the Truman era, was sharper-looking, its chinks filled in with ten-year-old (not thirty-year-old) 'plate. The paper—although running much the same content—was edgier, tighter, and McGuire—who had threatened to quit the day the first blacksmith order came in—was bored stiff. After the saddest two weeks in Gallagher's life, with a farewell lunch nearly every day—mostly just the two of them, sometimes Bohan, Kennedy, and Tamburino tagged along—McGuire was gone.

But before news of his departure was public, the *Times* staff convened for the solemnization of the Mullins-Oakley vows, reception following at the Chateau d'Etoile. It was a huge affair—400 head, mostly family, and the twenty-odd Timesmen herded together at two rear tables. Sal was married in St. Rose of Lima Church, her train extended half the length of the center aisle, dragging over the sheeting the sacristan had unrolled to the curbstone. Gallagher and Miss Toohey watched as the broad-backed bride, swathed in silk and lace, tackled the church steps. Bent at the waist, she raised and lowered a tottery foot within the compass of her gown's gauzy hoops, and brought the other foot up next to it. No one was available to help her. The ushers were busy pulling the eight bridesmaids, swallowed in pink or violet net, out of a fleet of limousines. The bride's mother and aunts received the maids and—alarmed at the way the net gapped and swelled—slapped at their dresses. The bride watched the pandemonium from the top of the steps.

Then the wedding began, and Sal and Arty were joined in marriage for all eyes to see. Smirking at his friends, the bridegroom swaggered down the aisle holding up his bride's fist like a prizefighter.

Much later, McGuire showed up at the reception with Aerial, in palest yellow. Blonde Aerial, eyed for the first time by the newsroom, shimmered, chic and shapely. She clung to her boyfriend's arm and they swept down the reception line. Everyone gaped, Bohan and Tamburino swearing that never before had they seen such a delectable dish. Miss Toohey scrutinized the frock, the posture, the delicate features and cornsilk hair. "Some peach! Hats off," she said, "to the 'Fly."

When the receiving line broke up, and the cash bar opened, Gallagher lost sight of Miss Toohey and the A.C.E. She was cruising the tables looking for her own place card when she felt the pinch of her editor's bony fingers: "She's just a dumb cluck, Catherine. I went and spoke to her. Had nothing whatsoever to say for herself."

"Really?" Gallagher lamely said. And how much, she wondered, did Toohey know?

In all that time, McGuire had not detached himself for one minute from the yellow dress, much less greet or even seem to see the Women's reporter. Gallagher had swallowed her third glass of punch, with Miss Toohey sipping next to her. McGuire had warned that Aerial had received an invitation and meant to come to the wedding, forcing the live-in boyfriend to play along and be cool. But suddenly he was making a break from the yellow girl, who was swiftly circled by Timesmen. He loped over to the tables set aside for news staff. Gallagher watched him read the place cards, then switch one with another. In relief and triumphant joy, she grabbed another wine from a passing waiter's tray.

And so, at the sitdown dinner, there they were, side by side—Aerial across, but busy with the fast-talking Bohan and Tamburino, faces burning, beading with sweat, so long had it been since they'd lapped up a dish of this sort. So McGuire was free to wind his leg around his writer's and hold hands beneath the tablecloth. Their shoulders and arms pressed, but they talked little. Gallagher's eyes were glassy and unfocused, and McGuire freely held forth, addressing the whole table.

And if that weren't enough for the gossips, the couple made off—when the music started—to dance in a corner, while the yellow girl was traded off among the staff, Dayside, Nightside, married and single: some had brought and already dumped their dates—even the bridegroom was in line to dance with Aerial.

But no one cared about that; all news eyes were trained on the cheaters. Maybe they'd suspected, maybe they hadn't, but now they knew. And that Cathy Gallagher, O'Callahan was saying to Mrs. O'Callahan, seemed like such a lovely girl. People shook their heads: it was a shame. She might have been a crack reporter, but fame—and the flattering buzz-bombing of the Shitfly—had swelled her head. Those few dances, so sweet, so intimate, in her lover's arms, could cost Gallagher—even Toohey knew this much, but when did young people ever listen?—all the credit earned by the series.

And how could the girl have known that McGuire was fixing to quit, and she'd be left—with the scandal *and* the losses—to rot on Women's?

PART TWO

CHAPTER 6

It began when John B. McGuire, late of the *Long Island Clipper,* now resident blacksmith at Gross Smythe Village, Hampshire, and freelancer for *Industry Metal Works,* with two days to go on the job in Wampanoag city, dropped a rolled-up copy of *Editor and Publisher* on the Women's desk, and caught the limpid gaze of the reporter's big, myopic eyes, whispered a hot nothing so that Miss Toohey could hear, called the lunch date for 11—even earlier than the day before—and pointed his grimy, calloused finger at an ad on the classified page. "Get the job," McGuire said. "It's got your name on it."

It was 9:45 A.M., all the obits were in, and that day's paper—except for late-breaking wire—was the lookout of Composing, booming and crashing underfoot, so that the Women's reporter, C. A. Gallagher, was—in a word—free. She unrolled the magazine and spread it out on a fashion layout. The job was on a big daily in Depointe, Michigan, a paper she had never heard of, but 350,000 circulation, huge! The Wampanoag paper even in its heyday never topped 25,000, and it was lucky to hit 20,000 in the lean recessional years when the New England economy collapsed and the newshole shrank to nothing. The *Depointe Bullet,* edited by a whiz-kid (he'd left the ad world to take one of the A.C.E. desks, rapidly moved up to City, then leapfrogged over the next three levels of editorial command to dictate the contents of the entire paper), was booming: ad space bloated as spreading zones of well-heeled readers from South Bend deep into Canada and as far north as the Superior shores clamored for the paper that was making, as its TV campaign put it, "yesterday's keyhole into tomorrow's laser." Even the *Bullet*'s newshole was bullish. It didn't seem to matter that Michigan was mired in stagflation, or that

Depointe had never rallied from race riots, whose fires and terror had driven out legions of taxpayers and gutted thriving retail blocks; where armed gangs patrolled the vacant lots and burned-out streets, or else ambushed cars on the ramps of the freeways named after automotive titans. Even that industry was running on empty: Americans were buying smaller cars cheaper from Japan, and the Big Four had stripped Depointe of its car-making might, relocating plants overseas and in the Sunbelt, where unions were poison.

It was in *this* unpromising climate that the 35-year-old Rolf Luck had beefed up the news staff, updated the format, retooled from hot to cold type, and doubled circulation in two years.

McGuire knew of the miracle-working Luck and his disciples, flogging the corrupt, crime-ridden and wasted city for the benefit of its new-found suburban readers. Luck was the darling of a rich syndicate with papers, small and large, east of the Mississippi and from Florida to New York, with the *Bullet* as flagship.

The classified page of *E&P* lay open on the Streamline table amid the cups and hot-dog plates. The *Bullet* sought an "entertainment" writer—extensive clips, competitive salary, start immediately. "Call them!" McGuire said, his mouth stuffed with his second New York–System dog. "Don't fiddlefuck around."

Gallagher read the other ads, but nothing looked so tempting. The Streamline was doing a brisk business, but Wampanoag was sinking deeper into sludge: cuts in federal grants for redevelopment had brought the city to near-bankruptcy—a full quarter of potential taxpayers now drew their checks from welfare or unemployment. The latest arrivals in the newsroom, interns who hoped for full-time, were finding pink slips in their pay envelopes.

"Gallagher!" McGuire snapped his fingers. "Are you still with us?"

"If I go to Depointe," she said quietly, "what about—?"

"What about what?" he said. "You think I've got nothing better to do in life than dump broads?"

This was funny but Gallagher didn't laugh. "So why send me to Mongolia?"

"Depointe is a hole," he returned. "It isn't Mongolia."

McGuire reached over to uncurl Gallagher's hand from the coffee mug, sniffed its palm. "You smell like a donut," he said. "Sweet and cheap." He leaned across the table. "Get the job. We'll deal with the other stuff."

"Try and keep me away," he added. "I'll stick like paint."

"Nice," she said sarcastically.

"You bet your ass it's nice."

They talked until after 1. She had talent, he said, and drive! She even had guts, but she couldn't do it alone. Her writing was raw; she didn't know how to go out and get it, fast and accurate. She needed careful handling. And those editors in Depointe were sharks. They were snapping up all the prizes. No one else was hiring, they were laying people off. Newsprint was sky-high, the biz was shrinking.

"It's one hell of a long shot," he said, trying another tack. "You don't have much to offer compared to what they'll see. Do it for my sake, Gallagher. Instead of taking a decade to crawl to the top—I don't think I could live through *that* again—you'll be there *tomorrow*. What do you say?"

When Gallagher had blocked Wednesday's fashion page, she watched Miss Toohey lock up the biscuits to go home; then waited till, at the dot of 4, Dayside stampeded out of the newsroom. Only then did she roll, and crooked, a sheet of yellow newsprint into her machine. "Dear Mr. Luck," she typed.

Phrases arch and sinuous tried to fall onto the page, but Gallagher choked them back and waited for better ones. Nightside arrived in the form of a sallow, slit-eyed Clip and his rumpled editor. Gallagher kept her eyes on the letter, dated May 21, 1975, "Dear Mr. Luck." Cone dropped his raincoat and rifled through the assignment sheets, then tracked out with Clip for a quick one before the round of meetings. Police was already squawking about domestic battery on Chokeberry Street, a barroom melee at Trigger's Tap, attempted suicide from the roof of the Y, but Nightside still had a free hour, with good old Gallagher covering (in case of an earthquake, nuclear attack, or a call from the mayor's office), to soak up a beer and shot.

"Dear Mr. Luck," Gallagher read back. "Where did you get a name like Luck?" She yanked the page out, and recommenced. "There are obvious reasons why you wouldn't hire someone like me," she typed. "And I've heard them all from my editor, John McGuire. I decided to apply anyway. Enclosed please find my resumé and a series I wrote for the *Wampanoag* (R.I.) *Times*. I'm assigned to the Women's desk. But I don't think you need a genius to cover TV and movies, if that's what you mean by 'entertainment.' I don't watch TV, but when I first came to Wampanoag, I knew nothing about cooking, housework, or weddings, but I fit right in here. I write and edit my daily pages, and string for City, doing color and human-interest stories.

"If you're interested, call me at home because my paper would hate to hear I'm on the job market. Thank you."

She yanked the sheet out of the roller. In the heat of composition, she hadn't noticed that the text was slanting up on the page. To hell with it. She found a *Times* envelope, and dropped the letter in the slot.

Exiting the office, she ran into O'Callahan, phlegmatic as ever. No backlash had come as a result of the spooning at Sal and Arty's wedding. The bigger news—that the Shitfly was on his way out—put other gossip in the shade. McGuire was quitting, yes, said Miss Toohey, and not a minute too soon because the publisher meant to "kick his ass out." But McGuire had the knack for foiling management, through second-guessing and timely interventions. He had saved his staff many a heartache in pay cuts, layoffs, and firings. In return, management had been building an arsenal of evidence against the prize-winning troublemaker, and time was on its side.

What it hadn't known was that McGuire would once again play his hand early, penning a stiff note of resignation on the very morning that O'Callahan planned to axe him.

"O happy day!" Gallagher could hear McGuire's gravely voice from the rear of the newsroom. And then, a minute later (Bohan and Kennedy), "O happy day-ay-ay." After a beer-and-chaser lunch, the short-timer and his boys killed the afternoon on spitball tennis, smut, Three Stooges routines, and calls to Women's.

Altogether, McGuire's last ten days passed in such pandemonium that it was only trained reflexes that got the paper out every day. People were too busy to remember the wedding, much less the sight of the on-the-job romance.

Once a day Gallagher met the 'Fly in hideyholes a few blocks' distance—sometimes less—from the newsroom (if Gallagher happened to be working) or from the Gallagher house. They met in alleys or doorways, kissed, then tore off in McGuire's sky-blue MG.

In learning his new trade, McGuire scavenged the mill towns built along the now-filthy Wampanoag river system. In these villages you could see, and pocket, hand-wrought parts and shards left to rust in the junk heaps of gutted factories, every windowpane broken. Built before 1800, it wasn't until the end of the century, during the second industrial boom, that these fabric mills, fully capitalized at last, were at peak—spinning, weaving, and dyeing raw wool and cotton for the nation. The cloth barons built towns to house the farmworkers and immigrants arriving in droves to work for peanuts.

The couple spent long afternoons cruising these red-brick villages and walking their treeless streets, while McGuire sketched bits of wrought-iron filigree on gates and stoops, picked up old glass, and pointed out the many styles of bricklaying and stonework. It was an odd pastime for lovers. McGuire was charged with talk and ardor; his fever kept them on their feet, tracking every square foot of town, or rolling in an oversized motel bed. They picnicked—in the car or on the industrial carpets of rented rooms—on wine and bread, cherries, cheese, Napoleons, brownies, sometimes whole cakes. Mostly they drank, always they made love, sometimes jumped in the bath, if the tub looked clean. Wherever they were, McGuire filled the hours with his talk: leaving the news biz at last and equipping the forge, splitting up—or almost (she was still on the farm, but looking for work)—with Aerial. The sting of the old Shitfly—even on the subject of Aerial—was gone. The new McGuire was defanged, declawed, all heat and sweetness, salty waves of passion and a tide of talk.

Gallagher had known men whose aim in sex was fusion—burial, if they could get it. You could feel, even in tender moments, a lunatic force at work—not just to get in, but to come out the other side. McGuire had this aim, and the lethal fury that went with it. For him passion was fatal. In the cooling off, he was prostrate. For long minutes, it felt like lying under a fresh, heavy kill.

McGuire was quick to crow about how great they were in bed: how wild and supple, how fierce, when it was all him. He was the one who turned himself inside out. Gallagher loved McGuire, better as time went by, utterly, more than any other man, and told him so. But during the furious unions, she felt a little alone, like a bystander at an accident.

McGuire was happy; he said he was happy and he seemed to be happy but they both knew (didn't they? Gallagher wondered) that it couldn't last forever.

For a few weeks after McGuire left the Swamp, life was simple, even sweet. A new city editor was hired to keep the staff up to snuff. O'Callahan was no fool; he knew the spike in notoriety and circulation (if not in ad lineage per se) was due to upgrades by McGuire—the gut-wrenching features, the hound-like reporting on beats, the barbed heads and striking graphics. The *Times* would continue, the publisher had announced post-McGuire, on this winning streak, but without—he paused—"the Shitfly." So, the new man, Billy Arnold—mild, amiable, fresh from a PR job for the diocese—went along. He kept out of people's hair, and edited with a light hand. For a month or two, or until McGuire's old posse got fagged, forgot, or left the paper entirely, a bit of sting remained to goad the Timesmen, and to keep the coverage sharp.

Gallagher liked Billy Arnold, but Billy Arnold was leery of the spitfire on Women's, so quick with the backtalk. The McGuire trio was, for the moment, incorrigible, so he left them alone. Bohan, Kennedy, and Gallagher worked together: they drummed up story ideas, honed them at joint lunches, and worked like hounds to bring in the work on deadline. But it wasn't quite the same without their chief, and the sharp blue pencil that had saved them so many times from ridicule, libel suits, disaster. His bully-boy style notwithstanding, McGuire had always known where in Wampanoag the line was, and he had shaved it closer than anyone had ever done. Billy Arnold could also see that line, but kept himself—and the timeservers and yes-men he edited—as far away from it as he could.

When Gallagher handed McGuire an issue where all three delinquents had bylines, he read a few grafs, then handed the paper back. "You don't know which end is up, and neither do those helmet-heads." Gallagher pressed. Couldn't he see the legwork, the enterprise, the unpaid overtime—and no help from anyone!—that went into this work? McGuire just laughed: "Do yourself a favor, Gallagher. Take the job in Depointe."

When Gallagher replied that the job hadn't been offered, he said, "So what are you waiting for? Get off your slats and get the offer!"

And then, one day—after reading until 5 A.M., because she was now working the 4-to-11, replacing Al Clip whose wife had just had their third child ("What wife?" everyone had said. "I didn't even know he was married!")—her mother wrestled her awake at 9 for an urgent call. It was Luck from the *Depointe Bullet*—or was it? She was half awake, and the guy had such a low, growly voice—it couldn't be Luck. The voice was saying—what *was* it saying? Gallagher was thrown, and trying to control the wobble in her voice. Yet when she hung up she knew that something big had happened. Her mother, who had heard the ballooning voice, was hovering. She laid a place mat on the kitchen table and some silverware. A fresh pot of coffee was on the burner.

Mrs. Gallagher was amazed that a newspaper near Chicago would call up Cathy just because of a few articles on diners and poor people. How had they heard of Wampanoag? she asked her daughter, who explained again that it was *she* who had contacted them. In the news business, they couldn't care less, she told her mother, where you came from, or what burg you covered. What mattered was the writing and, as O'Callahan would say—even he knew this much—the caliber of the mind, the drive. Who could know, just from reading the *Times,* she added, that only one person had that kind of drive? Don't run yourself down, Mrs. Gallagher told her daughter, before you have to.

Catherine let her mother talk—she talked so rarely, and the call had upset her, too—while she roped in her stampeding thoughts. She wanted to call McGuire—now!—but Aerial might be lurking. (Aerial still didn't see why she had to go: she had her rights. And why did "John," so ardent, such an extrovert, want to live by himself all of a sudden?) Well, there'd be time to work all that out, because Gallagher—although the job had yet to be offered—was going to Depointe! The *Bullet* editor said how amused they'd been to get the cockeyed letter on newsprint, telling them why they should ignore a Women's-page writer from a paper in Podunk. They'd already screened 300 applicants—at least a hundred were at the top of their form, seasoned reporters from papers 100 times the size of—. "What'd you say the name was? Wampum?" Yet they were snagged by the very moxie of it. Some there knew Jack McGuire. How long had she worked for Jack?

In short, they wanted the candidate "who rejected herself"—"Is it Cathy or Cathleen?"—to come out for a weekend. They wanted to see her, talk, have her take a few tests—it was all legit. Would she want to come out for a trial?

Reporting this story to her mother, Gallagher wasn't sure if she'd even answered. She must have said yes, because the *Bullet* was calling back later with flight reservations for the upcoming weekend. Gallagher screamed. The phone rang: McGuire. Before Gallagher could squeeze a word out, McGuire was saying that, although they'd just seen each other and—for the sake of the suspicious live-in and other newsbags—were supposed to hang fire, he *couldn't!* He'd pick her up for a drink at 9, okay? Gallagher heard, but her brain was racing too fast to say more than yes. When she hung up, she realized that by the time she saw McGuire at 9, the weekend in Depointe—and the future—would be arranged.

Returning to where her mother was pouring coffee, Gallagher picked up a cup and saucer. They rattled in her hand. "Pull yourself together, kiddo." her mother said.

"I *am* ambitious," Gallagher said, thinking of poor McGuire. "I was wrong to think I wasn't."

Yet it was only *after* the weekend—not right after, when the dust of dazzlement was still settling, and stunning the way each silvery speck touched bottom—that Gallagher realized it wasn't ambition only. In the course of those forty hours, under the close eye of the Bullets—the smoky lights and potent drinks, the rich and exotic dishes, the challenges, insults, and furtive touches: pats, strokes, caresses, even (unbelievable as it seemed back in Wampanoag) kisses and clasps—a second self emerged, first seen as it was flushed from its night flight into the Depointe airport, then startled by the lupine gaze of the sub-editor dispatched to meet it.

Ralph Bluestem, the sub, had laid his plans for the hick babe, whose silky phone voice had promised, in its quickness and candor (that unbeatable quality), complete pliability. Bluestem was newly divorced and the defunct marriage, nasty as it was, had addicted a virgin bachelor to the luxury of regular sex. The stream of dates, affairs, and one-night stands that followed did nothing to make up for the loss of a wife who'd run off with a reporter from the competition. This girl from Wampum was earmarked for him, and he had spent the day casting and recasting images of her fresh face and opulent body. When the real thing issued from the gangway and into the glare of Depointe Metro, the sub-editor nearly shrieked in pain.

Stunned, floored that the Wampum babe was just a girl—lanky and cute, yes, but not the soap-ad beauty, rosy odalisque, wildcat, French slut, sleek-toned surfer girl of his mind's eye—Bluestem lit right into her. "I asked if you were gorgeous. And you said yes!"

At first, Wampum—face wreathed in a professional smile—didn't hear.

Then, as if replayed, she heard. "What?"

Back on earth, Bluestem laughed. He embraced his candidate, who *was,* after all, still a girl. "I'm warming up to you," he said, "even if you did lie on the phone."

Wampum looked Bluestem in his glittery eyes—he wasn't dogmeat, but no dreamboat either. "What did you say to me?" she said. "Are you cracked?" But it was said in jest, and Bluestem wasn't the least embarrassed. He took his charge by the arm and led her through the vast space of the airport. Wampum/Gallagher was trying to remember the long-distance calls. One had come over the hook phone shared with Miss Toohey, whose eyes and ears were alert—and the newsroom still as a tomb. After a few details—arrival time, flight number—Bluestem wanted to chat a bit: what color hair? height? long legs? beautiful? "Why are you asking me this?" Gallagher had said, but wondered if this talk was just McGuire raised to a higher power. Whatever wisecracks she'd made, she couldn't recall. Wasn't this part of it?

Bluestem drove his hireling-elect into the city, a long, nearly silent ride. Always cautious, even methodical, Bluestem was busy with his fresh impressions and the laying of new plans. And Wampum, this altered self, refused to seem anxious, eager, or even willing to talk. The weekend was for that, and there'd be plenty of time, as McGuire had warned, for them to get at her. "Keep a lid on it. Let them do the talking."

Once downtown, Bluestem eased on the brakes in a block of restaurants and glassy buildings. "What do you say to a drink?" he said. "Are you old enough? You look about 13. Is that the drinking age in Wampanoag?"

Gallagher studied the editor's square, meaty face with its trim beard. "You wouldn't have remembered Wampanoag," she said, "if you didn't like me."

"We like you," Bluestem replied, sounding irritated, as he would whenever he sensed he was being worked. "We wouldn't have invited you if we didn't at least 'like' you."

Gallagher waited in the tiny car for Bluestem to trot around and open her door. "You're big!" he said, as they stood on the sidewalk and she could see clear over his head. "Not for a Wampanoag," she returned, and the Wampanoag theme was struck a third time. When the more mundane and professional subjects were tapped out, the personal and insinuating tested and rejected, they could fall back on Wampanoag and laugh: they never got tired of it, tickled by its smallness and insignificance. They would never forget Wampanoag, one Bullet told Gallagher, even if they never laid eyes on the envoi again—and they might not, she was warned repeatedly, given how obscure her paper was, and how laughably small. They said this so often that Gallagher took it as another kind of test, and worked it herself. She had some chances, in the two days, to hone her part in the jest. She thanked her hosts often for the honor of the junket, which could be but fruitless for them.

That first night, Bluestem took her to a private club, appointed in green leather and mahogany. Famous faces and notable events—shot by the foto hotshots of the *Bullet* and competition: fires, handshakes, floods; parties, bathing beauties, touchdowns; trenches, blizzards, murders, niteshots, funerals, riots, and parades—lined the paneled walls. Under the green-globed lamps was a handsome wraparound bar where a dozen men in dark suits or raincoats leaned into their drinks—not much beer, mostly straight spirits. Inside the quadrangle, the bartenders were mirrored against terraces of bottles. The Depointe press club, Bluestem had announced, and Gallagher was duly impressed. No paper in Wampanoag or even in Providence had such a club, or dreamed that newshounds could claim such a ritzy joint.

Gallagher was the only woman present. She sat, in her pale blue dress, between Bluestem and a slight man in a black blazer whom Bluestem had introduced, but Gallagher—shaking hands with still another writer, the *Newsweek* stringer—hadn't caught the name.

Wondering what to order, Gallagher could feel many pairs of eyes inspecting her flanks. What was wrong, she wondered, with the picture? Was her dress, so crisp and sail-like, too summery? And her hair, never styled in any definite way, just cut and left to itself—was it too casual? And was the face itself, with a little makeup but nothing you could see, too plain? Bluestem's centerfold ideal notwithstanding, there was still much to criticize. She was too unpolished, too unimproved. Why hadn't she thought of this, and what could she do to make up for it? She looked left at the black blazer drinking something yellow, and right at Bluestem, who was waiting his order on hers. What did a woman order in such a club? And how many would she have to drink before they'd call it a night?

Gallagher asked the bartender what he'd recommend. Dumb, yes, but it popped their balloon: why make a drink order into a contest? Her stiff-necked partners laughed. Gallagher ordered wine.

"Oh, God!" the left-hand man groaned. "Don't order wine here."

"The young lady," continued the man with a voice so penetrating it jolted the whole bar, "will have Pinch and water. Or do you like rocks?" he asked, and the recruit got her first look at the face that had pumped 300 Bullets, that had goaded, teased, and cuffed them, pulled their scabs and pinched their bruises, probed their skulls to see where in their squishy brains they were weak and helpless and how many buttons they had that he could push, how hard and how often.

The face was homely: tight mouth, lynx eyes, and large nose fitted to a head so thin it looked starved. The Wolverine, they (the ones who'd been skinned and disemboweled, their buttons pulled, their circuits busted) called him. Everyone else called him—and Gallagher heard it first from Bluestem's prayerful lips—Rolf. "Rolf," he said, giving it a mouthful of air, "this is our girl from Wampan-oog."

Rolf offered a narrow hand to squeeze hers, then turned back to his drink and what he'd been saying to the trenchcoat on his left.

Taking the cue, Bluestem left the bar to speak to the *Newsweek* man, now sitting at a back table. Gallagher's scotch was set down. She looked around, but even the bartender had turned his back and wandered over to the other side of the bar. Gallagher could see him, over the bottles of booze stacked on the island. She tried to think of at least one drink you could make with each liquid: silver, gold, maroon, and green. Thus occupied, she sipped her scotch, until Luck—for it was Luck, all that time it'd been Luck—ordered her another, and turned from his left to show the Wampanoag a jeering grin. (Later, Bluestem told her that she had passed the first test: not to chatter, and to sit like a man, not some nervous twit.)

It was long past midnight when Bluestem divulged to Gallagher this and other such secrets. They were in her hotel room, after he had invited himself up for a nightcap. Bluestem hadn't intended to spill for the recruit (it was always better to keep them squirming), but the Wampanoag was not really in the running, and he needed someone to pay attention to him for a change. There were tips he could give her, if she'd just warm up a little.

They drank their brandies, Bluestem smirking, when he wasn't describing—in that droll way he had—the crackups, suicides, divorces, and arrests that followed the scoops, prizes, syndications, bonuses, and triumphs, as the paper (under the Wolverine) had broken records in both newsstand and circulation. The Bullets, according to Bluestem, had always bled (twenty-hour days, seven-day weeks) for their glory.

Gallagher had drunk so much scotch she was content simply to sit still, safe now from the peering and jeering of the press club. Bluestem crowed about how well she'd worked it, how wowed people were, what a hellcat she could be—so bitchy, but funny! Never, Bluestem claimed, had they planned to consider a tyro, but now even Luck was rethinking. He was smitten, Bluestem claimed. "Not once did he insult you!" Bluestem, bleary-eyed, gaped at Gallagher, sunk in the armchair. "I wish you'd come closer," he said. "I can hardly see you." Gallagher didn't move.

Ten minutes later, the sub-editor lurched off the bed, carefully landing his glass on the dresser. In the mirror he saw his own blotchy face and a distant Wampanoag. He pointed: "You know what? You're better-looking than I thought. When I saw you at the airport, I thought—shit! I gave myself all that grief to bring in this clothesline!" Bluestem winked, then steadied himself. "You know what you reminded me of?"

When Gallagher didn't answer, the sub-editor did. First he laughed. "A kangaroo. Have you ever seen a kangaroo hopping off an airplane?" He was choking with laughter.

Bluestem turned away from the mirror to look at the Wampanoag. First, he faced the wrong corner. "I'm leaving now. I like you, Wampanoag. I want you working for *me*. I'm a little in love with you, you know that? So is Rolf."

Bluestem stumbled over to the armchair where Gallagher had slumped, but then he halted, and aimed for the door. "I'm not going to kiss you," he muttered. "I can see you're not ready."

"Tomorrow," he said, facing the door, "get a wakeup call. The testing starts at 9. Sure you can find the place?" Bluestem had the door opened. He closed it behind him, but not all the way. "Hey, Wampum," he said, his red face showing through the slit. "Sleep tight. You're going to need those furry little balls tomorrow." The door closed.

Gallagher eased out of the armchair and lowered herself onto the bed, her head sinking between the pillows. And that was fine, until the room—steady till then—began to revolve. She sat up, and it stopped. She'd had many drinks and no dinner—too crazed for the plane food, and nothing had been offered since then. They had spent the first few hours in the press club, then moved off to a second, even plusher joint. When Luck, drinking scotch like water, failed to get the rustic girl drunk, or even to make her cry; when every dig and crack was ignored or returned, he faced Bluestem. The perky Bluestem craved Luck's attention, and reddened to the tips of his ears and down his neck.

"Hey, shorty," Luck yelled, "how much d'ya pay for that Jap car you just bought?" (Earlier Bluestem had treated them to the specs on his new Hobbit, how spiffy and quick, snug and silver, how much in hp and gas mileage, and what an improvement over the last clunker.)

"Just under five grand," Bluestem said, clearing his throat. He replayed the car salesman's clinching argument, when Luck cut him off. He had something to say, but first he ordered another round.

"Five grand!" Luck bellowed, when the drinks were set down. "You cut-rate little piker! I spend more than that for a suit!" He winked at Gallagher, then roared with laughter. The exchange set the tone for the night. The jokes were on Bluestem, for the benefit of the rustic—and the crueler they were, the sharper they cut, the more Bluestem (or 'Stem, as Luck called him) gobbled it up.

By midnight, when Gallagher had excused herself to find the ladies' room, the 'Stem was so hopped up he hid behind a pair of velvet drapes, then ambushed the recruit coming out of the john. His face was stretched with smiles. After a hearty kiss, he put his arm around the startled Gallagher. "You're wonderful!" he crooned. "Do you know how wonderful you are? Everyone thinks you're just wonderful!"

But when they reached the bar, where Bluestem meant to showboat his catch, picked by himself from a heap of rejects, Luck was gone. He was on the other side, talking to a beefy man introduced as Police. Bluestem dropped his arm, told Gallagher to hold their places, then scurried off to join the confab. It was Luck who slipped away first and returned to the recruit.

After angling himself so that his knee bumped Gallagher's leg, Luck asked if she could come up with one good reason why they should hire a Women's-page flack from that Indian newspaper, he forgot the name. "You don't even know how to write. I saw your stuff. It's smart, but it's raw. You take a lot of editing—I can see that."

Gallagher, who'd heard this before, took a sip of scotch, but the glass was empty. Even the ice was gone. Luck lifted the glass to signal the bartender; Gallagher declined. He waited until a fresh glass was placed in front of her, then he leaned onto her shoulder. He whispered (Bluestem and Police had gathered round): "Can't take it, huh?"

Gallagher lay back on the pillows. The room swung a little, but didn't twirl. A few minutes later, she rose, showered, and got back into bed, only to lie there the rest of the night brooding. Why would a newspaper shell out for the flight and the swank hotel—gilded lobby, marble bathrooms, gigantic bed (although no chandeliers)—just to get her pig-drunk the first night and shipped home the second? Did they do that to everyone they wanted to hire?

The next day, staggering out of bed, faint with exhaustion, she shambled down for the breakfast buffet, spread in four corners of the marble lobby, but it looked expensive—Gallagher didn't yet know that the *Bullet* expected her to eat, and on their tab. She exited the hotel, wandering down a boulevard lined with skyscrapers, some clear glass, some black or golden glass. Depointe was famous, in places like Wampanoag, for how bankrupt, firebombed, husked and perilous it was, but none of the famous blight was visible in this part of town. Here the streets glistened from a fresh washing, and bustled in rush hour with smart-looking citizens, black and white, hurrying to work. Gallagher gazed at the gold- and green-glass walls, where she could see the crowd in motion, as in some sun-shattered fishbowl.

Gallagher circulated until her stomach felt steady enough for coffee. She had passed the *Bullet* building, an art-deco pyramid skyscraper, crowned with a strip of lightbulbs: DEPOINTE BULLET, the bulbs flashed, READ BY 351,894. Beyond the revolving doors and past the newsstand was a luncheonette from that same era—tile floor, wraparound marble counter, low ceiling, aromatic and steamy. Gallagher bought a copy of that day's *Bullet,* along with the *Times, Newsday,* and the *Chicago Tribune,* and sat at the counter. A quick read proved that while the *Bullet* was 50 billion times better than the Swamp product, it was eclipsed by the others. The movie column, bristling with nicknames and epithets, traded in behind-the-scenes Hollywood tidbits. In stark contrast, the music critic, reviewing a piano recital, ruminated on phantom aural corrections in Debussy's chain of parallel fifths and octaves. It was a subject obscure and rarefied enough even for Dana Falkenberg. The theater man reported from a Shakespeare festival in Ohio, with kudos for the Bard's excellent script. And that was the day's entertainment budget—no, there on the back page was the TV column. The TV critic was, to judge from the pic, about Mrs. Gallagher's age, with the same bleached helmet of hair. "TV Day" was an omnibus piece: switches in time slots; a graf on ancient movie actors doing cameos on daytime TV, and briefs on celebrity golf and an old sitcom recycled from England.

Gallagher folded up the papers. After half a dozen coffees and the heartening read, she felt ready. Besides the tests, there were two meals to be eaten with Bullets, and innumerable hours of drinks. She shouldered her way past the throng of reporters—as chic as the business class—waiting for elevators. The older ones were mute and sour-looking; the younger, all pumped up for the day, filling the vaulted lobby with their feverish talk and glassy laughter. When the elevator landed, Gallagher's courage had run out.

The news staff poured out of the elevator on 7, where Gallagher—staying on alone—could see a cavernous room lined with a hundred desks. Just as the elevator doors were closing (the chamber was washed in perfumes, spicy and floral, from the cadre of female reporters, released in a rustle of silk), she spotted Luck, or Luck's back, in the $5,000 suit, parting a mob of reporters as he advanced. The doors closed and reopened onto a fresh scene: a warren of mint-green cubbies and the sudden clatter of adding machines and typewriters. Walking past the cubicles, Gallagher scanned pastel pantsuits, rumpled jackets, yellowed shirts, and loud ties familiar to any Wampanoager, along with the bald or permed heads, clip-on earrings, and pearl chokers. It was a heartening sight. Gallagher slipped into PERSONNEL, where a woman with eyeglasses on her face and a pair hanging around her neck ushered her into the sound-proofed test room. Two men were already there, bent over thick booklets, filling in ovals on answer sheets.

The personnel lady told Gallagher she was late, but it didn't matter; nobody ever finished the test, so just do as much as she could. Mr. Moon, the M.E., would pick her up at noon, and bring her back for the afternoon session. Gallagher took two pencils and the test booklet, and sat next to an older man, who was sighing, and across from the younger, who was beating his foot against the chairleg. No one had said how many tests, or how long. When Gallagher had mentioned them to McGuire (just the thought of his sweet name, so Wampanoag, brought a flush to Gallagher's cheeks), he laughed: "Don't be an ass. What do they care about tests? Can you write and can you take orders—that's what they want to know. I told them you can write."

McGuire mentioned one test he'd taken back in his reporting days. The job was in the bag, he said. All that was left was to meet the M.E. He knocked on the editor's door: no answer. Walked in:

empty. So he sat down, cooled his heels. 10 minutes, 15. All along, McGuire said, the editor was there, crouched under the desk. Part of the test was to find him, and then hunker down with him. McGuire flunked. He stayed seated. The editor kept saying, "Hey, Mister. Speak up. I can't hear you."

"Never," McGuire said, "sit taller than your editor. Remember that, Gallagher. It may sound obvious, but Depointe will see if you know it."

McGuire was wrong, though. The tests were real: IQ in the morning, then math and English; general knowledge in twelve areas, and some final test, not specified. Gallagher took up a pencil and looked toward the frosted window, then bent over page 1: analogies.

She finished the first part an hour early, and handed the booklet to the stunned personnel lady. After asking about the ladies' room, Gallagher wandered downstairs instead, pushing open the fire door to a scene of chaos, as deadline stalked the city room. Nothing in Wampanoag had prepared her for this. Gallagher had seen film clips of the NYSE the day before Christmas: it was on that scale—shouting, charging from desk to desk; the drilling of hundreds of electric typewriters, screams of phones; there was a PA system, too, and messages booming out.

This was the brain of the paper, a hive that Gallagher would rarely enter, because all the soft news was slowly digested and pushed out (or so the City desk thought) in the Sunday room, which shared a quiet floor with the test kitchen and the publisher's suite.

Gallagher tried to exit through the fire door, but it had locked shut. She snuck down a side aisle, where two reporters were reading a ribbon of tickertape, and a third was on the phone. She marched past a nest of writers tearing sheets out of their typewriters and racing—it was ten minutes to deadline—up to the barrier reef of A.C.E. desks. The editors were stacked by rank: four aces close to the reporters, two cities, and behind them—shielded from the hubbub in his own special cell—was Luck, now on the phone, with his feet up on his desk. The executive editor was bathed in a softer, brighter light from the rest, and shielded by thick glass that was soundproof, and (as Gallagher learned later that day) also shatter-, fire-, and even bullet-proof. Gallagher saw him stand and gaze over the sea of his frenzied workers. Before his crosshairs could reach the spy, Gallagher found the elevator, and was in it.

Later—when it was clear that her entry had been seen by many—Moon explained to Gallagher that no unauthorized person entered the newsroom, especially at deadline, and that the receptionist and Luck's private secretary could have tripped an alarm. There was an armed security force at the ready. Gallagher apologized for her mistake, but wondered why—with their extreme fear—they would leave the fire door unlocked. She didn't ask, though, because McGuire had proscribed remarks, ironies, observations, or anything else that might imply an independent eye at work. Such sharpness would never count in her favor. "Don't sit taller, and don't feel free to speak your mind. Never let them know what you're thinking." Gallagher absorbed this advice, but feared that this strange ordeal might make her forget herself.

She needed no help with lunch at the Motor Bar. First she and Mr. Moon had drinks, but since it was midday, Moon had only two (not counting wine). Gallagher, with more tests to go, had one. Drinks, she'd noticed, were a must for Bullets: they were so high-powered, so wound-up, that to sit and feed (and they fed only with each other) called for tranquilizing darts, and they took them straight up in a string of doubles or even triples. Moon, who was by nature stolid, had ordered a double Cutty.

The Motor Bar was a relic of better days, when the auto industry had tyrannized over the city, but also supplied it with a flood of cash, jobs, and brains. At one time all downtown restaurants—when not owned outright by the car-makers—were named after models, designers and manufacturers, steel and tire barons. The Motor Bar, lined with silver paper and smoked glass, was fitted out with black leather banquettes. The fabric, Moon explained, all remnants from the T-Bird interior, late '50s model. Moon was chatty, amiable, and so mild that Gallagher wondered if he himself might be a test, the "good" cop, into whose ears last night's unspilled beans might freely pour.

The M.E. touched on highlights of *Bullet* history, its recent spike of growth, its ages-old war with the *Depointe City Blade,* which, up to now, had always been first in everything: scoops, numbers, talent, cash, overseas bureaus, circulation, and ads. Now the *Bullet* was shaving the *Blade*'s edge. These were exciting times, especially so, the M.E. added, given the recession, and how hard—with the inflated price of newsprint and oil—it had hit the industry. Moon was a realist: the boom couldn't last forever; there was only so much growth in the region, and they were near the limit. "Things," the M.E. said glumly, "will get ugly then, and Rolf will go after the *Blade*. He's already cutting into their columnists, and he's raided Sports." Moon laid down his fork. "You're young, so you don't remember how things used to be. News was still a profession ten, even five years ago. Now I don't know what you'd call it." He picked up the fork and guided its tines into a pile of peas. "When I started out, this city alone had four dailies and a weekly tab. To beat the competition, we had to get out there and *hustle*. Now—." He put the fork down again. "There's nothing out there now. Rolf's kids don't know this yet, because Rolf has them all hopped up on something. The game is all him." Moon, his face pallid and slack, looked at Gallagher. "I shouldn't be telling you this," he said.

Moon then asked if she'd care for dessert. He flagged the waitress. "Does this interest you at all?"

Gallagher said it did, but Moon seemed doubtful. "It's slim pickins for kids like you. The joy of it is over. That's why things are so cutthroat. They weren't that cutthroat when I started out. Or I never would have wanted in."

Gallagher nodded.

"You look," Moon continued, "at our competition on any one day. Tell me if you see any difference between them and us. They're talking now about merger. I say: why not? What difference would it make?"

Gallagher was thinking about McGuire, and what *he* had said. The *Bullet* and the *Times* were on two different planets, but what Moon and McGuire had seen happening to the news biz was the same.

But there was no time to sink into that reflection because Moon was on to something else: the test scores. At first, Gallagher didn't follow. He couldn't mean (could he?) that the morning tests were already corrected, and—as he was now saying—the *Bullet* abuzz with the story about the candidate from Flatsville who scored a genius IQ. When did *this* happen? Gallagher asked—and was he hired? Mr. Moon smiled: "Wouldn't you be the one to know?" he said. Gallagher's face fell. The weekend was not even half over and the job was bagged.

The waitress spent some time arranging cups, saucers, and pots. Gallagher was surprised at how deflated she felt—had she been counting that much on this job? Moon was trying now, as soon as the waitress left (he had seen the look on the girl's young face), to change the subject. But first—just out of curiosity—he asked if she'd decided against the job, and—if he wasn't being too nosy—why had she? He added that he didn't know that it had been offered yet, but he wouldn't be sorry to hear that it was: they had never, to his knowledge, had a genuine egghead at the *Bullet*. It might be fun.

"You're saying," Gallagher said, as a new and wholly gratifying picture was forming, "they could offer it to *me?*"

"You have to take the other tests first, and they'll all want a crack at you." Moon looked at Gallagher. "If it was up to me, I'd take you," he said.

Gallagher's face bloomed with pleasure, but the lunch was soon over, and at 2 sharp she was back in the test chair. She finished early (the general knowledge/current events quiz was so obvious you'd have to be dead not to be up on it), and took the elevator to the luncheonette to drink the day's ninth or tenth cup—none as good as the Streamline. She felt her attitude toward Wampanoag shifting. How smart could they be at the *Bullet* if they needed these dumb tests—and so many! All Mr. O'Callahan needed was one obit.

Then back she went for the last five subjects. Raced through history and art; slowed down for music, slower for geography, and stopped short at sports. There were two sections—legendary and current. She put down the pencil at "SPORTS: Current." There was no point in going further. And all I'd have to have done, she thought, is crack open the sports page once in a blue moon. What would Ox say?

Feeling dizzy from no sleep, a drink at noon, and six hours of tests in the stuffy room, Gallagher wanted out. But it wasn't over yet: there was one last test. Although this test was untitled, it wasn't hard to guess what it was. Dire crises and nerve-wracking dilemmas were narrated in short paragraphs. You were asked to pick, among multiple choices, the likely outcome, then evaluate the outcome, identify with one of the characters; sometimes correct the situation, and finally report on any emotional reactions. It was a test of sanity.

Gallagher was fagged. She didn't buy any of the fake stories. They were just there for you to find your place on one or another nut scale. You were a certain percentile more ruthless than average, cruel, a bulldog; or, short-changed on ego, a moody wimp, crying towel, enslaved to others. There was no middle ground here; all the answers were loaded. Thoughtlessly, Gallagher veered toward a low Authoritarian. But even before she'd blacked in the last oval—the test lady hovering—she saw her error. A high A was probably hired on the spot; a low A thrown on the junk heap. The instrument was blunt, but it would insure the news engine was never weakened by anything too soft or thoughtful. Depressing, though, to rip through tests of intellect and memory only to crash on case histories. Cases had always been a problem for Gallagher. She liked cases: a case, with all its oddities, seemed more compelling than any point you could make about it. But in newspaper work, as she well knew, cases were fodder. You went out and found them to support a point your editor was after. Otherwise, you only needed a case to flavor a story, color it up, make it seem realer than real.

Both male candidates were absent from the afternoon tests. What did that mean? Gallagher was alone in the mint-green room and, after flunking the sanity test, she put her head down on the desk. When Personnel returned to claim answer sheet, pencils, and booklet, Gallagher told her to tell whoever was interested that she was going back to the hotel. Personnel shook her head: "They just called up here—Mr. Bluestem and Mr. Luck—and they want you right away. You don't have time to go back. They've got plans for you!"

Gallagher sank into the chair.

"Don't get comfortable. They're waiting." Gallagher didn't budge.

"I don't make the rules here, honey," Personnel said. "Go to the ladies, put on a little lipstick. You don't look too good."

Gallagher nodded, but still didn't move. Never in her life had she felt so whipped.

"I'll get you a drink," the lady said. "Pull yourself together, okay? They'll blame me!"

Gallagher took the cone of tepid water, then trudged to the elevator. The lady was behind her. "Don't forget your coat. Please take it."

The lady patted her. "You'll be fine, honeybun. You did a beautiful job. Nobody here's ever seen tests like yours!"

After Gallagher had slid down to 7 to meet Luck and Bluestem, but before they'd whisked her off to the press club, she'd heard the one about the "genius of Wampanoag": the chick who'd scored in the high 3s on IQ (better than any living Bullet), then went and funked the nut quiz. She was flat as a pancake when it came to personality.

Luck was the one to tell her.

"You're a mental case," he said, as she closed the glass door to his bulletproof cell, having bypassed the triple checkpoints of A.C.E.s, City, and the guard. Gallagher was still pulling the door-handle, forcing it, although the door shut only of its own vacuum-powered will, and slowly, so slowly that at least three rows of desks could easily hear, in the quiet of the day, how Luck had put it to the genius. There were, even then, office wags at work ("There once was a genius from Wampanoag") on the fresh material.

Gallagher released the door handle, then turned to face her inquisitor. In a black blazer and white linen shirt, a twice-shaved face and freshly clipped head, Luck stood out bright and sharp, as if he had been hammered out of gold. Behind him, on the oak shelves, was—beside the methuselah of champagne—a bank of phones and six clocks giving the time at global hot spots. On the left was a wall of TV screens and a circle of black leather chairs. Wire and tickertape machines were nested on the right. They were quiet—no, one of them was churning up a story, but silently, behind their own thick glass walls. Gallagher's shoes touched the fringe of a blood-red Turkish rug. She did not move. Peering over the polished terrain (black-metal desk set, black marble paperweight, silver pens and paperknife) of his table, Luck's eyes looked bored and tired. "Sit down, little woman. Take it easy. I've been up two nights straight and you look like you haven't slept this month. Want some joe? I also have," he said, opening a panel door and pulling out a bottle, "something better."

Luck poured out the something into two tumblers. Then he lay back in his bouncy chair, propped his loafers—so new even the soles were clean—on the desk.

Once settled for a cozy chat, he was silent. He rearranged his feet and sucked on the glass. Gallagher's stupor was now pierced by wires of nervousness—but where, she wondered, were they coming from? Riding the elevator, she had given the job up, then talked herself into the slump that came with the prospect of a life sentence in Wampanoag. Yet those wires kept stabbing at the exhausted matter of her brain.

"I'm waiting," said Luck.

"What are you waiting for?" Gallagher returned.

"What am I waiting for?" he repeated. "Well, normally I wouldn't waste four seconds on a reject."

Gallagher's heart and stomach were in free fall.

"So, why am I waiting?" he asked himself. "I'm waiting," he said, expansively, "because I want to. I'm beat and it sort of feels good. I'm curious to see—," he said, sweeping his feet off the shiny desk to stand. He was short, so Gallagher was able to command a full view without stretching her neck.

"Go on," she said.

"You think you're really something, don't you?" he snapped. He was pacing and stopped behind her chair.

Gallagher took her time. It was easy now. The new self, miraculously rested and blasé, was buoyed up from the deep where the low-A psyche—too human, so stupidly benign—had sunk. "I wish you'd light somewhere," this new self commanded. "I can't talk if you're buzzing me."

Luck laughed. He turned his back on Gallagher and faced his newsroom. "Is this better?"

"Sure," she said. "This is not for my amusement, so get what you can out of it."

Luck strolled back and lowered himself on his chair. "You'd kill for this job," he said quietly. "If you don't get it," he went on, "you're back in the Dark Ages. No one's going to take you seriously. It was a fluke you got this far."

"Why was it a fluke?"

"You don't want to know why," Luck said, bouncing back. "And why should I bother to tell you? You're hurt enough already."

Gallagher snorted.

"But I'll tell you," he said. "Because I like you. And you're a bright girl. God knows you're bright."

But instead of explaining how a Wampanoag had ended up in Depointe he just shook his head. He had one thing to say: although she was talented "in the raw," the *Bullet* no longer had room for amateurs. "Full-blown talents are banging down our doors," he said. "Even someone who's never heard of me wants to work for me." He smiled. "If I gave you the chance."

Someone was knocking on the glass door. Gallagher turned to see a wilted Bluestem. Luck waved him off. "But I'll tell you what the big problem is—and it's something that not even a little hellion like yourself can talk your way out of."

Luck turned to the wall of phones and picked up the simplest model. "Send Bluestem over to the club. Tell him to pull his socks up."

"He likes you," Luck said, when he hung up. "But that's *his* tough luck. He likes children. Anyway, to continue, what we need is staff with a proven track record. Fire-eaters! This city's a powder keg, in case you hadn't noticed. You might have it—who knows?—but that's not what the test says."

She listened, she took it. "Okay," she said, "I've just got one question."

"Shoot," Luck replied, lowering himself deeper into the chair.

"What I don't get is why a newsman needs a test to tell him who's got it and who doesn't. I thought you prided yourself on instinct." She took a breath, focusing. "So, are you lazy or just thick-witted? Whichever it is, it's nothing to brag about."

Luck smiled. "I like you," he said. "You've got that going for you."

"I don't think you do like me," Gallagher replied.

Luck sniffed. "Let me get my coat. We're going now and we won't be back. Strap on your armor, Wampanoag. I'm just starting to like this."

Luck pushed his arm through Gallagher's for the walk over. At the doors to the press club, he halted. "You think you're tough," he said, "but you listen to me." He tightened his grip on her wrist.

"No matter what you say or do now, you can't rewrite history. That test spelled it out. You're indecisive, soft, a thumbsucker." He opened the door of the club onto a repeat of last night's scene. "You don't cut it."

Gallagher walked in.

"Get the picture?" she heard, as a knuckly hand pressed into her back.

"Get it?"

CHAPTER 7

The weekend trip to Depointe came in the fall, and now it was the dead of winter, the second week of February. Mrs. Gallagher offered up her daily Mass for her daughter, who was still waiting to hear from that paper in the Midwest—although why Catherine would want to go out there and live alone, just to work on a bigger paper, Mrs. Gallagher couldn't fathom. It wasn't a matter, as the husband had pointed out, of more money. The Gallaghers had heard nothing but bad about Depointe, burnt down, on the skids, crime-infested: it wasn't called "Murder City," Mr. Gallagher said, for nothing. She'd have to rent a place, buy furniture, her mother added, and no one to cook dinner—and what was she going to do about Dan Juscik and that editor she liked?

Mother and daughter were walking to church together. Catherine kept her mother company on Thursdays: eight o'clock Mass, breakfast at Bell's, and a trip to the dime store or the A&P. By then, 11, 11:30, it was time for bed with McGuire, because it had become mostly bed (especially after the Depointe weekend) and fewer trips to the mill towns; bed and a lot of drinking. Everybody drank, Catherine noticed, except her parents, who took an occasional nip, yes, but no more. Was drinking, she wondered, what divided a world like the Gallaghers'—where people were content with little—from the *Bullet,* where they were content with nothing?

Gallagher had never been much of a boozer, but now could take three or four drinks in an afternoon. McGuire would bring a bottle to the motel room. It was a different scene: instead of the picnics and French wine, it was now a quick infusion of the "goldens," as they called them: the Turkeys, Granddads, the Jacks, Jims, and Johnnys.

Catherine was startled to hear her mother bringing up "the editor." How did she know about him? Catherine asked, as they strolled out of church. Mrs. Gallagher zipped her rosary beads into their case and pulled a tissue from her pocketbook. "He calls you every day, Cathy. Don't you think I *notice?*" The mother marched the length of the churchyard and down the steps to the sidewalk.

"Not only that," her mother continued. "I happen to know he's married."

"He *isn't.*"

"Your father told me."

Catherine stopped short. "How does *he* know?"

"See?" her mother crowed.

"He isn't married. He has a girlfriend, that's all."

"Oh, *that's* all," her mother said sarcastically.

They walked down the avenue, past the dress shop, bakery, cobbler's, and funeral parlors that Catherine had passed every day for nine years trudging to and from school.

"Do you still want to go out for breakfast?" her mother asked.

"I admit he has a girlfriend," Catherine said. "But that's all."

Once settled in a shabby booth at Bell's, and after Eddie Bell, who went to first grade with Catherine, had taken their orders and slapped their table with a filthy rag, Mrs. Gallagher said, "I'm worried about you. Is that so bad?"

Catherine stirred the coffee Eddie had brought. He returned with the metal basket of condiments, and laid two bent and spotty forks on the oilcloth.

Mrs. Gallagher waited. "How can we let you go to that awful Depointe when you look like a scarecrow? Your clothes are falling off you! I know you're drinking with that guy. And God knows what else—I don't even want to think about it!" She tried to catch her daughter's eye, but Catherine's gaze was fixed on Dukie, Eddie's brother, flipping eggs on the grill.

"Well, don't think about it then," Catherine said.

"I *thought* about it," her mother said, "and this is what I thought: You can do a lot better."

The plates of twin eggs and hash browns, and the side order of bacon, were brought to the table, along with two saucers of pale toast. Eddie pulled a dozen containers of butter and jam out of his pocket and tossed them on the table.

"How?" asked Catherine.

"You know what I mean," said the mother darkly.

"No, I don't, exactly. Tell me."

"Well, you don't have to see married men. Why can't you ever find a *single* man, someone who can take you out in public? I don't like the sneaking around. Do you?"

Catherine buttered a slice of toast and laid it down.

"Eat it!" her mother insisted.

Catherine picked up the slice, limp and cold.

"If you don't eat, you're going to die. Ever think of that?"

An hour after the breakfast, spoiled by the usual wrangle over food—how little Catherine ate, what that meant, and what it could turn into ("Don't treat me like a child!" "Well, grow up then!")—the *Bullet* called. Bluestem. Just then—Catherine was dressed, with her raincoat over her arm—McGuire pulled up by the back door (it was the closest he'd ever come to the Gallaghers', although he still didn't cross the threshold).

Mrs. Gallagher spotted the car and ran to the telephone, scribbling a note ("He's out there!").

Catherine ignored it. Bluestem was inviting her to come out to Depointe for a two-week try-out. The mother dragged a chair next to the phone and pushed her daughter into it. "We hadn't forgotten you," Bluestem was saying. "Rolf was away. Up to yesterday, he was still deciding. I told him we should get you out here, see what you can do.

"Are you there?" Bluestem said. "Hello?"

He went on. "So it's partly my doing, although Rolf makes his own decisions. Everyone liked you," he said solemnly, still waiting for a response. "Wampanoag, you should know that I personally went out of my way to make this happen. Based on what we had, you wouldn't have gotten the job, period."

Catherine looked at her mother, waiting.

"I miss you," Bluestem said, shifting ground. "I've been thinking about you ever since you left. You were *my* first choice."

Cooling his heels now ten minutes, McGuire tapped his horn, an MG horn, tuneful, but you could still feel the impatience.

"Can I call back?" Catherine said finally.

"Why are you pulling this?" Bluestem demanded.

"I'll call you tomorrow, okay?"

"No later! And promise you'll say yes." He paused. "We all want this to work out, Gallagher. You owe it to yourself." He paused, and in a different tone said, "You owe it to *me*."

Rushing to the motel, cruising 20, sometimes 25 miles over the speed limit, and jabbering non-stop, with a giant beer wedged between his legs, McGuire offered Gallagher a swig, and she gulped it down. It was a Canadian beer in a quart can and now it was empty. "I love you," McGuire was saying, "I crave you, I love your legs and your hair, I love your virgin's body, I love your voluptuous mind, your sick laugh, I love you in the sack, I love you drunk, I love you stone-sober working at your double desk across from Miss Two-wheels.

"Hey," he shouted. "How *is* old Two-wheels? Does she miss me? One of these days I'll give her a ring.

"I noticed you didn't ask about my new forge. Just for that, I'll tell you." And he went on to name make, year, the geezer who'd sold it, the equipment needed to haul it from Shrewsbury and place it in the barn; how fuck-friggin'-*fab*ulous it was, how much he loved to feed it, stoke it, to hammer in the red eye of its fiery oven. Did she know how much it weighed? No, not that much. Think, think how much—dense, solid *iron*. He had a new supplier of pig and scrap, too. And she should see the nails and tools he'd already crafted. Did she want to see it sometime?

"Hey, Gallagher," he barked, "still alive? You should get a little more shut-eye." He grabbed the quart can out of her hands. "Whoa," he said, shaking it, "you sucked up *this* baby!"

Parked in the motel's empty lot, McGuire didn't, as usual, jump right out. "Feeling punk, huh?" he asked. "You're not on the rag, are you?"

Without waiting, and before her face could crumple into the mash of misery that few had noticed—certainly not McGuire—but that had been her everyday face since (after returning that Sunday from Depointe, fagged, baffled, but full of a wild hope) the hope had been pounded into nothing by the months of waiting, McGuire turned the key in the engine and barreled out of the parking lot. "Let's blow this joint!" he yelled. "Let's go to Boston! No, Gallagher doll," he wailed, "let's hit the Apple for a couple of days!"

Before a word of protest could pierce the air, McGuire's lead foot had wheeled the small car onto the rustic roads of North Wampanoag and was racing south to the interstate.

"Stop!" she yelled into the wind, but seeing the tense grin, McGuire was unfazed, until Gallagher let her face sag into the miserable mash, showed him, and, eying it, he exited, circled round the interstate and re-entered, heading north. "Whatever!" he yelled. "Whatever the hell you *want,* Gallagher! Just tell me!"

Half an hour later, the sky-blue car roared into the south end of the city, coughing and shimmying as it slowed to 60. Thus began a full day, like the first one, of amusements, pleasures, delicious treats, oysters and white wine in a penthouse saloon with a view of Boston harbor, lunch at the Ritz with a quartet of waiters; strolls along the alphabetic streets of Back Bay where an exalted McGuire piped of his love and his freedom, his love of freedom and his love of love, his perfect joy and unquenchable passion. They roamed the Public Garden; they ate fudge at Bailey's, they walked to the MFA for a look at the Copleys and the Sargents. They ate chowder and fried clams; peanuts, candy apples, chestnuts, and only the day's increasing chill sent them rocketing south to Haymarket, where they shared a hot grog and warmed up for the drafty ride home.

Sitting on a wooden bench angular as a pew, Gallagher said that never before ("I know what you're going to say," McGuire interrupted, "but go ahead anyway") had she had so much fun, or eaten like such a pig. She was laughing, he wasn't. Solemn, stiff even, he murmured, "It's yours, girlie, for the asking."

Gallagher stared at the blacksmith. He was already looking the part: thick in chest and shoulders, rosy and coarse in the face, but those icepick eyes still sharp.

"What are you saying?"

"I'm not saying, I'm asking. Maybe I'm begging, I don't know yet."

"This is the best day," Gallagher said, "I've ever had. And you're—."

"Say it."

He waited, but she didn't say more.

Then: "I can see right through you!" he said in the driest tone. His face had knotted into the snarl familiar from Swamp days.

"And thanks, by the way, for the patronizing. You really know how to dig in the knife. You always did."

The mood of the day had thus soured. An offer, to be made, was blocked: she had heard it, she knew what it entailed, but all that day's sweetness could not charm the *Bullet* from her retentive skull, a skull so crafted by McGuire that it was an ideal medium for a bullet—and the charge that went with it.

There had been little discussion of the *Bullet,* no news about the two-week trial had reached McGuire: Gallagher hadn't had the time, or the heart, to tell him.

The blacksmith had long grown sick of the subject. After the initial phone calls, he lumped the Bullets with "journalists," that club of creeps who needed master's degrees to wipe their noses. But when Gallagher returned, with stories from the test weekend, McGuire really blew his stack. He could see right through those thugs; they were egomaniacs, cheap-ass peddlers, *ad men.* Gallagher had gotten no farther than an account of the first night when McGuire stopped her. He would hear no more. To think that a gangster like Luck, and the sheep who answered to him, were out to wreck a fine old newspaper like the *Bullet*—it was enough to make you weep.

That day Gallagher and McGuire had been sitting at the Streamline. They often stopped for a coffee after polishing off a bottle in the Tiptop Inn in Attleboro or the Pines in Woonsocket. Gallagher was waiting for McGuire to rally after the upsetting story.

"Never mind me," he said. "If you want to be a player in this game, you'll have to roll with it. Don't think I'm going to talk you out of it. I just want you to know what you're up against. There won't be a thing I can do," he said grimly, "to help you."

"But," he added, sounding more like himself, "when they run your scurvy ass out of town," winking, "remember your home in the Swamp."

"Don't do it, though," he warned, a minute later. "Don't come back, Gallagher. Look at me," he said, taking her chin in his hands. "Learn from my mistakes. I don't give a rat's ass about this trade," he said. "I'm happy to be where I am. But you remind me of myself ten, fifteen years ago. A tank division couldn't have stopped me. Don't come back, Gallagher. For your own sake, stick it out."

All this was ages ago. McGuire forgot he'd said it, and also forgot how much depended (or maybe he never knew) on the job in Depointe. In the weeks of waiting for the verdict, McGuire had been distracted. He'd furnished his barn with the new forge, a couple of anvils, heaps of cordwood and iron; then he built an adjoining shop to work the nonrusting metals. He loved all metal, but only the corruptible was truly noble. He had also worked on Aerial, encouraging her to pack her bags (she was doing her best, with the help of a couple of boyfriends, to find a livable place). Meanwhile, enough freelance editing had been scared up to finance the apprenticeship, but in the future McGuire saw nothing but forging. As life had simplified, the bright idea of replacing Aerial with Gallagher had taken hold.

In this interval, Gallagher sensed that the subject of Depointe was irksome, even painful to McGuire, so she rarely mentioned it. But McGuire, whose antennae forever bobbed and pulsed, hadn't *really* forgotten; he needed but a sign to see that Depointe came first, and life on the blacksmithing farm a distant second, if any place at all.

The fishhouse meal lay sodden on the plates, heaps of opened clams puddled in their saltwater. "So," McGuire asked, pushing his plate aside, "what's up?" and Gallagher told him the latest. When she finished, McGuire had lit a cigarette and was studying the crowd hunched around the oyster bar.

"Can we still see each other?" Gallagher asked.

McGuire didn't answer. He paid the check. It was while scooting out of the booth that, in his harshest voice, he said, "I'll stick by *you,* Gallagher." Halting at the bar, where oysters were shucked by men in rubber gloves, he grabbed her by the arm. The shuckers and customers turned to look. "Why the fuck wouldn't I?" McGuire said bitterly. "The question is, whether it'll be worth your while to stick with *me!*"

During the try-out, Gallagher published fifteen stories: three think pieces, seven reviews, and five shorts. She put up in a dreary hotel a few blocks from the *Bullet,* and fell asleep at night to the sound of a woodshedding trombonist. "Mood Indigo" she recognized, and "Goodbye Porkpie Hat," as the jazzman modulated to fold a dozen familiar melodies into a continuous ribbon of sound. The view from the window was of a back street, whose huddled buildings were rinsed in moonlight, and backlit by the reflected glare of downtown towers. The chain of hollow blue notes lent the scene a chilly glamour.

It was a romantic place, Depointe, however grimy and decayed. The stagelit backstreet spoke of that hopeful time after the war when a generation came home and moved into these crowded streets: steam heat, el trains, and a sea of hats careering homeward at sundown. Neon signs, faded orange, flame blue, flared over the doorways of a bar, drugstore, Chinese laundry, although above street level the windows were dark. Rising over a weedy lot on a brick and cement wall was an ad for Gilda's Golden Ale, rubbed to dust.

Depointe had struck it rich in the early '40s when the Allies had ordered tanks, jeeps, and trucks by the thousands. Even before the soldiers came home, the plants had converted back to cars. The demand was heavy, and swelled into the 1950s, when families, with regular paychecks and bonuses, left their walk-up flats for Monopoly houses on newly cleared tracts. Yet still more humanity (from the grain belts and abroad) flooded in, and the central city was flush until the '60s, when the riots drove out everyone with the money to go.

When Depointe was just beginning its rise, Wampanoag had long fallen. The city's eighteenth-century shell (stone churches and mills, clapboard houses) had been razed, and nothing so solid or stately built to replace it. Wampanoag missed the Jazz Age. Its fate was to be rebuilt in the 1950s and '60s, when the burst of indigenous style—the rugged retail monuments that had ennobled downtown Chicago, Depointe, and Manhattan—was long over. Where Depointe read like a page from the '40s, Wampanoag was a jumble: whole blocks of reinforced concrete—outdoor malls and parking garages, department stores built like prisons—with here and there a fragile hull from the early textile days. These mills, rat-infested but weirdly impervious to vandals, kept their honor: three or four stories high, with each stage clearly marked and pristine in its ornament; rows of delicately paned, arched windows, Gothic cornices, the occasional clocktower or lantern.

In America, nothing lasted very long, so Gallagher wondered when Depointe would expunge all traces of *its* brief Golden Age.

Already there were plans for a riverfront development—the new downtown—a spawn of glass and steel towers. The race was on, one of the older reporters told Gallagher, to see which would come first: the bust or the towers.

There weren't many geezers left on the *Bullet*—that was one of many differences between its modern plant and the rattletrap *Times,* churning out the same old line on the same old subjects, staffed by loyal sons, who'd grown up, as had their grandfathers, puzzling out the world with the help of their trusty paper of record.

Gallagher was assigned, with the few old-timers, to the Sunday room. In Sunday—two newsrooms joined by a broken wall—there were no real deadlines. If not a single story was filed—no celebrity interview or TV column, no squib on a dinner theater or rock concert, no write-up of a children's show, no record, film, or book review—the copy desk, ranged under the broken wall, was happy to fill the entire hole with wire; they had a ton of it, all usable. The *Bullet* was supplied by every news service in the country—and by French, German, and British wires in the city room. A hundred papers could be filled every day with the bright, terse reports that chattered over the machines, clumped in their cages all over the paper—including the seventh-floor glass cage where Luck handpicked the day's top stories.

If, however, the Sunday editors, seated around their horseshoe desk, dared fill even the chinks with "canned," Luck would fly down on his broomstick (as someone put it) spitting nails. Rolf Luck switched, demoted, and fired editors as often as possible, to keep the low dogs hungry and the top dogs anxious. Thus any Sunday copy chief fond of his job had to pull reams of copy from the arty (but retentive) souls who had flocked to Sunday, precisely because *there,* they thought, the heat was off.

In his first year, the new E.E. had purged the city room. First, he cleared deadwood (half the staff—most, aged 50 and over—were pensioned off or fired), and put the remainder on notice: file a story a day—producing enough copy to fill three papers with just city news—or walk. Then Luck would take his pick from among his favorites; how much play their work got depended on assignment and on an ever-changing estimate of their worth.

Taking the cue from Luck, each embattled editor lashed his staff for more copy than even the best could honestly produce, then shamelessly played favorites—or girlfriends. ("It's a kennel in there," an older dog had been heard to say.) Everyone felt the backdrafts of envy and hatred, the flare of hellish lusts. The human field was so hectic and conflicted that you couldn't always tell a red-hot coupling from a vendetta. One thing was clear—all passion was wired into Luck's seventh-floor brain center. In turn, the E.E.'s signals—public humiliations, sudden demotions, pay slashes, forced retirements, automatic and absolute blackballings from the press world west of the Atlantic and east of the Rockies—jolted every nervous system.

As a raw recruit on a derided section, Gallagher counted for nothing, yet even she could feel the blast from the seventh floor. In her quarter, people were edgy and volatile: deep gloom one minute, exultation the next, as their stock (in Luck's eyes) kept rising and soon crashed. Gallagher spotted this pattern the first night, but it took a few days to grasp the system, because no one seemed to be noticing—or, if they did notice, they weren't saying.

Arriving at the *Bullet* that first day, Gallagher found her place by the window, where two masses of flowers—red roses and an even bigger, mixed bunch—were arranged in vases. Bluestem pushed the flowers aside and dropped on her desk a stack of index cards, with ideas—often in the form of a question—for feature stories, four or five of which she was free to work up. She was also, in the course of the try-out, to review several movies, a play, and cover at least five shows. When he met her that morning at Lamont House, Bluestem explained that she would write the main story for Sunday's pages, but was also expected to cover anything the regular critics—movie, theater, music (popular and classical)—couldn't make. "You're the pinch," Bluestem said, "but you're all mine for Sunday." He nuzzled her neck at the *Bullet* revolving door, in clear sight of a clump of city room gladiators. The news went out that instant that Ralph Bluestem had bagged the new one, some drip from Long Island.

At lunch Bluestem passed on the tidbit. "People think I plucked you for private use." Gallagher laughed, but the editor wasn't even smiling. After a sip of his whiskey sour (Luck had ridiculed this partiality for "faggotty" drinks), Bluestem said, "I know you must feel attracted to me." He paused, sipped. "You wouldn't have been so eager to come if you didn't."

Gallagher was preoccupied with story ideas, and anxious too, about the dozen movies and shows she had to cover (and how to get there, since she didn't know where anything was). There was a movie that night in a mall cinema twenty miles out of town. The film critic, who hadn't so much as looked her way, had shed the assignment through Bluestem.

Having a critic-at-large was Luck's idea, but the first-string critics didn't much care for it, so don't expect them, Bluestem said, to be helpful—and be wary if they tried to be. "The last thing they want is an eager beaver breathing down their necks," Bluestem said, "even if it's just you. At first, they'll stiff you. You'll be lucky to get the runoff."

Tonight's film in the far-flung suburb was a bio of Moses, B-picture, shot "on location" in the San Fernando Valley, and on an old backlot built for a more famous Bible flick. The theater critic, relieved that the "intern" had been assigned a movie, told Gallagher to beware the freeways; the juvenile gangs that had terrorized the city in past months liked to ambush motorists in underpasses and ramps, beat them senseless, or just shoot them. In the last flooding rain, several freeway victims had been hospitalized, one dead.

For all his wiles and warnings, Bluestem wasn't able to hold the attention of his try-out reporter, so he ordered a second drink and lobbed a few questions: Married? Engaged? If not, who'd sent the flowers? Family?

"What flowers?" Gallagher nearly said, but then recalled the lavish bouquets shading the desk where she'd arranged the story ideas. And with them came the image of Juscik and McGuire—the likely donors—now roped together like a couple of farmhands, caught forever in some silent-movie still.

To dodge the tide of homesickness, Gallagher took a manly swig of bourbon.

"You don't have to tell me," Bluestem offered.

But it was too late, for McGuire and Juscik, now put into play, were primed to pry into everything that didn't concern them. For the rest of that day Gallagher was haunted by their takes (like scenes from *Modern Times*) of the hellish Bullet machine, its automated workers, brutal foremen, and head maniac.

That night Gallagher barreled out to Northfield via the Methanol Freeway, sat through two showings of *Aaron, My Brother,* picked up a sandwich in the mall, and gunned back to the Lamont. There she drafted the 250-word review and, after four frenzied rewrites, was in bed at 3, awake and so wired that her body seemed to arch above the scratchy hotel sheets.

Up at 6 and out by 6:45, she bought a coffee-to-go and raced up the stairs to type the piece in the shadowy Sunday room, cavernous and still. Then she dropped original and carbons in Bluestem's empty basket. It was a funny review—at least it seemed funny—and though no one had said, "Make fun of this if it stinks," it seemed the right thing to do.

At 8:30 sharp, the lights bubbled up and the three copy chiefs marched into the room. At the horseshoe desk, they gathered the heap of wire that had chattered in overnight, and edited away in the hope that the day's ton of in-house copy would fail to materialize. One of them nodded to Gallagher, now shivering with cold and fatigue. It was then she caught, out of the corner of her eye, an envelope ranged among the thorny stems, and realized that she didn't *know* who'd sent the flowers. In her still-dusky niche, she opened the envelope with trembling hands: empty. This one went with the roses, still tight buds, and she placed the envelope against the green vase. Then she found and opened the second one—same message, but on a blank card—and laughed. The theater critic happened to be passing by.

"I'm glad to see you've found something funny here," he said, holding out a hand to Gallagher. "Lawrence K. Langton," grasping hers. "Just don't let them see it."

Langton's desk was behind Gallagher's. She swiveled around. The theater critic was tall, a thatch of graying blonde hair on a big, handsome head. He wore a tweed suit with a belt around the waist. Lawrence ("Call me Larry") slipped the jacket on a cedar hanger, explaining, as he went along, why cedar and from what county in Ireland his suits had been shipped—last summer, by the way, he was critic-in-residence at the Abbey. His desktop was cleared and gleaming. On the dustless surface was a cup and saucer of thinnest china, patterned with tiny shamrocks. The matching teapot was on a tray with more cups, creamer, and sugar bowl. Larry had taken up a silver watering can and was drizzling his flowers: paper-white narcissus, he told Gallagher, and pots of pink and white cyclamen, a violet, and Delft bowl of shamrocks. This profusion was arrayed behind Gallagher all the day before, and the handsome theater critic, too, seated among his utensils; he had even taken the time to inform her about freeway perils, but Gallagher had missed the whole cozy set-up. Had she been that distracted? "I didn't get any sleep last night," she confessed to this friendly face, so poised. "Really?" he replied. "I never sleep."

Gallagher would have liked to hear more (up close the face was deeply grooved, its eyes hollowed-out in their sockets), but the stroke of 9 had brought in movie, book, and TV critics, music briskly following, and then Bluestem's rubbery tread. There was little talk as the critics manned their stations, spread out as far from each other as possible. Larry had boiled some water, and was now arranging glossies of stage stars on his desk. He had stopped over in New York just last week, he said, and was preparing the season's "praeludium" on new plays.

Gallagher swiveled back. A glance showed Bluestem hanging his jacket on a wall peg, then picking up the review in his basket. He left the cubicle, returning with a steaming cup of coffee. He got up again to sharpen a fistful of pencils. Gallagher's eyes had nearly closed with weariness when she saw, peripherally, a small, dark figure stealing up close. The figure was already chattering when it reached the try-out's desk, but what—for it was the movie reviewer, dressed in black, whose razored hair came to a point on her forehead—was she talking about? Gallagher turned to look at the pale face with black-ringed eyes. Bluestem had introduced them, but the movie critic, Devra Kazin, had turned from her work for only a second, and Gallagher had caught just the sharp-edged profile, wreathed in blue smoke.

It wasn't until Devra had pivoted and clicked back to her own desk, hidden by bookcases, that Gallagher got it. In the torrent of speech was an invitation. ("Maybe you'd like to come, maybe you don't have time. Maybe you'd prefer to keep to yourself this week. I don't know. I know that asshole [Did she say that?] has given you enough for a year, and he expects you to file it in two weeks. Fine. Just tell him to fuck off. That's what I'd say. I'm not telling you what to do. That's your business. If you're free, fine. And if you feel like it. If you have the energy. I'll pick you up. I know where they put you. It's where they put everyone. It'll be an early dinner. Nothing fancy. Seven o'clock. No? Yes. Yes? Let me know. Only my husband and children. Quarter of seven, right. Ciao!")

Gallagher, pleased at the unexpected welcome, picked up her index cards and shuffled. She dealt out the cards in the space between the two vases (a few of the roses had unfurled into dense, velvety cups) and picked one. She carried the card to the ladies' room and sat on a dusty lounge chair. Some famous songs, the card read, were written by plain folks, who never again in their lifetime had another brainstorm. Who? What songs? How? Where do they think the creative itch went? Be kind and *be simple,* Bluestem had scribbled at the bottom. That meant: Go light on the sarcasm. Both he and Luck had detected sarcasm in the coffee article. It could be, Luck said at the time, funny, but too abrasive for a readership of over a quarter-million. After skimming six or seven *Bullets,* Gallagher could see that the quarter-million liked a joke, but they liked it soft: a pun, soft satire, but no slice, no stab. There was a tone (light but not flippant, ironic but not slighting) to please the quarter-million, "the people," as Bluestem called them—as in "Talk to the people, Gallagher!"—and it was up to her to figure it out. "We can't just slice and dice," Bluestem had warned en route to the office, "like you guys in Wampanoag."

Wondering whether—and how—to sweeten what O'Callahan liked to call her "pickling" style, Gallagher nodded off, until the movie critic burst through the door: "Caa," she said in speed talk, "Stem's look—." But when Gallagher followed her back to his cubicle, no Bluestem. She found on her own desk, instead, a sealed note, taped to the carbon of the Moses review. "Bull's-eye! I love you," it said. "B."

Gallagher studied the carbon: a few epithets had been cut. (Movies were sensitive terrain, apparently, no matter how cheesy.) The lead was modified from a two-clause sentence joined by a "but" to two sentences. Nonetheless, Gallagher's name had been printed on the review, and underneath: "*Bullet* Special Writer." Gallagher burned with pride. She set aside the glorious page-and-a-half. The review would run tomorrow in the back pages, and then all here would know.

Gallagher went to the morgue to scan the ASCAP and BMI volumes, and spent a few hours hunting down big hits by nobodies. When she returned to show Bluestem the gems she had mined, no one was there: the Sunday room had emptied out for lunch.

After a lonely walk downtown, lunchers flocking into heavily draped restaurants and windowless bars, the *Bullet* hopeful spent the afternoon making calls to one-shot lyricists in Fort Wayne, St. Petersburg, Redlands, and Tempe.

. . . It was back in the '50s. Just your average housewife coming home from the grocery store. Her eye caught by a headline: "Frank and Ava: Splitsville." Drops her bags on the kitchen table. Collapses into a chair. Poor Frank. Weeps. Then pulls herself together, one thought comes back: "I want to be around," sniffs, "to pick up the pieces. . . ."

"And isn't that," chirped that same housewife, twenty years later, to the Depointe reporter, "just what poor Frankie was thinking when the two-timer dumped him? He was nuts about her. 'I want to be around to pick up the pieces,'" she repeated, singing it this time, "'when somebody breaks your heart.' Honey," the woman went on, "my heart *bled*."

The reporter was scribbling it all down.

"Are you going to print this? Hello?" she said.

"You sat down," the reporter said. "And you wrote the whole song?"

"I poured it out."

"How?"

"With paper and pencil." She paused. "Ever hear of Johnny Mercer?"

A thrill went up Gallagher's spine. She could picture the graf, with *this* in it.

"I scribbled it on the back of a shopping list," the lady went on. "I didn't have any paper handy."

"And then?" asked Gallagher.

"I sent it."

"To?" Gallagher thought to ask.

"I just wrote 'Johnny Mercer. Hollywood, California.' I didn't know his address, and I had to get it out of my system."

"And it got there!" Gallagher shrilled.

"They wrote back to ask if he could use it."

Gallagher was taking it down word for word.

"'I want to be around,'" the lady sang into the telephone line, "'to pick up the pieces,'" and Gallagher joined in: "'when somebody breaks your heart.'"

"Thanks," said the reporter, listening again while the story was retold, with a few extras thrown in: name of the grocery store; the call placed to the husband at LeTop Ford, not being able to find an envelope, crying like a baby that whole day long. "I still feel bad," the lady said. "But that's life, isn't it?"

Gallagher had the gist of it and hung up. Then she called two other parties still collecting royalties on a hit single: a local man, former boxing ref, who'd written a teary ballad for Billie Holliday, and the sisters who'd had the bright idea to pen a birthday song—they had the tune, but it "took ages" to get the lyric just right.

The story was shaping up like a dream, and tomorrow a bylined review would run in the morning edition for the eyes of the quarter-million. No one who could read would be caught dead buying a ticket for *Aaron, My Brother.* The movie laid an egg in Depointe, ditto for everywhere south of the Canadian border.

"Good night, Miss Gallagher," sang Larry Langton as he swept past Gallagher's desk, followed by the TV critic, who waved, and the book critic, who didn't; after an interval, even the movie critic, in her spidery dress, sprang from place and fled the room. Seeing that the day had turned dusky, and the barn-like Sunday room was still, Gallagher stacked her notes and drafts. She was going to collect both bouquets to take home, and was just pulling out the roses when, in a rush of hot breath, Bluestem surfaced.

"Put 'em back," he said.

The flowers were out of the vase and dripping onto the wood of the desktop, the thorns biting into her hand. "Put 'em back!" said Bluestem, moving closer. Gallagher, whose long night and day of work had muddled her, froze in place. Bluestem reached to snatch the wet bouquet, but she whipped it away.

"Put them down!" he said, louder. "Why are you so stubborn?" Then he dropped the coat he'd been holding and snatched the flowers, shoving them back into the vase. It took several tries, but at last he managed to poke all the stems in. Gallagher stared; her hand was stinging from scratches. Her arm was still bent at the elbow. She dropped it, careful not to get blood on her skirt. "Are you out of your mind?" she said.

"I could say the same thing about you," he returned. "Why wouldn't you put those bloody things *down* when I told you to? Is there something wrong with your hearing?"

Gallagher retracted the wounded hand that Bluestem tried to grab, hiding it behind her back. "They're *mine*."

Bluestem stepped back. He was shaking his head, now grinning. "Oh, you!" he said. "Wait'll I tell Rolf. He said you were missing a few screws, but he had no idea!"

Bluestem held Gallagher's coat. She reluctantly dug her arm with the closed fist through the sleeve. From the back Bluestem wrapped his arms around her. "I *loved* your review. I laughed. You're *my* kind of writer, Wampanoag," he said, turning her around and putting his face near her face. "I like you," brushing her mouth with whiskery lips reeking of cigarette smoke, "screwy or not."

Leaving the Sunday room, Bluestem said, "Now do you see why I wanted you to put the flowers down?"

Gallagher didn't answer.

"I'm not taking you back. We're going out. Can you see now, you stubborn Wampanoag you, why I didn't want you lugging the flowers?"

Gallagher was tired, she was going home and was ready to tell him this, when she considered the likely effect of a rejection. "I'll have a drink with you," she offered, "if you want."

"You'll have a drink and then we'll have dinner," he said. "You need it. You're dead alive. I also," he said, lowering his voice, "need to knock heads with you."

He waited, though, until they were in the Hobbit to say more. Gallagher was stiff with dread. "You've got guts, Gallagher!" he crowed. "That's just what we thought you didn't have. I was right. Instincts. Hey," he said, "lighten up," kissing her cheek: "We're going to celebrate!"

The review of *Aaron, My Brother* was budgeted for Tuesday's paper, and the one-shot songwriters was Sunday's feature. On Wednesday, Gallagher went to a tedious play about seals evolving into humans, and, on Thursday, to the opening of Ice Caprice. Thursday afternoon she spent a few hours researching styles and themes of old ice shows. She'd never been to an ice show, she told Bluestem, although she'd skated as a kid, in the Ice Age. He laughed—she could always make him laugh—and listened to an account of the old days in Wampanoag with their arctic winters; now, she said, winters were like Miami. Why? he wanted to know, and Gallagher—anxious to get going—told him she'd explain it in the article.

"You're going to work the Ice Age into your story!"

Before leaving that night, the Lamont switchboard relayed a long-distance call. It was McGuire, lonely, anxious, and curious, too. Gallagher said she couldn't talk; she was going to the ice arena. And *not* for hockey, she added.

When he heard the rest of it, McGuire groaned. It was outrageous, he said, gross stupidity to waste a real writer on stuff an ape could cover. "That dump of a city is falling apart at the seams, but they've got the gall to send *you* to an ice show!" This confirmed his impression of Depointe. Fuck 'em, he said, and come home.

Gallagher smiled at the idea, hung up, and shot through the Lamont corridors, thick with smoke and the residue of boiled dinners. What McGuire refused to see (and why?) was that, on an entertainment beat, Ice Caprice—and everything popular and lowbrow—was all hers! The *Bullet* editors had been quick to detect, from the tests and interviews, the underside (arty, egghead, hoity-toity) of the genius of Wampanoag. They weren't hiring her, as Luck said, for her brains *or* her ideas. They had no slots (like Larry Langton's, or classical music's Peter Rappaport) on the culture beat. They were grooming her, the foreign-film buff from Kings, to write to every sector of the quarter-million about things it knew and loved: like Neil Diamond, for instance, but also Wayne Newton; *Chorus Line* and dinner theater; Top 40 and Ry Cooder, Shaft, Sly, the Duke, the Chairman, and the Galloping Gourmet; Gore Vidal and Vidal Sassoon. That first weekend, Luck had dropped the names of a few Vegas headliners just to see how they'd strike the snooty Wampanoag. In the girl's favor, she was up to speed. Thanks to Juscik, she'd seen a couple of blockbuster movies, the Mathis concert and Steve Martin, and could stretch it.

Her job now was to spin this fluff, and flavor it just right. That this job might take skill and even art was something that McGuire—ever the purist—failed to see. Coming up the ranks in the old days, McGuire had covered only hard news: explosions, robberies, riots, and killings; or the bloodless battles of law, politics, and state. Ultra-hard was still best. You started out chasing fires, and ended up covering wars. And yet, she thought, exiting the Lamont's gloomy lobby, the "naked city" beat had never exactly been offered to her—not even by McGuire himself.

Readers lapped up these gritty stories—this was the stuff they needed and wanted to know about the shadowy, perilous world around them. But did they really think that reading gave them any control over this world? What, she'd asked McGuire one time, was the point of reportage, what did it do—besides supply a few thrills? McGuire's reaction was swift: he leapt out of bed like a spring. "Get up!" he barked, scooping his clothes off the floor. "I'm taking you home. I'd like to throw your scurvy ass out the window, but we're not up high enough. Are you just playing dumb, or are you as cynical as you sound? I should have nailed you, Gallagher, when I had the chance."

Stark naked, McGuire glared down on the bed. "You don't have the integrity to write for a newspaper, Gallagher. Your kind never does."

He was dressed and halfway to the door. He seemed to have something more to say. What was it? A few minutes later, without a word, he stripped and crawled back into bed. He lay on his back with arms folded over his eyes. Gallagher could see the pain her tactless remark had caused. Still, he'd missed the point. McGuire, who had the guts to take almost everything else at true value, was soft on newspapers. He'd left the profession "for good," but he was still in deep.

So she continued, without McGuire's help, to think about it. The hometown papers, lousy though they were, offered the man-on-the-street news about himself: his weddings and funerals, for instance, his 50-years-wed; minutes from his clubs, unions, troops, societies, circles, auxiliaries, and legions—no meeting too small or trivial to merit a write-up. This kind of coverage flattered and comforted in a world where the local counted for nothing. In place of this friendly attention, the great papers—the *Times,* the *Post,* the *Tribune,* the *Bullet,* even the sleazy *Daily News*—printed the press releases generated by big government and industry, political parties and unions. Occasionally these papers looked under the surface, dispatching their professional hounds to sniff out, kick up, and test the muck. In McGuire's case, it worked like a charm: a corrupt town government had been exposed, the crooked pols sent to the slammer—but how often, she wondered, did a news story spark this kind of cleanup? And wasn't it true, when historians studied a purge or crackdown, that the bad governments, the corrupt parties and banks were ready to collapse on their own, without any help from newspapers? Did the eleventh-hour coverage make that much difference?

And time worked against a newspaper in other ways. Even the welfare series—a small effort, yet blown out of all proportion—was forgotten as fast as a tuna-fish feature, with the next day's forty pages of updates and boilerplate: what good did the series, or the furor it caused, do either its subjects—still on welfare—or its welfare-loathing readers? Things *did* change (although just as often they changed back), but how much did the newspapers have to do with it?

Lying there that afternoon, Gallagher could hear McGuire's breathing, at first shallow and quick, then gusty. Had he dozed off? She leaned over and looked at his flushed face. He was now above it all: without guilt or doubts, single-minded and courageous. And maybe he was right; he had, at least, the grace to love what he believed in, and to believe in what he loved. Good faith protected him like a charm.

The ice show was endless—the music, soft rock and treacly ballads, deafening, and the routines, all the same: one-legged skating, spins, twirls, leaps, sharp turns. The figures etched into the ice were fun to watch until they overlapped and melted into a frosty scrawl. During the second half, Gallagher moved to a better-lit spot and wrote her story, leaving space for the finale—a big ensemble number in honor of the nation's 200th. First, a couple danced onto the ice: Betsy Ross on (just as everyone always thought) George Washington's arm. Then a cake floated out shaped like the Declaration of Independence, followed by a speedy re-enactment of the first Thanksgiving (and wasn't that Thanksgiving, she thought, a colonial event?). The big number involved everyone—Uncle Sam and the Statue of Liberty as principals (Uncle seemed to be on stilts, and Liberty skated with lights on her hat), mobbed, at intervals, by Green Berets, grunts, flyboys, sailors, WAVES and WACS, followed by vintage soldiers: Doughboys, Johnny Rebs, Minute Men, cavalry, Red Coats—representatives of all sides from all the wars. A big number—anthems, pledges, flags, firecrackers: raucous, gaudy, and inane. Even the crowd, now dwindled, seemed listless, or just stupefied from staring at the dazzling block of ice.

Before climbing into bed, Gallagher glanced at the review, scribbled on a legal pad. She could see, even in the afterglow of composition, that the piece was a botch. Effete, disdainful, it was the too-thoughty view of a bluestocking (as Bluestem had called her) on a dumb but friendly show. Ice Caprice never came to Wampanoag, too small, so Gallagher hadn't the aid of nostalgia's rosy glass to soften the critical glare. Ice Caprice would have been big, she thought, in Wampanoag. The natives loved a splashy show, patriotic theme, familiar tunes. People would remember it forever, like the time, many years back, when Frank had come to the Tent and few but politicians and high-rollers could get tickets, even from the scalpers.

Gallagher tore out the pages and dropped them in the wastebasket. After opening the window (the jazzman was out, so it was quiet except for the occasional car or clumsy drunk stumbling out of the Lamont Lounge), she sat down at the desk, then strained for the sentence that would convey to her audience a driblet of enthusiasm for the long, tedious show. But each time she ventured a phrase, irony would creep in; a single syllable would give it away. She tried imagining Juscik as her reader, but (except for hockey) Juscik wouldn't be caught dead at an ice rink. Then she pictured her mother, Annie Gallagher, reading the article, and that helped, although by the last graf it was clear that the draft for Annie wasn't slick enough for Luck, or even for the sentimental Bluestem. The thought of Bluestem, though, did the trick. Bluestem was both cynic *and* naive enthusiast. Holding onto the 'Stem, Gallagher crafted twenty grafs of perfectly poised "light and bright." Mindful of cost and effort, the review lauded patriotic love of spectacle, glancing back at the modest blade shows of yesteryear, deplored the hawkish, ear-splitting confusion of the finale, but cheered the strength and acrobatic grace of the skaters.

Finished at 2, Gallagher reread the three fluent pages, her face and neck stiff, eyes stinging. It was a brilliant sham—smart *and* slavish—just exactly what Luck thought the simpleton from Wampanoag (Kings' egghead) couldn't do! I can reach any level, she whispered to herself—any segment.

Too wired to sleep, she skipped downstairs to the Lamont Lounge, a dive so dark she had to inch along for fear of stumbling over customers. She ordered red wine—no, she said, make that Jack Daniels, ice, and carried the glass to a table. Once settled, she felt, through the smoky darkness, the borings of many invisible eyes—the lone men, travelers and locals alike, she'd seen so often sliding into this joint. When she spotted one making his careful way in her direction, she was out the door.

When she shut the padded lounge door, she heard something bump against it. She locked and chained her own flimsy door. The notes of "Satin Doll" were floating up into the window. She sat down to listen. But before the song was over, she shut the window, went to bed, and fell asleep.

CHAPTER 8

Gallagher peered through her round window to see, through a feathery bed of cloud, the brown and green-tufted earth, glassy pools with suns and, as the plane turned in tighter circles, the shadow of a wing spreading over the golf course. The aircraft burned its rubbery feet on the runway, skidded, and screeched up to the gate of Wampanoag–Ocean State Airport. Gallagher notified neither family nor friend to meet her at WOSA. She wanted to part the curtain of air—which was mostly Wampanoag salt, mixed with a few cupfuls flown in from New York, Los Angeles, and on her own Flight 199 from Depointe—alone, with no one to see how strange she was. Two weeks of poor sleep, nights of drinking with Bluestem and Luck, many stilted dinners with Sunday staff, and the production of fifteen stories in ten days had done it.

Most of the pieces were already printed, read, and tossed—although Rolf (as Gallagher had come to call him) presented his reporter, "our Bullet," as Bluestem said at that last dinner (*my* Bullet, Luck corrected him) with an envelope of her clips: reviews, features, short takes, and six columns, together with his typed critiques—sometimes as long as the article itself, often monosyllabic. He had found much to fault, but was—like Bluestem—amused by the girl's flair for satire, for an ironic twist, an innocent-seeming epithet. Just the way she aligned things was mean. And exposing costly, overmanaged shows and flicks, stars and impresarios made for a good read—so long as it didn't end in a lawsuit or an embargo for the first-string critics.

Overall, Rolf liked the Wampanoag's work and even kidded her on the heft of copy—usable stuff—that had cost the paper so little in salary and time. A theater company *had* yelped about the shafting their seal play had gotten. Luckily, it was a visiting troupe, and the acid squib (the show had closed the next week) was not the handiwork of the theater man ("L.L." as he was known on Broadway), but rather the rip-job (said Bluestem, quoting L.L.) of the little Kings girl trying to get hired. Mr. Langton had phrased it more tactfully to Miss Gallagher, as he called her, but with the warning that certain big doors would be slammed in her face if any such cocky sideshow ("I could do that, too, you know") was repeated.

Jealousy, Rolf—when he heard this story—had said. "Ride right over his face. If this paper could dump Langton, he'd be gone."

"Without Larry," Devra Kazin begged to differ, "this circus would fold!" The movie critic was trying to wise up the recruit at dinner in her penthouse apartment. "In Bluestem's eyes, you're just dandy," she said, "but don't overdo it or people'll turn on you." Gallagher had nodded. "You don't get it," Devra insisted. "I don't mean *us*. You could live with that. I mean the rest of this town and beyond! In your case that means theater owners, actors, talent agents, even the goddamned restaurants—you lose *them*, you're out of a job, lady."

Devra, Gallagher could see, was a straight-shooter. She had already explained ("Ashby's a drunk") why her husband, Ashby Connors, sports editor at the *Blade*, was drinking nothing but soda water. Dinner was served by a butler and maid in a glassed-in bay overlooking the Depointe River. Devra gave Gallagher a few minutes to adjust to the splendor (vast living room walled by abstract paintings, adjoining conservatory with a forest of flowering trees; ultramodern metal furniture among freestanding marble columns), then explained that she'd inherited *both* grandparental fortunes and was, thus—and *here* was the point—the only staffer who could not be bullied or blackmailed because she had her own money, and tons of it! "I don't need that laughable paycheck!" she sneered. "And if I *did*," she continued, "Dr. Rolf Mengele would be the last schlockmeister on earth I'd hump for."

Thrilled by the torrent of contempt and abuse aimed at one who seemed invincible, Gallagher was ready for more: why, she asked, was Luck the *last*? But the rich critic clammed up. Devra, the husband said, didn't like being "fished." She'd much rather "punch you in the head"—he went on—"unasked." Devra ignored this remark, but shot the husband—handsome, but puffy and nicked like an ex-boxer—a slit-eyed look. It was true, she said, that she was unresponsive to pressure.

"Still," she continued, catching Gallagher's eyes scanning the husband's muscular build: she believed in doing her best for the paper, even if that meant cultivating useful parasites. That meant, she said (anticipating Gallagher's question), anyone from the talent to the money men. "Who'd be dumb enough to overlook something so basic?" the reviewer sniffed, laying down her fork (her dinner—a fan of bright sauces pooling around hills of tiny vegetables and a veal chop—was untouched, although the meat had been stabbed) and letting her blackened eyes rest a moment on the husband's bored face. "Enough already," she said suddenly, ringing for the salad, and a glass of wine for the guest. "Can we change the subject?"

Rolf smiled when Gallagher offered an extract of this conversation. "She's prudent," he said. "It's always up to the writer to know where the limits are, because it's my job to try and push you over them. But," he continued, "if you overreach and they dick you, it's your funeral." He paused. "Way to do it is stroke them with one hand," he said, poising his small fist in front of Gallagher's eyes, "and squeeze them with the other!" He winked. "But that comes naturally, doesn't it?"

Sniffing the salt air of Wampanoag, Gallagher wobbled through WOSA terminal where, suddenly nauseated and light-headed, she crumpled to the floor. The floor rose to meet her, restful and cool, but pain from the one folded arm alerted her to her position and to the onlookers. A man rushed forward. "Should I call an ambulance?"

Gallagher said no ambulance, but allowed herself to be helped to a seat. The knot of travelers stepped back. Did she have cancer? Pregnant? Maybe a death in the family, someone whispered. Gradually—although still curious—they went about their business. The samaritan fetched a cup of hot coffee. Gallagher sipped it and promised him—an older man and kindly the way a Wampanoager could be to strangers—she would call her family. But when he was gone, Gallagher slumped in her seat. She drank the coffee. Trundling into the ladies' room, she was struck by what was in the mirror: liver-colored eyes, rings so black they looked furred, fish-white skin, parched lips. When she laughed—no one else was there—a patch reddened on each cheek but the eyes still looked like oily marbles. She rubbed her cheeks with a water-soaked handkerchief, patted them dry, and dotted on some pinkish makeup, a slick of lipstick, left the scary eyes alone.

For two weeks she'd been ravenous, yet unable to force anything more than cottage cheese or mashed bananas down a gullet squeezed in protest. Her stomach, at first noisy and active, had shrunk and hardened: it seemed asleep, zippered, with no food to occupy or irritate it. So it was with extreme caution that Gallagher returned to her seat, opened the container of blueberry yogurt and started to spoon it in. First she prepared. More than 500 miles separated her from Luck and Bluestem (the names alone, however, tripped an alarm and sent out a spurt of natural speed, but the body was too depleted to do more than race its engine). She might buy a magazine or newspaper—but no! she told the reckless brain: no news products, nothing but the cool air of West Wampanoag and the container of solid milk. Slowly, as she spooned the glop into the empty cone, the shut-down works, the cold insides filled and commenced the novel chore of digestion. A wave of energy, subtle as breath, vitalized the moribund, giving it strength to pick its pocketbook up off the floor.

A few minutes later, however, the abused stomach was knocking and heaving like an overloaded washer. Gallagher tottered over to a bank of phones and, clearing her throat, called home and got Mrs. Gallagher, whose pleasure at hearing a familiar voice kept her from detecting its odd quality. The Gallaghers would be at the airport—"lickety-split" was the quaint phrase Mrs. Gallagher heard herself using, because something of the pulverized daughter *had* come through.

And it wasn't just the booze, the frenzy, the diet of air that felled the newshound, returning from the heroic trial: it was flu, bronchitis, and pneumonia which, flying in with Gallagher, hit like a three-eyed hurricane within the week, at the end of which Rolf Luck called to offer her a job. Mrs. Gallagher told him to call back when her daughter was able to talk, or even to hear any news. "Don't tell *me*. I'm just the mother," Mrs. Gallagher told Luck. "Call back later," she said.

And he did, as did Ralph Bluestem from Sunday, and Personnel, too, and they called almost every day for a week, until Gallagher was able to take the message, if not the call itself. Mrs. Gallagher told them yes, her daughter would accept; she'd go to Depointe, but not right away—not for a long time, the mother made clear to Bluestem, who then assured his boss that they could reclaim her faster if they wanted. Never had they seen such drive, such zeal. Guts, Bluestem said, killer instinct. Pliability, Luck added. "She can write the whole damned back of the book!" Bluestem howled. "Don't kill it," Luck warned, and the subject of a Sunday staff replacement—one of dozens of hirings and firings on Luck's monthly docket—was dropped.

Gallagher lay like jello on a bed in her mother's house. Everything hurt, burned; her bones were lead. What do I have? she asked her mother after Dr. Maher made his first house call. "A bug," said her mother. Then, after several feverish nights, he returned. "You've got another one," her mother said. In her weakness, Catherine imagined these bugs joined by strings of slugs and maggots, armies of flies and malarial mosquitoes, all buzzing, flying, stinging, flicking, biting, swarming, and boring day and night in the body's tropical hive. At noon one day Mrs. Gallagher entered the room with an ice pack, removing the hot, sodden cloth from her daughter's forehead. She mentioned that "Rob" Luck had called with news. Hearing this, Gallagher commanded her bugs to evacuate: get out, march!—and out they went, hurrah, hurrah, down the steps, out the door, picked off at last by the Wampanoag late frost, the killjoy that came every year to turn spring back to winter. The bugs were not yet routed, but soon would be, and Mrs. Gallagher gave her daughter—visibly better; the dark flush had cooled and the eyes less swollen—more news.

By next day, Gallagher was out of bed, seated by the window, and—watching the handsome, lethal bluejay that housed in their bare maple—planned the stages of her move. In her hands was a letter of resignation, drafted weeks ago, full of grateful flourishes and regrets, most of which had been scratched out. What remained was a simple statement: the kind of kiss-off a Rolf Luck might pen, testing the springboard for his stratospheric leap.

Each day she felt keener, stronger, and returned on Monday to give notice to the Swamp. The Timesmen were beside themselves.

Except to croak, no one had ever left the paper before retirement. Though some of the younger reporters were wowed, even jealous of the obvious promotion, few could picture asking—even if invited—for active duty outside of Wampanoag. It would involve, for one, moving out of town. No native could conceive of life in that trackless waste, and if positively forced out, a Wampanoager was likely to come right back.

Each working day of the last two weeks, Gallagher was treated to lunch by a different staffer. After the first lunch, when the soon-to-be big-time reporter sketched in the paper, her assignments, the editors, building and day-to-day life, the news spread far and fast. Soon even the non-lunchers were experts on the *Bullet* mentality, the oddballs and routines, the number and types of stories Gallagher had filed. They'd heard about the tea set on L.L.'s desk and the dust-up about the seal show. They knew it all, but each fresh luncher wanted to hear it again, from the top. So the story filtering through the *Times* every afternoon was always a variation, but beefed up as versions were meshed and edited. In time the two-week trial became so familiar that even Miss Toohey felt she had reviewed the flicks and traded cracks with Rolf, as well as "lived through" the climax of illness and triumph. People loved the story. Gallagher had never expected such a flood of interest and sympathy.

What she didn't know was that the Timesmen were being tactful; they were curbing their horror at the pitiful, backward working conditions in Depointe. Just who did those sweatshoppers think they were, and in what century were they living? Were they all mental? In Wampanoag, the Yankee plutocrats, slavedrivers, and skinflints had been driven out. The newsmen and printers had built up the strongest union shop in New England. Management—from O'Callahan to the ad director—were all average Joes with at best an M.A. from State. No bluebloods, no stockholders need apply.

Those Depointe editors were living in the Dark Ages. They didn't comprehend that people had their lives to live. They couldn't work all the time and socialize. The socializing—this poaching on private time—was the limit! No union shop worth its bylaws would tolerate that trick. All those drinks and forced fellowship—did they think they were in Russia? The mystery was why that brassy little Gallagher, no sissy—and with six months on a Guild paper, whose fifty-year struggle with the bosses had won them ironclad contracts, double-time-and-a-half, full staffing—would brook such an outrage. "She never had the pleasure," Miss Toohey told the A.C.E., "of working for Mr. Seeley at 10 cents an hour."

What was the draw? the A.C.E. asked Toohey, who'd sat with the girl on Women's all these months, but Toohey said she couldn't fathom it. They were about to chew over the sad fate of the Shitfly, recently canned and now jilted, when the A.C.E. spotted Gallagher standing in the doorway with Mr. O'Callahan, fresh from a prime-rib lunch with old Mr. Seeley. So typical, Miss Toohey remarked: the girl had jumped the gun on what should have been the highlight of her news career—a luncheon at the Wamp-An-Oag Club, where few beside the old publisher had the bloodlines and wherewithal for membership.

Even for one like Gallagher, so recently wined and dined in the swank chophouses of Depointe, it had been a memorable lunch. There was a formality, a timeworn elegance at the 200-year-old New England dining club that no upstart eatery in the flatlands could hope to match. In thanking Mr. Seeley for the treat, Mr. O'Callahan detailed, for contrast's sake, life on the big daily in the brash French-Canadian boomtown that auto money had made. Yes, he said to Gallagher, he'd heard those "tales from Dee-Pointe."

At first, Gallagher seemed to be the only woman (apart from waitresses in black taffeta) present and enjoying the refinements of the club's Georgian dining saloon with its Chippendale chairs and lace tablecloths. A line-up of grim-faced colonials and signers was broken by arched windows swagged with red velvet. There was no portrait of Mr. Zechariah Fayerweather, merchant and first governor-general—but he was remembered anyway. In a codicil, the first citizen had provided for clubmen to be served in perpetuity with the state's quohaug chowder in summer and johnny-cake in winter. Twice yearly the club's active roster decamped to the seashore for an all-day clambake, firing the same beachstones their forefathers had gathered a hundred years ago. It was still gentlemen only, as the former publisher put it, except for the Tuesday luncheon when, as she could see, club wives made use of the side entrance.

After a year on Women's, Gallagher recognized not a single face among these prominent club wives. Mr. O'Callahan wasn't any the wiser, but old Mr. Seeley knew everybody. He made introductions; an affable matron, who claimed to read the *Times* religiously, was sorry not to recognize Gallagher's name. A broad, plain face under a blue-feathered hat commented on the editorials, how she found herself in fundamental agreement with them. Gallagher accepted the compliment for lifetime Wamp-An-Oager Camden Goddard Chase, the right-winger who scripted the unsigned editorial page. Only oldtimers bothered with this page, where a flag of the thirteen states ran with a quote by a colonial pundit. O'Callahan laid it out himself, and the anonymous opinionmaker roared—if so much as a word was changed—directly to Mr. Seeley. Goddard Chase's axe was ground to a pin on the same few heads: lawlessness of an imperial presidency, havoc wreaked by meddling courts; glory of states' rights, divine logic of governance by the elite; perils of peacetime mentality, and the God-given right to military aid for backward countries fending off indigents, rebels, and international schemers.

Returning to the *Times*—after leaving Mr. Seeley to his chauffeur—Mr. O'Callahan discoursed on the city and how skilled it was at surviving hard times. He never worried about Wampanoag *or* the paper, oldest in the state and one of New England's senior dailies. In his own time he had seen constant flux: from a postwar heyday of fifty to sixty pages, stuffed with local news, photos, and ads, to pamphlet-size ten years later, as the last vestiges of industry fled the city. A bounce-back in the '60s when the feds ordered the city to self-destruct and rebuild. Now, once again, the paper was on its uppers, about as lean and hungry as could be. Wampanoag was in a depression; the municipal budget broke, yet burdened with ever more dependents. The manufacturing base was gone, consumer spending zilch; pickings were so slim that half the ad department had been laid off. Things, in short, had never been worse. "And yet," the M.E. said, when they had hit Times Square and stood on the lonely traffic island (the editor scanned the height of the red-brick tower to where, just under the eaves, "Wampanoag Evening Times" was painted in bold cursive), "I'm sorry to see you go." Wampanoag was a one-paper town, and in this system, he said, lay the future. Even folks who got their main news from TV relied on the *Times* for everything else, especially—

now more than ever—a sense of reality. (Gallagher recalled how defunct columns like WHY GROW OLD? and ASK DOROTHY had been snuck back on the Women's page.) And as long, Mr. O'Callahan went on, as Wampanoag lasts, the *Times* goes with it. Wampanoag, he reasoned, *is* the *Times*. "Where you're going," he warned, "there's no such thing as civic spirit, no tradition, no respect for memory. Worse," he said, shaking his head, "they don't take care of their own."

O'Callahan lowered his gaze, sighed. "Don't think," he said, glancing at the third-floor windows, "I don't see what's wrong here. Our friend McGuire saw—although no one would give the bastard the satisfaction. *This,*" he said, pointing to the third-floor windows, "is no place for ambition."

He took a moment to catch his breath. "Yet look at that poor blackfly, or whatever they call him. He's a common laborer now, with no market for his product. He couldn't move forward, so he fell back." O'Callahan smiled (if you could call that pumpkin cut a smile). "It's a goddamn shame," he said. "He was the best—although for us," he quickly added, "a disaster."

Gallagher nodded. She gazed up at the windows, too.

"He'd lost something, even by the time he got here," O'Callahan said. "Too much booze. That's what happens to the good ones. You should have seen that kid fifteen years ago, when he went out to New York. Only a bomb could've stopped him." O'Callahan tightened the pumpkin cut. Then the muscles sagged to become the jowly, hound-dog face that hung like a hammock from his ears. Gallagher could picture McGuire, standing on his chair, slapping the steel ruler on his hand: "Bring me the carcass," he'd yell (checking to see the M.E. deaf in his glass cell) "of Benedict O'Callahan!"

To celebrate the new job, McGuire was treating Gallagher to a shore dinner on Rock Point. The sun was low. Seagulls walked the deserted beach. The tide was going out; high on the beach was a black scrawl of seaweed. McGuire took Gallagher's clammy hand—since the triple illness she was clammy most of the time. The setting sun dazzled their window, and only slowly did the blue sky reappear. Then the fireball rolled up and fell over the horizon. "It's going to be fine," McGuire said, squeezing the damp hand.

Gallagher said she wished it would just get started; the agony of waiting, the goodbyes were murder.

"People're happy for you," McGuire said, opening his menu. "Don't begrudge them their time."

Gallagher said she was tired, not begrudging.

"You don't have time for tired, girl," her former boss said. "If you go out there with that attitude," he said, "you won't last long."

"I'm not going with an attitude," Gallagher explained. "It's physical."

"Same thing."

"Why are you doing this?" she asked.

McGuire drew the pack from his jacket pocket, and lit a cigarette. The waiter popped the champagne cork. Gallagher thought McGuire looked older. His skin was yellowish, leathery, and the caves around his eyes deeper.

"I can't stand this soda pop," he said, flicking the wine glass. "I got it for you."

Gallagher was softened by his sad look. No matter what he said, he couldn't hurt her. What he thought about her prospects mattered, yes, but only while she was here, and because they were in love.

"I don't get it," he said, glancing out the window at the sea's dark stripes and single whitecap. The ash on his cigarette was hanging.

"You don't get what?"

McGuire squashed the butt so hard, the paper split. He was smoking the unfiltered kind and too many. He drained his glass and poured another. "We'll need another bottle," he said, "or would you mind if we switched?"

"I don't care."

"That's your problem, Gallagher," he said. "You don't care."

"If you're going to talk this way," Gallagher snapped, "why are we celebrating?" McGuire turned toward the sea-filled window. The plates of steaming fish and side dishes arrived. The champagne bottle was replaced by a pitcher of beer.

After McGuire had driven her home, she undressed for bed but couldn't sleep. At dawn, she awoke from a fitful doze. She had been dreaming she had to walk to Depointe, and waving goodbye from the window was McGuire.

Was it McGuire or Falkenberg? In that soapy light, they were easily mixed up. Gallagher opened her eyes to the bare wall where the crucifix used to be, hung with its braided palm.

She pulled down the shades until the room was dark, a bar of light bubbling at the windowsill. She closed her eyes. First on the lids was a flotilla of boxes, rings, and neon stripes. When the pattern cleared, she remembered something—sitting on a park bench in the arboretum—Falkenberg sprawled on the grass.

What was he doing? He never stopped working, never wasted time, or if he did, it was to consult something serious: musicology, theories of art, long poems untranslated from the German or Italian. But he had no book in hand, and was lying with his eyes open. She remembered this scene as the last; when she saw him after this—to return a book or collect clothes—he was himself again, preoccupied and cool.

Graduation was a few weeks off and it was this that had touched something off in Dana, and brought things to a head. Dana had been brooding—at first he wouldn't say about what, then he said he saw the end in sight, no matter what she'd promised about staying on and finding a job in town. "You're young," he told her. "You don't know what will happen. I've been through this before." When she asked what he'd been through, he wouldn't say.

A few days later, she was stacking her college texts for sale (only math and science; the novels, art books, and poetry were still shelved). Taking a breather, with her head resting on a pile of books, Catherine was startled to see Dana burst in the door. He had somehow gotten into the building and raced up the stairs. "I never see you," he said. "They've disconnected the phone. You promise to come over for dinner, then you don't show up."

He knelt on the floor, next to the stack of books. "Sit up," he said, and Catherine perched on her mattress-bed, tucking her feet under her. "You're cold to me," he said, and sat down next to her.

"No, I'm not," she said mildly.

"You can't get away from me fast enough. Why am I so repulsive to you all of a sudden?"

Through the open window, Catherine saw the sunlight fanning the quad and felt the chill wind. Sun-lovers were already spread out on the winter grass, flat on their backs or grouped around card games, snapping Frisbees from corner to corner, reading, napping, or otherwise gathering the fine wool of the waning school year. Catherine hadn't in four years experienced much of this sweet idyll—and maybe none of them did, until the end was in sight and, with it, the sudden expiration of childhood.

She had eased out of Dana's grip. It was too fresh a day, the sun now broken free, spinning clouds of dust. But Dana wasn't easy to ignore. He stood, peeled off his clothes, and stretched in the light. Now naked, he crawled onto the low bed, folding his arms under his head.

He was waiting for something. The room warmed in the now-cloudless day. Catherine fetched a bottle of apple wine and they passed it back and forth. Light arrowing through the green bottle caused colored flags to quiver on the walls, and by then—some powerful amp was pumping a Mozart concerto through the quad—they yielded to the slumbrous pleasure of it.

When they'd finished off the bottle, the air had grown chilly again; Dana covered himself with the bedspread and Catherine went back to sorting books. The sun dropped behind the west quad, filling the room with marine light, the pure blue of a New England dusk, warming wood and reddening glass. When Catherine looked up, the sky was inky. Dana was asleep.

There was a point there, she remembered, of harmony, and they had reached it. Then Dana's eyes—he wasn't asleep—opened, and he pulled his friend under the spread. Thinking he too had found his moment, he rolled on top of her, but soon rolled off in frustration. They lay on their backs watching the dark sky release its first stars. Then he could swallow his anger no more. She'd never given him what he wanted, she was selfish, cold, immature. He leapt up, walked to the far wall.

When he turned from the wall, his face was in shadow. He let the bedspread he'd wrapped around him drop to the floor. Catherine could see him clearly enough, although he reached to switch on a lamp. "They can see you out there!" she whispered. But he was pleasing to look at: pale and hairless, slim as a medieval Adam.

He switched off the lamp and paced in the dark. The moon puddled on his back and streaked his legs. He pulled out a dresser drawer and stood over it. "I want to ask you something," he said.

"Okay."

"Can I wear something of yours?" he said.

He was still hovering over the drawer and now dropped his hand into it. She thought of the contents—small stacks of panties, bras, a half slip—and what it might look like in the moonlit room. "Please," he begged. She watched as he drew something out—what?—and draped it on his shoulder, then bent over, drawing on his bird's legs something small and silky. He stroked his hips where the flimsy fabric was stretched. Then, just as slowly, he stripped the panties off, pulling the slip from his shoulder. He was in profile, but Catherine remembered that his eyes had closed tight and his mouth opened. When he tried to climb back into the bed, she shoved him away. "Get out!" she said in someone else's—an animal's—voice. "Can I take something?" he'd asked. After a while he'd dressed and shut the door behind him.

An hour later, it was Else at the door. Catherine waited for her friend to make her way to the low bed. "Are you sad about something?" Else sat with her—she was never in a hurry—and they listened to the shrieks and laughs of students parading through the quad. Else stayed for an hour. "I guess you're not up for coming? I hate to leave, but—."

"Go ahead," the animal voice said.

"You *are* crying!"

"Leave me alone."

"Put the lights on," Else had said. "It's dreary in here."

Next day, Dana came back early. Mornings you couldn't just invade the dorm. Someone sat at the reception desk and could easily spot a stranger charging up the steps. (So how did he get in?) Catherine hadn't slept much, but enough to feel refreshed. She remembered yesterday, the blissful afternoon and ghostly night. The strangeness of it was still vivid. In all the weeks spent snooping in Dana's apartment, how had she missed something like this? Somewhere beneath the hard skin of his sophistication, and tucked in the slack hours of those art-packed days, was this other creature with the strange hungers.

And there he was in the doorway, camera and lenses slung around his neck, his shooting jacket on, just like any other day. "Get up," he said. "We'll eat breakfast somewhere. I want you to come out with me."

The morning was cloudy, colder than the previous day, and nothing at all ghostly about it. Off they went, like old times, not to the grass at the Basin, but to the Kingstown Arboretum, where Dana shot tree trunks—mainly the dark, smooth bark of fruit trees. By afternoon, they had settled on a bench to admire the different plantations of naked trees. Even in winter, Dana explained, you can tell them apart by the outline and distinct pattern of branching. The sun slipped from its cloudbank and Dana lay on a patch of grass, stretched at his ease in the warming light.

Catherine opened her eyes in her own bedroom. Daylight soaked through the shade, stark and bright. She burrowed under the blanket, but she could still see the park bench.

She considered the scene. It should have been dramatic, shattering, but it wasn't all Dana's fault that it had fallen flat. She was hung up on the "irregularities," as her mother might say; too much the prude, Dana said, an "emotional dwarf." For all those slick art films she had seen, she didn't begin to understand men. Dana had offered this view in his usual levelheaded way so, far from feeling hurt or patronized, she conceded the point and waited for the kiss-off, something that should have been mutual and easy.

This didn't happen. "I love you," he groaned, pulling her down to the ground to lie beside him. "Will you stay with me?" He buried his head in her neck. She waited. Maybe because the afternoon was almost over, the big park so lonely, the thought of the soon-to-be depleted college and the solitary summer so sad—time seemed to stop and Dana's question expanded to fill up that time. After fifteen minutes, or maybe an hour: "Why won't you answer me?" he said.

She waited still longer, then told him how strange it was to hear him talk of staying together when they had never been together. They were total strangers. "You don't even *like* me," she said.

Now he was the one to feel something. She remembered the wounded look he gave her—years of experience and cynicism were wiped from the artist's face and, although not understanding or liking him any better for it, she could see she'd caused him pain.

For the next few days Catherine had holed up in the dorm—"thinking," she told Else. Dana didn't call until he was prepared to ask for his books and to insist that she come and take her things, too. Else tendered many invitations—different kinds of nighttime fun, or just a walk and lunch. They were all rejected. Finally, seeing that something radical was needed or Catherine (as Else told the troubled-looking girl, once installed in the hotel) would still be "in the fugue state," Else took action.

She teased out the Dana story but felt strangely short-changed when she heard it. It didn't add up, Else said: Catherine either refused to tell all or, more likely, had already repressed it. Did it amount to a proposal? If she'd turned him down so easily, why was she still mooning? And, if he was so revolting, what was the big deal? In spite of the bracing questions, the luxury setting and treats, Catherine was still in the fugue—if that's what it was. It was like carrying around a heavy egg; sometimes, Else said, she could see the egg boiling in the girl's eyes! But Catherine claimed to feel better, and—unlike Dana—younger, greener every day, until she felt barely old enough to graduate from high school, much too immature to figure out why a 30-year-old artist wanted to dress like a woman and have a girlfriend.

Else soon put Catherine on the bus to Wampanoag. From that hour forward, Catherine could never finish puzzling over the question of who, in those last scenes with Dana, had done what to whom. Who was to blame for how sore and rattled they both felt? Even now—she heard her mother in the kitchen, and could smell the frying bacon—what more did she understand about men? Not much, except that she and Dana were probably even. For months he'd treated her like a bedwarmer, but in one day she wiped out all his credit.

During the early morning, both sharp memories—of Dana and of McGuire—tangled in the airless bedroom. Waking again when the sun was above the roof, and a cool light lapped at the shades, Gallagher sensed how keen she was for Depointe. Luck, Bluestem: she was more like them—hard, rotten, cold. It was they, and *not* McGuire ("Eat 'em up, dogs!" he would rave, driving on his trusty Wampanoags, and yet—only a few years after his journalistic triumph—he was gone, run out on a rail, making horseshoes), who were the real newsrats: sharp-fanged, sleek, and pitiless. Gallagher wondered if she could hope to be that healthy and sleek. She sat up in bed. Leaning toward the dresser, she stretched her lips to see, in the mirror's silver pool, all those razory rat teeth.

CHAPTER 9

A week later she drove the sleek, white-rat car, packed with a few cheesy belongings, northwest to Canada, then west to Depointe city. After spending a few days in a budget motel on the outskirts, she discovered turn-of-the-century Apley House situated on the Depointe River. There, borrowing a fold-up bed from the manager, she assembled her kit in a ground-floor cubby. For three weeks she hunkered, skittering daily to and from the *Bullet* and the hole. The days had a painful angularity. Was it caused by snubs from Luck and Bluestem, for whom the arrival of a third-string writer meant less—now that the slot was filled by a scribbling body—than she'd hoped? Or by the walls that had sprung up to divide the lonesome, single reporter from the engrossing familial worlds of Devra, Larry, and others on the Sunday staff? There were no dinners, no drinks, no lunches; not much more than a nod in the morning—if someone saw the rat slink by.

That first week the rat presented her silky face in Bluestem's glassed-in cage, but Mr. Bluestem was busy and felt, moreover, that the probationer—having everything to learn—should treat her editor more formally. Gallagher was stung by the brushoff. When had he changed? (Nobody else, Larry Langton remarked, had noticed any change: Bluestem was still Bluestem, an ape, and what else did she expect?)

But compared to the 'Stem who, at the close of the try-out, had wined and dined the triumphant Bullet, ambushed her for kisses in dark niches, escorted her to work and back, this ape *had* changed. He informed Gallagher first day back that he'd fallen in love and was soon to be engaged. "What?" Gallagher had said. A nurse, Bluestem said; he'd met her, he added, not even a week after Gallagher had left. "Strange, huh?" he said, cocking his head, a smile playing on his thin lips.

Bluestem was booked every night with the nurse. He was never free for lunch. The entertainment page was now low priority; his mandate was to retool the Sunday magazine, jazzing it up with shopping features to lure suburban advertising.

At first, Gallagher herself was less than busy: it was late in the season and the regular beats were covered with ease, no overflow. Bluestem didn't have time for coaching, as he put it, so ideas and "enterprise" had to come from her. She pitched a few ideas, but they were vetoed: too eggheady, or too low-life; too arty, too Wampanoag. Gallagher turned to the index card from the try-out. She called a handful of rookie film directors: What had it taken to break into the biz? Contacts, film school diploma, visibility on the lots? She did a quick rundown on radio call-letters, stringing all the cute ones—WWOW, KISS, KCOP, and KUKU—into one big, silly graf. She covered a Javanese puppet show, and interviewed a now-ancient Mr. Wizard, on tour with a children's host from early TV. There was a novelty tune that hit the charts "no. 1 with a bullet." The lyric was a how-to on scoring during your coffee break. Bluestem wanted Gallagher to mimic the song's steamy tone, but Gallagher—for the first time since arriving and dashing off a hundred takes without a snag—was stumped. Her head ached from the strain of crafting snappy sentences, and loading every rift with variants on the word "quickie." The time-out gave her a chance to eavesdrop on the Sunday room. She listened to the idle hum and sudden volleys of typewriter keys. It didn't sound like easeful composition, but no one was stumped, either.

In the two months since Gallagher's first visit to Depointe, the *Bullet* had begun the conversion from hot to cold typography. Metal and manpower were on the way out, electronics and photography moving in. Reporters were learning how to type a story so a scanner could read it and spew out "camera-ready" columns, cuts, heads, and subheads. Composing had already been stripped down and retooled. A handful of compositors who'd manned the bulky linotype machines, punching out slugs for molten-metal casting, were now pasting paper spills on plywood dummies. At every level the printing process was losing weight. In the newsrooms, bulky items like paste-pots, pencil jars, and scissors were jettisoned, as were all manual typewriters. The scanner couldn't read lead marks, much less grapple with a scroll of pasted sheets: stories had to be typed on single sheets of paper with characters punched by electric machines using magnetic tape.

The principal gain, the staff was told, would be in speed: the process that took twelve steps would now take three, or four at most. Yet Gallagher was not alone in thinking that something was lost in the compression. The labor-intensive rigmarole that struck a story into metal, then pressed it on paper, was neither flexible nor fast, but it ensured that the news would pass through many sets of hands before it reached the reader. In the good old Swamp days, everyone in Composing had a tub of pencils, and used them. A single article might travel from a Toohey to an A.C.E., through a McGuire, and sometimes double-back to an O'Callahan, and then the proofreaders in Composing would have a go at it. If they didn't get—or *like*—what they were reading, the compositors *themselves* would call to complain or correct. Even after the grimy copy was cast in metal and bolted onto the press, a mere phone call from O'Callahan—on, say, the day when the president was shot, or, once, when a factory burned down in Centredale—to "remake page 1!" and those plates would be unbolted and melted down.

The days of handcrafting the news were over. Now the reporter's raw copy (with a glance from the editor, who was armed only with correction tape) went right into the paper. And even this quick process was soon to be further streamlined. In a few months, the typewriters would be turfed and each writer hooked to a video-display terminal, to keypunch stories onto a screen. The day's stories would be "mailed" to the editor's screen, and from there to the compositors, who'd have their own set of screens. Only layout, with spills for paste-up, would ever touch paper. At every stage, the printing process was dematerialized, made as simple and speedy as possible, but there were snags—especially at this transitional stage. One of these was the effect of a sloppy scribe like Gallagher—whose copy was grimy, thick with correction tape—on sensitive machinery. In the old days, any kind of rewrite was just dandy, as long as it was legible. There was room in the old system for heavy cuts and redraftings. Now everything had to be done once, and right. If the copy wasn't clean, the computer choked. Luckily for Gallagher, the workload had been light, so—adapting her elaborate methods to the new system—she had the extra time for retyping. Composing, notwithstanding, was forever on the horn to Sunday, beefing about computer snafus because someone's copy was filthy, miscoded, thick with layers of tape.

When McGuire called (and he did nearly every night), Gallagher ranted on about this nerve-wracking new method. She was sorry to hear that—although people expected flak from the unions—every newspaper, even a pokey rag like the *Times,* would convert to cold type. The savings in salaries alone made newspapers profitable again. Half the pressmen could be pensioned off; any extra labor needed could be hired under new contracts. The few old-timers who finagled a renewal would learn to love paste-up. For all the system's short-comings (cost in jobs, blow to the unions, certain death of an ancient craft), digital, McGuire insisted, was the future. The paper could be gotten out twice as fast at half the cost. When Gallagher pointed out that stories were now written and edited by the same person, McGuire scoffed: the biz, he said, had always been heading in that direction, even at the best places. That's why, he added dryly, he'd gotten *out* of the business. "It's a goddamned typing job!" Gallagher groaned one night. "Get used to it," he barked. "And don't blubber. Master that bonehead technique, Gallagher, and write your stories!"

To make up for time lost in retyping, Gallagher started her day early and left after everyone was gone. Her stories continued to jam the machines and sometimes Composing itself would retype them. Yet the new writer still managed to publish a byline three or four times a week—the stuff, bright and breezy, if slight, was paid the rare compliment of being read by other staffers.

After two months on the *Bullet,* Gallagher had met everyone, but was rarely asked out. Then, one Friday, two city reporters she saw at breakfast every morning invited her for a drink at a night-spot favored by bankers, lawyers, *Bullet* stars and editors. Housed in a glass highrise, the bar was called—"believe it or not," Gallagher told McGuire—"the Money Tree." McGuire sniffed. "Don't you get it?" Gallagher demanded. "You're such a fool," was his reply.

Gallagher said she wasn't a fool. She'd simply observed that, as everything in Depointe (and at the *Bullet*) was about money, they'd named the bar of choice the Money Tree, and—even if such a tree really existed—it was too droll. McGuire was silent. Then he said he didn't want to hear about new boyfriends. "Tell me about work, Gallagher, but skip the bars."

These days McGuire tended to be glum. He had found no ready market for his handmade tools. He was forced to take editing work just to pay the mortgage. And Aerial was still on the farm. She'd found apartments she liked, but none she could afford. "What do you expect me to do, chum?" said McGuire when Gallagher snorted: "Throw her out on the street?"

Maybe, said Gallagher.

"You're hard, friend."

Suddenly the newsroom was crackling—Gallagher snapped out of her funk. Typewriters started, ionized words pounced onto sheets. Gallagher looked up to see Luck shadow the doorway, now making his way up the aisle from the magazine, past the copy desk, Bluestem's cube, and into the Sunday pen, stopping—Gallagher's hands had not touched her keys: a blank sheet was rolled in, slugged WAMP/KWIKI take 1. Her eyes had tracked Luck on his path. Every other head was bowed; she saw all the bent necks as he walked, glancing neither right nor left. He dropped a hand on Gallagher's machine: "Taking a siesta?"

Gallagher saw Bluestem hovering at his glass door; she could imagine his eyes straining on their stalks to see.

"No," Gallagher replied.

Luck turned to grin at Bluestem, who had slipped out of his cage. "What're your plans today, Gallagher? Free for lunch?"

Gallagher considered. She couldn't remember any plans, so nodded yes. Luck moved closer, to grin in her face: "You're cheap," he said, "but you're not free."

Turning on his heel, "Be ready at one!" he said, then marched down the aisle, ducked into Bluestem's tank, in and out, then gone.

Bluestem approached his minion's desk, a gleaming smile stretched on his face. "Where are you going?" he sang. "Suppose *I* can't come along?" He stood behind Gallagher's chair with one hand kneading her shoulder. "We'll go out to the Tree later tonight. You have time?" Gallagher felt newsy eyes on her back, taking silent stock of the development. Bluestem tapped the blank, coded sheet in Gallagher's machine and sat down on her desk. "Hey gal, where's my story?" he crooned. Then, in a lower voice, he hinted the piece could be reassigned to the food writer—avid, lusty, "eats men whole," Luck had said over one of a hundred drinks. Gallagher covered the sheet of paper with a hand. "Attagirl!" said the editor, giving her a fatherly pat. "Don't forget," he whispered. "Wrap it up by five. Be ready at five."

In a burst of electric keys, the squib on the sex song was shaped, with no typos, into something playful for a Thursday box (Bluestem wanted it ASAP, and as the entertainment page was already locked with columns and movie-star pix) on Food. At 12:45, Gallagher applied a coat of color to a tense face, whose normal ruddiness had paled in the weeks of ten-hour days and no-cook dinners. (Gallagher shopped for her nightly cottage cheese and fruit right at the Apley's own moldy deli, a favorite with elderly tenants, fresh from the beauty parlor and reeking of perms and sets. She had tried a supermarket in the neighborhood—a strip of riverfront apartments flanked by automotive mansions at one end, and war-torn gangland at the other—but the sight of armed guards stationed in the doorways took her appetite away.) The long days of desk work made it hard to sleep. Her nights were broken by dreams, homesickness, and a cold dread of living alone in Depointe. But the saucy squib, dashed off like a pro (*hack,* she could hear McGuire say), had cleared her eyes and brain of fatigue. Luckily, she'd thought to wash her hair and put on a decent dress. Thus, she was only mildly cowed by the scene at the Pomeranian Wine Cellar, Depointe's premiere restaurant, and by Luck's dark tailoring and freshly barbered head.

His table was in an alcove flanked by columns. The cellar's stone walls were washed in a spectral light; the genius of the Pomeranian was to cast this luminous dust, like sun in a fogbank, allowing diners a divine vision of their partner, but of little else. The place was infamous as a rich cheaters' haven: you had your sumptuous lunch or dinner in near-seclusion—there were no windows, the artfully contrived niches, columns, and half walls screening even the guiltiest diner from scrutiny.

A half-moon banquette anchored Luck's table. Gallagher slid into the middle, until she saw Luck moving himself over. They were, she saw, to sit flank on flank, facing the obscure depths of the restaurant. Luck kept inching over until his leg touched Gallagher's; he grinned—his head a little lower than hers. "Slide down," he ordered, a hand pressing her shoulder, and she slid until their heads were even. "I can see you in there," he whispered, "hiding behind your mask. That's fine. Peek through the bars till you feel safe." Gallagher picked up her menu, a leather volume with silver corners. Inside, on blue sheets, was a polyglot legend of dishes and wines, penned by the Pomeranian, famous for his cooking and a beautiful hand. Luck allowed his reporter a moment to read, then closed her menu, tucking it, with his own, under his elbow. "Don't think about food. We'll have a few drinks first."

And so the first pair of martinis arrived at the table. Gallagher tried to angle her body away from the leg—small and thin like a child's—pressed against it. "Don't be allergic to me," Luck warned, his hand gripping her arm. Gallagher sipped the frigid, oily cocktail—there was something perverse about this iceless, colorless blend of alcohols. Still, it was an alluring drink, she thought, staring at the translucent surface, silky washes lapping the glass. Luck was drinking his second and considering a third when Gallagher, glancing at her watch, saw that the lunch hour had elapsed, although no food had been consumed. Luck hadn't even touched the little loaf with the knife in its back. At first, Gallagher avoided it too, but the drink poured into an empty stomach had her hacking at the bread, until Luck, with a laugh ("You're a rough article, Gallagher"), took the knife and, from the other end, carved off a neat slice. He hadn't, in the hour's time, said much, although he had favored the reporter with many a stare and significant smile. He didn't seem to want to talk, or to listen either. At one point, he clapped a hand over her open mouth to stop an account of Jack McGuire's last days at the *Wampanoag Times*.

"I'm not interested in other people's problems," he said, before removing his hand. "Your face is hot, Gallagher. Is something wrong?"

Gallagher, sipping her second martini, touched her face, and it *was* hot. "Am I red?" she asked.

"You'll do," said Luck, leaning over to flick the skin. "Have you ever seen a doctor about this skin?" he asked a minute later.

"What about it?" said Gallagher, the words furred, but intelligible.

"You could use dermabrasion here," he said, touching a cheek, "and here," flicking the other. "You look a little shop-worn."

Gallagher asked why he was always so personal.

"What do you mean 'personal'? Take it as a compliment."

Gallagher might have said more, but a stupefying wave, languorous, like a breeze over a pond, made it seem irrelevant.

"Have another," he said. "The third one clears the head," he paused, "if it doesn't kill you. I'm enjoying this, Gallagher. Can you tell?"

Gallagher nodded. Her head felt heavy, yet the earth seemed to exert no gravitational pull.

"You're a cool customer," he went on, "and I like that. I don't know where you come by it, though, coming from nothing."

"Where do *you* come from?" Gallagher burst out.

Luck ignored the question. "I'm worth twenty of you, and I'm no more than five, maybe ten years older."

Gallagher drank deeply of her ice water, fizzy and garnished with a lime disk.

"How old did you say you were?"

Gallagher was getting the hang of this kind of lunch.

"I can't be more than 10 years older than you. I'm 36. How old are you, Gallagher?"

"You're older," she said.

"How much older?" The waiter brought his fourth, her third. Luck hadn't ordered the fourth, or third—he had considered it, but hadn't given the order—so he sent the drinks back. "Get me a bottle of 'zz-zz-zz,'" he said in the ear of the barman.

"What's *that?*" asked Gallagher.

"What do *you* know about wine?" he sniffed. "How much older?"

"Thirteen," she said.

"Thirteen years?"

"Thirteen years," she said, adding, "if you're not lying about your age."

Gallagher excused herself (if she could trust her eyes, he'd flushed at the remark) to go to the ladies room, but was detained. "Pay the toll," Luck said, forcing her back to face him. Then he pushed his face forward.

"Don't be absurd!" said Gallagher, struggling to get away.

"What gives you the right to talk to me that way?" he said, his face even closer.

Gallagher returned the stare.

"We'll see who's absurd," he said, releasing her. "Come back here. Don't try to skip out."

Gallagher picked her way through the maze of columns and alcoves. It took two sets of directions to find the ladies' room. She stood in the glare of the all-white room, but couldn't force her eyes to focus. There in the mirror was an egg where the face should have been. She leaned forward, and the egg stretched and waved, black puddles for eyes. She commanded it, but not a muscle budged. She laughed at it, but that only made it weirder. How could she keep that gangster in line if she couldn't manage the egg on her own neck? She flopped into a chair. After a peaceful interval—was she asleep?—she stood up. Fingers clutching the sink, she sent a clear signal to the face. Better, clearer—and, in all, it took only fifteen, maybe twenty minutes, thirty minutes at most. She tottered out of the white room and reentered the dusky grotto to seek Luck's alcove. The "zz-zz-zz" had been decanted, and the empty bottle lay in a basket with a napkin tied around it. Something mud-black had been poured into two of the half-dozen glasses arrayed on the table. Jarred by the sight of fresh drinks, Gallagher leaned her head against the stones, squeezing out a hot tear. She felt relieved to be rid of one at last. Luck passed her a wine glass full of blood, then retrieved it. "Take it easy. We'll order some lunch." The waiter appeared and dropped fresh menus on the table. When he left again, Luck gathered his reporter in his arms and kissed her with a hard, suctioning mouth.

"Hey!" said Gallagher. She wriggled away. "Get away from me!"

"Are we going to order?" he asked, if as nothing had happened. "Are you hungry yet?"

After three coffees, Gallagher felt better, but Luck was glum, so he started on the wine. A multicourse lunch—Dover sole, mixed grill—had been ordered and laid, but it went back to the kitchen nearly untouched. Gallagher ate the salad, purple and green, and picked at the dessert: a dense, sweet mound floating on a pinwheel of colored sauces. The sugar made her mind race with ideas that, although all tangled up, she was anxious to express. Luck appeared to be coming out of his sulk. He grasped his reporter's hand in arm-wrestle position. "I'm *interested* in you," he said emphatically. "I think you'll do well for us."

Gallagher thanked him.

"What I want to know," Luck continued, "is what *you* want to get out of it. Just tell me what you want, and I'll get it for you."

"Okay."

"Okay what?"

"I'll think about it."

"You'll think about what?"

Gallagher grinned. "I don't know what the hell it is you're talking about."

Luck had full access, he explained, to the city of Depointe—government, industry, arts, society, courts, crime, feds, media, you name it. Would she like, for example, to see the line at Ford? the Henry Malcolm Mustang estate? the woods where Hemingway used to go camping? The U.P. was beautiful, especially in summer. He had a place up there. What did she want to see? He could do anything.

"I don't know enough about it to decide," Gallagher chirped. This was the first friendly talk she'd had since coming to Depointe for good, and she now felt she understood Luck—better than anyone: he was powerful, yes, but decent and could be generous, if you played him the right way, and didn't ask for anything. But she *did* have something in mind.

"What?" he asked.

"Is this all I'm going to get to do?"

"Do what?" he asked.

"You know. The kind of assignment I get from Ralph."

"What does he give you?" Luck was using a different tone now. It was the tone Gallagher would've expected at lunch with the E.E. "Do you have a problem with him?"

"No."

"You're just like everybody else, you know."

"In what way?"

"You just want to climb. But you know something, Gallagher? Actually this is something I thought you *did* know. There's nothing up there but me."

"I wasn't talking about that."

"Talk to Bluestem about your assignments—unless you're after his job, Gallagher."

They rose, left the table, Luck saluted the Pomeranian, and they climbed the steps to daylight at 4:45 P.M. "You going back to the shop?" he asked.

"I'm going to the Tree."

"Tonight?"

"With Ralph."

"I'll go, too."

Arm in arm they walked back to the *Bullet,* but Luck, as it turned out, had calls to return, people to see, so Bluestem and Gallagher set off alone—but they weren't alone for long, for the cream of the city room was already settled in the Tree, and Luck showed up an hour later, although he acknowledged no one from Sunday. He arrowed straight to the bar, where his city editors, like the Red Sea, parted to make his place.

For a month after the Pomeranian lunch, Gallagher saw nothing of Luck. After drinks that night at the Money Tree—when he dredged every detail about the four-hour lunch—she saw very little of Bluestem. "Rolf only has lunch," Bluestem told Gallagher on the way over, "with 'intimates.'" In the hour they sat by a window in the beautiful Tree, a shallow room with recessed spotlight and walls stamped in brass, he repeated it a dozen times. When Gallagher mentioned that Luck had offered her a tour of the assembly lines, the Mustang estate, the city vault, Bluestem dropped his head ("O Jesus!") to the table.

Gallagher was drinking glasses of soda water with cuts of lemon, but she still felt drunk. Eventually, Bluestem left the table to remind Luck of "something important. I'll be right back." But Bluestem stayed at the bar until one of the editors crowded around Luck turned to see him hovering. Even after he'd been spotted, no move was made to include him: the editors addressed an occasional comment over their shoulders, but the 'Stem stood alone, glass in hand, his baby face glowing with the pleasure of standing so near the elect.

Gallagher studied the scene. Not once did Bluestem glance back at the table where he'd left his invited guest. This was standard practice at the Tree: you might go over with "friends," but if something better walked in, all bets were off. Gallagher knew this but still felt shafted. After thirty minutes nursing another fizzy drink, trying to hold out, Gallagher, steadier now, hungry and very dry, groped around the floor for her purse and exited.

After that night, Gallagher heard from Bluestem through memos. Her assignments, when accepted, were tossed on top of his in-box. The Sunday editor was jealous of the unearned tribute of a lunch with Luck, and also fried, she supposed, because the last-hired, low dog from the "back of the book" had up and bolted the Tree before he did. A day later she heard from a staffer how Luck had roared with laughter when the gullible 'Stem saw how his reporter had walked. "For me," Luck brayed, "she'll swallow a quart of gin. For *you,* she didn't cool her heels five minutes!"

A week later, a group from Sunday was sitting at the Tree "d'Été," a few tables set up on the sidewalk. The magazine editor, Roberts Hackenflecker, was talking. "Luck was bragging about you. 'She drinks like a camel,' he said.

"A camel," the long-faced Hackenflecker repeated. The staffers at the table laughed and Gallagher laughed. But just how funny was it? And what would happen, she wondered, if Bluestem decided to get even?

After this episode, people were chummier (Luck had never called any of *them* camels!) to the new Sunday writer: she had stood up to the "Reich," she had thrown down the gauntlet. "Win the battle with the 'Stem," Hackenflecker had said, "and you write your own ticket here. You can have Bluestem's job if you want it."

"What battle?" asked Gallagher.

"They're trying to see," said Hackenflecker (who enjoyed immunity at the *Bullet* because, although he edited a major section, he never drank with Luck), "if you've really got the rocks. You called their bluff," he went on. "You can't back down. The eye'll be on you night and day.

"You didn't have to play it so close—and so early," he continued, a few minutes later, "but this is just how it's played."

In four swift passing months, through spring and into early summer, Gallagher worked, grinding out more than her weekly share of copy. There was no regularity; each week brought a different spread of backup work in theater, movies, concerts, books, and records, along with puffs on visiting actors and celebrities, coverage of shopping-mall events and children's shows, along with the odd think-piece: Why were there so few roles for black actors? Why was television suddenly able to showcase a divorcée in a sitcom? What made the tedious, low-rent "Bowling for Dollars" such a stunner in the ratings?

Gallagher took whatever came her way, and made the most of it, dregs or not. The regular reviewers softened, and many times passed on a major film or play only to have Bluestem spike it rather than assign such a plum to the "compacter" (as Gallagher was called), who could crunch any kind of trash into hard, bright little grafs. Bluestem was cool; he was thoughtful; he could be charming, he wasn't *always* mean—but Gallagher was sidelined. Worse, her pieces were slashed, buried on classified, or guttered next to a big movie ad. Gallagher felt the editor's slights: this was upsetting, unfair, but still better than the "battle" forecast by the magazine editor. War had been averted. Gallagher did her work and lumped the rest; she posed no threat—as anyone could see—since after the famous Pomeranian lunch Luck hadn't called again.

Still, those in the know—the veterans who'd seen Luck put the match to the newsroom tinderbox time and again—saw that this calm was just a time-out. All ingredients for a big blow were there: Luck's megalomania, Bluestem's envy, Olympic sexual rivalry, Bluestem's mute rage, growing every year he was passed over for a natural (even well-earned) promotion to A.C.E., only to be—cruelest cut of all—pitched to Sunday. Although at Sunday the 'Stem rose to the top, it was never the same. From the onset, people had figured that hiring the chit from the Blackfoot paper was an opening move in Bluestem's overdue revenge. The recruitment itself was a clear win over Luck's public veto.

But once news of the Pomeranian lunch had spread, battle lines were replotted. Word had it that the couple was gone for twelve hours, and the Pomeranian could only account for one. It could mean only one thing. Bluestem was routed—and, if *that* wasn't bad enough, the Mohawk, or whatever she was, stiffed him that very night at the Tree, ran out on him in front of the whole world. And would the little squaw's reckless bravado bring them together, Luck and Bluestem—as they had always come together before—or was Luck fixing to have a little fun with the 'Stem?

Things had simmered down since that eventful day, but no one was fooled. Luck and the Wampanoag were lovers, and Bluestem was publicly licking his wounds. Now it was simply a matter of months, maybe weeks—hardly worth the money the sharps (from City, one from Sunday) had put on it. One question remained: who would be forced out—the redskin alone, or Bluestem with the turncoat native? Was it conceivable that the Wampanoag stay—and Bluestem walk? At the *Bullet,* anything was possible. The paper did have a history, though, of backing the top dog.

In those quiet weeks of toil, keeping her head low, both on the job and off, Gallagher had begun—aided by hints from friends—to worry about Bluestem and the heavy atmosphere, like a thunderhead, that her presence could create. Even on days when Bluestem was up, brisk, joking with staff—if Gallagher happened to glide into the glass cube, his mood instantly darkened. He was blunt, clipped, and, if she pressed for assignments or advice, surly. The change was marked and seemed to date from the Pomeranian lunch. As time went by, no improvement. Desperate for a sign of the former friendly 'Stem, Gallagher entered his office one day, and, uninvited, waited for his gaze to rise from the desk, where it seemed glued. Then, catching his eye, she grabbed his penholder, a quartz block big as a skull, and thrust her fingers into its holes. (Did he flinch?) Her fingers sunk up to the knuckles. "See?" she said to him. (What was that look on his face?) "I'm stuck. I'm at your mercy."

He smiled, if the weak curl of his lips (and the stones that were his eyes) could be called a smile. Then the stones swiveled back to their papers.

"Want to get a drink?" Gallagher asked another day, defying (by low man speaking first) the natural order of things.

"Don't have time," the answer came back.

"Tomorrow?"

"Tomorrow's Saturday."

"How about Monday?" she persisted.

Bluestem hauled his gaze—his eyes seemed hung on weights—upward. "Sunday night might be okay. I'll take you to dinner." He paused. "If you want to have dinner with me."

"Yes!"

The eyes dropped again. "Fine. I'll call you at home."

That night, Gallagher told McGuire (who called every night, but *not* to talk shop) about the jam she was in, and how she was finally, thank God, fighting free. McGuire had heard the story of the Pomeranian lunch, the Tree, and the aftermath. "What's up, Gallagher?" he said, when she finished. "I don't get it." She explained further. "How's your work going?" he asked, after a pause.

"What work?"

"What pieces are you working on?"

Once more Gallagher explained the system: how she got only the castoffs (drive-in movies, dinner plays, youth symphonies), and the dreary feature (line dancing, rollercoaster design) Bluestem threw in, and so blah that it took a feat of hydraulics to pump out a few good grafs.

McGuire was silent, but Gallagher could hear his breathing.

"So much," she said, "for the 'writing.' "

He still didn't speak.

"Are you there?" she asked.

"You dumb fuck!" he bellowed through the wire. (Gallagher was lying on the rough carpeting, her head resting against a table leg. She sat up.) "You're a total washout, Gallagher. And you wonder why they're 'exploiting' you! You're lucky they've found a way to exploit a lazy crap-artist like yourself."

"Oh, thanks!" she shrilled into the line. "I needed that. Tell me what I did to deserve it!" She paused to breathe. "You're not here—you know nothing about the situation I'm in!"

"Take it easy!" McGuire was quick to say, although his voice still crackled with anger. "I can't talk to you anymore. You're always flying off the handle. Did I say something offensive? If I did, I'm sorry."

Gallagher stared out the window at one of the Apley courtyards—a green square and an apple tree; even in the dusk, she could see the small, dark birds pecking in the grass.

"You're sorry! You jump down my throat for making the best of a lousy situation, and say you're *sorry!* It's too late for sorry! *I'm* sorry!"

"Okay," he said. "I was trying to help. What have I ever done, Gallagher—*when* have I ever done *anything* to hurt you?" His voice was harsh, pleading. "Tell me so I'll know. I'll hang up right now if you say I've ever said a word—."

Gallagher stood, phone in hand, gazing out the window—it was a low window and broad, making the grassy square seem like a connecting room. She could never look at that green patch without feeling relief; if she opened her window and stuck out an arm, she could pat the grass and dig up a fistful of Depointe earth, rich and wormy. McGuire didn't know it, but he was right; she was grinding in the gears of the flesh-eating machine. He knew those gears; he'd done his time.

"Are you still there?" he asked.

He'd kept himself free of it for a long time; she'd thrown herself right into the works. That was the difference.

"Are you listening?"

But no one had ever condemned him to the sludge beat—for life.

"Well, listen good, because you may have only the one chance, Gallagher, and you've got to use it. You're got to go out and *prove* yourself as a writer. That's your trump card. You've got to fight for some meaty stories—not the piffle you've been doing. Any fool can do that. Get *control* of the situation. Do some work, Gallagher, and get the hell out of politics!"

Gallagher listened. "They won't give me any 'work,'" she said. "They might have before, but they won't now."

"Don't wait to be handed it on a platter!" McGuire howled. "Do you want to get canned? What the hell's happened to you?"

Gallagher could no longer see the courtyard. Now that she had the chance, and months of tears built up, she meant to cry them all out. McGuire waited for the flood to ease, then began to talk. When he said all he could, and as many times as he needed to, Gallagher was flattened—eyes swollen and lids stuck together. When he finally hung up, she fell asleep with her head under the table.

She woke an hour later to the grainy light of a full moon. Why was she sleeping on the floor like a bum? Had she slipped that low? She got up, switched on all the lights, then scavenged for food. After eating everything she could find, and gulping a quart of milk, the newest model Gallagher—all ramrod spine and hard-plated head, every weakness leached out in the flood of tears—had hatched. Good, she croaked to the reflection in the black window, and to the quiet telephone, still under the table: good.

But before Monday's gallant remake could begin, Sunday night's dinner—which Gallagher, in her tight hood of decision, had almost forgotten—must play out with its hidden motive. For why else, in his present coldness, would Bluestem have set aside a weekend night for one he begrudged even a minute of his work-day time? This was the question.

After the late-night feed of applesauce, cheese, and stale Oreos, Gallagher slept in her alcove from earliest birdsong till after noon. She had remembered to wash off the sticky mask of tears, so her face felt smooth and cool, her body peacefully slack. She lay back on the narrow bed to enjoy the midday business on the lawn. The tree was leafy; dark-bodied birds were rummaging through the bright grass. Above the wall, the sky was blue but furred with humidity and pink gases from the city furnaces. Gallagher padded into her kitchen to make coffee, carried a cup back to bed, and opened a steno pad, where she had been keeping a log of the weather. It was foolish—who cared, even one day later, what yesterday's weather had been?—but it made the time served in Depointe seem less penal. She entered the date, June 24, 1976, and the sky's condition, the temperature, the degree of summer's advancement, the birds seen and—using yesterday's *Bullet*—the sun's rise and set, the tides (although these tides, and those who cared about them, were a distant reality). When she had exhausted her impressions of that Sunday, seen through the screen, she set the pad aside and picked up a new book, the recent work of four U.K. poets, not one recognizable name. They were all young, English, Irish, one Scot, and the writing was quiet, drab: simple accounts of time wasted in damp, woebegone places with no money and nothing to do but sit in a pub or walk on the downs. You could hardly imagine what it was these poets did for a living; they were never in love—too glum. The introduction was written by an English critic (also a poet), who supplied an account of the lives behind the writing. They were teachers, doctors, civil servants, newsmen, but nothing professional had filtered into the poetry. The poems—like the weather log—were cool, clean, and remote. Who, in reading that log, would guess the cut-rate films, gaudy shows, movie stars, sitcoms, and TV bowling that really filled the diarist's days? Gallagher felt someday she might write one of those U.K. poems, all impersonal and hollowed out.

But unlike the news biz, poetry would be slow. It was meant to be slow. A whole year's worth of weather might yield nothing, or maybe a few lines. Nothing good could be rushed or forced.

Gallagher closed the book and gulped the dregs of cool coffee. McGuire had advised using every spare minute to read the competition, to gather ideas, to research the ideas assigned, but there was time enough for that tomorrow. She wanted to have a day like the ones those lonely men in England had—or thought they had. The trick was to have it, and not be swamped, or killed, by it. She was thinking about this when the phone rang. Roberts Hackenflecker wondered if she'd ever seen the *Bullet* shop at night when the day's news was spinning off the presses? Gallagher said she hadn't. Didn't she think, the editor said, it might be worthwhile? So, the editor went on, in his steady way, how about tonight?

"Tonight?"

The plan was this: dinner at Hackenflecker's—a bunch of people: friends, no writers—then the magazine editor himself would drive Gallagher down to the plant where they could watch the first edition as it was printed, folded, stacked, tied, loaded on trucks and then hurled onto the streets by 3:30 A.M. "Sound good?"

Gallagher held her breath.

"Okay?" he said.

The dinner and outing would cut short the English-poet's day, but Gallagher figured, when the time came for dinner, she'd be glad of the break. The poet's day would start now with a cigarette (she kept a pack on hand for just these moments). Then, sitting in her nightgown on the floor, just to think: a good beginning.

Later that day, she drove out to Wheel City, a town she'd passed en route to the movies. It was an industrial town like Wampanoag, not as old, but just as run down. Here one of the first auto plants started up, but was long gone.

Depointers, nonetheless, were proud of Wheel because it had already been "renewed," and a full decade before the Model Cities era. A new downtown sprung up on landfill, home to a few smokeless industries and corporate offices. The old downtown, where Gallagher was headed, was all but chucked; a building or two rented for municipal offices, a few others leased to the state college extension. Even on weekdays, when the coffeeshops were open and a few stragglers loitering, Wheel was bleak. On weekends, with the shops dark and offices closed or boarded up, it was a ghost town. How, Gallagher wondered, had an industry younger than the century left so much wreckage? She walked the main street, passing a gallant, Beaux Arts bank, then walls of homely, yellow-brick offices, hole-in-the-wall coffeeshops and ragbag stores. No person, on foot or wheels, passed. After five blocks of steady pacing, Gallagher began seeing something. On the opposite side of the street were thousands of dustballs or cat fluff blown up against the windows. Further on, she crossed the street to study the windows of a TV repair shop.

Strewn against the darkened glass were—not dustballs!—but dead moths, wings extended. The moths had struck the glass at an angle and were rayed in even, slanted lines. The wings were white, translucent, some not entirely dried. Gallagher found window after window striped with insects until, coming to a block of houses whose first-floor windows were screened, they stopped—but in the next block of offices, there they were again.

What had happened? Gallagher halted, sat down on a bus-stop bench. How did they die all at once? Was it a plague? The street was treeless, and hardly any grass—where had they nested? If they'd sailed—in a wind-driven cloud—from the farms, or maybe from some far-off prairie, how did they all end up in Wheel?

Gallagher got up, retraced her path. The moths were on the left now, slanting upward. The sky—so bright this morning—was already clouded. Gallagher felt the chill, but couldn't bring herself to walk faster down the desolate street. In Depointe, even the streets were weird: they weren't black asphalt, they were yellowish-white and pebbled; you could scan their flat grade clear to the horizon.

It was late. Gallagher figured it must be late, because the sun, which was out again, flung its low fire at the store windows. Looking back, two golden roads, broken at intervals, ran the length of the street. She sat on the steps of the bank watching the fiery light slide down the glass and over the millions of moths. Gallagher stood up to see better, shivering with excitement. This was it, wasn't it? This was what those U.K.s would see in their minds, but turn it down low in the writing, so low you could hardly see, but you could feel it. She could feel it—but could she turn it down low enough?

It was a long drive back, but in her exaltation, she hardly noticed.

Later, Gallagher stood near Roberts Hackenflecker in the thundering vault where four presses rolled their immense wheels, sending the wide thin sheeting over and under, and into the teeth of the machine. An unbroken skein of printed page snaked along the track to be chopped; then the sheets were twisted and folded—for a while, you couldn't see—then sections of Sunday's first edition rolled down a rubber track to flop onto the baling table. Hand balers were tackling the thicker sections, but there was also a machine baler that wrapped and tied normal loads. At several tables paperboys stuffed in ad inserts.

For an hour the two Bullets watched. Roberts would lean over to yell some salient fact (pounds of paper, barrels of ink, roller rpms) into Gallagher's ear. After satisfying their curiosity—and when the noise had become intolerable—Hackenflecker guided Gallagher through the pressroom, past the loading decks and into the dark alley. It was almost three, but the editor knew of an after-hours bar, a comfortable place not far.

They drank single-malt scotch in a saloon so dark, Gallagher could barely see her glass, but she could feel Roberts' eyes intent on her. He was not a talker. They listened to recordings—bebop and hard bop, Roberts explained—of Parker, Davis, and Gillespie, Thelonious Monk, Charles Mingus, John Coltrane. It was beautiful, Gallagher thought, but too rich and vital for the drab poets.

Leaving the bar after another drink, they sat in the parked car at Apley House, and stared into the dark. It was nearly five—Roberts walked around to open her door. "You're good people, Gallagher," he said, breaking into the long silence.

He watched as she unlocked the heavy wood door and disappeared.

That night Gallagher dreamt about the printworks. The presses were huge, silvery. Someone kept turning them off. Roberts came through a door to explain, but it was too loud. Luck and Bluestem, she saw, had blown in to straddle the top of the press, and what movie did that come from? She woke, suddenly, to a cloudy, humid day. It was late, almost twelve. Today she felt too foolish to write in the log; it wasn't worth it to try and remember the movie quoted in her dream, or what it meant. It was almost Monday and what had she done toward the serious stories needed to rescue her career and her self-respect? Nothing. And everything, she thought—gazing at the low sky with its filthy wad of cloud—went against making that effort now.

But Gallagher set out to buy a dozen newspapers and magazines: *Bullet, Blade, Times, Tribune,* and *Daily News,* along with *Vogue* and *Glamour, Esquire, Time, New York,* and—for laughs—*TV Guide* and *Soap Opera Digest.* She spent the day reading periodicals spread on the bed like a jigsaw puzzle. By 4:00, head aching, she had twenty ideas that seemed Bullet-proof, but also sophisticated, up to date—even a little advanced—but nothing far out or too deep. Gallagher flopped on the bed and closed her eyes. An hour later she woke with a start. Outside was a darkening summer day. A pod of storms pounding the plains was barreling into the city. The air was disturbed, the sky lurid. It was 6:45, and Bluestem due at 7.

CHAPTER 10

Some of the ideas—fleshed out into stories over the next weeks (full summer, scorching sidewalks, sun boiling the long stripe of river)—were perfect. The longer pieces were sent over the wire, and Gallagher's byline appeared in thirty different papers, including a few page 1 teasers. People were noticing, and Bluestem took credit for spotting talent in out-of-the-way places.

Gallagher assigned some credit to her former editor, but McGuire warned against resting on laurels; the battle had just begun. She was busy, she told him, on all fronts: taking drafts home to polish, logging hours of TV to spot fresh trends, scouting art and student film festivals. She assigned herself to the Grade Z flicks no one on the staff had heard of: "wall-to-wall blood," and exclusive inner-city runs. Only in daylight, Gallagher told McGuire, would she dare creep into the vast, musty theaters, whose floors glittered with broken bottles, gummed with food, used condoms, soda, and dried vomit, to find a seat in the rear, near an exit. Just last week, she told him, she had ventured into the thousand-seat Majestic for a lightly attended matinee of *White Trash Massacre, Part II.* (No, McGuire said, he hadn't seen it.) There was no story, she said, no characters. A remote mountain people, starved and fiendishly inbred, was hit, in a few months' time, by blight, rabid animals, and feuds. Highlights included a hillbilly skinned alive; another was hung upside down so ravenous dogs could eat his face; and the climax: a family of cretins bricked alive in a cave with bears, jackals, and a nest of vipers. (In every case, she told McGuire, the audience rooted for the animals.)

McGuire sighed. "What did you say?" he asked. She'd filed twenty inches, Gallagher replied, about the experience of sitting there, glued to the seat, while the audience, maddened by the sights, shrieked with joy as each fresh batch of honkies was dispatched. "I left before the end," she confessed, but in fact she'd fled when a sharp-eyed viewer spotted "whitey," right in the audience, big as life.

Sure, she told McGuire, that kind of story is only good once. So she kept her eyes peeled, reading the slicks and tabloids, for new faces—actors, singers, models—anyone worth a call for a picture-interview. On free weekends, she drove out to college and regional theaters to talk to the odd matinee idol "sent to Siberia." These faded names got top billing and drew sellout crowds. And yet, however eager the old-timers were for a hit, they shied away from the splashy publicity local newspapers were happy to give them.

Why are they like that? Gallagher had asked the theater critic, after a bruising phone session with Adele "Peach" Perkins, a three-decade ingenue, beloved by Mrs. Gallagher's (and *her* mother's) generation. Covering "Hollywood-in-exile," Larry Langton confirmed, was no picnic. The old movie idols had been burned and humbled. The last thing they wanted was to dredge up the past, only to be pitied or patronized. And same goes, he said, for filmography, Broadway runs, the marriages, divorces, shack-ups—*anything* people were still interested in. They'll clam right up, he said, unless you stick to the play of the moment, and ask them about "stretching."

And what's wrong with that? asked Gallagher.

"If you write up that gargle," Larry said, "your story gets the nail. No one's interested in sunset ambition. Readers want to hear about the moguls, the casting couch, the Brown Derby, the dirt, the agony! Or what went sour and when, and how they ended up in a dump like Eagle, Michigan. That's your story, kiddo."

Wasn't that, Gallagher said, a bit *too* cynical? "No kidding!" Langton said. "What's worse is you have to slice deep to get the quotes. It isn't pretty. They've finally got it together, they're all dried out or tanked up, and *you* come along to prick their balloon. Even if you don't do it right there and then," he added, "you'll get them in print. There's no other way."

Larry, sitting in the Tree with Gallagher, was tanked up himself. Any day now he expected a transfer to Travel; *that* writer had been shipped to Moscow when the *Bullet* Sovietologist had moved up to the *New York Times*. Larry couldn't wait. Theater in Depointe was a joke; the principal houses recycled sludge from the '50s and the odd musical; there was no writing talent on the horizon, and name actors weren't exactly beating a path to Depointe. Even the money men were pulling the plug—the city was too wild after dark to draw the serious pocketbooks.

Gallagher was surprised to hear this and said so. When she'd first arrived, the drama desk seemed so glamorous, so—. Larry interrupted. "I put a good face on it. You newsfolks are always the last to know. Funny, isn't it?"

Langton ordered another gin—no mixer. It was late, after nine, and the Tree was empty. From shop talk, he swerved to the subject of home life: how his clever wife had stripped, papered, painted, and varnished the shell of an ancient brownstone they'd bought in a homesteading program. The house had cost peanuts, but they were locked into a five-year stay—no slumlording and no leasing—in a precinct where even the roaches were armed. Was it worth it? he asked himself. They'd find out.

In the last half hour, Larry had been called to the phone twice. Shortly after the second call, Louisa May Child Langton, "the Lady Langton," as Larry introduced her, sailed into the Tree. A strawberry blonde, Louisa May wore layers of white linen, her curls framing a face pretty enough for a soap ad. Her fingernails, Gallagher saw, were gnawed close, on fingers like chicken bones. Which was worse, Gallagher wondered, finding the husband in a bar with a girl, or just finding him (fresh off the wagon) in a bar?

Louisa May no sooner whisked through the doorway when the spills of bright chatter began. Mostly she talked of Lawrence—his residencies at the Abbey, his plans for books (first families of the American stage, an introduction to the Kabuki), the fundraisers he had hosted for twin Old Actors' homes, in Depointe and County Clare. In matters of loyalty and human kindness, the man was, she said, a nonpareil.

The pretty face and compliments that so lulled Gallagher only seemed to nerve the critic up. Larry swallowed his gin, chewed his ice, and started on Louisa's drink. Then, getting up to order another round, he sat down at the bar.

Gallagher left the Tree with the Langtons to spend a festive evening at their home. On hand-embroidered linens, Louisa May spread a medley of odd dishes:

paté, tongue, Alaskan crab legs, black bean soup, caviar, bouillabaisse, roast capon, shrimp toast, petit fours, candied fruit, and cheesecake. She adored company; cooking was her passion; and all these, she said, sweeping a hand over the banquet, only the fruits of the last day or so. It was a treat, she added, to have Larry Langton at home, don't you know?

Not once during the hours-long feast did the hostess light at her table. She rushed to freshen wine and water, to put on records, to heat and reheat dishes, to ladle gravies, chutney, sauce. When Larry uncorked the cognac, Louisa brought out swatches of fabric (she also designed clothes and slipcovers), including the plaids the critic had brought back from a walking tour of Scotland. She unfurled wallpaper samples and paint schemes, blueprints for gardens and additions. Finally, ashen-faced, exhausted, she leapt up, then—apologizing for a headache and inexcusable lassitude—sank into an armchair.

Gallagher was saying good night at 1:30, when she noticed the theater critic had fetched his own coat. She wasn't going straight home, Gallagher told the Langtons; she had calls to make. Louisa took the coat from Larry and was closing the front door behind Gallagher when Larry squeezed through to the porch. Gallagher dashed down the steps, but Larry grabbed her arm. He had something to say; couldn't she wait a minute? Louisa May, perching on the arm of a wicker chair, was waiting on the porch there, too. But when her husband whispered something in her ear, she shot off.

Taking over the Travel desk, Larry whispered to Gallagher, was simply a ruse. He was leaving Louisa, and leaving Depointe, too, if he could. His aim was to string for a fashion or maybe an airline magazine and live abroad. If all else failed, he could patch together a living importing woolens.

But then—before Gallagher could ask a question—Louisa May reappeared with an uncut pie, three glass bowls of ice cream, a beaker of claret sauce, and a bowl of shaved chocolate, all arranged on a lacquered tray. She whisked back inside to drag out a table, coffee pot, liqueurs and glasses, cups and lace-edged napkins.

When Gallagher finally tore herself away, it was past three. Tired and dazed, she still refused the Langtons' offer of the guest bedroom and breakfast in bed. The question forming in her mind—why Larry Langton, longtime newsman, syndicated critic, and theater nob, would chuck it all: and for what, to shill for the airlines?—was answered. He had to. In the course of the evening, Gallagher had heard how Louisa May, in addition to countless acts of mercy, had rescued him from the demolitions of a boozer's life. She'd stood by through the weekend benders, the disappearances, the rages, the scary blackouts, the climbing on—but mostly falling off—the wagon. It was Louisa May who kept him sober, Larry admitted—when he *was* sober. But he never wanted to be sober again! *This* was clear.

That weekend, Gallagher drove out to Eagle to meet the actor who'd graced with his elegant villainy scores of classic horror films. Randolph D'Aart, his British wife, Reenie, and his best friend, child star, and talk-show staple Dodie McArdle were currently headlining a traveling production of *Dames at Sea.* While the *Dames* director chalked up the stage, Gallagher led McArdle and the D'Aarts to seats in the stifling theater. She'd already offended both wife and friend by focusing all her questions on Randolph and on yesteryear's bumper crop (Did he like working with Corman? How much directing did he take? What started the Poe craze?) of scary flicks.

The haughty actor—smoking Dunhills in the ancient, tindery firetrap—kept his cool. At most he sneered or ground his teeth. It was the friend who flared up.

Mr. D'Aart (the child star was saying) was not here to discuss "cult" films to which his person and talents had added so much luster. Had the girl seen the press the D'Aarts had garnered when *Dames* previewed last winter in Duluth? Was she aware of the book—treatise, D'Aart corrected—the actor was writing on the erosion of Baja? Or the charity Reenie had chaired in the spring for handicapped actors? Really? Very few people, he said, cared about those silly, campy films, least of all their star. Where, by the way, was Larry Langton? Was L.L. still writing about the stage?

Stifling in the fiery, hot theater, Gallagher let McArdle ramble. Then the director, bellowing from the stage, said that Randy, Reenie, and Dodie were wanted, chop-chop. Gallagher used the last minutes to fire off a dozen questions: special effects, makeup, how much of the dialogue was ad-libbed? Which was the biggest grosser? The actor and his wife stared at the stage.

"Randolph might be too much the gentleman," McArdle snapped, "to contend with a pushy little starfucker, but," he added, "I'm certainly not!"

The D'Aarts, drifting down the steps, took their leave. The child actor lingered. Eying the reporter scribbling in her pad, he growled: "If you print any of that garbage, I'll make it my personal business to have you expunged!"

Gallagher wrote the story in one day—a corrosive portrait of a washed-up, aging gargoyle, whose slight talent he now deigned to scorn; spoiled by success, cosseted by flacks; snooty, addled, and conceited. The thirty-incher ran that next weekend on the entertainment pages of twenty-eight dailies. That Monday Gallagher received a phone call. "Delmore McArdle," the *Bullet* operator said. "Go ahead, please." Gallagher held her breath. "Listen, you fucking vampire," he hissed. She waited and heard. "You have no more friends in Hollywood!"

But she was already a star, Roberts Hackenflecker insisted, when he heard the story: she didn't need those friends. Roberts and Gallagher were driving out to the country so Gallagher could see her first automated truck plant. "Don't worry about it," he said.

From a balcony, glassed in and soundproofed, they watched a double line of silvery robots installing radiators. From there, the *Bullet* staffers were taken to the showroom to see the late-model pickups, then to the executive lunchroom. Everything else, the Great Motors' spokesman told them, was off-limits to the press. But they weren't on assignment, Roberts explained; they weren't even *reporters*. He had visited the plant before and been taken all round, he said, even through the R&D labs. The GM official was unmoved. ("Maybe if we call Luck?" Gallagher suggested. "Forget it," Roberts replied.)

Instead, the two writers spent the afternoon cruising the leafy fringes of northern Depointe County. In a wealthy hamlet, under the canopy of interlaced beeches, they found an old-fashioned tea house. They ordered lunch on the wisteria-draped porch. "You've read the situation correctly," Roberts said, starting—as he always did—in the middle of a thought. "You've acted in time," he added. "Keep it up."

"Keep *what* up?" Gallagher asked, but she knew he must mean the five weekly bylines, the excellent play her work was getting, her popularity on the wire, maybe even the way she'd finessed the Luck-Bluestem problem. It was all fine and dandy, she said, trying to conceal her pleasure, but it wasn't exactly *real* writing. "Compared to what?" he asked. And she mentioned the poems and essays she'd been reading—and how formulaic the *Bullet* seemed next to that.

Roberts listened.

So, she went on, maybe she was shrewd, or maybe she was lucky. In any case, it was a minor accomplishment.

"You've got drive!" Roberts said, his eyes bright with anger. "You've got talent, and you're working for a first-rate paper. What more could you ask?"

Gallagher gazed at his flushed face, dappled by wisteria leaves. "What if the work you think is so great," she said, "is just meaningless slop?"

He said nothing. Then he shook his head. "It's not easy to be consistently good at this."

"Maybe not," she said. "But don't you ever question it?"

"Never. And I don't think I'd want to. But I wonder if you aren't getting a little ahead of yourself. Your work is good, but it isn't what it could be."

Roberts poured tea into Gallagher's cup, then a trickle of milk and spoonful of sugar. He even stirred the tea. "I think what *I'm* doing—" he began, then stopped. "I'm not defending myself. There's no need. I'd never say 'meaningless,' but it's not what I'd pictured myself doing, either."

"Did you want City desk?" Gallagher broke in. The waitress approached their table with a fresh pot of tea. "That's what everybody wants."

"Is that what *you* want?" he asked.

"I hate news," Gallagher said.

Roberts's eyes widened. "Why are you *in* this business?"

"I know other people here love it," she said mildly, "but I like angles, not facts."

"You like play," he said. "You want to be a star. That's okay, but you have to be awfully good, you know." He paused. "Let me ask you a question. What's the point of a press, if it's not to report facts—to make sense of them?"

"If that's the point," Gallagher responded, "why aren't *you* working on City desk?" The tea was strong; her skull bones felt tight under their skin. She glanced around the porch: a bowl of roses on each cloth, ferns and pale lanterns hanging from the ceiling. Beyond the garden with its paths of trellised archways was a dense green hedge.

"I've been there already," he said glumly.

She'd barely heard him. "What?"

"I don't want to get into it now," he said. "Don't ask." He followed her gaze through the whitewashed arches. "It'll be all over the paper tomorrow, right?"

Gallagher considered. "You're the only one I talk to."

"What about Rolf?"

"What about him?"

He pushed his cup away, napkin and spoon. "Well, you asked."

After rolling up its light, the afternoon sun hovered on the horizon. The garden released its coolness. During the '60s, he'd signed on with the AP, following stints as State House correspondent for the *Toledo Telegram* and the *Minneapolis Horn*. He ended up in Washington. There was plenty of competition then—it was a different scene. (Roberts was about McGuire's age—maybe a little older—so the story sounded familiar.) Like McGuire, the magazine editor was a newsman from birth.

"Is that it?" asked Gallagher.

"I'm not finished."

By 1971, he was filing stories from South America, when—.

"South America!" exclaimed Gallagher. The memory was unraveling slowly, the material strangely fresh—raw even—and jumbled together. Had he ever told it before?

"Mainly there," he continued. "But I was also in Eastern Europe for a year."

The sun flared one more time, firing the editor's face. Roberts shaded his eyes. By then, he was his own man; he could follow his instincts; he was free to cover anything in bureaus that were fast and fierce. Where exactly? she asked. Bogota, La Paz, Caracas, Quito, he said, São Paulo, even Rio for a while. And doing what? Covering politics—the regimes, parties, military, the sudden swings from left to right; the coups, the juntas; arts, sometimes, high society—later, the big peasant migrations; multinationals, too, to the extent that it was possible.

"So then?"

Roberts lifted his cup and Gallagher filled it. "Nothing," he said. "That's it."

"Really?"

"Don't kid yourself!" he snapped. "You think I'd be in a dump like Depointe if that was the story?" Roberts glared. "Can't you see that I'm not finished?"

"You're finished," laughed Gallagher.

"Thanks," he grinned.

"You laughed!" she said.

"I laughed. Now listen."

When Gallagher could tear her eyes from the editor's haunted face, dusk had become night. For two hours—longer—they had sat over cold tea. A workday was wasted—no story was drummed up, no draft written, no pages edited—yet it seemed like a lot had happened.

Normally dry, Roberts had given a surprisingly rich account of life as a leg man. After transfers to bigger bureaus in the northern cities, he'd became a rover, then a chief—Southern hemisphere. Even toward the end, he was still reporting, filing a column, "The Americas," that ran on hundreds of foreign-news pages. His last story should have been the kicker. He was there for the final days of a ruling dynasty, whose name had once been the country's, and whose ancestral tree was rooted in medieval Spain. There was no coup, no violence. The family's base—soldiers and ranchers—good for so many generations, had suddenly eroded. An upstart family, whose vast wealth was rooted—not in crops, but in high-yield factories and mines—had campaigned for full-scale industrialization, state-controlled farming, a centralized police force, and stringent population control. Rock-ribbed Stalinists, Roberts said. Not that the royal family wasn't just as proud to back Hitler.

It happened, Roberts added, on his birthday, his fortieth. He was on his way to tape an interview with the fleeing family. (Where were they going? "The States," Roberts replied. "Where else?") The night before he had attended a farewell dinner, 500 guests. The wine cellars were drained. The party lasted till morning. Half the time Roberts was on the phone working on entrance visas.

"They must have trusted you!" Gallagher exclaimed.

"I knew the son. We were the same age."

"So, it was the next day, right? The day the family left?"

That morning, he was racing up the palace steps. Helicopters were on the lawn, with the sharp-shooters. It was stiflingly hot, 105 degrees, the palace shimmered like rock candy. Hundreds of officers loitering in the square. They were starting to cordon it off. Roberts was alone—no other press invited. He was late, out of breath. The climate was bad for his asthma.

"I forgot to tell you," he said, interrupting himself, that for months—almost a year—New York had been badgering him to come back. (Come back where? Why?) They were consolidating bureaus, shutting some down—the service was hemorrhaging money. What they needed then were experienced home editors. They were eager to set him up in D.C., Manhattan, or maybe Chicago. But, he said, however prestigious, it was a desk job. He'd die before he'd let them nail him to a chair. He was a born legman, that's what he was trained to do. That's what he did best. The hours, the travel, the danger—none of it fazed him in the least. He was made for it.

He glanced up. Fast? He was fast as he'd ever been at 20. He was faster! He was the best they ever had in the hemisphere—. He stopped, peering at Gallagher. "Do you think I'm bragging?"

Gallagher shook her head.

"I am a little," he said. "But you get it. Good." What happened was this: he tripped—his shoe came untied, or he was going too fast. He fell, tumbled down the flight of steps. When he landed, his kneecap was cracked, his hand broken, the whole back of his head bleeding. He lay there frying in the noonday sun. He felt no pain. It was over. It was the end.

Gallagher waited, but the magazine editor had finished.

When he spoke again, it was only to say that—like everything else—he learned it the hard way. What they had been trying to tell him, but he was too dense to hear—was that he was old, too old and too beat up, for a young man's job.

Gallagher let her breath out. It was horrible, sad—not just flubbing the story of a lifetime and landing in some fleabag hospital, but how final it seemed. But *why* was it so final? Couldn't this happen to anyone, wasn't it an accident?

Roberts just shook his head. If she didn't understand, he could never explain.

"It's a young man's job." McGuire had said this—it was his story, too. Thinking of McGuire, Gallagher pictured the Swamp city room, wall to wall with geezers and whitebeards, every one of them a legman. "In Wamp—" she started to say, but Roberts cut her off. It wasn't some Indian paper he was referring to; he was talking about the inner circle—New York, Washington, London, Paris, Moscow—places where the fight was to the death, where you couldn't be too young, too fast—.

But wasn't there *less* competition now? Gallagher asked. Why was it such a young man's job when, as McGuire had so often insisted, "there was nobody out there left to beat?"

Roberts didn't seem to hear. His eyes were hollow, his lips dry and pale. Was he reclimbing the steps?

She repeated McGuire's remark. Yes, Roberts agreed: the old story—consolidation, chains, the shrinking wire services. Of course, this was a new element, but it had *nothing* to do with what had happened to him. These days, if anything, you had to move even faster! There was TV and radio to beat, don't forget. And it was too easy, he said, to hide behind the big picture. The big picture was beside the point. It had nothing to do with day-to-day reporting.

"That's *so* naive," Gallagher insisted. "You're agonizing about that day, and you refuse to see what was behind it."

Roberts was silent. The kitchen had long closed, but no one seemed to mind the couple sitting out on the porch. "Why do you insult me? What could you possibly know about it?"

"I know this. It wasn't about turning 40," Gallagher said. "Or if it was, it's because the rules changed. It used to be okay to grow up. It meant you knew something. Now the less you know the better you are."

Roberts waited. "Tell me something," he said. "If the big picture is so ugly, how come only a little squirt from Sunday can see it?"

Gallagher considered: how *did* she see? McGuire, of course, had, from the moment he'd decided to quit—and before—

ranted day and night about how flabby, corrupt, impotent the biz had become. There was no real competition (McGuire didn't count TV), nothing to keep a man on his toes. It had always been dog-eat-dog, he'd said, but now most of the dogs were eaten. There were a few places left for the biggest, meanest dogs and they'd all kill to get there.

Gallagher was spelling out the dog system, but the magazine editor wasn't interested in what some sour-grapes loser had to say. "You think you're tough, Gallagher," he said, leaning in, "and you *are*. But two-bit philosophy isn't going to make your life any easier. You can't be a good newsman by running everything down. There's something to be said for good faith. You're a cynic," he added, "and cynics never make the grade."

Inside, the last lights went out and still they sat.

"Concentrate on the work, Gallagher. Do good work and let others worry about the big picture."

You did good work, she felt like saying, and look what happened to you! But what did happen to him? He fell down the steps in some banana republic a million times more backward even than Wampanoag—and bam! Life was over. Why? What had he done wrong? (McGuire would say: he didn't get the goddamned story, fool!)

Gallagher felt (they had left the tea house, and were groping their way to the old Saab) that she didn't—even at times like this—understand men: if they were such hard-headed realists as they claimed, how could they be so gullible? Why was some impossible code always driving them into martyrdom? Who was holding them to this standard? She didn't have standards: she was flexible. No matter how the course changed, she'd be on the boat.

"How are things going with Ralph?" Roberts asked, as the old car swerved on the curling, country roads.

"You mean Bluestem?"

"He still your boss?"

She didn't want to think about Bluestem. What code did he have?

"You seemed to be getting pretty thick with Rolf." He paused: "That makes a difference."

Gallagher looked out the window at the streaming darkness.

"How are you getting along with Bluestem?" he asked again.

"Okay."

"Take care, Gallagher," he said. "Be a foot soldier for a while. Don't alienate Bluestem. Don't make things *too* hard."

In silence they drove back to Depointe. When Roberts pulled into the Apley lot, he said, "I'll think about what you said, Gallagher. *You* think about this. I've been in this business twenty years, and if I've learned one thing, it's this: you won't get anywhere blaming something else. It's just *you* out there," he said, holding her by the shoulders. After they kissed, and kissed again: "Remember this," he said, "it's just you."

With all the lights out, Gallagher lay on the bed, an arm covering her eyes. Why, she wondered, did some newsmen, the good ones like Roberts and McGuire, think it was "just you," your work, enterprise, and drive—while everyone else knew it was all Luck? McGuire was long gone from the biz, so his views were irrelevant, but Roberts was still a player. Luck, oddly, never acknowledged the magazine editor's existence. How had Roberts managed to find and secure this outpost? Gallagher could only think of one reason: the old ways were still ingrained in Roberts. And now that his best days were over, his vanity and ambition were nobody's business; he was, therefore, untouchable.

It was Bluestem, a *real* player, who was the ace at the new game. At the famous Sunday night dinner, he sketched in highlights of recent *Bullet* history. The time was right, he seemed to feel, for Gallagher to know just how much the game had changed. First to get the boot was the old City staff. The veteran hounds knew too much, they had too many friends, they were hamstrung, Bluestem said, by a lifetime's cozying up to power. Some of these dogs had been around since the New Deal, and had seen the city of autoworkers make history by voting in a full slate of Democrats. Muckraking stories in the *Bullet* had exposed a network of deals and kickbacks linking car-makers with City Hall. But the auto men, Bluestem went on—the Mustangs, Butzes, DuCoops, and Dexter-Coops—got the last laugh. They had themselves, mansions and riverfront acreage, zoned out of the city. They seceded, took their millions in tax money, and incorporated their own township.

But city politics, Bluestem said, had changed, and the old newsroom just didn't get it. The story had shifted: it wasn't Big Business versus the little guy. As the unions began to flounder—and the subcontracting began—organized labor lost its clout. The meaty stories the old hounds used to carve out (union-busting, graft, the machine, and the racketeering) were old hat. Politics and the industry were more intricately connected; only the legal eagles could thresh it out. And to what end? Bluestem said. It wasn't a story readers could understand. Government, more and more, was left to police itself. No one paper could follow all the transactions. Luckily, the man on the street seemed savvy—even cynical—about government. He knew he didn't know, and he didn't care! The only ones who still cared were the old hounds sniffing the old trails. They had refused, he added, to keep up with a new world, and a new kind of reader.

So although the old legmen dearly loved the paper, some were willing to retire or be phased out. Young talent, fresh from the J-schools or suburban papers—locked out for years because of Guild policy on forced retirement—flooded in. Luck trained them, every "man John." The new teams were put to a specially devised test: they were switched weekly from beat to beat, and had to file every day, if it took them twenty hours to do it—and no whining to the union rep. Job descriptions were irrelevant in a newsroom this fluid. There wasn't time for the slow bonding of reporter to beat. Politicians and institutions were in flux, Bluestem said; nothing lasted very long, so the deep fund of knowledge and mutual trust fostered by the beat system was a waste of resources. Once job descriptions were voided and beats nullified, the Depointe Guild's back, for all intents and purposes, was broken.

"And who gives a shit about unions!" Bluestem brayed that Sunday night. Like medicine or law, news was now a profession, and newsmen—if they were good enough—could take care of themselves. "We don't need any backup," he sneered, "from labor."

For hours, in breathless bursts, Bluestem relayed the stagings of Luck's new *Bullet*. "When things got really hot," Bluestem continued, "people either leapt aboard, or took a dive. We were always," he said, "a good paper; now we were a *smart* read. We aimed the product at the educated, upscale reader, and, thanks to Rolf Luck," he said, "that was what we got."

Politicians, he said, were still leery, for Luck was a wild card. He had a knack for sniffing out juicy scandals and had assembled investigative units ready to dig deep. The paper retained a fleet of top libel lawyers, all the better to defend, as Luck would say, the public's inalienable right to know "whatever!"

In their own clumsy way, the pols tried to soft-soap the executive editor, and he let them. He might return the favor by covering a pet project; but, more often, he didn't bother. He was motivated, Bluestem said, by one thing and one thing only—"the *pure story value.*" If the piece was a grabber—shocking, hot, pitiful, funny—it ran; if it was dull or too hard, it got the spike. That was *Bullet* practice, and politicians made the adjustment, and survived—or they didn't.

Throughout the paper's overhauling, and up to this minute, Luck and Bluestem were, Bluestem said—showing Gallagher two fingers squeezed together—"like this." The Sunday editor reached across the table, unfisted Gallagher's hand from her wine glass, and entwined his fingers with hers. "Or like *this,*" he repeated, squeezing.

Gallagher laughed.

"What are you laughing at?" asked Bluestem, in the languid, husky tone that usually preceded a romantic move. Gallagher was beginning to get the idea. This move was necessary wherever and whenever two Bullets of unequal rank met. If it happened to be two men, they worked out a cruder variation. While the move had the air of romance, it was no more than a salute.

"I'm laughing," Gallagher explained, thinking fast, "because I'm becoming just like you and Rolf."

"In what way?"

"I like to drink," she said, thinking faster. "I'm a camel."

Bluestem had both of her hands in his. "Shh," he said, kissing the back of one hand, and the palm of the other. "Let me enjoy you. I think," he added, his voice muffled, "I'm falling in love with you again." He looked up to check.

"You want to know what *I* think?" she said, taking a gulp of wine. "I think you're off your nut."

Did she say that—or just think it? Even if she said it out loud, it was still okay. Bluestem, like his mentor, could take it. In Luck's book, flak from a woman—

whatever the context—was always a come-on. In his decade at the *Bullet,* Luck had rarely been crossed; he had gotten very little lip. But when he did, he took it as a sign that the poor fish had only one thing left to offer.

Bluestem drove Gallagher to the Apley, and made the obligatory grab. He was tough and wily, but she broke free, slammed the car door, and raced to the building. After catching her breath, she hoped he realized, as she did, that it was nothing personal.

CHAPTER 11

A Sunday-room ceasefire followed. The entertainment writer drummed up stories, fresh, all of her own devising, and Bluestem was content to showcase his writer. The new work was bright, snappy, stuffed with quotes and odd facts. The tone was chummy yet cool, knowing but inclusive, arch but never mean; the style suited any kind of show and all "readers," from the naive ticket-buyer to the armchair voyeur.

Gallagher filed several stories a week. Long or short, in-depth or on-the-spot, the copy was always printable and nearly as is. (Easy? It was like falling out of bed, she told McGuire.)

Then suddenly, it got hard.

Bluestem was assigned a sub-editor to handle arts and entertainment. Ackley, the new editor, liked Gallagher and her work, he said. But—to show he was making his own contribution—he assigned his own stories. There was a difference between Gallagher's ideas and John Ackley's; and if Gallagher failed to see this, the new editor—on occasions when his writer resisted his or pitched her own—was quick to spell it out. They already had, he emphasized, adequate coverage of movies, books, records, TV, and music. And the "sleazeball acts and strange carnivals" she hunted up for her own purposes were of little interest, he claimed, to the targeted reader: professionals, young parents, persons interested in themselves, their jobs, leisure, their houses, health, and self-esteem. Couldn't she find more wholesome, upbeat material? And, by the way, there was a smug "know-it-all" tone in the work; brittle and snobbish—not at all, he emphasized, the way she was in person. "Be nice, be yourself," Ackley advised. Gallagher had one question for the new editor—mild-mannered, soft-soled (even his car was egg-shaped): Was it Luck who'd criticized, or was it Bluestem?

"Are you trying to undermine me?" Ackley said.

What had happened? wondered Gallagher, a week after Ackley, plucked from Women's—mad as a hornet, some said, although the rage was muted in public—was reassigned. The trouble started with Ackley, no doubt; but it didn't end there. The new sub, it turned out, was just one of many whips for a new program: to attract even *more* affluent suburban readers—thought to be too busy to waste time and energy on the mess they left behind every night, when, swarming the carmaker freeways, they roared home to Southchester, Northport, Westhaven, and points beyond.

What *did* they want to read? Gallagher groaned in frustration, as the sub-editor hashed, slashed, and spiked her already filed stories: a mandolin orchestra from Charlevoix (cut to five grafs), a sweep of downtown dancehalls (no art), and a profile of an old-time screen hoofer who was launching a dress line for K-mart (rewritten five times, and still in limbo).

It was *her* job, Ackley pointed out, to find out what they wanted to read. Hadn't she been working this beat for over six months now?

Gallagher knocked on Bluestem's door. He was sympathetic. Yes, he said, Ackley rubbed people the wrong way, everybody knew that. The guy had started out, Bluestem explained, in the city room—and look where he ended up! But Bluestem would say no more. "Soften him up, Gallagher," warned Bluestem. "We want this to work out."

It was Roberts who passed the word on Ackley and his blasted career hopes. There was a story, unconfirmed or at least not publicly acknowledged, that he had faked interviews in a life-in-a-teen-gang essay, run on page 1. It was a bad business, made uglier by the fact that it was Ackley's wife, a *Bullet* photo assistant, who tattled. She was sleeping, it turned out, with another reporter. Nothing official was done. But Ackley was barred from the city room—stripped, in effect, of his credibility—and stuck at a desk in Women's. One day, the top "color" writer on City; the next, editing Erma Bombeck. But it wasn't quite so bad, Roberts added, as it seemed. Luck wanted to overhaul the Women's page, jazz it up, without sacrificing recipes and weddings, the handful of agony columns and the crossword. Most of the older staff quit or retired within a month of Ackley's posting. But that was okay, too, Roberts said. The page was dreary. Four young women were hired on the spot, one right out of school. In a year, the successful one—who'd dated, then dumped Ackley—got a plum City assignment; another inherited Ackley's job when he was bumped over to Sunday; the third, a nice girl, Roberts said, but maybe too nice for a tough racket, had quit and gone home; the fourth was dead—but, Roberts added, there'd been other problems. Suicide? Gallagher asked. She drove out to Fairlane Island, Roberts said, and piped a hose from the exhaust into the window.

It wasn't, Roberts admitted, a sparkling record, but it wasn't *all* Ackley's fault either. He was a nice enough guy, Roberts said, but weak.

Yes, he was weak, Gallagher said. And because he was weak, he needed to push the knife in harder, give it an extra twist.

Gallagher *wasn't* looking for trouble, she told McGuire. It was Ackley. He took every piece she wrote (even ones he had assigned himself) and butchered them. Ackley wanted nothing new or fresh. His top priority was to build up "listings," so Gallagher compiled blurbs for movies, plays, TV, and pop concerts. He wanted regular Q&As with visiting stars and promoters; he wanted hard-news coverage of all big-ticket entertainments, including auto and boat shows, food courts, water and theme parks. Readers had children, he'd explained, and they needed help finding things to do. This stuff could be big. But it was drudgery, Gallagher told McGuire, because it had to be done straight—no personality, no angle, no commentary.

McGuire let Gallagher bitch and moan. Then, for the first time in over a year of pep talks and sermons, the former editor had little to say. Things weren't working out. It wasn't what he'd expected from a paper of that caliber. "Chuck it," he told Gallagher. "It's not a total loss. You can use it on your resumé."

Before McGuire had the chance to explain, Gallagher, shocked and stung, hung up on him. When he called back, she hung up on him again. The third time, "You got it all wrong!" he yelled. "It's not *you!* God knows you've tried!" Gallagher listened. "You're publishing what—twenty, twenty-five bylines a month? You must be writing the whole goddamned section! It can't be you. It's got to be them. Cut your losses, doll, get ready to dive. That's the best I can give you."

In late summer, a string of pop stars with platinum singles sang to sellout crowds at the Depointe Cheetahs stadium: Neil Diamond, Barry Manilow, Elton John, the Captain and Tennille, Wayne Newton, and Olivia Newton-John—in the first two weeks. Profiles of these mega-singers had to be "thoroughly researched," Ackley memoed to Gallagher. Real fans would know ten times more than the reporter, and they wouldn't be gulled by a "seat-of-the-pants" or "off-the-wall" take on their idols. "Be enthusiastic! Go with it," he said. "Write like you believe what you're saying."

After scanning the memo, Gallagher walked it back to Ackley's desk. "This sounds like a hard sell," she said. "Are they taking out full-page ads?"

Ackley smiled. "You're forcing my hand." Okay, if that's what she wanted. Before he arrived at Sunday, he said, he'd read through her clips. Entertainment writing, he said—inviting Gallagher to sit down—was not Tuesday night at the zoning board; it wasn't a workaday beat. You needed spark, zip. You had to love what you did; you couldn't be a wet blanket. And their readers didn't like to feel patronized. *Our* readers, Ackley went on blandly, were special. When they opened their paper, they didn't jump to foreign news or editorials. Fans of "Shows and Stars," as Ackley had renamed the page, also read comics and horoscope. They weren't always the brightest. Finally, he reminded her that they could always get stringers to cover the extra movie or play; that Gallagher's duty was to make "S&S" a success.

By the way, he said, he was planning a new feature for her page. He'd work it up in a memo, but she might as well hear about it first. Research showed that their readers tended to be hardcore TV viewers, especially daytime. So why not—he had already run it past Bluestem—compile plot summaries of the soaps for viewers who missed a day? "With your literary flair," Ackley remarked, "wouldn't this be a natural?"

When Gallagher reached Bluestem's cubby, she found him cooler than ever. Are things getting out of control? he asked. Was she trying to force his hand? To put it bluntly, John Ackley, a sixteen-year veteran, meant more to the *Bullet* than someone right off the street. They had more invested in him—salary, seniority, and so forth. And he had his points. Gallagher had to work things out with Ackley. "We're giving him a six-month try-out, and from what we can see, his only problem is you."

For four weeks Gallagher labored to strain all traces of sarcasm from her tone. When she succeeded, the prose was tight and dry, or completely flat. However brief her takes, Ackley always cut, rewrote the lead, and edited so heavily that the stories were unrecognizable. Instead—as Luck had said during their last talk—of the typical Wampanoag rich meat, half-raw, half-cooked, the latest clips were pap. "Who *gives* a hoot?" Luck said. "It's just filler anyway. We get better stuff from the wires!"

They were sitting in Luck's office, at Gallagher's (who'd rushed in, sailing over the heads of both Ackley and Bluestem) request. Although she'd vowed never to give way before those saurian eyes, Gallagher started to cry. Luck suggested the Tree. "Let's hoist a few," he said. He needed the break and—from the looks of it—so did she.

"So," Luck said, sitting at the bar. It was early, and the Tree was empty except for a table of young lawyers, who'd been there, the barman said, since eleven. There were six—fired that day—and although their table was littered with glasses and ashtrays, no sound came from their corner.

"What did you want to ask me about?" Even Luck's voice was muted. That morning Gallagher had sent a note ("You asked five months ago what I wanted. I want to talk to you ASAP"), but hadn't expected so prompt a reply, especially these days, when no one—except Hackenflecker—seemed to give a damn about Gallagher or her plight. She had fallen so far off, she thought, that she might, paradoxically, be more secure—except that once in the limelight no one ever seemed to slip back to the shadows: it was limelight or extinction. Ordering a scotch for himself, Luck let Gallagher speak her own choice—a bad sign?

But when Gallagher said she wanted to talk about her work, Luck said, "What work?" She'd filed virtually nothing worth reading, he said, in a month. (This was true, but couldn't he see the straits she was in? And if he couldn't, she added, she was telling him now.)

"So," he said, slapping a fifty down on the bar top, "what else do you want to ask me?" (The barman tucked the bill under the cash tray and stacked the change on the bar.) Gallagher waited, then vented. The problem was all Ackley, his lousy judgment, his sellout mentality; how fast he was running the section into the ground, sucking out its life and juice. Even the newshole, she said, had shrunk, while ad space ballooned. Worse, as she had mentioned to Bluestem, was how he treated his staff: harassment, vengefulness, spikings, scapegoating, gas-lighting, a "textbook case," as Larry Langton confirmed, of passive aggression. And Larry *liked* him.

Luck cocked an eyebrow. "So," he said yet again, after the tirade. "What do you think I should do? Fire Ackley and maybe Bluestem, too?" He had ordered them fresh drinks. "Do you imagine I'd fire two overpaid editors just to keep *you* happy? If you think that, you're overdue for a reality check. I could see it," he added, "if you had something really superfine to offer. Do you think you do? Tell me what it is.

"By the way, what are you doing to Ackley? Never mind," he said. "I'll tell *you* a secret. I don't know if we're going to *keep* 'Slops and Shops'—or whatever it's called. I've considered gutting the whole back of the book. Start all over."

Luck gazed a moment into his gold drink. "Don't you know enough to sit tight—a year, say, year and a half at most? I don't know how Ackley's low-ball game will play. All I know," Luck said, pinning Gallagher with his eyes, "is that ad lineage is through the ceiling, and we hardly need to lift a finger to sell papers. All we do," he said, grinning, "is give these sharks a lousy *mention* in the vicinity of their ad, and the cash floods in.

"But maybe it won't fly," he said. "People might get sick of it. For all we know, not even the dodos read your page. They just look up movie times."

Luck swirled his scotch and ice. "Where entertainment's concerned, who cares anyway! Five years from now, the whole section—Langton, Kazin—might be turfed. None of it's critical to anything."

Luck was showing off, wasn't he? Could he really picture a newspaper without reviews and features, or was he just putting her and her section in its place?

A while later Luck offered Gallagher a loan—or maybe it was a gift. "You need cash? Here," he took out his wallet. "Take what you need. Five hundred, a grand—take it!"

Gallagher was stunned. She told him it wasn't money she needed.

"Well, just let me know. I'm prepared to give you what you need, just as I said. But I can't fire Ackley just because he's breaking your balls. Don't even think of it."

Gallagher said she wasn't thinking that far ahead, but Luck shook his head. "Why else did you go over his head, if it wasn't to knife him in the back? You might as well go and tell him what you told me, Gallagher. We keep no secrets here."

Gallagher stared.

"Want some advice? It's good, but I don't think you can make use of it."

"What?"

"Just listen. Quit this job in your mind. And get yourself off the hook.

"Quit in your *mind,*" he repeated. "That way, you can mentally cancel out Ackley and Bluestem, and then write whatever the hell you want. If you're fired, you got there first. If it works—."

Gallagher listened.

"Quit in your mind," he repeated. "Maybe you can beat that weasel at his own chickenshit game."

"I think you're telling me to quit, period," Gallagher said, knowing, at last, that the sky was falling, that the ship was sinking, and that never for a minute had her feet been securely on deck.

"Quit," he repeated (loud enough for the barman and the table of canned lawyers to hear) "in your mind. It's a mental discipline, Gallagher. You won't believe how good it'll feel."

A week later, ignoring the magazine editor's terse warning to lay low till things cooled down, Gallagher played her last card and begged Bluestem for a drink. "If you want to," he sighed, without looking at her. "Birdcage at the Butz, 4:30."

High in the Butz-Impala building, a glassy tower, housed in its fiftieth floor, was the Birdcage, Depointe's bar with an escort service. Glass-domed and hung with hundreds of elaborate swings, cages, and nests (but not a single bird), the bar turned slowly on its thick concrete disk. Bluestem and Gallagher sat at a window table, well off the rotating core. Below them stretched the North side, Depointe River, and the Canadian flats. It was a hot, cloudless day so they could see clear across the lake, where air met water in a woozy line.

Bluestem was drinking an iodine-colored champagne drink. Gallagher ordered it. Bluestem chatted about his recent trip to Disneyland, with fiancée and children. He and Lindy had set their wedding date, planning a honeymoon in Aruba. The kids started school in a week, and, shortly after, when things settled, Bluestem would move in. He'd sold his house and bought into hers, although they planned, he said—as soon as possible—to build. He'd never been happier in his life, and recommended it to Gallagher—family, marriage, "the works."

"You should try it," he exulted. "See the difference it makes."

Bluestem had never before alluded to his girlfriend, or his life away from the *Bullet*. Why the sudden intimacy? Were they planning a big wedding? she asked. Would he adopt the children? But Bluestem, although he responded (yes, and not first thing), seemed suddenly bored by the subject. Looking out the glass wall, he asked if Gallagher felt settled in Depointe.

Here was her chance. Bluestem had always been a friend. He loved her. She could count on that. Yes, she told him, very much so.

"I'll be frank with you," Bluestem said, pushing a cigarette into his mouth and letting it droop, unlit. "I'm surprised to hear it."

Feeling the chill, Gallagher followed his gaze out the window and over the flats.

"I've been here a good five months," she said. "I'm as settled as I'm going to be."

"But can you see yourself," he said, in a counseling tone, "five, say, ten years down the line, reporting the news?"

She nodded hard.

He tried again. "Do you see yourself doing this for the *rest* of your life?"

He was letting her down easy. She didn't want it: easy *or* hard. "Yes!" she said. "Yes!"

Bluestem flicked an ash from his lip. "I've been in this business fifteen, almost sixteen years now. I'll die in harness." He couldn't grasp the fleck, so picked at his lip, stretching it to see.

"Of course you will!" she said.

It was a few minutes after five. The streets below suddenly swarmed. Office workers fled the Butz-Impala, crossing over to the block-long parking garage. Gallagher watched. The narrow streets filled with cars, although only the occasional horn blast reached the fiftieth floor.

"What do you make of it?" mused Bluestem.

"Of what?" she said, her voice a little too high.

"Of *this,*" he said, pointing to the clogged streets, the teeming sidewalks of Depointe.

"I *like* it here," she said, still hoping it could be, ever so carefully, turned around.

"I don't mean 'here,' said Bluestem. "I mean: what do you think of *them?*" he pointed down. "The folks you write for?"

Gallagher had to laugh. "Do *you* think about them?" she asked. "Does anyone at the *Bullet?*" As soon as she said it, she was sorry. It was exactly the wrong thing.

Bluestem checked his watch, flipping it around his wrist where it hung loosely on a linked bracelet. "You know something, Cathy Gallagher?"

She looked up; no one here had ever called her Cathy.

"You have never understood—you probably never *will* understand," he said, looking up, "the mass mind. That's your problem. Or rather, that's been *our* problem."

Bluestem reached over to take her hand, and squeezed it.

Had she been fired?

"Say yes," he said, "because nothing could be truer, and you know it."

Gallagher's gaze dropped fifty flights to the street. The crowd had thinned, scattered, some already on the freeways and over the bridges, leaving Depointe, and the Butz-Impala, as fast as they could roll out.

"You're a highbrow, Gallagher, face it. You're a bluestocking. And this is a stretch, this is an awkward fit for you."

"There's a problem?" she asked, suddenly feeling the full force. She was out. It was over.

"You tell me," he said.

Even Bluestem was washing his hands. Was it too late to quit in her mind? What did that mean anyway?

In the next two years, there were big changes at the *Bullet.* Bluestem moved on to *Parents* magazine, then to a top post at *USA Today;* Luck went to Hollywood, first as a producer, then as a studio head; Roberts Hackenflecker was tapped to run the Orange County bureau of the *Los Angeles Times,* before starting up his own weekly. Devra and Larry Langton stayed put, although Larry was single again.

Within five years the *Bullet* was bought by General Tire. Circulation plunged in the '80s and the paper was sold again, finally merging operations with its rival, the *Depointe Blade.* It continued, even with reduced costs and capital influx, to hemorrhage readers.

Gallagher hung on one more month.

Bluestem never officially fired her; she quit on her own, in fact. As her assignments, ever more trivial, started to dry up—and after she'd decided, in guilt and shame, to break up with McGuire, and leave it *all* behind—she quit the *Bullet.*

That day, Gallagher dropped yet another in a series of moronic assignments—a new card game called "Trivial Pursuits"—on the sub-editor's desk, and was sent to Bluestem. Instead of reporting to Bluestem, Gallagher went back to her own desk and wrote an obit—to be sent, *not* to a flack like Bluestem, or to an operator like Luck, but straight to the top, to the publisher: whoever he was, headquartered elsewhere, and fully out of touch with reality. "Dear Sir," it read.

Gallagher was shortly after on the road in her small car. She packed a few things: books, clothes, the typewriter McGuire had sent through the mail—she couldn't just leave it there. Once—twice at most—speeding east, the car swerved toward the shoulder. The third time, Gallagher skidded to a halt, brakes screeching, horns blaring at the sudden, inexplicable mid-road halt. She pulled over.

It was the beginning of autumn, a cool September day, and the unemployed hound had buckled the weather log in the seat beside her. It was dusk, no streetlights to mar the westward view of flames scoring the Depointe skyline.

"Catherine Frances ('Genius of Wampanoag') Gallagher," the letter to the top had said, "24 years of age, formerly on the Women's desk with old Toohey of the *Wampanoag* (since 1805) *Times,* and of freelance ironman Jack McGuire—." But it stopped there; it wasn't fun, and Gallagher didn't want to waste the time. She had quit in her mind: this is what he meant. In a simple note dated 10/6/76, and addressed to Rolf Luck, she resigned her position. At three that afternoon, she left her desk, no goodbyes. She didn't hate them; she'd liked Roberts Hackenflecker very much, but what could she say to him?

Ahead there was nothing but an hour's worth of traffic. She steered the white car, steadier now, onto the interstate. In the rearview mirror, many miles back over the flatness, lay Depointe still burning. Like McGuire, she knew exactly what was back there, and what she was leaving. It wasn't a tragedy; it was just the end.

FICTION TITLES IN THE SERIES

Guy Davenport, *Da Vinci's Bicycle: Ten Stories*
Stephen Dixon, *Fourteen Stories*
Jack Matthews, *Dubious Persuasions*
Guy Davenport, *Tatlin!*
Joe Ashby Porter, *The Kentucky Stories*
Stephen Dixon, *Time to Go*
Jack Matthews, *Crazy Women*
Jean McGarry, *Airs of Providence*
Jack Matthews, *Ghostly Populations*
Jean McGarry, *The Very Rich Hours*
Steve Barthelme, *And He Tells the Little Horse the Whole Story*
Michael Martone, *Safety Patrol*
Jerry Klinkowitz, *"Short Season" and Other Stories*
James Boylan, *Remind Me to Murder You Later*
Frances Sherwood, *Everything You've Heard Is True*
Stephen Dixon, *All Gone: Eighteen Short Stories*
Jack Matthews, *Dirty Tricks*
Joe Ashby Porter, *Lithuania*
Robert Nichols, *In the Air*
Ellen Akins, *World Like a Knife*
Greg Johnson, *A Friendly Deceit*
Guy Davenport, *The Jules Verne Steam Balloon*
Guy Davenport, *Eclogues*
Jack Matthews, *"Storyhood As We Know It" and Other Stories*
Stephen Dixon, *Long Made Short*
Jean McGarry, *Home at Last*
Jerry Klinkowitz, *Basepaths*
Greg Johnson, *I Am Dangerous*
Josephine Jacobsen, *What Goes without Saying*
Jean McGarry, *Gallagher's Travels*

Library of Congress Cataloging-in-Publication Data

McGarry, Jean.
Gallagher's travels / Jean McGarry.
p. cm. — (Johns Hopkins : poetry and fiction)
ISBN 0-8018-5634-5 (alk. paper)
I. Title. II. Series: Johns Hopkins, poetry and fiction.
PS3563.C3636G3 1997
813′.54—dc21 97-7002
CIP